# RIGHT YOUR WRONGS

**KINGS OF THE ICE 6**

Also in the *Kings of the Ice* series
by Kandi Steiner

Meet Your Match
Watch Your Mouth
Learn Your Lesson
Save Your Breath
Stand Your Ground

# RIGHT YOUR WRONGS

## KINGS OF THE ICE 6

KANDI STEINER

First published in the United States in 2026 by Kandi Steiner, LLC
This paperback edition published in Great Britain in 2026
by Renegade Books
an imprint of Quercus
Part of John Murray Group

1

Copyright © 2026 Kandi Steiner

The moral right of KANDI STEINER to be identified as the
author of this work has been asserted in accordance with
the Copyright, Designs and Patents Act 1988.

Cover illustration by Rachel Lawston.

All rights reserved. No part of this publication may be reproduced or
transmitted in any form or by any means, electronic or mechanical,
including photocopy, recording, or any information storage and
retrieval system, without permission in writing from the publisher.

This book is a work of fiction. Names, characters, businesses,
organizations, places and events are either the product of the
author's imagination or used fictitiously. Any resemblance to actual
persons, living or dead, events or locales is entirely coincidental.

A CIP catalogue record for this book is available
from the British Library

PB ISBN 978-1-40875-124-4
EBOOK ISBN 978-1-40875-125-1

Typeset in Georgia

Printed and bound in Great Britain by Clays Ltd, Elcograf S.p.A.

Papers used by Quercus are from well-managed forests and other
responsible sources.

Quercus
Carmelite House
50 Victoria Embankment
London EC4Y 0DZ

John Murray Group
Part of Hodder & Stoughton Limited
An Hachette UK company

The authorised representative in the EEA is Hachette Ireland,
8 Castlecourt Centre, Dublin 15, D15 XTP3, Ireland (email: info@hbgi.ie)

To the ones who clawed their way out of the dark,
    who learned to breathe again
    after the world tried to steal the air from their lungs,
    and who dared to open their hearts
    when it would've been easier
    to keep the door closed.

This one's for you.

Scan the QR code to enjoy Kandi's
*Right Your Wrongs* playlist as you meet
the sexiest hockey players around . . .

## A NOTE TO THE READER

This story contains themes of domestic violence, emotional abuse, and coercive control.

While these elements are integral to the journey of healing, resilience, and reclaiming one's life that unfolds in these pages, I want to acknowledge that they may be difficult or triggering for some readers.

Your well-being matters.

Read at your own pace. Take breaks when needed. And know that this story was written with care — for those who have survived, and for those who are still finding their way forward.

With love,
Kandi

# PROLOGUE

### BOUND

Shane

If a heart was tied to a person, mine was inextricably bound to her — and it stopped beating the day I left her behind.

Ariana Ridley had tried desperately not to be noticed when we were in college, but one look at her and it was clear how impossible that mission was. She was like a diamond buried deep, and her beauty was the volcano that unearthed her. It wasn't only her piercing blue eyes or snow-white complexion. It wasn't just her heart-shaped lips or her goddess-like curves.

It was the untold stories in her gaze, the way she wore her trauma like a cloak.

She called to me in a way I couldn't fight, because I saw what everyone else overlooked.

Ariana was a survivor.

She was just like me.

We fell in love too easily, too quickly, at a rate that should have foretold how bad it would be once we finally hit the ground.

I was young and stupid when I let her go, when I chose my dream of hockey over her because I thought I was doing the right thing, and because hockey was the only thing I'd ever been able to depend on. I hated myself for the choice I made, and I regretted it every day.

I saw her once after that, years later, when I got injured and watched my dream go up in smoke. I begged for her forgiveness. She rightfully denied it.

I never thought I'd see her again.

Which was why I was grinding my teeth together to keep my jaw from dropping now, my heart kicking back to life in my chest with a force strong enough to take me to my knees.

Because here she was, in front of me again.

My Ari.

Standing next to my new General Manager.

As his wife.

# CHAPTER 1

## RESILIENCE

### Shane

Her hand shot into the air, and with it, she knocked my whole world off balance.

It was January 2006. I was a junior at Boston College, playing hockey for the university's team and counting down to when I'd have my psychology degree in hand on my way into the NHL. I'd already been drafted by the Jacksonville Barracudas, my rights held by them while I attended college.

Four years to hone my skills on the ice with the Eagles, earn my degree, and enjoy a little bit of a normal life.

And then, it was off to the races.

I'd had a plan ever since I was ten years old. That was the year I realized hockey was everything to me. That was also the year I stopped treating it like a game and started manifesting a career.

I'd play my ass off through high school. I'd get drafted. I'd make sure the team that drafted me understood I wanted to go to college, and they'd hold my rights until I graduated. I'd go the full four years, get better and stronger on the ice, and make sure I had a backup plan in the form of a degree that could be used for a future career.

So far, I'd checked the boxes.

I'd played like a beast through high school, securing a spot in the USHL when I turned sixteen. I garnered scout attention early and was drafted the summer after I graduated high school, with the understanding that I would attend college, but the team would retain my rights. And here I was, the top-scoring winger for the Eagles and just three semesters away from graduation.

I had a plan.

And I was following that plan perfectly.

Until the second that girl raised her hand and ruined everything.

"Is resilience an individual trait, or is it built through community?" Professor Reid asked, scribbling *Nature vs Nurture in the Home Environment* on the whiteboard as he did. It was the first day of my Human Behavior in the Social Environment class — an elective I'd selected with team leadership in mind.

If I wanted to be a leader, not just on this team but on the ones I'd play for in the future, I needed to understand how humans ticked. I needed to know how to work with players from all backgrounds and upbringings.

Again, all part of the plan.

Two rows in front of me in the lecture hall, a hand bolted into the air.

I had a clear view of the girl the hand belonged to — or at least to the back of her head. She wore a white t-shirt, and her dark blonde hair was plaited into a thick braid that she had pulled over one shoulder. Even from two rows back, I could see that her nails were bitten short.

And she had a scar — right in the middle of that hand suspended above her.

"Yes," Professor Reid said, nodding to the girl as he clasped his hands behind his back. "Miss?"

"Ariana Ridley," she answered, lowering her hand. Her voice shocked me. It was smooth and raspy, like that of a woman twice her age. "I believe it's an individual trait."

Professor Reid nodded. "I see. Can you explain your reasoning?"

"Resilience is about the fight inside you — even when no one else is there to help or bail you out. It's born out of necessity, out of circumstance, and out of a will to survive. You can put two people in the exact same situation with the same community around them and they'll respond differently."

Professor Reid jutted his lip out in thought, bobbing his head side to side as he considered.

"Support systems are nice, but they're not what gets you through. *You* get you through," she finished.

A ripple of murmurs echoed through the classroom.

Before I knew what I was doing, my own hand was in the air.

Professor Reid's brows shot up, and he nodded to me. "Go ahead, Mr...?"

"Shane McCabe, sir."

I didn't miss the flutter of noise at my name. The students sitting in my section had already noticed me, but now the whole class knew they had Boston College's star winger in their class.

"I disagree with Miss Ridley."

As soon as I said it, she turned around, balancing her forearm on the back of her chair as she looked up at me.

And once again, I felt my world tilt.

5

She was a knockout. There was just no other way to describe her. She had the kind of beauty that robbed a man of common sense — smooth, alabaster skin, golden hair, heart-shaped, rose-colored lips.

But it was her eyes that had me speechless for so long it was embarrassing.

They were piercing, a shocking bright blue like two glowing pools of spring water.

And they were haunted the way only a survivor's can be.

"Go on," Professor Reid said with a smirk when I didn't elaborate.

I thought I heard a few chuckles near me, but I blinked, swallowing and tearing my gaze from Ariana and back to Reid.

"I don't disagree that survival comes down to what's inside you," I said slowly. "But I've lived enough to know sometimes what's inside isn't enough. Sometimes, you're standing in the wreckage with everything you thought you could count on gone."

I paused; the weight of those words heavy on my ribcage.

"And the difference between drowning and making it to the surface isn't how hard you struggle in the waves." I leaned forward, tapping my desk for emphasis. "It's how graciously you accept the hand that reaches for you. It's the steady voice of a coach, the encouragement from a brother on the ice." I shrugged, sitting back again. "It's your team — whatever that may look like."

The room went quiet, and my eyes flitted back to Ariana's. She was frowning at me, and I wasn't sure if it was because she was annoyed I was arguing with her, or because she understood the point I was making.

"But hey, maybe it's a bit of both," I conceded, and really, I was speaking only to her then. "Maybe, sometimes, resilience is what you carry inside. And sometimes...it's who carries it with you."

"Very good points, Mr. McCabe," Professor Reid said, and then he tapped the white board and transitioned into his lecture.

But I was still looking at Ariana.

She was still looking at me.

And when her lips melted into a soft, breathtaking smile; I knew I was a goner.

## CHAPTER 2

### THIS IS IT
Shane

At forty-one years old, I was having my patience tested as a coach in a way I imagined it might have been tested had I ever been a parent.

It was mid-September in the most chaotic opening of a season I'd yet to experience. As head coach for the Tampa Bay Ospreys, I'd seen a lot over the years — suspensions from offseason debauchery, rookies who just never showed up to camp, rookies who *did* show up and then underperformed in a way that had us all wondering why they were ever drafted.

But this season felt like my own personal hell.

Our goalie, Will Perry, affectionately known as Daddy P, was the best in the league. There was no debate. Irrefutably, he was the best — and all summer, he had been sitting on the Ospreys' offer for a contract extension next season. He'd promised me he'd seriously consider it, but I had a feeling he was leaning toward retirement.

And I couldn't blame him.

He'd put his body through hell for decades, won himself a Stanley Cup with the team a few seasons ago, and had played one hell of a career, in general. He was married now to his former nanny, Chloe, and they were ready to give his daughter a sibling.

But just because I could understand his choice didn't mean I had to love it.

Perry had his struggles — the same hip that had carried him through two decades of saves now protesting every drop to the ice, his stamina fading with it. But all in all, he was still incredible. He was a powerhouse and a team favorite. He was the heart and soul of the team.

And everyone knows if you kill the heart and soul of anything, it doesn't take long for the rest to decay.

So, I walked into the first day of preseason training camp with a promise from Perry that he'd have an answer for me. It was the first time since my rookie year coaching that anxiety thrummed through me on the first day of camp — coffee full in my hand, stomach too tight to take a sip.

If I had to rebuild our team around our backup goalie or, worse, a new goalie altogether — I was in for a tough season ahead.

To add to my misery, we'd lost our General Manager unexpectedly over the offseason.

Richard Bancroft, or "Dick" as we all called him, had been a jolly old man. He was everything you might think Santa Claus might be in his down time when he wasn't running the North Pole. And though a bit eccentric, he'd helped me turn this program around. We went from a losing team that could barely fill half the arena to a championship one that frequently had sold-out games. Between his off-the-wall marketing and my knack for bringing out the best in players, we had what it took to achieve greatness.

And we did.

Up until the very moment he passed from a sudden heart attack.

Grief didn't like to play by any rules you tried to set out for it. I'd learned that at a very early age. Still, now that camp was here, I didn't have the luxury of grieving my old friend anymore.

Because I had to prepare for his replacement.

The Tampa Bay Ospreys had scrambled to get us a new GM before the season started, but by the time negotiations were settled, we were right on the cusp of preseason. That meant this new guy was walking into a team already settled for him. There was no time for him to make any of the changes he might want to, unless he decided to do so in the middle of a season, which wouldn't be the most ideal situation for anyone.

I didn't consider myself a very religious man, but I did pray. I'd been praying since I was a kid, since the day I lost my parents in the most unfair way imaginable.

And so, when I walked into camp that day, I was praying — that somehow my goalie would stick around for a couple more seasons, and that my new general manager wouldn't be a prick.

Fortunately, once I stepped behind the bench and heard the familiar slice of skates over ice, my nerves settled. The rink was alive with motion — pucks clanging off the glass, coaches barking drills, trainers hauling gear across the bench, the low thud of sticks meeting the boards. The smell of fresh ice and sweat was like a candle scent poured just for me.

We were off to the races, transitioning from rookie camp, which had taken place over the summer, to seeing the full team together for the first time. The energy was different now — the rookies trying to impress, the vets not giving a shit what the rookies thought at all. The veterans didn't move like the kids did; there was rhythm in their stride, muscle memory in every pass and stop. You could almost feel the rookies shrinking under the weight of it.

But some of them were inspired, lighting up from the inside out and chasing the challenge. Those were the ones I had my eyes on the most.

I scanned the ice, watching for chemistry, for hesitation, for anyone who looked like they'd forgotten what it meant to belong here, and anyone new who might be hungry for a chance. It was my job to know who was ready and who was bluffing it.

I caught sight of Perry at the far net, mask off, water bottle tipped to his lips. He was laughing at something our defenseman, Jaxson Brittain, said, that familiar crooked grin making him look ten years younger than his body felt. But when he dropped back into the crease, I saw it — the hesitation, the guarded way he planted on his left side. It wasn't enough for anyone else to notice, but it was plenty enough to make my stomach knot.

The vets were ribbing him between drills, tossing a few "old man" jokes his way, and he was giving it right back, glove raised in mock salute. Typical Daddy P — the heartbeat of the room. And yet, under all that noise, all that routine, I could see it in his posture. The heaviness. The finality.

He hadn't given me his answer yet, but I could feel it coming.

I turned to Kozak, one of my assistant coaches, nodding toward the net. "Soon as this drill's over, tell Perry I want a word."

Because whatever decision he'd made — it was time I heard it.

My assistants took the reins when Perry skated over to me, and he hopped off the ice and walked back to the locker room with me guiding the way. We slipped into my office, the quiet *snick* of the door closing behind us setting my nerves on edge again. I gestured for him to take a seat before I did the same, and then I leaned forward, elbows on my knees, gaze leveled with his.

"You're going, aren't you?"

Will Perry was what I would call a man of stoicism. He'd always been laser focused on the game and this team, with the only soft spot in his heart being reserved for Chloe and his daughter, Ava.

So when his eyes welled, his jaw tight, a loud sniff breaking the silence of my office, I knew.

I closed my eyes, letting out a long breath before I sat back in my chair. "Fuck," I murmured.

"My hip is going," Will said, and I didn't miss how his throat bobbed at the admission. "No one hates that fact more than I do, Coach. But I have a family. I'm already looking at a life of rehab. The last thing I want is to not be able to play with Ava or her future siblings."

I nodded. "I understand, Perry."

And I did. Goalies weren't the only ones who suffered injuries that followed them for life. I still did physical therapy for the career-ending one that turned me from a player to a coach far younger than I ever anticipated.

That memory had the next question rolling off my tongue.

"Would you ever consider coaching for us? You and I both know you'd do better than ol' Romanov out there."

That made Perry bark out a laugh, which melted some of the tension in the room. "That man hasn't taught me shit, not in all the years I've been here. I've learned more from Ava than him."

I chuckled. "I don't doubt it. So, you'll consider?"

Will was silent a moment before he nodded. "I'll think on it."

"Good." My eyes flicked between his, the corner of my lips curling just a notch. "So, this is your last season?"

"This is it."

I shook my head, hand finding my desk to help me stand. Then, I extended that hand for Perry's, taking it in a firm shake when he stood to join me. "Then we better fucking win the Cup."

"Hear, hear," Perry echoed.

I considered hugging him, but decided I'd save that for the spring. For now, we still had one last season, one final ride — and I didn't intend to let him off easy.

"Now, back on the ice, Pickles. Time to show these rookies how it's done."

The rest of the day blurred past in a rush of drills, video review, and media obligations. My assistants rotated players through testing and conditioning while I bounced between the ice and the meeting rooms, checking off boxes and trying not to think about what Perry's announcement meant for the rest of our season.

Around noon, the rink had quieted. Most of the guys were in the gym or showering off. I was halfway through reviewing tomorrow's drill plan when Kozak poked his head into my office.

"Coach," he said, breathless from the walk. "They're setting up for the press conference. PR says the new GM just arrived — they're almost ready for you."

I scrubbed a hand over my face and exhaled. "Great."

The word came out flat. I wasn't ready for this, not after the morning I'd had. But ready or not, I had to meet the man who'd be running this circus with me.

"You good?" Kozak asked.

"Yeah." I stood, tugged on my jacket, and squared my shoulders — game face in place, the same one I'd worn since my first day behind a bench as the youngest coach in the NHL.

We left my office and headed down the hall toward the media room — a space off the main corridor, just beyond the players' lounge. I could already hear the hum of reporters setting up, the clatter of camera equipment, the low buzz of conversation bleeding through the walls.

I'd done a hundred of these, but something about this one felt heavier. New leadership meant change. And change rarely came without casualties.

I pushed open the door, ready to shake hands and smile for the cameras even as my stomach rioted.

My gaze found him immediately — Nathan Black, the new general manager. I hadn't taken the time to research him past the photo and short bio our PR team had supplied me. I liked to get to know people for who they were, not the laundry list of accomplishments they boasted — though, this man did boast quite a bit. He was the kind of executive the league loved: a golden boy with a finance degree, a Harvard certificate in sports management, and a knack for turning struggling franchises into profit machines.

Physically, I noted immediately that he was tall, polished, and in his early fifties, if I had to guess. His hair was dark, threaded neatly through with silver and cut like a Hollywood actor's — short on the sides, a perfect swoop at the top. His navy suit was tailored, cuff links shining at his wrists. It was jarring, compared to Dick, who often showed up to press conferences with the buttons of his dress shirt straining against his belly, and rosy cheeks glistening under the harsh light.

Even from across the room, I could tell this was the kind of man who never raised his voice because he didn't need to. Power followed him in a quiet way— in the calm confidence of his stance, the precise movements of his hands as he spoke with PR, the faint smirk that seemed permanently etched into the corners of his mouth.

His grin, when it landed on me, looked practiced. It was polite and professional, but it didn't reach his eyes.

I assessed all of this in just a few seconds, because immediately, my attention was drawn away from my new general manager to the woman standing beside him.

My heart stuttered at the first sight of her blonde hair, swept into a neat twist. My breath faltered next when I took in her dazzling blue eyes, the very ones that used to undo me with a single look. It didn't matter that decades had passed, I'd know her anywhere — how could I ever forget those lips, the graceful shape of her, the haunted gaze that had been a wraith in every nightmare I'd had since the day I walked away from her.

Ariana Ridley.

The only woman I'd ever loved.

Like she felt me before she saw me, her smile that was aimed at Kozak wavered, her brows pinching together just slightly.

Then, her eyes snapped to mine.

# CHAPTER 3

## AFTER ALL THIS TIME

Ariana
Present

I realized with acute agony that it didn't matter how long I'd had to prepare for this exact moment, no amount of time or composition could properly brace me for Shane McCabe slamming back into my life.

It was like being struck by a steel beam picked up in the winds of an F5 tornado, the way his eyes latched onto mine, the rest of the world fading to black around us. I blinked and saw him as a twenty-one-year-old kid sitting two rows behind me in a lecture hall. I blinked again and saw his eyes squeezed shut, his brows pinched together as he kissed me reverently with shaking hands. Another blink and I was drenched in rain, screaming at him not to leave me, heart breaking when I realized he'd already made up his mind.

A final, rapid set of blinks had me back in the present, where I did my best to school my features and bury every memory right where they belonged — in the past.

But my eyes betrayed me, dragging slowly over the man he'd become. Shane stood tall and solid in his tailored suit, broader through the shoulders than I remembered, his frame carrying the unmistakable marks of discipline and care. The years had filled him out, hardened him in places, honed him in others.

His dark hair was trimmed shorter now, brushed back neatly, though a few rebellious strands still fell forward, softening the severity of the look. Faint lines bracketed his eyes when he focused, proof of laughter and strain and everything life had carved into him since we were young. And when his gaze met mine again — steady, piercing, achingly familiar — I felt it in my chest, the same way I always had.

He looked like a man who knew exactly who he was.

And worse — like a man who still knew exactly how to undo me.

"There he is!" my husband said, opening his arms like he and Shane were long-lost brothers as opposed to complete strangers who would now be forced to work together. Fortunately, he had the good sense to drop that wide embrace and extend a hand for Shane's in the last moment, when Shane finally unglued his shoes from the ground and made his way over to us. "Coach McCabe, your reputation precedes you. Nathan Black."

"A pleasure to meet you, sir. Excited to work together." Shane's voice sounded odd when he said the words, though no one in the room would notice but me. I hoped they also wouldn't notice how his eyes flicked to me, his jaw flexing before his strained smile was back on my husband.

"We're going to make magic, you and me," Nathan promised, still grasping Shane's hand in his as he clapped him on the back with his free hand. "Just you wait and see. I've got some tricks up my sleeve."

The way he grinned with that comment made my skin crawl.

What an unfortunate thing to feel around my husband, and yet I knew him well enough to know when he was joking, and when he was making a threat.

I was well versed in the latter.

As if he couldn't help himself, Shane's eyes slid to me, and this time, he indulged in letting them stay there. And because it would be impolite to look anywhere else, I held his gaze.

It sliced through me like a razed wire, even after all this time.

"Ah, yes," Nathan said, standing straight before he curled his arm possessively around my hip and tugged me into his side. "This is my beautiful wife, Ariana."

Shane's nostrils flared at the word *wife*.

His eyes didn't leave mine, the gaze piercing through me like a spear.

And then his hand came forward.

That little motion shouldn't have had my throat tightening. It was just a handshake, a polite formality that was natural and expected in that moment.

But the world went silent as his fingers reached for mine.

I told myself to breathe, to be normal, to remember where I was and who I belonged to.

Still, my pulse betrayed me, drumming so hard in my throat it blurred my vision.

And when his palm met mine, the years between us disintegrated, heat blasting from the point of contact and sizzling every nerve in my body.

That hand was warm and rough, but worst of all, it was familiar in a way that made my knees threaten to give.

For a second, neither of us moved. Shane shook my hand before holding it too long to be professional, too short to ever be enough.

He hesitated when it was the appropriate time to break the contact, eyes flicking between mine, and then his fingers tightened around my hand, his pointer finger gently pressing into my wrist like he was trying to speak some sort of secret code to me with just that touch.

And here we were, standing in the moment of truth.

Would he pretend like he didn't know me, or admit our history?

My stomach twisted with a fear I couldn't quite name. Part of me braced for Shane to speak — to say my name like he used to, to expose the history I'd buried so carefully — and the thought sent a sharp spike of panic through my chest. I could already imagine Nathan's hand tightening at my hip, the warmth of his possessiveness tipping into something colder, something dangerous.

But there was another fear just as unsettling.

That Shane wouldn't say anything at all.

That he'd let go of my hand, step back, and pretend I was nothing more than the woman standing beside his general manager. A stranger. A closed chapter. The idea hollowed me out in a way I didn't want to examine too closely.

I stood there, caught between dread and disappointment, unsure which outcome would hurt more.

"Ariana," Shane said, sending a wave of goosebumps over my skin. His lips curled at the corner, like he saw the effect he'd had and loved it, and that made my gaze harden. Because although my body seemed intent on betraying me, I refused to let it drag me down memory lane like Shane and I had only joy between us.

We both knew that was *far* from the truth.

"It's a wonderful surprise to see you here. How have you been?" Shane seemed reluctant to drop my hand, but he finally did with that question, and I immediately folded my fingers together in front of my waist.

Before I could answer, my husband arched a brow. "You two know each other?"

"We had a class together at Boston College," I said, and I hated how low my voice was when I said it, but I wasn't surprised. I didn't know how Nathan would react to this news, which had me hesitant to speak too loudly. I hoped to brush it off quickly and not make a thing of it, but I could tell by the way my husband's gaze narrowed that I wouldn't get off that easily.

"Is that right?" he asked, that perfectly practiced grin of his sliding back into place easily as he turned to Shane. His grip tightened as he pulled me even closer to him, and I winced against the sharp dig of those fingers into my hip. "Sweetheart, why didn't you mention this before?"

"I honestly didn't realize it was the same Shane," I said with my own practiced, nonchalant laugh. I was aware of how ditzy my husband believed I was, so I played my part. And even though it was the last thing I wanted to do, I leaned into Nathan, placing a hand over his chest as I smiled up at him. "You know how crazy our life has been lately. And that was ages ago, another lifetime it feels. It was just one class together, after all."

I knew the lie was thinly veiled, but fortunately my husband was a man of discretion. So, he kissed my hair and turned his smile back to Shane. "Well, I look forward to hearing stories of the good ol' days in Boston."

Shane's smile was tight as he slid his hands into the pockets of his slacks, and when a member of the public relations team came over to steal Nathan away and prepare him for the press conference, I was ready to slither back into the shadows and watch him from a distance like I always had. I waited for Shane to excuse himself, knowing he'd be a part of this press ordeal, too.

But he just stood there, rooted like a tree, his eyes fixed on mine.

When he looked at me that way, I couldn't help but soften. It didn't matter how my heart was still broken from his actions, the cracks splitting fresh in my chest at the sight of him as if to remind me not to get too close. *Danger*, my common sense whispered. *Stay away*.

And yet I couldn't move, either.

Shane finally shook his head, the motion subtle, his eyes trailing down my modest navy-blue dress to my nude kitten heels and back up. "I'm sorry for staring, I just... I believe I may be in shock."

I didn't want to smile, but damn it if I could fight against the tilt of my lips. "Like seeing a ghost, huh?"

"After all this time, life has brought us back together."

With that, my stomach soured, and finally, the cold resolve I'd been wishing for found me.

How dare he?

How dare this man look at me this way, all reverent and wonder-struck, and say those words like this was some happy reunion?

"Yep," I snipped, standing taller and smoothing my hands over my dress. "And you can't get away from me this time, unless you quit your job. And we all know nothing is more important to you than hockey."

I held the emphasis on *nothing* so that he understood what I meant.

And by the way his face fell, I knew he had.

"Ari," he started, but before he could plead whatever sorry excuse for a case he had, Nathan was back at my side.

He reached for my face to pull me in for a quick kiss, but instinctively, I flinched.

It was only a micro-second of a moment, a reaction that no one should have noticed. Nathan surely didn't. He smiled post-kiss and told me to wish him luck before he was following the staff to the room where the press was waiting for him.

But when I turned back to Shane, his face was ashen, his jaw slack.

He'd seen it.

And I shouldn't have been surprised.

This man had always seen right through me, since the very moment we'd met.

## CHAPTER 4

### YOU DON'T KNOW ME

Ariana
2006

I'd like to say I didn't pay one single ounce of attention to Shane McCabe after that first day of class, but it would be a lie big enough to grow my nose four times in size.

Curiosity raked through me like claws as I walked back to my campus dorm, and it was all I could do to pause long enough to pee before I was at my laptop and googling him.

The top of the search revealed instantly that he played for the university's hockey team — that must have been why the room *ooh'd* and *aww'd* when he said his name.

A few more scrolls and I discovered he was drafted to play in the NHL at eighteen, and he'd be on his way to Jacksonville as soon as he graduated.

Then, in a gut-wrenching surprise, I stumbled upon an article about the death of his parents in an ice storm when he was just seven years old.

That one sat with me long after I closed my laptop.

Each week, I'd walk into the classroom and sit in my same spot. I always arrived early — it was just part of who I was. But Shane was the same way.

He'd take his seat just minutes after I did, always two rows back.

And he'd look at me the whole way into the lecture hall, offering me a smile and a wink just before he was out of view.

I never turned around to look at him.

I knew better than to entertain whatever fantasy my stupid girl brain was trying to get me to latch onto. I'd seen firsthand what *love* was, and it wasn't anything like the story they painted in the movies and books.

Love wasn't passionate kisses and thoughtful dates planned from beginning to end.

It was fists to the face and bruised ribs, often paired with a cheap piece of jewelry and a hollow apology.

And I wanted nothing to do with it.

But one month into the semester, Professor Reid blew up my attempt to stay away from the dark-haired, gray-eyed boy.

Reid clapped his hands together at the front of the room, the sound snapping everyone's attention forward. "All right, folks, listen up. Your first big assignment is a field observation paper. You'll spend a few hours volunteering at a local school, youth center, or after-school program of your choice. Then, you'll write a paper connecting what you observe to the theories we've been discussing in class."

A low murmur rippled through the room, some groans mixed with a few intrigued hums.

"Now, this will be a partner project," he continued, voice carrying easily over the chatter. "You can choose your own partner today and let me know on your way out of class..." His mouth curved into a mischievous smile. "...or, if you don't, I'll happily assign you to whoever's left. Your choice."

The room erupted instantly, desks hinging and voices overlapping as everyone scrambled to claim their friends.

I turned instinctively toward a girl a few chairs away who was already angling her notebook in my direction. But before I could say a word—

"Hey!"

The voice carried above the chaos, unmistakable.

I glanced back just in time to see Shane McCabe vault two rows like it was nothing, his long legs eating the distance until he dropped into the empty seat beside me. His boyish grin was lethal, his gray eyes flashing like he'd just scored the game-winning shot. With one smooth sweep, he shoved the hair out of his face and stuck out his hand toward me.

"Partners?"

What could I say but yes?

• • •

Shane let me pick the location for our assignment. I chose Girls Inc, the after-school program I'd grown up in — a place that offered tutoring, mentorship, and a safe space for girls who needed somewhere to land after the school day ended. It was where I'd learned how to take risks, how to speak up, how to imagine a future bigger than the one waiting for me at home.

He didn't question the choice.

He did not, however, let me drive myself there.

Instead, he insisted we ride together, picking me up from my dorm at two o'clock on a Thursday afternoon. I told myself not to read into it, even as a flutter of nerves — and something dangerously close to excitement — settled low in my stomach. He was just being nice. That was all.

Still, when he pulled up in a black Pontiac Grand Prix and I spotted two smoothies waiting in the cup holders as I ducked inside, my pulse kicked up a notch.

"Strawberry banana or berry blast?" he asked, weighing them in each hand.

"I'm not really hungry."

"You don't have to be hungry to enjoy a delicious smoothie from the one and only Smoothie Guy."

"Smoothie Guy?"

He stared at me like I'd just insulted his entire lineage. "The Smoothie Guy. The one with the cart when you get off the B Train at Commonwealth?"

I blinked, which only made his insistence grow.

"Okay. Now you have to try both. And I'll be bringing you a new flavor every week until we find your favorite."

"It's freezing outside."

"I would hardly call fifty-eight degrees freezing."

"Well, it's still cold."

"So?"

"What if I don't like smoothies?"

"Come on. Everyone likes smoothies."

He flashed that stupid, sexy smirk, and before I could protest — or remind myself not to overthink the fact that he'd gone out of his way for me — I was tasting them.

And damn him, they were the best smoothies I'd ever had.

"Berry blast," I said after tasting both, and Shane smirked, handing me that one and taking the other. Then, the car was in drive, and we were off.

The Fray played softly over his speakers, and Shane thumbed the steering wheel while quietly singing along.

"So, why did you pick Girls Inc?" he asked after a while.

"I like that they create a safe place for girls to take risks and grow."

He nodded. "You ever been there before?"

"Not this location."

"Where?"

"There was one where I grew up."

"And where was that?"

"Connecticut."

"Ah," he said. "You used to volunteer there?"

I swallowed, looking out the window. "No."

Shane glanced at me, but didn't ask me to fill in the blank. And when he took my cue to end the conversation and reached forward to turn up the music, I was thankful.

We pulled up to Girls Inc forty minutes later, and before I could even touch the door handle, Shane was out of the car and had jogged around to my side. He held the door open and took my book bag, slinging it over his shoulder without letting me protest.

I'd never had a boyfriend. In high school, everyone knew me — which meant everyone knew my family. And there wasn't a boy stupid enough to try to get near me when they knew who my stepfather was.

Still, I'd had crushes before. I wasn't immune to teenage girl hormones.

But when Shane took my bag and then, without hesitation, took my hand in his — I experienced something I never had before.

My stomach erupted with a flurry of butterflies, their wings tickling the inside of my ribcage. I flushed so warm that sweat prickled the back of my neck.

And I smiled.

Because how could I not?

It was unfair, how effortlessly attractive he was. He didn't even have to try. He was in athletic sweats and an old hoodie that said Waterloo Black Hawks on the front, his hair disheveled beneath his beanie like he hadn't cared to even run a comb through it. But he wore his confidence and swagger like an accessory, and he just looked so...

Cozy.

Like he would be the perfect place to curl up and rest.

• • •

Inside Girls Inc, the bright chatter of afterschool chaos met us at the door, along with a smiling staff coordinator who quickly split us up. Shane got waved toward the gym, where a group of girls were setting up for a basketball scrimmage, while I was sent to the art room.

The art room smelled faintly of glue and paint, the long tables littered with paper, scissors, and half-finished collages. I slid into an empty seat beside a pair of girls bent over a poster. They glanced at me with the wary curiosity reserved for strangers, but it didn't take long before their chatter carried me along.

One girl talked about her dream of designing clothes, her voice sharp with certainty. Another shrugged like she wasn't sure when I asked what she thought she wanted to do when she grew up, then admitted she wanted to be a lawyer because her cousin said she'd be good at arguing. They asked me questions in return, but I kept my answers clipped, redirecting them back to themselves.

And as I listened, I couldn't stop the ghosts that rose.

It was hard not to think about me at twelve years old, at a table like this, looking at the clock and wishing the hours would slow down. I knew once my mom showed up, the warmth of this room would evaporate. At Girls Inc, I wasn't the girl from the broken house. I wasn't defined by where I lived or who I lived with or what money I did or didn't have. I was just... me.

And I had a chance at a future.

Still, in my mind, the credit didn't belong to the program. It was the kids themselves who clawed their way forward. Just like I'd answered Professor Reid when he asked, the girls beside me weren't thriving because someone gave them crayons and a safe building. They were thriving because they had grit, because they were strong enough to keep going even when it seemed impossible to do.

At the end of the day, all of them had to go home.

And that was where true resilience was born.

When our time wrapped, I found Shane in the lobby, hair damp with sweat, his grin easy as the girls he'd been with clung to his arms to say goodbye. I felt myself bristle at how natural it was for him, how much they clearly adored him already.

"So," he asked once we stepped outside, "what'd you get?"

I hugged my arms around my notebook, even as Shane took my bag again. "They're really smart and driven. They have dreams. Even though they go home to who knows what... they find a way to look to the future with positivity and light. That's what stuck out to me."

He nodded. "Yeah. But what I heard most was how much they leaned on each other — on the mentors, the program, the whole community. One girl said she never would have stayed in school if it weren't for the people here."

I shook my head. "Well, maybe that's what she said, but that's not entirely it. It was still *her* who had to stay in school, you know? It was her who had to stick with it."

Shane pulled us to a stop in the parking lot. "You don't think she had help?"

"She succeeded because she didn't quit. She kept going no matter what. It's about resilience — what's inside her, inside all of them. Not what's around them."

Shane tilted his head. "You used to go to a Girls Inc, right? That's what you said."

The air in my lungs thinned. "Well... yeah."

"Do you not think they helped you?"

The question hit like a slap — not because it wasn't valid, but because he had no right to ask it. He didn't know what I went home to every night. He didn't know the way my stomach sank when my mom's headlights pulled into the parking lot, or how I'd count the hours until I could come back.

My throat tightened. "You don't know me, Shane McCabe, and I'd really appreciate it if you stopped acting like you did."

I snapped the words, and then I grabbed the strap of my bag off his shoulder and yanked until he released it.

I stormed toward the car, heat flooding my chest, fingers shaking. I felt sort of stupid once I got there, seeing as how it was *his* car, and I didn't have the keys. I was half-tempted to catch a bus back to campus when I heard his footsteps behind me, steady and unhurried.

Wordlessly, he opened my door for me.

I didn't look at him as I slipped inside.

The ride back toward campus was too quiet, and the longer I sat and stewed, the more I realized how cruel I'd been. He'd just been asking me questions, just arguing his side of our assignment the same way I was.

But he'd triggered me, and I hadn't known how else to react than to push him away.

"I'm sorry—"

"Hey, I'm sorry—"

We said it at the same time, our eyes snapping to each other as we both let out low chuckles.

"You shouldn't be," I said next. "It was me who bit your head off."

"You had every right to. I shouldn't have assumed I knew anything about you." Shane paused, switching hands on the steering wheel. "But, for the record, I'd really like to change that fact."

His eyes met mine again, and the sincerity there nearly killed me.

"I don't think you'd like what you discover," I whispered.

Shane frowned, and then without hesitation, his hand was reaching for mine. He curled his fingers around my own, holding tight, as if the notion hadn't sent those stupid butterflies into a frenzy inside me once more.

"My parents died when I was a kid."

He said the words unflinchingly, like he was just telling me the weather report for tomorrow. Meanwhile, my jaw had unhinged, my heart stalling in my chest.

"It was an ice storm. We lived in Georgia and, well, let's just say snowstorms really mess up the roads down there. It's not like here where they have plows out within the hour. They had pulled over, the snow coming down too thick for them to see. And I guess it was too thick for the semi-truck that hit them, too."

I closed my eyes, letting out a slow, pained breath.

"I grew up with my grandparents after that. They put me in hockey mostly because they didn't know what else to do with me. I was seven, and by the time I turned ten, hockey was my whole world. The coaches, my teammates... they're who got me through."

He glanced at me before his eyes were on the road again, but his hand never left mine.

"So when I talk about how important community is, it's because I lived it. It's because, for me, a team is everything." He paused. "And I realize that you probably feel the way you do because you didn't have that. You fought your battle alone." He looked at me, holding my gaze. "You may still be fighting alone."

My throat constricted, and my gaze flicked between his eyes, my chest aching in a way I hadn't expected. There was something in the way he looked at me — not pity, not judgment — just a quiet, unsettling understanding. It made me want to turn away, to shield the parts of myself I'd learned to keep guarded.

But another part of me felt something shift, fragile and unfamiliar, as if his words had reached into the corners of me I didn't even know existed. It was unnerving... and somehow comforting, too, to realize he saw the fight I'd always believed no one noticed.

"So, maybe we're both right," he said, looking back at the road. "Maybe resilience is born inside us, but maybe it's fostered by the ones around us who give a shit, too."

I squeezed his hand.

He squeezed back.

We presented our findings the next week in class.

And we got an A.

# CHAPTER 5

## WHAT A PLEASANT SURPRISE

Shane
Present

"Goddamnit." I blew the whistle after the curse left my lips, frustration boiling in my veins. Preseason was officially here, and I had the guys playing out a scrimmage in our last practice before we'd take on our opponents tomorrow night.

And as of now, we looked more like a group of giraffes on ice than a professional hockey team.

"Tanev, are you in need of contacts, or did you just blatantly refuse to pass the puck to Fabri, who was wide the fuck open?" I asked, hanging my hands on my hips.

"Oh, Tanny Boy for sure needs glasses," Jaxson Brittain said, skating around his best friend, who spit on the ice while giving Brittzy a proper glare. "Explains why he missed that one-on-one shot against a rookie earlier, too."

"What is it you Canadians say?" Vince Tanev asked, thumbing his chin and looking up before he snapped his fingers. "Oh. I remember. *Nize it*, Brittzy."

"Hey, go easy on him," Carter Fabri called from where he was bent over catching his breath. "The poor guy has a ten-month-old going through a sleep regression."

"He'll be going through an ice-time regression if he doesn't get his shit together," Daddy P quipped from the net.

Aleks Suter couldn't resist himself. "All right, Grandpa. Not sure you should have much of a say in the matter, since you won't be around this time next year."

"Yeah, you'll have a cane by then," Fabio chimed in. Then, he started using his stick like a cane, hobbling on his skates with a hand on his back as he moaned in fake agony.

To the outsider, it might have all seemed a bit harsh — but this was how the team was, especially this particular crew. Chirps flew between the five of them like rice flew on a wedding day. And if one of them was getting picked on harder than the others in today's practice, you could bet someone else would get the lashing tomorrow.

But it was all in good spirit. They were a family, these guys and the women they'd found over the years. Any time I was invited to one of their group barbecues or other events, I saw firsthand how much they all meant to one another. They even pulled me into their little community; when they could tear me away from the rink, anyway.

The rest of the Ospreys, rookie and veteran alike, smirked from the sidelines or skated around staying warm while these five battled it out. When I'd had enough of their shenanigans, I blew the whistle to signal it was time to get back to work, and they did without hesitation.

That was what I loved about them more than anything. They goofed off, yes, and they'd tested my patience more than once with how they'd sneak in rounds of golf even during the season when they knew they were forbidden from playing any other sport, due to the chances they might hurt themselves.

But at the end of the day, they were damn good players. They held each other accountable. They pulled out the best in one another and in every other player on our roster.

I was lucky to have them.

My stomach tightened a bit as the scrimmage kicked up again because I realized they'd be like a monster without its head next season when Daddy P was gone.

Across the rink from where he guarded the net, our backup was in place for the other scrimmage team — Ben Sandin. He was young, twenty-fucking-three to be exact, but he was also hungry. He'd come to us fresh out of the USHL at the ripe old age of eighteen, and he'd been training under Will Perry ever since.

The kid had heart, too, which was what I loved about him most.

His father was sick. He had aggressive pancreatic cancer, and Ben had been splitting his time between the rink and hospital rooms for the better part of the last six months. I knew too well the devastation that came with losing a parent, and I hoped the kid wouldn't have to experience it. I hoped, somehow, his father made it through.

But for now, I was happy he was still focused on hockey. I wondered if it was saving him the way it had saved me as a kid.

He had his own style, but he also took it in stride when Daddy P gave him pointers. That was all I could ask for when it came to a young goalie — that he was driven, passionate, and willing to learn.

Still, he was a quirky, young kid with half the life experience that Perry had. He would struggle to lead a team until he was older, I imagined — and I wasn't so sure he was the right choice to be Perry's replacement.

There were trades we could make to get a goalie from other teams in the league, but I wasn't so sure that was the right choice, either.

Honestly, the only thing that felt right was to beg Will to stay, and I knew that option wasn't even on the table.

My thoughts were swirling as I watched the scrimmage play out, my assistants taking over and blowing the whistles when they saw something they wanted to call out between plays. I held mine between my teeth, arms folded over my chest, gaze darting from one end of the rink to the other.

And that's when a flash of golden hair caught my eyes.

Ariana Ridley — er, *Black* — was standing in the front of one of the box suites, her hands braced on the top edge of the plexiglass that surrounded the seats as she peered over and scanned the arena like she was looking for something.

When her gaze snagged on me, my heart leaped into my throat.

Without thinking, I lifted a hand in a wave. She returned it hesitantly, and then tried shouting something to me. I couldn't hear her over the scrimmage, but I held up a finger, letting her know I'd be right up. Then, I signaled to Kozak before bolting through the locker room and to the closest elevator.

I knew this arena like I knew my own house. I could get anywhere I wanted to be without even thinking about it, knowing which back routes to take, which elevators, when it was necessary to cross into the fan-facing areas. I made it to the suite Ariana was at in under six minutes.

She'd stayed put, her hands still on the plexiglass as she gazed down at practice. I paused at the top of the suite, taking in her silhouette with the bright ice illuminated in front of her. The last time I'd seen her in an arena was when she was watching me play two decades ago.

Ariana must have heard me, because she turned over her shoulder, and she smiled.

It was like a fist to my gut.

"I'm sorry," she said instantly, wrapping her long cardigan around her tighter as she climbed the stairs up to where I stood. "I didn't mean to take you from practice."

I shoved my hands in my pockets and tried to mirror her smile, all the while shoving down all the words that wanted to tumble out — like *call on me any day, any time, and I'll come running, Ari.*

*I'm still yours.*

*I never stopped being yours.*

"Ah, no biggie. Kozak has it handled down there. Besides, I could use the break," I said instead.

Ariana nodded, her arms tightly crossed as she glanced at the ice and then back at me. "I was just looking for my husband."

At this rate, her words were fucking MMA fighters, and I was their punching bag.

My mind, unhelpfully, flashed back to that first day — to the way she'd gone rigid when Nathan kissed her before the press conference. It had been just a fraction of a second, but she'd been far too stiff. I'd clocked it immediately, the way you notice a missed step or a blown coverage, and I hadn't been able to stop replaying it since.

Every interaction, every glance, every touch between them was dissected in my mind like game film I couldn't stop studying.

"He wasn't in his office," she added when my dumb ass didn't reply. "And I don't know this arena well enough yet to guess where else he might be. I thought maybe he was peeking in on practice."

"Well, he did earlier, so your guess was a good one," I managed, and then I nodded toward the door of the suite. "Come on. I bet we can find him."

I opened the door and held it for Ariana, watching her go every step of the way. I couldn't help how my hand hovered at the small of her back, guiding without contact, though I reverberated with the urge to touch her just to see what she'd do, just to feel her again after all this time.

Thirteen years. That was how long it had been since I'd last seen her.

Eighteen since I'd last held her in my arms.

I cataloged those lost years in her features, in the soft lines at the edges of her eyes and mouth, the way her hair had changed in texture, a few sneaky strands of silver threading in with the gold. It had my chest tight, the way I felt robbed by not being able to witness those changes in real time. But her eyes were still that shocking bright blue, and I knew her smile would be the same, too, if I ever got the chance to see it on full display, and not just a slight curl of her lips.

We walked side by side in silence for a moment, me pointing the way to the elevator that would take us back down to the guts of this place. I had a few ideas where Nathan might be, and more popping into my head as we walked. I'd seen him spending quite a bit of time with our analytics team earlier — which, if I was being honest, had kind of rubbed me the wrong way. I didn't like the way the intern nodded and looked as pale as snow when Nathan was talking to him, one hand clamped on his shoulder with a politician's grin in place. I also hadn't loved how Nathan had insisted on getting to know all the players since he'd joined.

I was aware that didn't make sense. He was our new general manager. He *should* get to know the players. But this guy set off all my alarms when he walked into any room I was in. I just didn't trust him, no matter how friendly he was to me and everyone he met.

*It's because he's with Ariana and you're not*, my common sense tried to tell me.

But I assured myself it was something more.

"So, what do you think of Tampa so far?" I asked after pushing the button on the elevator to take us down.

Ariana seemed lost in thought, but she blew out a breath before shrugging, her eyes casting up to mine. "It's hot."

I chuckled. "Yes, that it is. Wait until you have to suffer through a summer here."

"I've heard the winter is nice, though."

"It is. January to March is the best. Great time to go to the beach, too, if that's your thing."

Ariana folded her hands together and nodded, and I felt supremely stupid.

*Was I really talking to this woman about the fucking weather right now?*

This was Ariana Ridley, the girl who had me spilling my guts about my parents' death within hours of spending time with her. This was the girl who'd felt more like my family than anyone else.

*Yes, but she's a stranger now,* my brain argued again. *Because you left her.*

"It's night and day to Boston," I said, not able to help myself. "No fall color changes or blistering winters here in The Sunshine State."

Ice slid behind her gaze at that, and she turned toward the elevator doors just as they opened. "Yes, well, I don't miss anything about Boston."

My next swallow felt like I had a throat full of razor blades.

Ariana shot out of the elevator, and then waited without looking at me until I joined her and gestured to the left. "Let's try the video review room."

She nodded and followed my lead. After we'd walked a few steps, I noticed her wringing her hands together, her lip between her teeth like she was a woman about to walk death row.

"You okay?" I asked.

Ariana glanced at me from the corner of her eyes before plastering on her best smile and forcing a breath. "Fine. I just... he's going to kill me for being so stupid."

I frowned, wondering what the hell *that* meant, but before I could ask, the man we were looking for found us, instead.

"Well, what a pleasant surprise this is," he sang, even as his eyes sliced between me and his wife like he'd caught us in bed together rather than walking with two feet between us. "Ariana, sweetheart, what are you doing here?"

Too quickly, Ariana was gone from my side and pulled into his. I heard them kiss even as I looked away with the excuse of saying a polite hello to Jeremy, Nathan's senior advisor. He'd been senior advisor to Dick, and because Nathan had rolled in so close to the season, he remained in his position, at least for now.

"We'll continue this conversation later," Nathan said to Jeremy then, and the way he leveled a gaze at the man had the hair on the back of my neck standing on end. I'd never seen Jeremy look so ashen as he did in that moment, and his eyes skirted to mine only briefly before he nodded and excused himself.

*What the...*

"I'm so sorry to bother you at work," Ariana said. "I... I somehow misplaced my key and found myself locked out of the house."

I smiled at the innocence of that confession, at how many times Ariana had been forgetful when we were younger. I'd often teased her that her head was in the clouds, daydreaming about how to save the world when she'd leave her purse or phone at a restaurant we'd eaten at. She was always so apologetic, which I'd laughed at.

*Why the hell are you apologizing for something everyone does?*

Truthfully, I'd always loved when she forgot something. It meant I had more time with her. I remembered one night we got caught in the snow when we had to trace our steps back to a bar we'd been at near campus because she'd left her scarf. I loved the way the flecks stuck to her hair and eyelashes as we laughed and did our best not to slip and break our damned necks on the way home.

"You lost your key," Nathan repeated, and he was smiling, but it was as if that smile was a thin veil for his true feelings about this fact. "The one I specifically told you to keep on a keychain or hooked to your purse or whatever you needed to do because we have yet to have any spares made?"

He laughed as he said it, pulling Ariana into his side as he rubbed her arm.

I didn't miss the way she flinched, tucking her chin to her chest.

And I saw fucking red.

"I just misplaced it," she murmured in argument, but Nathan guffawed louder to drown her out, even as his grip on her intensified.

"Ah, women, am I right, Shane?" Nathan said to me, still laughing, like I was his fucking buddy, and Ariana was the butt of all our jokes. "It's a good thing you're beautiful, my love. And that I am a responsible man who doesn't misplace anything."

I watched Ariana at that — how her shoulders drew in a fraction, how she tucked herself closer to him instead of away, like she'd learned that smaller was safer. Her smile stayed in place, but it didn't reach her eyes.

Nathan's own smile fell instantly with that word, and he released her, digging into the pocket of his slacks. He pulled out a simple silver key ring and pressed it sharply into her palm.

"Huh," I said loudly, unable to help myself as I slid my hands into my pockets and grinned at Nathan. "So interesting to me that you have a key to your house instead of a keypad. What is this, 1980?"

Nathan blinked at me, clearly unsure if I was fucking with him. Ariana didn't laugh. Her fingers closed around the key instead, knuckles whitening before she seemed to catch herself and loosen her grip.

I stood my ground, shrugging. "Just saying, I don't know anyone these days who uses a key. I know you two just moved in. Do you need some help? I can stop by and replace the door mechanism in a jiffy. It's easy. Takes ten minutes tops. And then you can join us all in the twenty-first century."

Nathan blinked slowly, assessing. Meanwhile, Ariana's gaze flicked to him — quick and cautious, like she was gauging how he'd take it.

Like she was bracing.

"The lock isn't the problem," he said finally, forcing his smile back into place. "It's my dear sweet wife here who would lose her own head if it weren't attached."

He hooked his arm around her again and kissed the top of her hair, but she stiffened beneath him.

And all my fucking alarms were blaring now.

"Well, there wouldn't be a key to be lost if you had a keypad, would there?" I said, keeping my tone easy, friendly, like I wasn't cataloging every reaction in real time, and wasn't already deciding how much I hated this man. "Just a thought."

For a long moment, Nathan and I stood there in a quiet standoff. His eyes narrowed, flicking between my face and Ariana's like he couldn't tell if I was being amicable, or if I was being an asshole.

*It's the latter, you dumb motherfucker.*

"I better get going," Ariana said, carefully peeling herself away from her husband with her eyes on the key in her hands. "I have groceries in the car."

"Oh, wonderful, now we'll have spoiled milk and produce, too," Nathan said, still smiling, like if he pretended it was all a joke, no one would pick up on the fact that he was being a fucking bully to his wife.

I ground my teeth as the word flashed in my mind.

And I didn't care that I didn't know this man well, I knew enough to feel with urgent fervor that he wasn't good enough to call Ariana his.

"I'll walk you out," I said, but before I could take a step, Nathan slid in-between us.

"*I'll* walk her out."

He glared at me only a moment before he was all teeth with his fake smile, and then his arm was around Ariana, guiding her to the parking lot.

I had no choice but to watch him leave with her, and my hands curled into fists in my pockets, my stomach tied in the fiercest knot.

When Ariana glanced at me over her shoulder, I thought I saw apology in her eyes, as if she had anything to be sorry for. I also thought I saw her slightly shake her head, like she was telling me without words to leave it alone.

That's when it hit me like a six-foot-four, two-hundred-pound defender.

She was scared of him.

I was determined to find out why.

## CHAPTER 6

### FAIR TRADE

Shane
2006–2007

I didn't want to be apart from Ariana after that day at Girls Inc.

Instead of sitting two rows back from her, I'd taken to sitting in the seat right next to hers. I figured out when she walked to class and I'd meet her at her dorm, taking her bag over my shoulder.

It became a rhythm; one I looked forward to more than game day. Every Thursday, I showed up with a new smoothie from the Smoothie Guy — mango sunrise, tropical punch, peanut butter banana — and watched her wrinkle her nose before I convinced her to try a sip. By week four, I had a running list of her favorites scratched into the margins of my textbook.

Those walks to class were my time to shine. That was when I got to bug her without restraint. I asked her about everything: what music she listened to when she was sad (Coldplay), what her first job was (dog walker), why she always layered a lacy tank top under her shirts (because it's cool). She rolled her eyes at my endless curiosity, but she always answered. When fall semester was coming to a close, and I knew we wouldn't have Professor Reid together anymore, I innocently asked her which classes she was taking in the spring and made sure I had another one with her.

I didn't want to lose our walking-to-class ritual.

And from that ritual, Ariana came to know me better than most of my teammates.

She knew I was majoring in psychology, that it wasn't just a backup plan for when hockey ended, but something I already used in the locker room — to read the guys, to lead better. She knew we were clawing through the playoff race, one step from a Frozen Four berth if we could just keep the momentum. And she knew about my pregame superstitions and routine, everything from how I had to eat half a Hawaiian pizza to the precise way I laced my skates.

She told me she was majoring in sociology, that she wanted to work with kids someday. She didn't say it like it was some vague dream, either. It was steady and rooted, the kind of certainty that made me believe she'd actually do it.

By the time we'd reach the classroom, I was usually mid-question — sometimes serious, sometimes dumb — and she'd push open the heavy door with a sigh. "Class is starting, McCabe. You'll have to wait to yap at me later."

But then she'd shoot me this look, this small, reluctant smile that gave her away. She liked the questions. She liked me being there.

And I had every intention of staying.

One evening, I talked Ariana into a study date. Midterms were upon us, and it was the perfect excuse to spend time with her. She invited me to her dorm, since the library was packed, and I skipped over there like a kid on his way to Santa's workshop.

We had our books spread across her desk and the floor, two open smoothies within arm's reach, and Ariana was dead serious about cramming every last bit of theory into her head before our exam.

I, on the other hand, couldn't focus on a single word in that textbook or my notes.

School was important to me, and I wanted to do well on my midterms, but my mind was tied up. I was thinking about hockey, about how regionals were coming up, about how we had more than just a chance at the Frozen Four tournament. I was thinking about drills and video and staying mentally strong.

And more than anything, I was thinking about Ariana.

She was sprawled out on her stomach on the floor, gnawing on the end of her pen while she studied. Her hair was down tonight, still damp from a shower, and she was cozied up in a light pink sweatsuit.

It was my first time *inside* her dorm, as I usually met her on the sidewalk when I'd walk her to class. And while she studied her notes, I studied everything the room told me about her.

I saw the stacks of books in the corner of her room, not just textbooks, but fiction, too. Markus Zusak. Stieg Larsson. Stephen King. Virginia Woolf. Charlotte Brontë. Jane Austen. I saw craft supplies shoved hastily under her bed. There was a half-finished puzzle on her desk, now covered by notes we'd sprawled on top of it.

Unable to help myself, I snatched a black binder full of CDs off her nightstand and began thumbing through. Coldplay. Radiohead. Sarah McLachlan. Avril Lavigne. Fiona Apple. I hummed my approval when I came upon Snow Patrol.

"I can't wait for their next album," I said, pulling *Final Straw* from the slipcover and waving it at Ariana.

She glanced up in a study-haze, blinking before she frowned at me. "Are you going through my stuff?"

"Just looking at what music you listen to."

"You're supposed to be studying," she reminded me. "This whole thing was your idea."

"I can't help it. I'm distracted by you. Is that so bad?"

She rolled her eyes, but I saw the flush of her cheeks as she turned her attention back to her notes.

I picked one of her CDs labeled as *rainy day mix* and popped it into my laptop. When it started playing John Mayer, I smiled.

"We have similar taste in music," I told her.

"And apparently different taste in study vibes." She climbed up to where I sat on her bed long enough to turn the music off, and I didn't even mind — not with the view that little act gave me.

Ariana got right back to studying when she was on the floor, but I was still looking around.

My eyes caught on the one and only photo in the room.

It was of her and a woman I assumed was her mother. Ariana was holding a baby boy.

My stomach tightened.

"Who's that?" I asked, nodding to the picture frame.

Ariana looked up at me, then where I was staring, and the most genuine smile I'd ever seen graced her lips.

"My little brother."

Apparently, I didn't hide my shock well, because Ariana chuckled at my expression before turning back to her notes.

"Yeah, bit of an age gap, huh? He..." She swallowed. "Wasn't exactly planned."

"Care to elaborate?"

Ariana sat up, wincing against a pain in her neck as she rubbed it. "My stepdad is... a real piece of work," she said with a laugh that carried more weight than any I'd ever heard. "His favorite pastime is beating up on my mom and then making her forgive him with some elaborate, romantic gesture." She nodded to the photo. "That time, it led to an accidental pregnancy."

I gaped at her.

*Had she just said what I thought she had?*

"I was so upset at first," Ariana admitted quietly. "Shitty, I know, but I just... I felt like there was no way we'd ever get away from him now. If she had a kid by him." There it was, that smile again. "But then Georgie was born, and I swear, I'd never felt love like that in my life. My dad took off when I was a kid, so I never expected to have a sibling. I'm glad I do. He's the best thing in my life."

I blinked.

I was still stuck on the fact that her stepfather hit her mother.

Apparently, more than once.

"He's almost five now." She swallowed, looking at her nails. "I go home whenever I can. Not because I want to be in that house, because if it was up to me, I'd never go back again. But because I need to see him. I need to make sure he's okay."

"Fuck, Ari," I said, and then I was off the bed and on the floor right next to her, wrapping her hand up in mine. "That's... that's really heavy."

She nodded. "I told you, you might not like what you discover."

"I like everything about you."

She puffed out a laugh. "Even my toxic family bullshit?"

"Every piece." I frowned, sweeping a lock of her hair from her face. "He... he's never hit *you*, has he?"

Ariana's gaze slid somewhere behind me. "Not yet. But there was a night with a knife where I got in the way." She held up her hand, the harsh light of her dorm highlighting the shiny scar across her skin. "That's how this happened."

Her answer made the hair on the back of my neck stand up, and I pulled her into me without thinking, holding her close to my chest as she fisted her hands in the sleeves of her hoodie and hugged me in return.

"Why doesn't your mom just leave?"

"It's not that simple," she said on a sigh. "Though, trust me... I've asked her the same question many times."

"I get it now."

"Get what?"

I pulled back to look at her. "Why you believe resilience is born within."

Her smile was soft at the edges, her eyes searching mine. "You called me Ari."

"I did. Is that okay?"

That smile widened, and she nodded. "Yeah."

"Good."

"Can we talk about something else?"

"Anything you want."

"Well, we should probably be talking about stages of childhood social development..."

"Five minutes," I said. "Just a little break and we'll get back to it."

"Okay, then. Tell me about hockey."

I leaned back on my palms, but still stayed close enough that my knee touched hers. "It's all ramping up now. We've got regionals soon, then semi-finals. And then…" I shrugged, picking up the pen she'd chewed to bits with a grimace. "Championship game. Milwaukee. Ours for the taking."

She snatched her pen from my hand with a roll of her eyes. "You sound so sure."

"I am." I straightened, leaning toward her across the pile of notes. "Sure enough that I'll make you a bet right now. If we make it to the championship game, you have to go."

She blinked, then laughed — that soft, surprised laugh I was starting to crave. "You're insane. I'm not flying to *Milwaukee* to watch you skate around on ice."

"Why not?"

"Because that's ridiculous," she said, shaking her head. But the corner of her mouth betrayed her, tugging up. "Fine. What do I get if you lose?"

I tilted my head, and unashamedly, my eyes ran the length of her. "What do you want?"

My voice dropped an octave, suggestive, because I liked the way her breath caught when I teased like that. I liked how she pretended she was annoyed and unaffected by me, but her body told a different story.

And there it was, the reward I was seeking — the hitch in her breath, the parting of her lips, the slight widening of her eyes.

She stared at me for a second, color creeping into her cheeks, but then she smirked back. "Your smoothie punch card." She pointed her demolished pen at my chest. "I know you've been hiding it from me."

"*That's* what you want? Not dinner anywhere you choose, not me running laps around Conte Forum shouting your name — my smoothie card?"

"It's worth at least fifty bucks in free smoothies," she said primly, picking up her notebook. "Seems like a fair trade."

I shook my head, still grinning as I leaned back on my palms again. "All right. You've got a deal."

I extended my hand, and we shook on it.

I'd never been so motivated to win in my life.

•••

On March 25, 2007, right around midnight, I decided I couldn't hold back my feelings anymore.

I was on a bus full of my teammates, all of us buzzing after winning our regional game. I could still hear the roar of the crowd in Worcester even back at campus.

We'd buried Miami five–nothing. Frozen Four, baby. We were going.

And all I could think was that I had to tell Ariana.

The bus hissed as it pulled to a stop, brakes squealing against the quiet of campus. Midnight air bit at my lungs when I jumped down the steps, but I barely felt it.

I didn't even think about it — just took off running across the quad, grinning like a lunatic with my hockey bag thumping against my side. By the time I reached her dorm, my chest was heaving, not from the sprint, but from the thought of her on the other side of that door.

I knocked loud and insistent, and thirty seconds later, the door cracked open. Ariana stood there in a big sweatshirt and shorts, hair piled in a messy knot, finger pressed to her lips. "Shhh! My roommate's asleep." But she was smiling, and it hit me like a second victory. "What are you doing here?"

"Did I wake you?" I whispered, trying to catch my breath.

She was still smiling. The sight of it lit my chest on fire. "No. I was waiting up to see—"

She didn't get to finish before I had my hands in her hair and was kissing her.

The win against Miami, the way I'd thought about Ariana all the way to Worcester and the whole way back, the way she was all I *ever* thought about anymore...

It all snapped something inside me, and my patience was eviscerated.

She gasped against my mouth, surprised for only a moment.

And then, she melted, her hands finding the front of my hoodie and fisting there like she'd been holding back just as much as I had.

I could have kissed her all night. I could have survived off the little whimper she made, the way her body leaned into mine, how she pressed onto her toes like she wanted more. I framed her face, thumbs at her jaw, fingers curling in her hair as she parted her lips and my tongue swept in.

That had both of us groaning, and suddenly I was hungry for more than just a kiss.

When I finally pulled back, I pressed my forehead to hers, still grinning like a fool. "Be my girlfriend," I breathed, voice rough with hope. "Please, Ariana. I don't want this to be just... whatever we've been. I don't want there to be any question in your mind when it comes to how I feel about you." I swallowed, pulling back so I could look at her. "I want it to be you and me."

Her eyes flicked over my face, wide and searching, like she was trying to decide if I meant it.

I'd never been surer of anything.

And she must have seen it, because that smile was back, her cheeks flushed, lips swollen. "Yes," she breathed.

"Yes?"

She nodded.

And then she was in my arms, and I was spinning, feeling like I was on top of the world.

## CHAPTER 7

### LEAVE IT WITH ME

Ariana
Present

"Drops of Jupiter" played on the sound system as I slid a box cutter through the tape of another box. This one was marked *books*, and though I knew my husband would likely want me focused on unpacking the kitchen first, I reached for this box, instead.

I was trying desperately to feel some kind of joy.

I'd put on my favorite throwback playlist, one that reminded me of a time in my life where I felt full of possibility. And as I began plucking book after book from that box and placing them with care on the built-in bookshelves surrounding the television in our living room, I waited for happiness to hit me.

*I'm so lucky*, I thought as I pulled out my J.R.R. Tolkien collection. *So many women would kill for what I have*, I swore as I shelved my classics — Hemingway and Emerson and Salinger and Brontë and Austen. *I have so much*, I reminded myself as I thumbed my copy of *A Wrinkle in*

*Time*, the book that had served as my favorite escape as a child.

But each time I berated myself, it did nothing to change how I truly felt.

On the outside, I was the beloved wife of a successful man. I was rich in both money and love. I was beautiful and healthy and couldn't possibly ask for anything else.

On the inside, I was dying a slow, merciless death.

*This is because of Shane.*

I knew it and refuted it all the same, that being reunited unwillingly to the first man I ever loved — and the first to break me — had ignited all these feelings. Truthfully, I'd felt them well before that man had crashed back into my life. I'd been trapped in my own personal hell for years.

But seeing Shane again, marveling at the way time had changed him, wondering what would have happened if only he'd chosen to stick it out with me instead of run...

It stirred up my insides like a storm over a muddy river, all the thoughts of the past swirling with the realities of the present and the darkness of the future.

My hand hovered over the spine of *Angela's Ashes* once I'd placed it, and again I found myself remembering the first time I'd read it, when I was a teenager and felt seen by someone who also understood the reality of living in an unstable home.

I hadn't meant to end up here again.

But life rarely unfolds the way you intend.

After Shane left, I did everything right.

My mother was gone. My brother was now in my care. And I was preparing to fight an uphill battle against my stepdad. If all of that wasn't enough to bury me, the heartbreak I felt from Shane walking away when I needed him most would surely do the trick. Except, I didn't let it.

Just like the case studies of children we'd covered in my sociology classes, I was resilient.

I stayed in school, worked nights and weekends to finish my undergrad degree and then earn my master's. I poured every ounce of myself into becoming someone I could be proud of. I built a life for Georgie and me from the ground up. It was modest, but it was ours.

There were nights I fell asleep on the couch with his homework spread across my lap, the smell of burnt coffee in the air, student loan statements stacked on the counter. I was tired, but I was steady. I didn't need saving. I told myself that over and over — that I could do this, that love wasn't a requirement for survival.

But still, I'd catch myself lingering on other people's lives. I stared too long at couples holding hands in grocery store aisles. The sound of laughter from a neighbor's backyard would have my chest aching. The announcements from my college friends of engagements or babies made my eyes water. I told myself I didn't crave it — but God, I did. I longed for security, for comfort, for the soft kind of joy that comes from knowing someone else was there with you to go through anything.

And then, Nathan Black walked into my life.

He was everything I thought I wanted — calm, certain, dependable. He came to one of our nonprofit fundraisers for the youth outreach program I was leading at the time. Older than me by a decade, Nathan was there to speak on behalf of the financial organization he worked for, to talk about the importance of budgeting and how to get started even as a kid. I remember thinking how effortlessly he commanded a room, how safe he made everyone feel, including me.

He asked questions no one else bothered with, listened like he actually cared about the answers. He told me I was extraordinary — that I'd done what most people couldn't.

He asked if he could take me to dinner that night, and we ended up in a run-down diner at just past midnight, laughing as we bonded over our love for books and kids. And it happened so easily, how we went from strangers to dating. Nathan loved to dote on me, to take the weight off my shoulders in any way he could. He hired a housekeeper once a week to clean the apartment I shared with Georgie. He would often show up at my door with bags full of groceries. He'd cook for us and help Georgie with school projects.

For the first time in years, even though it was terrifying... I let someone take care of me.

The first few years of our relationship flew by, and they were as golden as a sun beam. Nathan would spoil me with dinners at restaurants that boasted dishes more expensive than my car payment. We'd take weekend trips to the lake with Georgie, where Nathan would grill and tell stories that had us all in stitches. He came to every event I organized, donated quietly to my programs, bragged about me in every room.

I felt seen and protected and cherished.

When he proposed, it was the easiest yes I'd ever said in my life — even if my mind did flash back to Shane. I knew it was silly, even then, to think about that boy. We had been kids when we fell in love. It had been so long since we'd even seen each other. I told myself it was just my heart holding onto the feeling of youth and innocence.

Nathan was my new path, and I was ready to walk it.

I thought I'd finally been rewarded for all the ways I'd fought and scraped and survived.

But slowly, the shine dulled.

It started with small things — the way he'd correct me when I told a story, as if I couldn't quite remember it right. The way he'd suggest I wear my hair differently for a fundraiser, or tell me a certain dress wasn't "professional." At first, I thought it was love — a man who wanted me to be my best.

Then came the comments about my friends, the subtle sighs when I made plans without him. He'd tell me I didn't need to work so much, that it was time to "enjoy the life he'd given me."

And when I bristled, when I reminded him that I earned my life — that I had before him and could again — his smile would falter, and I'd see the flash of something behind his eyes I didn't recognize.

By the time I did, it was too late.

Slowly, I found myself living a life I didn't recognize. I didn't work anymore — only volunteered for the organizations that were best suited for Nathan and his own professional goals. Nathan paid for everything — our house, our cars, our groceries, Georgie's medical school tuition.

Nathan took care of me. I couldn't remember the last time I'd had to take my car in for service or even pump my own gas. I never had to ask to buy a thing — the money was there, and he wanted me to spend it. *You don't have to worry about anything, sweetheart*, he said to me often.

But I did worry.

Because I never knew which version of him would come home.

I was a kept woman, and I should have been thankful. This was what I'd wanted — security, dependability, love. And he *did* love me. He loved me so fiercely he sometimes acted like a monster, only to grimace at his own actions and drop to his knees, crawling to me and clinging to my legs to beg for forgiveness and understanding.

Most of the time, my life was picture perfect.

But it didn't matter how rare the bad times were — they still screamed so loudly I couldn't ignore them if I tried.

And it felt like a repeat of how I'd begged my mother to wake up and walk away, except this time, I was beating on my own ribcage instead of her door.

My phone buzzing on an unopened box snapped me from my thoughts, and the first genuine smile of the day found me when I saw my little brother's face on the screen. It was a photo of us at his college graduation, him in his cap and gown, and me in a white dress Nathan had picked out for me. Georgie had me tucked under his arm with a proud grin, and I leaned into his side with a closed-lip smile.

"Why hello, Doctor Campbell."

Georgie's laugh made my heart squeeze. "Still have quite a few years before I earn that title. Haven't even gotten into rotations yet."

"Well, the title should be yours based off the amount of hours you put into studying alone." I put the phone on speaker before opening the next box of books. "I'm surprised you even find time to call me."

"You know I always have time for my big sis. How's it going in Florida? Been to the beach yet?"

"Have you seen how pale I am? Not exactly my scene."

"I think that's the whole point of going — to get a tan."

"I don't tan," I said with a laugh. "I was cursed with our mother's skin."

I regretted the words as soon as I said them, because of course that meant I was insinuating that Georgie's skin tone, so effortlessly bronze even in the wintertime, came from his father.

And I knew he wished he had nothing to do with that man.

It was part of the reason he was George Campbell now, the same way I'd changed my name from Ridley to Campbell after the whole ordeal, too. Campbell was our mother's maiden name, and we claimed it the way we wished we'd been able to claim her before it was too late.

"But, I will say, I'm excited to spend some time in our pool."

"Fancy pants," Georgie said with a whistle. "Got a pool in your backyard. Did you ever think you'd see the day?"

I chuffed a laugh. "Hardly. I still feel like I'm the same person I was when you and I were living off SpaghettiOs."

"I still love those things," Georgie said with a hum. "Don't judge me, but I have a whole stash at my dorm. It's the best late-night study snack."

"Would you advise your patients to eat them?"

"Absolutely not," he said. "But they don't need to know my personal business."

I chuckled. "I miss you."

"Miss you, too. You still going to come visit for your birthday?"

My stomach soured then. "Nathan thinks we should have a big party here, since it's the holiday and everything. Great way to get all the staff together before the playoff race really kicks in."

There was a brief pause on the phone before Georgie cleared his throat. "Well, Nathan certainly knows what's best for business."

The phrasing struck me as odd, stiff in a way Georgie rarely was, but I let it go. "Would you want to come here? I know you have your own friends and life there, that school has you tied up... but we have a room here with your name on it."

"Are you kidding, Ri? I wouldn't miss it for anything. My big sister is turning forty. I gotta party with you before your back and knees give out."

I balked, but was fighting off laughter of my own as my brother guffawed. "Oh, you think you're so funny with the old jokes, huh? Hate to break it to you, kid, but this will be you one day, too."

"Nah, I'm too beautiful to age."

"Keep telling yourself that," I said, still laughing.

"So... how was it seeing Shane again?"

That had my smile melting like snow under a blow dryer. I turned my focus back to unpacking. "What do you mean?"

"*What do you mean* what do I mean? Was it awkward? Exciting? Did your stomach fill with butterflies?"

I snorted. "Honestly, Georgie. I'm married."

"Yeah, to such a great guy," he deadpanned, and before the sting of that could sink in, he sucked his teeth and continued pressing me. "Seriously, have you guys had a chance to talk?"

"There's nothing for us to talk about," I said with finality, shelving a book a bit too hard. "Shane is Shane. He looks pretty much the same. He's the head coach and I am the wife of the general manager, it's not like we're hanging out all the time. He was a bit surprised to see me, I think, but he's been pleasant enough since. Professional. It's.... I don't know. It's nothing to talk about."

"Uh-huh," Georgie said. "And did you tell him you stalked his hockey career for years, or that you still have his Boston College hoodie?"

"Shh," I snapped. "I do not."

"I've seen it."

"I got rid of it years ago."

"I packed it into one of those boxes you're now going through."

That had my eyes wide and scanning, wondering which one. I'd have to hide it away before Nathan saw it.

Georgie laughed. "You're panicking now, aren't you? It's the one labeled keepsakes. I was fairly certain your darling husband wouldn't care to touch that one."

"You're a brat."

"You raised me."

I softened at that, smiling. "Yeah, I sure did. And I'm damn proud of you."

"Proud of you too, sis. All right, I gotta go, but I love you. I'll book flights for your birthday. Take care until then, okay? You're in a new place. Maybe it could be a new start. You know?"

That question was alluding to everything we'd never speak about out loud. Georgie didn't know everything about my relationship with Nathan, but I was certain he saw the pattern — the same one he'd witnessed with our mother before she passed.

He worried about me, even if he didn't have any proof or reason to.

He could tell just because he knew me better than anyone.

"I love you, too," I answered.

"Go to the beach," my little brother ordered, and then the call ended, and I was alone with the boxes once more.

When The Fray began to play, I swore I could smell that hoodie he'd teased me about.

The front door opened an hour later, the faint jingle of keys landing in the ceramic bowl by the entryway. I froze mid-movement, book in hand, pulse ticking in my throat.

*Shit.*

I'd meant to switch to unpacking the kitchen before he got home, but time had gotten away from me. I'd been lost in my thoughts, in the music, in the faint joy each book I unpacked brought me.

I was going to pay for it now.

"Smells like a hard day's work," Nathan called, his voice bright and booming.

I forced a smile before I turned. "Hey, you're home early."

He strode in still in his suit, jacket open, tie loosened. His grin was wide, almost boyish, as he crossed the room and caught my face in both hands, kissing me soundly before I could react.

"Big day," he said against my lips, breath hot with adrenaline. "You're looking at the man who just talked ownership into a full-staff restructure — mid-season. Can you believe that? They never do that. But I did it. I finally get to bring in my people. The ones I can trust."

"That... amazing," I managed, still caught between the press of his hands and the pounding in my chest. "Are you sure that's a good idea? To switch everything up when you just got here?"

Nathan stilled. "I think I know how to run a team, and that you should focus on unpacking and leave business to me. Hmm?"

He pulled back with the passive-aggressive comment, eyes scanning the room. His smile slipped. "Speaking of which, not much done in here, huh?"

My stomach dropped. "I was— I've been unpacking the books. I thought I'd—"

"The books." He looked past me toward the kitchen before walking over to the island. "You haven't even started on the kitchen? Ariana..." He sighed, pinching the bridge of his nose.

"I'll get it all done after dinner," I offered quickly. "I was thinking we could order in, anyway. Try a local place in our new home?"

Nathan was silent for a long moment, his fingertips drumming on the island countertop. He eyed the one box I had unpacked — filled with glassware — and then suddenly, his hand struck the counter with a crack that made me flinch. A mug toppled from the stack beside him, shattering across the tile.

For a long moment, all I could hear was Nickelback humming softly in the background, and my own heart pounding in my ears.

Then, like a switch flipping, his shoulders slumped. "God, look at me," he muttered. "Making a mess when you're trying to get things sorted."

He stepped forward, reaching out, and I instinctively stepped back.

His brow knit, wounded. "Sweetheart. I'm sorry. I didn't mean to— you know I just get worked up. We can order in. That's fine. The unpacking will get done. I'm sorry."

I nodded, though I was on high alert now.

Nathan sighed again, and then tried to smile and tease me. "Although, I don't see why you had to go get groceries this morning, if this was the plan." He shook his head. "I can't believe you lost your key."

"I found it," I said, hoping that would cheer him up. I ran over to my purse and dug out the key for proof. "See? It had slipped between my seat and the console when I grabbed my purse to go into the store. I didn't realize it. But once I got home and unloaded the car, I did a deep search. And here it is!" I dug back into my purse. "And here is yours. I'll put it in the dish for you so you have it for tomorrow."

His posture softened, and he shook his head on a smile. "You are adorable, you know that?"

My smile felt forced as he crossed the room and pulled me into him for a hug.

"I know this has all been unexpected and fast — the move to Tampa, taking over the team. And I know you were sad to leave Sketch In behind."

Sketch In — the nonprofit organization Nathan had not so subtly suggested I get involved with because it would look good for him. I did love the kids there, and I loved any chance I had to work with the community, but it hadn't been my baby. It hadn't been my choice.

Nothing ever was, anymore.

"But this is a big step, Ariana — for both of us. For our family. I want us ready. I want you to feel like you're part of it."

He pulled back and traced his fingers down my arms until our hands were clasped.

"You just need a little purpose again," he murmured. "That's all. I can help with that. I know what you need."

My stomach dropped, twisting sourly as a tight knot spread low in my gut. Part of me recoiled. I wanted to pull away, to tell him he was wrong, that he didn't get to decide that for me. But another part of me already knew it was useless. There was no winning here.

Shame curled through me like smoke, hot and suffocating, and I shoved it down, forcing my face into an expression of agreeable neutrality.

My throat tightened. "Nathan—"

"Leave it with me, my love. I'll take care of you." He hit me with the same smile that had swept me off my feet years ago, the one that promised safety. "For now, come to bed."

I hesitated, but the air between us had already shifted. I knew we were dancing on that delicate line between calm and mayhem.

So I nodded.

He brushed a kiss against my forehead and led me down the hall. My nostalgic playlist crooned on, muffled by the closing door. And as his hands found me, I floated somewhere far away — thinking only of the shattered mug on the floor and the way I'd sweep it up when we were done, pretending it was the only thing that had broken tonight.

## CHAPTER 8

### BACK TO LIFE

Ariana
2007

The next two weeks were the best two weeks of my life.

Shane was locked into hockey, the Eagles laser-focused on the possibility of clutching the championship. But any time he wasn't on the ice, he was with me.

Growing up, I was used to being ignored. My dad left when I was a baby. My stepfather pretended to like me only long enough to get my mother to marry him, and then he promptly showed his true distaste for me and all children. He preferred I be in my bedroom once he got home from work so he could watch TV undisturbed. Sometimes, I'd go out in the living room and try to talk to my mom, and he'd scream at me, and then at her, and sometimes the screaming would evolve into something worse.

I learned to just stay away.

I was used to being on my own. I didn't mind going to my room. It was safe there. I had my music and my books. I could make bookmarks and talk on the phone to the few friends I had.

But I got lonely sometimes.

When George was born, I spent a lot of time with him. My stepfather wasn't exactly thrilled at his arrival, and he didn't love when my mother doted over their son. He felt like the baby was stealing his attention.

So, most nights, I would be with Georgie — rocking him, feeding him, playing with him, getting him to sleep. He slept in a crib in my room, and I loved having him there.

"Sometimes I feel guilty for leaving him," I told Shane one night. We were curled up together in my tiny twin bed, his long legs hanging off the end of it. He quietly ran his fingers over my back and gave me space to talk out what I was feeling. "I mean, he's okay. Jay has never hurt him. But he's older now, you know? I think he's starting to understand what's going on around him. He hears the yelling, sees what Jay does to Mom." I shivered, tucking myself into a ball at Shane's side. I'd never told anyone the real, raw truth of my family dynamics. It felt both terrifying and liberating to have someone to share with now. "He's delayed in speaking. I think it's because any time he hears someone talk, it's bad."

Shane had sighed and tugged me closer, kissing my hair. He always listened. He never rushed me.

I confessed to him that same night that I'd gotten so used to being alone.

I'd also confessed I was glad to not be alone now.

Because every day after classes, every weekend, every night after practices or games — he was there with me. We studied and talked. We laughed and played.

We kissed.

*A lot*.

And it was sort of like walking in a dream. I'd never known what it was to be the center of someone's world until Shane McCabe.

True to his word, the Eagles made it to the Championship game. And true to mine, I followed them to Wisconsin. Shane refused to let me pay for my own plane ticket, but I refused to let him get my hotel room. We compromised, and my heart was in my throat, my eyes wide as I watched him skate in an arena swallowed by red jerseys and deafening Wisconsin chants.

They fought hard, but when the horn sounded on a 2–1 loss, the crowd roared, gloves and sticks flying from the Badgers as they swarmed their goalie. On the other end, the Eagles slumped over their sticks, stunned into silence.

Just like that, his dream of the Championship was gone.

Shane carried the weight of it visibly when he finally made it back to the hotel. I was waiting for him in the lobby as he dragged himself in, his shoulders slumped, hands shoved in the pockets of his hoodie. His headphones dangled, the cord snaking over the Eagles logo on his chest before disappearing into his pocket. His eyes were dark and tired, like the arena lights had burned the shine out of them. When he saw me, the corner of his lips quirked like he wanted to smile but couldn't quite manage it.

I opened my arms, and he fell into them without hesitation, this massive hockey player folding into me like a sad little boy.

"We were so close, Ari," he rasped, shaking his head. "One goal."

"I know," I whispered, hugging him tighter.

For a while, we just stood there, and I didn't dare be the one to break the hug first. After a while, Shane stood tall with a sigh, wrapped his hand around mine, and wordlessly led me to the elevator.

Without either of us saying it, we went to my room. Shane dropped his bag once we were inside, and then he fell face-first onto the bed with a huff.

I was going to suggest a shower, but judging by the damp state of his hair, he'd already taken one at the arena. So, instead, I climbed on top of him and started rubbing his shoulders and his back, giving him the space he so often gave me to work through his feelings.

"I know you're hurting right now," I said. "I know this loss must gut you in a way I'll never understand. But can I say something?"

Shane didn't answer verbally, but turned his head so his cheek was against the mattress.

"I'm proud of you," I said. "Win or lose, that was one hell of a game you played. I... I've never seen anything like it."

"To be fair, you've never been to a hockey game."

"And now I see what I've been missing out on." I smiled, still working his shoulders. "You... you were incredible, Shane. I don't think I got it before, but I see it now — how important hockey is to you, how much the game means. You come alive out there in a way you don't anywhere else."

Shane tapped my thigh to let me know to hop off him, and then he rolled to face me. He was laying down, head propped on his hand, and I sat next to him with my legs tucked beneath me.

"Hockey is all I've ever had," he admitted, his nostrils flaring a bit as he wrangled his emotions. "When my parents died, my grandparents threw me into it because they just wanted me to be busy and leave them alone. But they didn't realize that in their selfishness, they gave me my lifeline." He shook his head. "I've never had anything mean as much to me as hockey does." He swallowed then, his eyes searching mine. "Until you."

"Shane..."

"I mean it, Ari." He sat up then, one hand reaching forward to hook around the back of my neck and bring me to him until our foreheads were touching. "You being here tonight... it meant everything to me. I don't want to do anything ever again without you, not now that I know what it's like to be with you. Hockey saved me," he said, voice rough. "But you... you're bringing me back to life."

I winced as if the words had pained me, but they only lit a fire in my heart because I felt the same way for him.

And I only knew one way to tell him.

With my hands crawling into his hair, I tugged him closer, and I kissed him.

It was soft at first, a brush of lips that carried every unspoken word inside me. But when he sighed against my mouth and pulled me closer, I deepened it, climbing into his lap without hesitation. His hands trembled where they held my waist, and mine shook just as badly as they curled into his damp hair.

We stripped each other slowly, carefully, both of us eager, but somehow aware, that this was too precious to be rushed. My sweater went first, Shane's hands running up the length of my ribcage and hooking the fabric on his wrists before he pushed it over my head. His hoodie was next, my hands a lot less graceful as I tugged and pulled until he helped me get it off. We laughed when his elbow got caught in the sleeve, but it only made the moment feel more real. More ours.

When at last we were bare, he paused, forehead pressed to mine, chest rising and falling like he was trying to catch his breath. "Are you sure?" he whispered; voice rough.

"Yes." My answer came without hesitation. Because I was. Because for the first time in my life, I wanted to give myself to someone completely.

He reached for his bag, pulled out his wallet, and retrieved a condom from inside. My cheeks warmed, but my heart ached with how gentle he was, how careful, like he'd thought about protecting me before he ever let himself imagine this.

Shane laid me back into the bed, pulling the sheets over us and balancing on his forearms above me. My heart was hammering in my chest as he kissed me, one hand reaching between us.

When he entered me, I gasped, overwhelmed at the sharp stretch, the sudden rush of sensation. He stilled instantly, brushing his lips over my temple, waiting until I nodded, until I shifted my hips to meet his.

And then it was slow, tender, every movement deliberate. His arms shook with the weight of him, with the restraint he showed in taking me slowly. My breaths came in shivers, eyes stinging with tears I didn't want to blink away.

Because it wasn't just physical. It was soul-deep. It was the first time I'd ever felt like I belonged somewhere, like I was cherished instead of tolerated.

And as we moved together, as we kissed through the trembling and the laughter and the whispered promises, I realized there would be no untangling us now.

Our lives were forever woven, threads stitched in a night I'd never forget.

## CHAPTER 9

### SHAKING THINGS UP

Shane
Present

I sat next to Nathan Black at the team roster announcement press conference in early October, my arms tightly crossed, gaze focused on the microphone in front of me.

I was pissed, but had to act like every decision he was announcing was a team one that I backed completely. I hoped I looked relaxed and neutral the way I did during any press conference I wasn't exactly looking forward to — like the ones that came after a brutal loss.

This felt even worse than that, somehow.

It was the first time in my career with the Ospreys that my choices weren't just second-guessed, but overridden completely. Dick had always trusted my instinct on which players to start, which to send to the AHL for now, and which to let go completely.

Nathan, on the other hand, had smiled at me and patted my shoulder like I was some fucking kid, and he thought my efforts were adorable.

Then, he'd smashed my plans to pieces.

For the most part, our starters were the same. It was hard to argue that the guys on our first and second lines didn't deserve those spots. They were fierce, hungry — ready to go after the Stanley Cup after losing in the playoff race last season.

But from there, things went haywire.

Nathan chose to send players down to the AHL who I argued deserved a spot with the Ospreys. He put a veteran on waivers, someone who the fans assumed would retire an Osprey — me included. And perhaps the most controversial decision — he kept on a rookie who was vastly outplayed in camp.

As if I hadn't had enough of his bullshit explaining this to me and my staff, I now had to listen to him charm the pants off everyone in the press room and hope this didn't fall back on me in the end.

"We had some really competitive camp battles this year," he continued, answering a journalist's question about his decision regarding the rookie. "These are good problems to have — depth is a luxury. We want guys who play hungry, and Baranov earned his spot."

"And Wood didn't?" the journalist probed.

My stomach soured at the mention of our ten-year veteran, who was now on waivers, waiting to see if anyone in the league would take a chance on him before noon tomorrow.

"Wood has served this team incredibly, but all journeys must come to an end. I have faith he will find even more success with the team lucky enough to claim him off waivers."

Lights flashed, more hands shot up into the air, all of the journalists in the room clamoring to be the one Nathan addressed next.

A few minutes passed in a daze before someone asked me how I was feeling about the season ahead with the roster set, and I faked my best confidence as I answered that the team was strong and ready. Neither was a lie, but I was far from feeling my best with the way the rug had been yanked from under my feet courtesy of my new GM.

When the attention was back on Nathan, I let mine wander around the room.

I clocked every reporter, the ones furiously scribbling or typing, and the ones live streaming from their phones. I noted their expressions, which varied from shocked and disappointed to absolutely riveted.

And then my eyes found Ari.

She was standing off to the side, her back against the wall like she wished she could disappear into it. She was dressed modestly in a navy-blue pencil skirt and white blouse, the cuffs and lapel of which were lace. Her hair was fastened into a secure bun at the nape of her neck, her makeup light and flawless.

She looked sad.

I couldn't place why I felt that way. She was smiling, her hands folded demurely in front of her hips, her eyes sparkling as she watched her husband like he had hung the moon. One of our PR interns stood next to her, and when she leaned in to whisper something, it made Ariana laugh.

But there was something under the surface, something she was hiding.

As if she felt my gaze burning a hole into the side of her head, her smile faltered. She blinked, frowning, and then her eyes snapped to mine.

My next breath burned a little as I tried to smile at her, the corner of my lips ticking up before falling again. I wondered if it would ever pass, the strange sensation of both pain and longing that seared me when she looked at me. Decades had passed between us, and yet I could blink and still see her at twenty-years-old, wearing my hoodie, a pen chewed to bits between her teeth as she pinched her brows in concentration over a sociology book.

I thought she'd tear her gaze away, but perhaps Ariana was taking this stolen moment we had to let herself linger. Every interaction we'd had until now had been rushed, but in this moment, neither of us had anywhere else to be — and no one was paying attention to us.

Her lips quirked up, just marginally, and the prettiest flush crept across her cheeks.

The sight was enough to make me pant. I wanted so badly to get her alone, to ask her the millions of questions that had been plaguing me since her arrival.

But as quickly as that small smile had come, it was wiped away, her gaze turning cold. And I knew it without needing confirmation.

She'd just remembered that I'd left her when she needed me most.

I felt the ice she shot my way with that glare, the accusation, the hurt. I had only done what I thought was right, what I felt would be best for both of us — most of all her.

But now that I was older, I looked back at that young decision I'd made, and I didn't see a hero. I didn't see a man acting out of love.

I just saw a selfish, scared little boy.

And I hated him just as much as she did.

"Listen, I know it can be hard having a fresh face and new blood making decisions," Nathan said beside me. My focus was still on Ariana, who was watching me in return, though with more wariness now than anything. "We're making a few changes here at the Ospreys this season, yes. New faces, fresh energy — but we're also keeping the same values this organization, and this city, have always been built on. In fact, I'm proud to announce that my wife, Ariana Black, will be heading our Sweet Dreams Initiative this year."

Ariana jumped as though she'd been caught stealing a signed jersey from our trophy case when the attention of the room swung to her. She recovered quickly, her smile wide and lovely as she held up a hand in a polite wave to those looking at her.

But again, I swore I saw it — a slip in the performance, the mask faltering just long enough to glimpse the woman beneath it.

"It's a program near to our hearts, focused on rest and mental health for our city's youth. Thanks to a generous donation from one of our longtime partners, we'll have an expanded budget to reach even more families in need."

Cameras flashed again, a murmur breaking out among the crowd. Someone murmured, "Wow, that's great," as Nathan nodded with a beaming smile.

I looked to Ariana once more, and wondered why the joy looked performative to me. If anything I used to know about her remained true, this would be a dream for her. She loved to work in the community. It was all she'd ever wanted.

That only sent more questions swirling through my head. Had she ever finished her degree? Did she go into social work like she'd planned? Was that what she did now — or was this it? The fact that Nathan had her positioned front and center on this project made something uneasy twist in my gut. Did she have a job at all, or was she just another extension of him?

"We're not just building a winning team," Nathan added, his voice booming. "We're building a legacy — on and off the ice."

I felt my jaw lock as he continued, heat rushing sharp and fast through my blood. It took real effort not to react — not to shift, not to say something reckless, not to knock that polished grin straight off his face. I curled my fingers into my palm, nails biting into skin, grounding myself in the sting of it.

Then his hand came down on my shoulder, firm and proprietary, and I had to fight the sudden, vivid urge to shrug him off — or worse, to see how easily his fingers would break.

He squeezed, all smiles for the cameras, like we were allies instead of adversaries. "Me and this guy," he said, flashing the room that same confident grin, "we're going to bring the Cup home to Tampa this year."

I forced the best smile I could muster as the room erupted with more questions, but our PR team called the end of the conference, instructing the press where they could go for further information.

I stood instantly, fastening the button on my suit jacket before shaking hands with Nathan and posing for a few photos. Then, we were ushered out the back to the next room over, where staff waited to debrief.

Ariana slid in wordlessly, her husband cheerfully boasting about the press already. He had his phone out and was reading quote after quote about how he was being called a bold, daring visionary.

I exerted more energy than I ever had in the weight room just trying not to roll my eyes.

The moment Nathan realized Ariana was with us, he clapped for her like she was the star of the show, pulling her in for a swift kiss before hooking a hand around her hip.

"Well, did I surprise you, my love?" he asked, his grin a permanent thing.

Ariana's smile was demure as ever. "You certainly did."

"And are you pleased?"

"It's a lovely initiative," she answered.

"And the perfect thing to keep you busy and get you back in the swing of things," Nathan said, thumbing her chin. "See? I told you I know what you need."

Ariana wore a closed-lip smile, but leaned up on her toes to kiss her husband.

I watched all of this from the corner of my eye, all the while listening to Kozak fill me in on how Wood took the news earlier. My assistant was just as gutted as I was to lose Wood, but we had no choice but to take it in stride. I assured him we'd figure it out, one step at a time, and then excused myself from the conversation with a quick squeeze of his shoulder.

I swung to Nathan and Ariana next.

"Congratulations on the Sweet Dreams donation," I said to Nathan. "Maven has put so much into that, I know she'll be thrilled to hear there is even more to work with now." I slid my gaze to Ari next. "And I know she'll be over the moon to have you as her partner."

"Ariana will be leading, in fact," Nathan corrected. "As you know, Maven has her hands full these days with a nearly one-year-old. She has asked to take a significant step back. She still wants to be involved, of course, as well as Grace, but they will both take orders from our new general here."

He rubbed Ariana's arm with a prideful smile, and she leaned into him like she loved him more fiercely than anything in the world, like he'd given her the best gift.

*He has, you stupid motherfucker, and she does love him.*

*They are married, in case you forgot.*

The reminder was a stinging one, and it had me shaking my head at how foolish I was being, searching her for clues she was unhappy because selfishly, I hoped she never *could* be happy with him — or with anyone who wasn't me.

If my stomach was sour before, it was a rotted pit with that realization.

All those years ago when I made the choice I did, all I wanted was for her to be happy. Now, here she was, as happy as she could be — married to a rich, handsome man whom everyone adored, who took care of her, who knew giving her the Sweet Dreams initiative would bring her joy.

It seemed I was the only one who wasn't charmed by him, and I would be lying if I said I didn't know why.

Sure, I didn't agree with all the choices he was making for the team, but he was doing what any new GM would — shaking things up.

My disdain for him rested solely in the fact that he had Ariana, and I was jealous.

Once again, I was behaving like a selfish little boy. It was like I couldn't fucking help it when it came to her.

I internally shook my head at myself before taking a deep breath and giving a real smile, one I hoped Ariana could see was genuine. "I'm really happy for you, Ariana. I know the program will thrive beneath your charge."

"Thank you," she said, her gaze a bit questioning.

"If you ever need help wrangling the team to get involved, just say the word," I added.

"Oh!" Nathan snapped his fingers, as if a light bulb had just flickered on in his brain. "That's genius, actually. We could have the players out in the community, delivering mattresses and taking pictures with the kids. I like the optics here. Shane, can you work the first few meetings into your schedule and get on board with Maven, Grace, and my beautiful wife here?"

"I'm sure he's too busy to—"

"Of course," I answered, not letting Ariana finish her assumption. "It would be my pleasure."

And for the first time that night, I didn't have to force my smile or veil a lie.

It *would* be my pleasure.

Anything to have more time with Ari.

# CHAPTER 10

### DEAD END

Ariana
2007-2008

A year passed in a blur of stupid, incredible, all-encompassing young love.

Summer in Boston belonged to me and Shane. We spent afternoons sprawled out on the Charles River Esplanade, watching boats drift by as we listened to the new Snow Patrol album. We wandered Quincy Market, splitting lobster rolls I couldn't afford, but Shane bought without blinking, and on sweltering days we'd sneak into the rink just so he could skate while I shivered on the bleachers with a smoothie in hand. Nights were lost in each other, tangled in sheets until the sun cracked the blinds and we swore we'd lie there "just five more minutes."

Against his coach's advisement, we rented a tiny one-bedroom apartment near campus together. Shane had wanted to get something bigger and more modern, and he could, with the money his grandparents gave him. But I insisted that I be able to split the cost. And so, we ended up in a small, but quaint, place. The pipes clanked, the windows stuck, and half the outlets didn't work — but it was ours. We painted the kitchen a bright, reckless yellow because it was my favorite color, and even though it looked a little like vomit in the end, I still loved it. We bought mismatched furniture from thrift stores, piecing together a home out of scraps. And in that crooked little apartment, I learned what it was like to belong to someone — and to be chosen back.

That summer, I met his grandparents. I was terrified, since all I'd heard of them was that they didn't really seem to know what to do with Shane when he landed in their lap. But they hugged me tightly and asked me questions with genuine interest. They opened their home to us and seemed prouder of Shane than he realized. And, compared to my family, they were like angels on earth.

Shane also met my family that summer, though I'd rallied against his first suggestion that he come with me when I had a weekend planned to visit home. I thought the shame would kill me; thought he'd run the moment he saw the cracks in my family's house. But he didn't. He played with my little brother until he conked out for a nap, exhausted in the best way, and he helped my mom in the kitchen with the dishes after dinner. I overheard him telling her she'd raised the strongest daughter in the world, and I'd smiled so furiously my stepfather had raised a brow.

Of course, Jay didn't pay much attention to Shane when he was there. Other than a firm handshake that I was fairly certain was to ascertain his dominance more than to offer a warm greeting, he stayed quiet. He watched TV and left us alone.

But he also didn't scream or hit my mother, so that was a win in my book.

When fall rolled back around, Shane and I slipped easily into the rhythm of classes and hockey. Shane was flying, his eyes full of the NHL future that was just within reach now, every game another step toward the dream. And I was right there, chasing my degree, dreaming of the kids I wanted to help, the life I wanted to build. It felt like it was us against the world — and for once, I had hope.

But not everything was light.

There were nights the phone rang and my mother's voice came through the line, ragged with fear, begging me to come home, whispering that she thought this time Jay might kill her. Those calls cracked the perfect world Shane and I had built, shadows stretching into the corners of our little apartment. He would hold me afterward, whispering that I wasn't alone anymore, that he had me. But still, the darkness lingered.

Shane dreamed of his bright future, the NHL lights dazzling just ahead of him, but I couldn't stop the pit from opening in my stomach. Because somewhere in the distance, beyond all the magic, I saw a dead end waiting at the end of the road we were on.

And I had no idea how to stop us from speeding toward it.

## CHAPTER 11

### DROP IT

Ariana
Present

"So, as you can see, there are a lot of places the new budget can go," Maven Tanev said, her fingers steepled beneath her chin before she pressed a nude-polished nail to one of the papers spread out before her. "But I think this is where it would be best spent. The more beds we can buy, the more kids we can support."

"Second on that list would be the therapist support, wouldn't you agree?" Grace Tanev chimed in.

"Definitely," Maven agreed. "But we've talked for long enough. What do you think, Ariana?"

Maven and Grace were sisters-in-law, I'd come to discover. Maven was married to Vince Tanev, one of our star wingers, and Grace was engaged to his best friend and teammate. Apparently, it had been quite the scandal when the news broke, but everything seemed settled now.

I'd instantly liked them both.

Grace had bounded into the room for our first Sweet Dreams meeting like she'd just hopped off a plane and had espresso the entire flight — which, from our conversations since, might actually have been the case. She was a little jetsetter; though, it seemed she was excited to settle down in Tampa for the time being. As a petite woman myself, I appreciated that so much energy came in that small package of bronze skin and platinum-blonde hair.

Maven, on the other hand, had strolled into the room tall, poised, and warm, her bright smile making it impossible not to lean into everything she said. She was taller than both Grace and me by at least a foot, with brown skin and a halo of black curls. I could tell straight away that this initiative was her baby. She expressed the utmost care for it from the moment she began speaking, and I sensed the tinge of regret she held for stepping back.

"My daughter has proven to be my new obsession," she'd said in way of explanation when she opened the meeting. "I still love this community and want to give back whenever I have the chance, but I also want to focus on this baby whom I know won't be a baby for long."

I wasn't a mother, but I knew the truth of that statement. I'd watched Georgie grow far too fast for my liking, going from a newborn sleeping soundly in a crib in my bedroom to a med-school student. Sometimes it was hard for me to wrap my head around the fact that he was older now than I was when I became his legal guardian.

Maven's words had settled in my chest, stirring up my own thoughts of children. I'd loved Georgie fiercely and protectively, and I'd learned young what it meant to put someone else first, to structure your entire life around the needs of a child.

If I was being honest with myself... it had stripped any lingering romanticism from the idea of motherhood and left only the truth of it.

Add in the fact that I hadn't exactly had a beautiful childhood, and you could say my feelings on it were set in stone.

Nathan, on the other hand, loved the idea of a family — the way it would look for him, the way it would fit neatly into the version of himself he liked to present. But when he shared his hypotheticals, the weight of parenting had always landed somewhere outside him. He would talk about how great it would be to play with the kids and take them to work events to show them off, but it was always *me* in his vision doing the work.

The late nights. The sacrifices. The quiet, mentally loaded, unrelenting work.

He didn't want to be a father. He wanted a family for show — a doting wife who took care of everything, kids who were seen and not heard.

And that was when I learned that my husband wasn't the only one who could keep a secret or manipulate a situation. Because I had an IUD put in and I never told him.

"I think both of you are right," I answered, shaking off my thoughts. "Obviously, priority needs to be on getting as many mattresses and bed frames to as many families in need as possible. I also agree that the mental impact of living in those circumstances deserves attention. But I wonder if we could take it a step further — make it more than a one-time delivery."

Grace perked up. "What do you have in mind?"

"Maybe we start a 'Dream Partner' program," I said slowly, the idea forming as I spoke. "Each family we help is paired with a volunteer from the team — players, staff, even fans — who can check in, help connect them with other resources. It's not just about the bed. It's about stability."

Maven smiled, eyes lighting with approval. "That's good. I love that. It makes it sustainable."

"And maybe," I added, "we host a 'Sweet Dreams Night' at one of the home games — donate a portion of ticket sales to the program, let fans bring bedding donations. Kids we've helped could come to the game, meet some of the players. I think seeing familiar faces again, and realizing people care, would make a huge impact."

Grace tapped her pen against her notepad. "Oh, and we could do a short video series — player spotlights about what home means to them, or how sleep affects performance. Sponsors would eat that up."

My mind sparked with another idea, and before I could stop myself, I was leaning forward, words tumbling out fast. "What if we threw a gala in the holiday season? Between Thanksgiving and Christmas. We could call it the Sweet Dreams Soirée — black-tie, but warm and whimsical. We invite the families we've helped, the sponsors, the team. Ensure every kid who needs a bed for the holiday season has one, raise money for next season's beds, celebrate the kids who've thrived. It could become an annual tradition."

Maven's smile spread wide, eyes glittering. "You two are going to make me jealous I handed this off."

Her laughter filled the room, rich and genuine, and I felt something stir inside me — a flicker of pride, of purpose. For the first time since Nathan had dropped this initiative in my lap in the form of a control move disguised as a gift, I wasn't thinking about how it had started. I was thinking about what it could be.

The girls and I continued to hash out our ideas, namely focusing on whether just a couple of months was enough time to pull off a gala. Grace had zero doubts while Maven and I wondered — especially with her pulling back. I was new to the area, and I wasn't sure I had the connections necessary to make it happen on such short notice. But with Grace and Maven's help, and maybe some assistance from my husband... it was doable, right?

We were focused, heads bent together and debating logistics when there was a knock on the door.

We all swung to face it just as Shane McCabe let himself in.

"Coach!" the girls bellowed in unison, hopping up to hug him. He had his hands full — a cardboard drink carrier in one, a paper bag in the other — but managed to juggle it all with practiced ease, setting everything down on the conference table just in time to catch them each in a quick embrace.

"Brought peace offerings," he said, holding up the carrier with a grin. "I heard through the grapevine that this meeting didn't have snacks. Can't have that."

Maven peered over his shoulder. "Are those smoothies?"

My heart stalled in my chest.

"From JuiceFix on Kennedy," he said, tapping each of the cups. "Two mango dreams, one berry paradise, and one green machine."

"Ick," Grace said, her nose wrinkling. "Please tell me the green machine is for you. Pretty sure I speak for all of us when I say no thanks to kale in my sweet treat."

The girls laughed, swooping in to grab their drinks — both of them taking a mango — and continuing to tease Shane for his choice.

I stayed back, smiling but uncertain. I hadn't seen him in a setting this casual since... *God*, since college. And the last time he'd handed me a smoothie, it had been from our spot in Boston, the one that became a part of our relationship the way a song does for some.

Smoothies were our thing.

*What does it mean that he brought me one today?*

"I see the party's already started without me," he said, his voice easy as his gaze finally found mine. The grin softened, the teasing fading into quiet apprehension. "Hello, Ari."

*Ari.*

The nickname made my next breath lodge in my chest.

"Hello," I managed, and then Shane made the decision for both of us. He opened his arms — carefree and unassuming, like it wasn't a big deal — and I stepped into them before I could overthink it.

It was a simple hug, but the moment his arms wrapped around me, the years between us collapsed like dominoes.

His scent hit me first — that clean, familiar blend of mint, eucalyptus, and iron, like the rink itself had seeped into his skin. His chest rose against mine, steady and warm, and for a heartbeat, it was 2006 again. The way he squeezed me, the way a contented sigh washed against my neck the moment I was fully in his embrace...

It was only a second, but it felt like time had slowed just for us.

I wondered for that brief lag in time what it could have been like, if would have's and should have's mattered.

And then, as quickly as it began, it ended. We both stepped back with casual, professional smiles and distance — as if the air between us hadn't just charged with an electric current strong enough to power a city.

"So," he said, clearing his throat and gesturing to the table, "looks like I'm late to the brainstorm." He checked his watch. "The meeting *did* start at eleven, right?"

Grace laughed. "That's what you get for assuming *on time* isn't *late* to women like us, Coach. We were all here at ten thirty."

"Of course you were," he answered with a grin.

Grace picked up her smoothie and took a long pull before tilting it Maven's way. "Speaking of which, we need to get going. Our plan was just to get the ball rolling here and pass things off to your very capable hands." She looked at me. "I'll be at the next meeting, Ariana — maybe by then we'll have a venue locked in for this gala you've inspired."

"Count on me for calls and coordination," Maven added, gathering her notes. "I'll be more of a behind-the-scenes girl until the event itself, but you know I'll be there day-of, doing whatever needs to get done."

"*Or*...you could actually hand this off the way you planned and go spend time with that sweet baby girl of yours," Grace challenged.

"And *you* could set a date for your wedding."

Grace stuck out her tongue.

"Ariana, would you like to join us for a girls' night soon?" Maven said when they reached the door. "We have a little group that likes to get together for crafting—"

"*Some* of us craft. Others just drink and tell hilarious stories." Grace winked and pointed her thumb into her chest.

"We'd love to have you," Maven said with a chuckle, ignoring her friend. "If you'd be interested?"

My heart surged in my chest at the thought of making friends, which was a foreign concept to me these days. I used to have them — some from undergrad, some from grad school, many from when I worked at the youth outreach program in Boston before I met Nathan.

But that was the keyword — *before*. It had been a long time since I'd had close friends, or even distant ones.

"Sure," I said, my skin warm. "I'd love that."

I thought I saw something knowing in Maven's gaze as she tilted her head at me, but she just smiled and nodded before I could read it. "Great. I have your number, so I'll text you next time we have a date."

"Should we add her to the group chat?" Grace asked.

"Easy, killer. We don't want to scare her off before we have the chance to charm her." Maven hit me with one last wink, and then they were gone.

And it was just me and Shane.

The air in the room thickened, heating enough to make me tug at the collar of my blouse for a little relief.

We hadn't been alone in nearly two decades, and I felt every single one of those years like little zaps of electricity now.

Shane rubbed a hand over the back of his neck, eyes flicking to the empty chairs before finding mine again. Then, wordlessly, he reached for the berry smoothie and offered it to me.

"Thank you," I muttered, taking it with unsure hands.

"My pleasure," he said. His eyes searched mine a moment before he inhaled deep and rubbed his hands together. "All right. Catch me up."

He pulled out the chair beside mine instead of taking one across the table, the scrape of it against the floor loud in the quiet room before he sat. The nearness of him was immediately distracting — his shoulder close enough that I was suddenly aware of where my arms were, how I was sitting, how fast my heart was beating.

It helped, having something to do with my hands. I handed over sheet after sheet as I discussed how the program had been working up until now, what needed attention, and the ideas Grace, Maven, and I had briefly discussed. Shane nodded as he listened, following along with the attention of a coach going into a playoff game rather than one simply helping with a community initiative.

It was at least twenty minutes before I took my first sip of the smoothie Shane had brought, and when I did, I hummed, smiling. "Wow."

"Good?"

"Not bad," I said. "But also, I just… it's been a long time since I've had a smoothie."

Shane smirked, his eyes catching mine like he wanted to ask something but thought better of it. "Nothing compared to The Smoothie Guy, but it's a close enough fix. Sometime, I'll have to take you to the smoothie spot in Ybor. That's the one that might put our Boston go-to to shame."

That had my smile faltering a little, the way he was talking as if we were friends now. As if me suddenly ending up in the same city as him was going to erase years of pain.

"Anyway, I'm happy you're going to help with the players," I said, surprised by the coldness in my voice. But I leaned into it. "Do you have any idea which ones would be on board to do some of these events on top of their schedule?"

Shane was still looking at me in that strange way, like he wanted to say something but wouldn't allow himself to. "I have a few ideas. Jaxson Brittain for one. He had a strained relationship with his parents, and I think he'd be interested in helping out. Plus, it would make Grace happy, and he'd do anything for that."

I smiled.

"Then there's Daddy P. This is his last season." Shane cracked his neck at that with a sigh. "And I think he'd like to give back before he goes."

"Great. We can mark them down. Now, do you think the gala is a possibility? I mean, timewise?"

"It will be tough, but I think if we put our minds to it, yes."

"Do you have any idea where we could host it?"

"I'll talk to the PR team. I bet they have some ideas."

"And what about food. Do we have—"

"Ari, I'm sorry."

The words struck me like a lightning bolt to the chest.

My hands froze where I was jotting down notes, my eyes zeroed in on the ink on the page so I didn't have to look at Shane. I couldn't. Not with those words hanging between us. They'd shot out of his mouth quickly and breathlessly, like he'd been holding them back this entire meeting and couldn't fight them any longer.

"I realize I've said these words to you before, and I also realize they don't mean a thing after..." he continued quietly, his voice low and controlled, like he was holding it together by sheer force of will. "But I am. For whatever it's worth."

I didn't look at him, but I felt everything behind what he'd said — the restraint, the careful steadiness, the emotion he was keeping tightly leashed.

The apology itself was simple. The truth beneath it was not.

My heart was thundering in my chest, the temptation to look at him nearly eating me alive. But I knew if I did, I'd crash all the way out.

"I don't think we should talk about this."

"Why not?"

"It's in the past. It doesn't matter now."

"Doesn't it?"

"I'm married." I finally snapped my gaze to him with those words, and the way his jaw tightened, his nostrils flaring, I knew I'd hit my intended mark. "What happened between me and a college boyfriend twenty years ago is of no consequence. Okay? So let's just drop it and move on."

*Lie.*

*Big, fat lie.*

But I held his gaze like I meant every word, arching a brow as if to ask, *"Anything else?"*

For a moment, I thought he might call my bluff. Shane searched my gaze intently, like he was looking for a crack in the armor I'd quickly thrown up around me. But after a moment, he only nodded, wetting his lips before he cleared his throat and picked up a stack of paper in front of him. "Of course. You're right. It's all in the past."

I nodded, the sound of my pulse in my ears nearly too loud to think over.

For a moment, we were both silent. I was just about to launch into the next phase of our to-do list when Shane spoke first.

"How's Georgie?"

The question caught me off guard, and I finally let myself really look at him.

The edge I'd braced for wasn't there. Instead, his expression had softened, something genuine and unguarded in his eyes. It was the same care and concern he'd always had when it came to my brother.

Maybe the question should have stung. Maybe it should have made me angry. But it only warmed my heart, an easy smile finding my lips at the fact that Shane had asked about someone he knew meant everything to me.

"He's... *God*, Shane, he's incredible." My eyes welled with pride as I said the words. "He's in *med school*."

"*What*? Holy shit." Shane's jaw dropped before a grin split his face. "That's amazing."

"*He* is amazing. He's acing all his classes, chomping at the bit to get into the hospital and really dig in. He's leaving his options open, but thinks he wants to go into pediatrics. Specifically, oncology."

Shane whistled. "Wow."

"I know."

"You must be so proud of him."

My eyes stung again. "I am. I really am."

"He's lucky to have you."

That comment soured my delight. I wasn't sure I shared his sentiment. My poor brother had been unwanted by his father, had to witness horrible things happen to his mother, and then try to find normalcy with an older sister who had no idea how to raise a child. I couldn't give him half of what I wished I could.

And if it wasn't for Nathan, he wouldn't be in med school. There was no way I would have ever been able to afford sending him.

I sniffed, forcing a smile. "Speaking of family, how are your grandparents?"

Shane was watching me like he'd seen my train of thought, the doubt, without me even saying a word. He tried to smile, but it only reached the corner of his mouth before it fell again. "They passed several years ago."

"Oh, Shane... I'm so sorry."

"They lived a great life. Grandma passed first — just old age, as the doctor said. And Grandpa went right after."

I nodded, and without thinking, I reached for him, hand wrapping around his wrist with a squeeze. I knew how complicated his relationship with them was. He was thankful to them taking him in when his parents died, but they also hadn't known what to do with him, so they'd thrown him into sports and wiped their hands. They had been in their retirement era, ready for it to be just the two of them, and Shane hadn't fit into that narrative. But they loved him. They housed him and clothed him, made sure he was fed and had plenty of money for whatever he needed when he made it to college. Hockey was expensive, and they'd footed every bill without question.

But none of that made up for what he really wanted, what he needed, what he was missing.

Parents.

Family.

My throat constricted when I thought of how hard it all must have been for him.

I felt a tinge of hurt and jealousy, too. I wished I could have been there for him through it.

I wished we could have stayed in each other's lives.

Shane stared at where I held him, a muscle ticking in his jaw. When he lifted his gaze to mine, I felt stripped to the bone.

"Ari, I—"

A heavy knock on the door made both of us jump, and just as we retreated into our own space again, the door swung open to reveal my husband.

"Ah! I knew it. Hard at work already." He grinned wide, sweeping into the room without care and bending to press a kiss to my cheek, which flamed when my eyes skirted to Shane. "I was chatting with our rookies, making sure they felt good going into today's practice. And I remembered you were here, darling, so I came to take you to lunch."

"We were just finishing, anyway," I said, stacking up all the pages and slipping them into a folder. My neck was on fire, like I'd been caught with my tongue down my ex's throat rather than just sitting in a room with him. "Shane, thank you again for your help. Do you think you can get with the players, get a feel for who we can depend on, and we can discuss at the next meeting?"

"Oh, I'm sure all the players will be more than happy to help," Nathan answered for him. "And Coach here will thwomp them if they give you any grief. Isn't that right, McCabe?"

Nathan squeezed Shane's shoulders and shook him hard, all with a loud laugh that had always charmed everyone around him.

"I'm sure we won't run into any trouble," Shane answered carefully, and then he shrugged out of Nathan's grasp to stand, gathering his things. "I better get to it. Enjoy your lunch."

His gaze slid to me only briefly, enough for me to see there were still a thousand things left unsaid.

I hoped he could read my unspoken reply.

*Leave it in the past, Shane.*

*Please, just leave it in the past.*

Because I knew that was the only way I could survive being in his vicinity again.

## CHAPTER 12

### SUSPICIOUS CIRCUMSTANCES

Shane
2008

On a sunny day in late April of 2008, one year after we'd made things official, the little safe haven Ariana and I had built came crashing down.

I thought nothing could be worse than BC losing the championship yet again in the final game against Michigan, but even that had the silver lining of knowing I'd be starting my career in the NHL soon. There were still games to play, still titles to chase.

But the day we got the call that Ariana's mother had died, there was no silver lining in sight.

Everything happened like a car crash in a dream — painful and horrifying, yet blurry and hard to grasp. There were funeral arrangements and legal counsel, a girl in college who should have been thinking about her future forced instead to grieve the death of a mother she'd never quite known how to love.

And worse, it wasn't that her mother had been sick.

The police used careful language with us at first, choosing words like incident and investigation, as if they were afraid of saying too much. But it didn't take long for the truth to sharpen.

Ariana's stepfather told them he'd found her deceased. He said they'd argued, that he'd left to cool his temper while she stayed home.

He said she'd hung herself.

And the coroner confirmed asphyxiation — but there was more to it.

Bruising to the neck. Signs of a struggle.

Everywhere around us, there were two whispered words.

*Suspicious circumstances.*

There was no time to process it. One day, we received the call, and the next, I was watching the way Ariana's hands shook as she signed forms, collected her brother's backpack, and walked out of that courthouse as his temporary guardian.

I sat beside her through it all, but it felt like standing in the middle of a hurricane, holding onto someone who was already being pulled away.

I couldn't imagine what she was feeling. I couldn't even begin to try. All I knew was that the girl who had once leaned into me, who had filled our tiny apartment with laughter and light, was retreating into herself. She still let me hold her at night, but it was different now. Her eyes weren't on the future anymore. They were on survival.

The more I heard, the less sense it made. Her stepfather was under investigation for the death of her mother, possibly facing trial. Ariana would have to testify — to relive everything she'd spent her life trying to escape.

At the same time, she had to prove she was stable enough to raise Georgie.

And that was where the real nightmare came in.

Because Jay was Georgie's biological father.

Even locked up in county jail awaiting trial, his lawyers were already circling, filing motions, angling to argue that Ariana was too young, too unstable, too unfit to keep custody. Emergency guardianship was only a stopgap — proof of stability would determine whether it stuck. One misstep, one hint of chaos, and Georgie could end up living with Jay — or with another member of Jay's family, which Ariana made clear was no better.

We had an apartment, and we immediately made room for Georgie, but it was more complicated than just having a place for him to rest his head at night. Courts demanded roots, not chaos. Predictability, not press coverage. They wanted boring, steady, safe.

And I was anything but.

It was my coach who talked to me first, his brows pinched together as he looked at me with a mixture of pity and true sadness. "It would be impossible to keep this quiet, you understand?" he'd said. "You're a rookie, a hot one everyone expects great things from. And your girlfriend's stepfather being under investigation for murder isn't going to be something you can hide."

Ariana's lawyers had cornered me next.

"She won't listen to us, Shane," her counsel said quietly. "So you have to get through to her. You have to make her understand that being with you — with an NHL career about to take off — could jeopardize everything she's fighting for."

I hated them for saying it.

I hated that they were right.

My life was about to be airports, hotels, reporters, and cameras. Hers needed to be court hearings, steady routines, and bedtime stories for a scared little boy. I couldn't give her what she needed, and worse, staying by her side might cost her everything.

I lay awake at night, staring at the ceiling while Ariana's soft breaths whispered against my chest, and I thought about the choice in front of me. The truth was, I only had one.

The only way I could protect her, the only way I could love her the way she needed me to... was to let her go.

And I had no idea how I'd ever find the strength to do it.

# CHAPTER 13

## BRIEF BREATH OF TIME

Ariana
Present

Nathan was in a good mood when he got home.

I knew it the second I heard him humming as he kicked off his shoes in the entryway, the sound light and unburdened in a way that made my shoulders loosen. He appeared in the kitchen moments later, sleeves already rolled up, smile easy as he crossed the space between us and pressed a kiss to my temple.

Sometimes, when I saw him like that, I could remember why it was so easy to fall in love with him.

"Hey," he said airily, sweeping me up into his arms. I tried not to be stiff under his kiss. "I missed you today."

The words landed softly, warmly. I didn't realize I'd been needing to hear them.

"Hey, yourself," I replied, smiling despite myself. "You saw me this morning."

"Far too long ago." He glanced around the kitchen, taking in the clean counters, the candles I'd lit, the simmering pot on the stove. "Something smells good."

"I made your favorite," I said. "The lemon chicken."

His brows lifted. "With the pine nuts?"

"Of course. And I finally finished unpacking."

"Completely?"

I smiled in victory. "Not a box left in sight. I took all the cardboard to recycling, too."

"Well," he said, reaching for a spoon and stealing a taste from the chicken before he hummed his approval and wrapped me in his arms again. "I'm clearly under appreciating you. Thank you for taking such good care of me."

I laughed, the sound easy and real, and for a moment — just a brief breath of time — it felt like we were newly married again, like this house wasn't something I tiptoed through, like I wasn't constantly gauging his mood before I spoke.

We ate together at the island, knees brushing, his phone conspicuously face-down for once. He asked about my day, about how things were going with Sweet Dreams, about my opinion on the outdoor furniture we needed to buy.

After dinner, he surprised me by loading the dishwasher himself, swatting my hands away when I tried to help. "Go sit," he said. "You cooked."

I did, curling into the corner of the couch as he joined me a while later, draping an arm around my shoulders and pulling me in. His thumb traced slow, absent patterns along my arm.

"I want you to come to the game with me tomorrow night," he said casually.

I tilted my head back to look at him. "Tomorrow?"

"It'll be a big game," he said. "I think you'll have fun. Plus, it's important for the team and staff to see you there. Supporting, you know."

Ah. There it was.

*I want you to come with me because it looks right, not because I actually want to spend time with you.*

"Of course," I said, my smile weak. "I can do that."

"Good." He kissed the top of my head. "I leave for Vegas early the next morning."

I nodded, a strange mix of emotions stirring in my chest at the reminder. He was going for business, and him traveling for business wasn't odd. However, I'd never known him to go to Vegas, and as someone who'd never been before, I wondered what kind of mischief he'd get into while he was there.

And then there was the storm of emotions I felt at the prospect of him being gone for a while, of me having a weekend to myself.

Relief. Guilt. Excitement.

I could walk around the house without eggshells beneath my feet. I could do whatever I wanted.

There was a beautiful freedom in that.

"Oh, speaking of which," he said, still rubbing circles on my shoulder. "While I'm gone, the crew will be here to install our cameras for the house. It'll probably be Saturday."

"I forgot about those," I admitted.

"It'll be good, since we don't have a private gate. I know the community is safe, but it will make me feel better. Especially for when I'm gone on trips and you're here by yourself."

I smiled. "That was almost sweet."

He smirked back at me. "Gotta make sure my wife is safe."

For some reason, that wording made my stomach dip a bit. It almost sounded like a threat more than a doting promise.

I didn't let myself linger on it.

"I was thinking," I said carefully, "after you get back... Maven invited me to a craft night. Just something small with her and Grace and some of their friends. She does them once a month."

Nathan immediately stilled.

"Oh," he said after a beat. "So I get home from a work trip, and you're already making plans to be somewhere else?"

The warmth drained from my chest.

"It's not like that," I said quickly. "It's just one evening. I thought it might be nice to—"

"To what?" he asked, still calm, still aiming for a reasonable tone. "Unwind from being alone all weekend?"

"I didn't mean—"

"I just figured you'd want to spend time together," he said. "After I've been gone."

I swallowed. "I do. I just — this would be later. Like the next weekend. And I don't really know anyone here yet."

He sighed, rubbing his jaw. "I'm not saying you can't go, Ari. I just don't love the timing."

Of course he didn't.

"Well, let's see how we feel. Maybe I'll only go if you're busy with work that night. Otherwise, I'll stay home with you," I said because it felt safer than pushing back.

"That's a great compromise," he replied, the tension easing immediately. And then the moment passed, just like that, leaving me wondering if I'd imagined the manipulation of it all.

After about a half hour of watching a show together, Nathan stood and stretched. "I need to take a call. Work stuff. Should probably pack a little, too."

"Need help?"

"I got it. You relax."

He kissed my head and disappeared down the hall.

His office door clicked shut behind him.

After our conversation, I felt too uneasy to sit still and watch TV any longer. I turned it off, tidying up the kitchen before I padded down the hallway with the intent to wash my face, do a little light stretching, climb into bed, and read.

I hadn't meant to listen as I passed his office.

But his voice carried, and it was low and threatening

"I don't care what the odds say," he snapped. "That's not what we discussed."

He paused, and so did my feet. I stood just outside his office with my heart pounding in my ears.

"No — because that makes it obvious."

I frowned, carefully inching a little closer.

"I told you I'd take care of it. You're not supposed to move anything without clearing it with me."

*What is he talking about?*

"Jesus. Do you have any idea what that looks like?" There was a beat of silence and then — "Just—fix it. And don't call me about this again."

Immediately, I continued down the hall, walking as fast as I could while not making a sound. I ducked into our bedroom just as I heard his office door open.

Nathan stepped into our en suite bathroom behind me a few minutes later with his expression smoothed and polished.

"I think I'll pack tomorrow," he said on a tired sigh, already reaching for his toothbrush. "It's been a rough day, and I work with a bunch of idiots."

I nodded, my pulse loud in my ears. "Everything okay?"

"Yeah." He smiled. "Just people panicking about money they don't understand."

Something about the way he said it made my stomach twist.

Later, Nathan climbed into bed when I was reading, planting a tender kiss on my cheek before he rolled over and turned out the light.

He scrolled on his phone next to me, and my thoughts churned on with my e-reader stuck on the same page.

*What was that call?* It was so strange, and so *late* to be taking a call at all. Then again, he was about to be in Vegas for work, and they were three hours behind us... maybe that was all it was?

That led my thoughts to his trip, to the myriad of emotions I felt guilty for feeling about it.

I was looking forward to him being gone. To the silence. To not choosing my words so carefully. To breathing in my own house.

But I was also lonely here. I was in a new city with no roots yet. And for all our fractures and fault lines, Nathan was my husband. His presence filled space, even when it made me uneasy.

After a while, Nathan put his phone on the charger before leaning over to kiss my shoulder. "I'll miss you," he murmured. "While I'm gone."

"I'll miss you too," I said.

It wasn't a lie. I would miss him.

I also couldn't wait for him to go.

Both things were true.

And I didn't know what that said about me.

## CHAPTER 14

### DELUSIONAL

Shane
Present

**W**atching my star goalie puke had me wanting to do the same.

The poor bastard had barely made it over to the bench before he was forfeiting his pre-game meal, the fans sitting above us so they could peer into the tunnel as the players went in and out getting more than they bargained for. I heard the grimace ring out over the distinct sound of Will Perry's heaves, and I cursed under my breath.

It was only the third game of the season, and I didn't have full faith that Ben Sandin was ready to take on the beastly offense of the Baltimore Railers — who had won the Cup last season.

But we had no choice.

He was up.

*Fucking hell.*

"All right, Perry," I said, patting his back sympathetically as he spit the last of his vomit out on the floor and wiped his mouth with the back of his glove. "Go home and get some rest."

"I'm fine."

"You're not."

"I'm good now."

"You're dehydrated with food poisoning, at best, and going to get the rest of the team sick with a stomach virus, at worst," I combatted. Then, I shoved his helmet into his chest and pointed at the locker room. "Go. Now. I'll check in with you after the game. I mean it, Perry, I need you gone."

He was pissed, and he had no problem showing as much as he swiped his helmet from me and stormed down the tunnel to the locker room with trainers on his heels. Immediately, staff was cleaning up his sick, and I was launching into action.

There was no time for deep sighs. We had a game to win.

"Sandin, you're in."

He hopped off the bench immediately. Fortunately, we weren't far into the first period — he should have still been warm from warmups.

When Sandin nodded at me that he was ready, I could have sworn I saw his gaze slide up to the suite Nathan Black was in.

Our new general manager had been getting cozy with quite a few players — particularly the younger ones. If I were being a calm, rational coach, I'd see it for what it was. He was getting to know the team, earning their trust, convincing them that Tampa was a great place to call home, and this team would be all they'd need in their career. He wanted them to play hard and win for us, so of course he was investing time in them.

But the side of me that couldn't help but be suspicious wondered at it, at why he was so attentive to some players and virtually invisible to the others.

I didn't like the way my stomach twisted as Sandin dropped into the crease for his first play, like my body knew something my brain didn't.

That feeling only intensified as the game played on.

Sandin was completely erratic, and not in the "backup goalie nerves" way I'd expected.

One shift he was hyper-aggressive, charging out of the crease to poke-check a puck he had no business going after, leaving the net wide open and making the entire bench gasp. The next, he was late to track a shot he should have swallowed up without blinking — like his eyes were half a second behind the puck. Twice he froze when our defense shouted for him to cover it, letting play continue when any goalie instinct would have smothered the rebound.

And then, just to keep me from yanking what little hair I had left, he'd make some impossible, physics-defying save purely by accident — like the puck hit him because he wasn't squared to it.

Every shift was a coin toss.

Heads: miraculous.

Tails: disastrous.

The Railers didn't know how to read him, and honestly? Neither did I.

I kept glancing up at the suite, feeling my jaw tighten every time I caught a ghost of movement through the tinted glass. I didn't know what I expected to see. Nathan holding up flashcards? Signaling plays like a damn third base coach?

Ridiculous.

And yet...

I couldn't shake the unease crawling under my skin.

But hockey is a cruel game — sometimes chaos works. And somehow, we clung to a one-goal lead through the third period. The final horn blared through the arena, the crowd roaring, stuffed fish flying onto the ice as was tradition, and the scoreboard flashed a win we had absolutely no business earning.

Sandin skated to the bench like he hadn't just given me a cardiac event for sixty straight minutes.

The boys slapped him on the back, helmets knocking, gloves thumping. I congratulated them, gave Sandin an extra look I couldn't help — part suspicion, part genuine relief — and then ducked into the tunnel, my pulse still misfiring.

I took a second in my office, breathing deep before dialing Perry.

He picked up on the first ring.

"Well, that was a shit storm." His voice was croaky and worn.

"You're supposed to be resting."

"I am."

"He's not. He's been pacing and vomiting into a trashcan this whole time," I heard in the background. Chloe, his wife.

"Yeah, Daddy is bad at being sick," his daughter Ava echoed.

I chuckled. "How are you? Feeling any better?"

"No," he groaned. "I don't know what happened. I was fine, and then suddenly..." He trailed off, swallowing. "I just wasn't. I don't know, Coach. I'm sorry. I didn't see it coming."

Again, that twist in my gut, like there was something afoot that I couldn't quite put my finger on.

"Nothing to be sorry for. It happens, and this was just one of those times you couldn't play through it," I said. "I'm glad you're home. Get fluids. Sleep. Text me if you get worse."

"I'll be back for the next game."

"I have no doubts. Rest," I reiterated. "I'll check in tomorrow."

We hung up, but the call didn't do what I'd hoped. If anything, the pit in my stomach deepened. Perry getting sick out of nowhere. Sandin's bizarre performance. The way his eyes had flicked to Nathan's suite. The win that felt more like a warning than a triumph.

Something was off.

I didn't know what yet.

But the ice wasn't the only thing that felt slippery tonight.

The boys filtered into the locker room for the post-game talk, and I went through the motions — praising work ethic, highlighting key plays, calling out what needed tightening before our next matchup. They were buzzing, smiling, chatting with media, riding the high of a win.

And I tried to match their energy. I really did.

But the whole time, the wrongness gnawed at me.

Once the meeting wrapped and I dismissed them, I took care of my post-game to-do list as quickly as I could — including the world's fastest press conference — before I grabbed my jacket and started down the tunnel toward the parking lot, ready to get the hell out of my own head.

But as I passed the friends and family room, something made me slow.

A flash of long golden hair. A familiar silhouette.

Ari.

I never stopped in the friends and family room, mostly because I never had a reason to. I didn't have a wife waiting for me there. No kids were barreling out at the sight of me yelling, *"Daddy!"* I always slipped right by and out to my car, waving to players as they went left and I went right.

But tonight...

I stopped.

And I stepped inside.

"Coach!" Carter called out, his hair still damp from his shower. He gripped me in a big hug before pulling back and eyeing me cautiously. "What are you doing here?"

Fortunately, his new wife was holding their daughter just behind where he stood, the perfect excuse.

"Came to see my favorite girl, of course," I answered, reaching for Lennon.

Livia Young, our team dentist and Carter's unlikely companion, handed her daughter over with a serene smile. I felt like motherhood had softened her — not in a weakening way, but quite the opposite, actually. She seemed more at peace than I'd ever seen her, and the way she and Carter immediately reached for each other once her hands were empty, I knew they'd both found their person.

My chest tightened for a different reason then, a familiar ache squeezing my lungs as I wondered what that would be like.

It was hard for me to explain to myself, let alone anyone else, so I always kept it locked up — but I hadn't ever moved on after Ariana. I'd tried. I'd spent my fair share of nights with women who I thought could capture my interest, but they never lasted. It was like there was unfinished business with Ari, and until I got that closure, I couldn't move forward.

Even now, in this room, I had Lennon in my arms smiling and playing with the pin on my lapel as I chatted with Carter and Livia with apparent ease. But inside, all my focus was on where Ariana stood on the other side of the room, locked in conversation with Maven and Grace.

The apology I'd tried to give her, one too late and too little, had me rubbed raw. I wrestled with my guilt and frustration ever since she walked out of that room. If I were being honest, I felt helpless, because she was *right here* and yet I still couldn't reach her.

*It doesn't matter*, she'd said to me when we were finally alone.

*It's in the past.*

It should have hurt, hearing her say those words. It should have knocked the breath from me, should have thrown me back to the cold hard ground of reality.

But it didn't.

Because I simply didn't believe her.

What we had... it was young and passionate, yes, but it was real. It was fucking *everything*.

And I just couldn't accept that she never thought about it anymore, about me, about *us* — especially now that fate had thrown us back into each other's lives.

*She is fucking married, you dumb, egotistical prick.*

*To your boss.*

But it didn't matter. I was firmly in the land of delusion.

My common sense could try to reason with me all it wanted; the facts didn't change in my mind.

We had too many words left unsaid for me to leave her alone now that I had my chance.

Besides, there was just something about Nathan that I didn't like. Ninety percent of the time, he seemed like the perfect gentleman. I watched him sweetly kiss and hold Ariana, listened to him dote on her when she wasn't in the room, saw the way they looked at each other when they thought no one was looking.

He loved her. She loved him. That much was easy to see.

But I still didn't trust him.

And I didn't like her being with him.

*What the fuck is wrong with me?*

I was acting so unlike myself, it was terrifying. I was the stable, professional, level-headed coach of a national league hockey team. I'd always put hockey above everything. I committed my whole life to it, not even surrendering enough time to properly try to have any sort of relationship outside those I had with my team and staff.

And here I was, dreaming of my general manager's wife and hallucinating that I had any sort of chance in hell to win my second chance with her.

In what world would this turn out well?

That realization sobered me, and I found myself handing Lennon back to Livia, wishing both her and Carter a good night. I adjusted my messenger bag strap on my shoulder and headed for the door. I shouldn't have stopped in at all. I needed to go home and cool off. I needed to get a fucking grip on reality.

Before I could escape, a slender hand caught my arm.

I closed my eyes on a pause, exhaling and telling myself to keep it short and professional before I turned and smiled.

"Congratulations," Ariana said. "Not exactly the game I expected, but you pulled it off."

*Fuck*, she was stunning.

Her long golden hair fell in soft, brushed waves over her shoulders, not a strand out of place despite the hours she'd spent in the suite and working on Sweet Dreams tasks before that. I didn't recognize her sometimes, this poised, polished woman she'd grown to be in my absence, but I still knew it was her. I knew it was my Ari, the one twenty-year-old her dreamed of being, running a nonprofit and helping kids the way she'd always wanted to.

*Not your Ari,* my pea brain reminded me. *Stop being delusional.*

But then her piercing blue eyes lifted to mine, framed by delicate features I'd memorized long ago.

And it winded me.

I was knocked back in time again, and I didn't see the put-together, elegant woman in front of me.

I saw the girl she'd been at twenty — standing in the hallway outside her dorm wearing my hoodie and a shy smile. I saw the way she used to tuck her hair behind her ear when she was nervous, all the pen caps she destroyed from gnawing on them during our study nights, the way she laughed so loudly only to cover her mouth and blush like she'd stepped out of line, like she believed her stepdad's words that she should be seen and not heard.

That version of her flickered over this one, and it damn near leveled me.

"Thank you," I managed, my voice rougher than it should've been. "The boys did the heavy lifting."

Her lips curved politely, and I saw her eyes flick to the door before they were on me again.

"It was impressive," she said. "Sandin was... unpredictable."

"Understatement," I muttered.

My eyes betrayed me then, drifting over her like they had a mind of their own. Her style hadn't changed, but it was grown now, elevated. She wore understated neutral cashmere, a soft beige sweater tucked into tailored black slacks, and simple gold jewelry, nothing loud or attention-grabbing.

And yet she still lit up the damn room.

She was mesmerizing — soft curves under conservative fabric, alabaster skin that never needed makeup, but radiated when she chose to wear it.

That small, pale scar on her right hand, half-hidden against her side as if she could pretend it wasn't there, snagged my gaze.

I still remembered the night she told me how she got it, that she'd stepped in front of her mom when Jay was on a terror, and he'd snapped, driving a kitchen knife into the back of her hand where it was braced on the wall, her body serving as armor for her mother.

She'd been only fourteen.

Everything about her tugged on something in me I'd spent eighteen years trying to suffocate, and I felt powerless to fight against my natural urges for her.

She was off limits.

And yet I couldn't stay away.

"Are you heading home?" she asked, her voice gentle.

"I was," I said, grabbing the back of my neck. "Long day."

She nodded, her gaze dipping for half a second before she pulled it back up.

"You waiting for Nathan?" I asked, both a sucker for punishment and a fool for hope. As if there would be any other answer. As if she'd say, *Oh, Nathan? No. I've been waiting for you, actually.*

"Yeah, he should be here soon. He's got an early flight, probably eager to get home and get what little rest he still can."

That made my brow arch. "Oh?"

"Heading to Vegas for work," she answered with a shrug. "Which, I admit, will be kind of nice. I could use some free time to get the house settled."

Her smile was genuine with that, but then she balked, shaking her head.

"I mean, I'll miss him, of course, desperately. I just..."

"I get it," I said, smirking and holding out my hands to let her know she didn't need to defend herself.

Hell, I loved that she wasn't destroyed by him leaving town.

I was also committed to being the dumbest version of myself, apparently, because I opened my stupid mouth and asked, "How long is he gone for?"

"Just the weekend."

I frowned, wondering what business he could possibly have in Vegas, but I never knew what the general managers and team owners got into outside of the rink. So, I let my brain move to the more pressing question I had.

"Do you have any plans Sunday?"

Ariana frowned. "I... I guess just stuff around the house. Maybe treating myself to a Bravo marathon."

"Think you could spare some time to explore your new city with me?"

There it was, that beautiful blush that grazed her cheeks in the best moments: when our eyes locked in class that first day we met, when I'd stolen a sip from her smoothie and she'd realized we were sharing straws, when I'd kissed her without warning in the quad for everyone to see, when I'd whispered filthy words in her ear while she tried to study...

"I... I don't think that's a good idea," she said with a breath of a laugh, tucking her hair behind one ear as her gaze fell to our feet.

"Why not?"

At that, she sucked her teeth, her gaze lifting right back to mine to level me with a glare that told me she saw right through me pretending there wasn't a single problem with the two of us spending a day together.

"What?" I feigned innocence, pressing a hand to my chest. "You're *married*, remember?" I said mockingly, a knowing smile on my lips. "And I'm an old geezer who barely leaves the rink. What trouble could we possibly get into?"

Her brow ticked up like she knew the answer but wouldn't dare say it out loud.

"Come on. Let me show you around your new home."

Ariana's thoughts were unreadable as her eyes flicked between mine, but I noted that tinge of pink in her cheeks, the way her hands twisted together in front of her lap.

"It's one afternoon, Ari. As friends."

Her expression told me she didn't believe that.

I didn't believe it either.

She crossed her arms, uncrossed them, clasped her hands at her waist. "Shane..."

I stepped just a little closer — not enough to touch her, but enough to feel the gravity of her. "There are no practices Sunday. The guys have the day off. Your husband is traveling. And I'm not asking for anything except... a day. A little sunlight. A break."

Her eyes flicked down my chest, back up to my face. A tell. A warning.

Her silence stretched, and my heartbeat pounded so loud I could barely hear the conversations around us.

*Say yes*, I found myself pleading like an idiot.

*Please. Just let me have one day.*

Finally, quietly — like the word escaped before she could stop it — she whispered, "Okay."

"Okay," I repeated, trying and failing not to grin like a lucky bastard who'd won the lottery. "Sunday."

"Sunday."

Wordlessly, I extended my hand for her phone. Ariana hesitated only a moment before retrieving it, and I typed my number in quickly, texting myself so I'd have her number, too, before I handed the phone back.

Nathan swept into the room then, and for the first time since he'd arrived in Tampa, I found my handshakes and smiles genuine as we chatted about the game. It didn't matter that he had my hackles raised, that I still didn't trust him — I couldn't help but beam.

Because he was leaving.

And I was ready to make the most of his absence.

## CHAPTER 15

### NEVER LOVE AGAIN

Shane
2008

On the last Friday of May, 2008, the courthouse doors closed on the sound of the gavel and our whole world shifted.

Ariana sat stiff beside me through the hearing, her eyes glazed, her hands folded tightly in her lap. My grandparents had flown in to watch Georgie and help us figure out our next steps. But when Ari wasn't around, they were just more voices of reason that I didn't want to hear.

That courtroom felt more like a prison to me, like I was the criminal instead of Jay. Ariana and I were both barely hanging onto reality, but the judge's words cut through the haze like sharp shards of ice:

*"Guardianship extended, but provisional. Subject to review in six months."*

*"Any instability—financial, academic, or residential—could affect your petition."*

*"Remember, the child's father retains standing."*

It was clinical and felt heartless, like we were just paperwork to the court when it was our whole existence being shaken.

When we walked out, Ariana clutched the file to her chest like it was Georgie himself. I could hear her whispering to herself, a frantic litany of plans. "I can have a two-bedroom apartment by August... the job on campus is already locked down... I've got affordable childcare through that program for when I'm in school... I can graduate early..." She nodded as if checking off boxes only she could see. "I'll be steady, I'll be fine. I can do this. I'll make it work."

Her mind was racing, and my heart was breaking, because I knew exactly where those thoughts went next — to me.

She was already calculating how she'd fit my games into the schedule, how often she could fly out to see me, how many weekends I could spend in Boston before camp got underway and then I wouldn't have a break for months. She was trying to figure out how we could do it all without disrupting Georgie's routine. Her lips moved with the math of it. *Classes, job, childcare... trial prep... Shane.*

I squeezed her hand as we pushed through the reporters. There were only two now, damp notepads plastered to their jackets, cameras too fogged to be much use — but even so, the flashbulbs made her flinch. I pulled her closer, tucking her under my arm as the rain came down harder, guiding her past the curb and across the street until we were free of them.

The crowd thinned. The rain fell in sheets.

Ariana tilted her face to me, soaked hair clinging to her cheeks, her mouth curving in a trembling half-smile. "How poetic, huh? The pouring down rain."

I smiled, though it felt stiff. I couldn't help but reach for her, tucking her wet hair behind her ear as she leaned into my touch.

My heart was fucking shattering in my chest.

"I don't mind the rain, you know," she said, tilting her head up to the sky. It was like she was taking her first breath of the day, her lips spreading into a soft smile. "I like how it washes everything away."

My throat was on fire when I tried to swallow, and I looked up at the sky with her, but not in awe. I saw that rain for exactly what it was.

A reckoning.

Ariana's smile faltered when she looked at me again, her lashes blinking wildly against the rain. She saw it in my face, saw the way my chest locked tight, the way my jaw clenched, my nostrils flaring like I was fighting to breathe.

"Shane, don't," she pleaded, and the words were so rough, so broken that my knees nearly gave out.

My voice was just as pained when I replied. "You know I have to."

Her chin wobbled. "No, you don't. We'll figure it out," she begged, voice shaking, her hands clutching mine like she could hold the pieces of us together if she just gripped tight enough. "You'll travel, I'll stay here, but people do long distance all the time. I can still testify, I can still—"

"Ari." My voice cracked, but I forced it firm. "You know we can't."

Her chin lifted, defiant even through tears. "Yes, we can. You're leaving for camp in August, fine, but that doesn't mean—"

"It does." I swallowed hard, every word scraping my throat raw. "Think about it. The trial. The custody hearings. The advocate told you to keep a low profile, stay steady, stay home. If you're with me, you're in headlines the second a camera spots us together. You'll be the NHL rookie's girlfriend testifying in a murder trial. Do you know what his lawyers would do with that?"

"They'll do whatever they want no matter what I do!" she snapped, her voice breaking. "Why should I give you up because of him?"

"Because if you don't, you could lose your brother."

It was my voice that broke then, softer but no less brutal.

"The court will use it against you. His lawyers will call you unstable. They'll say you're chasing attention. And what about your safety? You think his family won't use me to track you down? To find you?"

She shook her head, over and over, but I could see what she wouldn't admit out loud.

She knew it, too.

All of it had been circling in the back of her mind, but she'd tried to ignore it, to block it out, to pretend it would all be fine.

But this was bigger than two people in love. This was justice for her mother. This was retribution for all Jay had put them through.

This was her future — and her brother's too.

I dragged a shaky breath into my lungs. "Ari... I know what Georgie needs because I was him once. When my parents died, I got thrown into my grandparents' house with nothing but the clothes I was wearing. I was seven years old, and my whole world was gone. Hockey saved me, but before that? I was lost. I needed someone steady and safe. I needed someone who wouldn't disappear no matter how messy it got. That's what Georgie needs now — not a sister splashed across tabloids, not uncertainty about where he'll sleep next week."

She shook her head more vigorously then, tears spilling down her cheeks and mixing with the rain. "I don't care. I just want you."

God, I wanted to believe her. I wanted to let myself say *okay, we'll fight it together*. But the picture was too clear — her little brother torn from her arms, her testimony shredded on the stand, her face splashed across tabloids instead of tucked safely away.

"This isn't about what you want," I whispered. "Or about what I want. It's about what you need. What *he* needs. And what I can't give you right now."

Her hands fell from mine like the last rope between us had snapped. "So that's it? You just decide? You break my heart and call it protection?"

My chest heaved. "Just because it's not now doesn't mean it's never."

Something I'd never seen before happened then. My girl who was always softness and light stiffened, her gaze narrowing, jaw set tight. I watched in real time as ice slid into her eyes. "If you walk away from me now, Shane, that's it. It *is* now or never for me."

That ice in her gaze pierced right through my chest, my heart, my lungs. My next breath was lodged in my chest. My pulse pounded unsteadily through my shredded heart. I knew what she was really saying: *choose me now, or lose me forever.*

"So you're asking me to give it all up," I said hoarsely. "To choose you over hockey. To forfeit my dream and stay."

Her lips parted, trembling. "No," she whispered, shaking her head, sobbing now. "No, that's not what I want. I just—"

But she didn't finish, because she knew. Deep down, she knew there was no other way.

And I knew, too.

I couldn't have hockey and have her, too.

So I pressed a kiss to her forehead, breathing her in like it was the last time — and I knew in my heart that it was.

"I love you enough to leave," I said. "Please love me enough to understand."

Just like that, I'd made my bed.

I was prepared to lie in it.

But I knew I'd never sleep again.

## CHAPTER 16

### THE ENDING OF US

Ariana
Present

We couldn't have asked for a more beautiful day.

Tampa in mid-October could still be sweltering. I'd discovered that with much chagrin as a girl who grew up in Connecticut and stayed in the northeast until very recently. I missed the leaves changing and the cool weather, but I had to admit — this wasn't bad, either. The humidity had dropped, it was pleasantly warm, and the sky was pure blue, not a cloud to be found.

That might have been the first sign something was off.

Days like this were meant to be uncomplicated. And yet, as I stood at the end of my long driveway waiting for Shane, my pulse skidded too fast, anticipation buzzing beneath my skin in a way that felt wholly inappropriate.

Shane pulled up and stopped short of the house, just where I'd asked him to. I hadn't wanted him any closer. The house loomed behind me, quiet and watchful, and something about leaving it like this — slipping away without a word of my plans to my husband — felt wrong.

It was wrong the way my excitement outweighed caution. It was wrong how easily I'd said yes. The fact that I hadn't told Nathan about it was all the proof I needed that this wasn't innocent, no matter how carefully I tried to frame it in my own head.

But I was just curious enough to ignore every warning sign and say yes, anyway.

"This is an upgrade from your old Pontiac," I mused with an arched brow, the wind blowing my hair as we cruised through the streets of Tampa with the top down in his Jeep Wrangler. It made me smile, that he could have picked any luxury car in the world, but instead he'd gone with something so unmistakably him.

The boy I'd once known — the one who lived for hockey and sunshine and any excuse to be outside — would have worshipped a Jeep. And somehow, it also suited this new version of him just as well: coach for the Tampa Bay Ospreys, easygoing, settled, sun-browned, and thriving in a life I never quite pictured him having without me.

"God, do you remember the summer the air conditioning broke in that thing?" He shook his head. "Grandma and Grandpa insisted I had to save up and pay to fix it on my own."

"Oh, how dare they," I mocked.

"Hey! I was too busy with school and hockey to carry a job," he defended, and then he hit me with a boyish grin. "And you, of course. Mostly you, in fact. I think I could blame the whole no-job thing on you, really."

My cheeks heated furiously, and I shook my head and looked down at my hands folded in my lap. "Hush."

He did, his grin still in place as he let his left hand hang out the window while the right thumbed a beat on the steering wheel. He used to lean the other way. He used to have his left hand on the steering wheel and the other on my thigh.

He had the perfect playlist on, one I couldn't help but wonder if he'd made just for today. When Snow Patrol came on, my smile mirrored his.

"Is music still one of your love languages?" he asked as we turned into Ybor. My eyes grew wide, the explosion of color hitting me instantly — candy-bright murals, wrought-iron balconies draped in string lights, a band warming up outside a bar even though it was barely ten in the morning. The scent of roasted Cuban coffee and hand-rolled cigars drifted in through the open Jeep, mixing with the humid Florida air.

"Always," I breathed, still looking around in awe.

When we stopped at a streetlight, someone pointed at us, and the group of what looked like twenty-somethings jumped up and down before one of them yelled out, "Hey, Coach! Great game on Friday!"

Shane smiled and waved at them just as the light turned green, and they nearly melted down at the acknowledgment.

It didn't seem to faze Shane, though, who just shifted hands on the wheel and asked me, "Do you listen to the same stuff you used to, or have you found new artists to love?"

"A little of both. I'll admit I tend to reach for the past, though. I find myself gravitating to Snow Patrol still, and The Fray, Kings of Leon... I don't know. I'm not sure music hits the same anymore."

"You took the words right from my mouth," he said. "Who are the newer ones you like?"

"Hozier, Vance Joy, JP Saxe, Lauv... I've really enjoyed Gracie Abrams lately, too."

"How about Maggie Rogers?"

I grabbed his wrist where it was resting on the console, my jaw hinged open. "I *love* her."

"She's incredible. I *knew* you'd like her, too," Shane said with a grin. "I saw her play live here last year."

"No! Really? Was she as magical in person as she seems online?"

"More so. Like a little hippie fairy spreading music glitter everywhere."

"I have to see her one day. Phoebe Bridgers, too."

"You know, I have an in with Mia Love," he said, arching a brow in my direction. "She and Phoebe are pretty close. I bet I could get us the hookup the next time she's in Tampa."

My jaw was on the floorboard now. "Who the hell *are* you?" I asked with a laugh.

Shane chuckled, too, and then turned us into the tiny parking lot of a small building, its stucco walls the color of warm sand. There was a deep red awning fluttering in the breeze that read *La Segunda*.

Shane cut the engine and hopped out of the Jeep, rushing around to my door before I had the chance to reach for the handle. "Ready to have the best breakfast sandwich of your life?"

It unnerved me a little, how easy it was to stand next to Shane in line while we waited to order, how natural it felt to point into the case of delicious pastries and laugh when we sat outside on the curb and watched chickens peck away at our crumbs by our feet. We talked like no time had passed. We laughed like we'd parted on perfectly pleasant terms, like we hadn't had our hearts put through a woodchipper.

It was like the day was too beautiful to sour it with any truths that might steal joy, like we both just wanted to ignore reality for one day and pretend this was normal — that we were just two friends back together after so many years apart.

But we *hadn't been* just friends, had we? From the first day we met, we knew there was something more between us.

And I felt that stark reminder as our day around Tampa continued.

When we piled onto the TECO streetcar to head downtown and found it packed to the brim, it left us no choice but to sit squashed next to one another.

I slid in next to the window, and then Shane took the seat next to me. We were an appropriate distance from each other until more and more people piled on.

"I've never seen it so busy," Shane remarked, and then he slid toward me, allowing a woman who appeared to be in her sixties to sit next to him.

It happened so quickly, without fanfare, just him scooting closer to me and smiling at the woman before offering her a seat. He continued chatting with her a moment, but I couldn't chime in, because I was all too aware of everywhere we touched.

We were connected from our knees to our hips, his leg warm against mine. When he finished his chat with the woman sitting next to him, he angled his body more toward me, and for no reason other than he had nowhere else to put it — his arm snaked behind me over the wooden bench seat.

Shane seemed to notice it then, too — how close we were, the heat that radiated between us. His eyes connected briefly with mine before we both shifted, but there was nowhere to go, no space to be found.

His scent surrounded me, that iron and ice and mint. Out of nowhere, a flash from our past hit me, and I remembered clinging to him in a fierce hug, his hoodie bunched in my hands, my nose buried in his neck and committing that scent to memory as I whispered, *"I don't know what to do."*

He'd held me just as tight and told me we'd figure it out together.

He'd lied.

I turned away from him, casting my gaze out the window as the trolley carried us to Channelside. I tried to focus on the palm trees, the people on bikes and scooters, the brief glimpses of water I got between buildings.

But Shane watched me in the window's reflection, and my skin burned beneath that gaze.

When we finally shuffled off the trolley at Sparkman Wharf, I guzzled the clean air into my lungs, hoping it would help clear the dizziness of being so close to him. Shane didn't seem fazed at all. He pointed toward the lively grouping of restaurants and bars, guiding the way through the crowd as I took in the lights hanging overhead and the sound of live music filtering through the air.

"Ah, so this is why it's so crowded everywhere," Shane murmured when we made it to the sprawling lawn of Sparkman Wharf. There was a giant screen at one end, people spread out in chairs or on blankets all across the grass. "There's a Tarpons game today."

The Tampa Bay Tarpons were the city's professional football team. I didn't know much about them other than they hadn't had a winning season in long enough to make the fans hesitant to want to buy tickets to any game. It wasn't fun to file out of a stadium after your team lost when you could have just watched the game from home or at a bar.

"Want to sit for a moment?" he asked, gesturing to two empty chairs.

I shrugged. "Sure."

"I'll get us a drink. Mimosa or Bloody Mary?"

"A little early, don't you think?" I laughed.

"Come on, it's almost noon now! And we've had breakfast. Besides, if I remember correctly, a Bloody Mary on a Sunday is one of your favorite things."

I bit my lip against a smile. "I can't believe you remember that."

"Extra spicy, too. Right? Like basically pour in an entire bottle of hot sauce?"

"Bonus if they have bleu cheese olives."

Shane wrinkled his nose, shivering like I'd scratched my nails on a chalkboard. "Animal, you are." But he winked, and then disappeared into the crowd.

I took in the view in his short absence, marveling at the ships in the water, the buildings of downtown sprawled all around us. Kids played games on the lawn, groups of friends shared drinks, people all over donned their Tampa Tarpons gear. By the time Shane joined me again, I was smiling ear to ear.

"You know, it may not be Boston, but Tampa is pretty cool."

"Oh, just wait. We haven't seen anything yet." Shane tapped his beer against my Bloody Mary. "To reuniting with old friends."

I gave him a pointed look, but grinned, anyway, as I took the first sip.

It was spicy and perfect.

"So, you stuck around Boston, huh?" Shane asked, his eyes on some kids who were playing tag.

"I did."

"Never wanted to go anywhere else?"

"I thought about Colorado once. But otherwise, no, not really."

"You did always seem happy in New England."

"It's home," I said, a soft smile on my lips. But my stomach twisted in the next second when I thought about how quickly we'd left, how Nathan had accepted this job without so much as speaking to me.

It wasn't that I would have said no. I loved him, and I wanted him to chase his dreams. I knew this was what he'd wanted for a long, long time.

It was that he didn't even think to consult with me, like I wasn't a partner in his eyes, but rather just an accessory.

"You did move, though," Shane said, his expression somber now. "Not long after the trial."

"I did," I answered carefully. "And again, when Nathan and I got married. How did you—"

"Hey, Coach!"

We both turned to the source of the greeting, and when Shane waved at the group of Tarpons fans who had recognized him, they were overjoyed. Suddenly, the people who had been oblivious to who he was in our near vicinity were paying closer attention, narrowing their gaze in question, some hopping on their phone. I wondered if they were googling to figure out who he was, if they didn't already know.

And I felt suddenly, acutely visible.

A familiar prickle of unease crept up my spine. I imagined a photo snapped at the wrong angle, a caption taken out of context, Nathan scrolling past it later, his rage boiling until it overflowed right onto me.

I forced my shoulders to relax, but I was anything but calm inside. *It'll be fine,* I told myself. *I'll just say we ran into each other. I was out running errands. Oh, why was I drinking a Bloody Mary? Well… I… they were free, actually. Yeah. There was a new bar opening and—*

The fact that I was already making up stories for an argument that hadn't happened yet had that *this is wrong* feeling lurching back to life.

"What do you say we walk a little?" Shane asked, shifting closer, his voice low.

Relief washed through me, quick and telling.

I nodded. "Sounds perfect."

We did a lap around all the shops, Shane stopping to tell me a little about each of the restaurants as we did. Once I'd finished my drink, he insisted we stop for a cone from Jeni's Ice Creams, and then we were on to our third form of transportation: rented bicycles.

It was just what I needed, that break from talking and being close to Shane. I rode in happy silence behind him, smiling at the sun reflecting off the water as we cruised Bayshore. Every now and then, Shane would pull to the side, stopping to point at something off in the distance and explain it to me.

He really had taken on the role as tour guide, and it made me think of when we'd walked around Boston that first summer we were a couple — how we'd watched the sailboats in the harbor, our days lost in the North End devouring the best Italian food the city had to offer, the nights we'd played tourist and followed the historical paths, reading about the men and women who'd helped found our country.

My chest ached fiercely with the memories by the time we parked our bikes in Hyde Park. There was an energetic market going on, white tents sprawled as far as the eye could see between the strips of shops on either side of the street.

And as if he didn't even have to think before he did it, Shane grabbed my hand.

Time slugged again as his palm slid into mine, his fingers curling around me with ease. Heat zapped from that point of contact, a warning sign or an invitation, I couldn't be sure.

We took only a few steps before I yanked away, tucking my hair behind my ear before I folded my arms tightly across my chest.

Shane frowned at the rejection, but quickly smiled and shook his head like he'd forgotten a cup on top of his car before driving off. "Sorry. I... I guess I..."

Instead of finishing the thought, he shoved his hands in his pockets and nodded his chin toward the market.

"I hope I didn't upset you," Shane said after we perused the first two tents in silence.

My throat was tight as I answered, "You didn't. It's just that I—"

"Am married," he finished for me, our eyes locking as we came to a stop in the crowd. "I know. It was... I don't know what I was thinking. I guess it just kind of felt..."

He swallowed, again shaking his head like he was an idiot unable to explain himself.

I couldn't help the smile that spread on my lips, even as my stomach tightened painfully. "I understand," I said softly.

And I did.

It felt natural, even after all this time, after all the pain and loss. I felt it, too.

"It's just nostalgia," I said, and even as I said it, I wondered if I believed the truth of those words. "We're old now. Easy to want to go back to a time when our knees didn't ache."

Shane barked out a laugh at that. "God, it's been a while for me on that front. I take aspirin like candy since my injury."

I frowned, the conversation paused long enough for us to smell soaps and lotions from a local craftswoman before we were walking again. "Does your hip still hurt? Even now?"

"Not all the time," Shane said with a shrug. "But, yes. Hip and knee, both. It takes constant physical therapy to manage the pain."

"That sounds tiresome."

"It's worth it to do what I love, even if not in the capacity I wish I could," he answered easily, and then he plucked a candle from the table we were browsing. He held it up, brows arching as I read where it said *bacon in the oven*. He opened it, inhaled, and then handed it to me to do the same as his eyes shot open wide.

I laughed.

It really did smell like bacon in the oven.

"I don't think I'd want that smell in my house unless there really was bacon coming," I said. "Seems like torture for my stomach."

"What about this one?" he asked. This candle was labeled *monstera that needs water*. We both laughed in surprise when we smelled it. It was actually quite delightful.

"What actually happened?" I asked as we perused the candles. "With your injury. If you don't mind talking about it, that is?"

Shane stiffened, his eyes darkening. "I don't mind." But he still paused a long moment before speaking again. "It happened late in the second period in a game against Toronto," he said finally. "I was on a break down the right side. A defenseman stepped up faster than I expected."

He lifted one shoulder in a small shrug, like the rest was obvious.

"I tried to cut inside. My skate caught. Knee went first."

My chest tightened, and a vision of him standing on the sidewalk in the freezing cold of Boston hit me like a truck — the crutches, the bulk of hardware under his clothes, the way he'd carried himself like a broken man barely hanging on.

"I heard it," he went on, voice even. "That pop everyone talks about. I didn't feel the pain right away, but I knew something was wrong."

He stopped walking, picking up a candle and turning it over in his hands before he sat it back down again.

"I still had momentum. Got hit from the side before I could go down clean. Took the boards hard. Hip shattered on impact."

The words sat between us, heavy and final.

"They helped me off the ice," he added. "I kept telling them I'd be fine. That I'd be back by playoffs." A brief, humorless exhale left him. "Turns out you don't rehab your way out of that."

I didn't know what to say.

Shane slid his gaze to me. "That's it," he said. "One bad second."

And then he reached for a candle, holding it up to ask the booth attendant how much it was.

In the end, I left with one called *old bookstore* and Shane picked *neighbor's freshly cut lawn* to take home. When we had our bags in hand, I turned the conversation back to his injury.

"I thought you would end up playing again," I said. "After the injury."

"I told you I never could."

That memory made my stomach twist, how we'd stumbled upon each other by chance in Boston not long after his career had ended in a flash.

"I know, I just... I guess I kind of thought somehow you'd find a way. You've always been so driven, so passionate." I swallowed. "I know hockey is everything to you."

Shane's expression went flat, like those words were an insult instead of the truth. "Yeah, well, I learned quickly there's only so far a *can-do* attitude can get you, and apparently it's not very far when you shatter your hip and tear your ACL at the same time."

I swallowed, eyes on where my hands were tangled together in front of me. "I'm sorry, Shane."

"Not your fault," he said. His eyes floated to mine as we came to a stop next to a jewelry tent. "We both know the blame is all mine."

"It was an accident."

He opened his mouth, then shut it again, a tight smile finding his lips before he gestured to the next tent.

I wondered if I was thinking what he was, if I'd read the implication of those words he'd muttered correctly.

He wasn't to blame for the injury that ended his hockey career.

But he was to blame for the ending of us.

## CHAPTER 17

### THE GUILTY ONE

Ariana

2013

Three knocks on the window next to our table made us scream.

I was out to dinner with my boss and two of my co-workers, celebrating a successful holiday fundraiser event for the family services nonprofit I'd been working with for a little over a year. I had childcare for Georgie for the evening, a rare occurrence, and was excited to have a glass of wine and eat as much pasta as I could without feeling sick.

But one glance at the man outside the window, and it was a futile hope.

I was sick instantly.

Shane McCabe stood on the other side of that glass, snow falling down around him and sticking to the brown beanie and dark green parka he wore over his hoodie. The six years that had passed since I'd last seen him were evident in his every feature, from the scruff lining his square jaw to the angular shape of his face. Gone was the softness of the young Shane I'd fallen in love with. He was all sharp angles now, from his jaw to the bones over his eyes.

Those eyes were somehow the same and so different I hardly recognized them. They were still that sharp blue-gray, as striking as ever — but they were haunted now, adding to the eerie image of him standing in front of me after all this time.

He truly was like a ghost, so much so that I blinked several times to be sure it wasn't my brain playing tricks on me.

His mouth was slightly open, his brows raised in surprise, like he couldn't believe what he was seeing, either.

Once my own shock settled, I realized he was slumped, that tiredness in his eyes evident in the lines of his face and the sad way in which he carried himself.

And that's when I saw what I hadn't before.

He was on crutches.

"Do you know this man?" my boss asked, one hand pressed to her chest like she was steadying her pulse. She was smiling a little now that we all knew there was no evident threat, but a strange man staring at us wasn't exactly comforting, either.

"I did once," I answered.

I apologized, excusing myself from the table and asking the hostess for my coat before I shrugged it on along with my hat and scarf. Then, I braved the winter cold.

The snow was falling harder now, softening the noise of the city. Shane stood against the brick, away from the window, the glow from Christmas lights painting a serene image for what felt like an impending car crash in my mind.

I stopped a few feet away from him, hands buried in the pockets of my coat.

For a long moment, we just stared at one another. The disbelief had passed, but neither of us knew what to say.

My body's natural impulse was to break down. I felt it in the sting of my nose, the prickling behind my eyes. I wanted to cry. I wanted to run to him. I wanted to hug him and be held and kiss him stupid and thank the universe for bringing us together again. I wanted to hit him and scream and look him right in the eyes when I said he's dead to me and has been for years, that I never want to see him again, that I'm better without him.

I stood frozen to the spot, instead.

"I can't believe I found you," he finally whispered, the words puffing out in a white cloud as his eyes searched the entire length of me like I was a mirage.

"Because I'm sure you looked so hard," I deadpanned.

*Atta girl.*

*Be cold. Ice him out. He left you. He doesn't get your smiles and "so great to see you" now.*

Shane frowned, wincing a little as he pushed off the wall and hobbled closer to me on his crutches. "I did. I—"

"Why are you here?" I asked, cutting him off. Again, I found a mixture of pride and sickness swirling in my gut for my ability to act so unaffected by him.

"By chance," he answered in a puff of a laugh. "I was just needing some fresh air and then I looked in the window and saw—"

"I mean in Boston," I rephrased. "Long way to be from Jacksonville in the middle of the season, isn't it?"

He swallowed, his jaw hardening. "Not exactly in playing shape, am I?"

My gaze flicked down to the bulky, square outline beneath his joggers — a knee brace, I guessed.

"What happened?" I tried to aim for apathetic again, but the words came out breathless.

"Shattered my hip. Tore my ACL. Ended my career."

The last three words had my eyes snapping to his.

I'd followed him for the first two years of his professional career. Even when it hurt, I couldn't help myself. I watched every game, every interview. I tracked his stats. It wasn't until a night that I drank myself into oblivion crying over him that I realized I was only torturing myself. I stopped cold turkey. I hadn't watched a game since. I'd done everything I could to avoid anything hockey related, in fact, which had been easy enough to do with my own career aspirations.

So I had no idea he'd been hurt.

I felt sick again.

Shane just shrugged, as if it didn't bother him, as if that wouldn't be the worst possible thing that could ever happen to him — to lose hockey forever.

"The team sent me here for my second and third surgeries. There's a surgeon here, Doctor Rovelli, who specializes in catastrophic hip reconstructions and has worked with a lot of Olympians and players from the NHL." He shrugged again. "Not that I'll play again. But I guess the team doesn't want me crippled for life, so that's nice."

I didn't want to show him any amount of sympathy, but it was impossible not to. My heart broke for him, for the boy I once knew and the man I knew nothing of now.

"I'm sorry," I said simply. I didn't trust myself to say more.

He nodded, his Adam's apple bobbing hard in his throat. "It's me who's the sorry one, Ari."

I let my gaze fall to the snow covering the sidewalk between us.

People walked by, muttering *excuse me* or so caught up in their conversation and laughter that they didn't notice us at all. Sometimes they brushed our shoulders or stepped over Shane's crutch at the last moment. All of them were oblivious to the two strangers they passed, how our world had halted to a stop on this cold December night.

"You look good," Shane said. "Happy."

"I'm trying to be."

He nodded again. "I want to ask you so many things."

"Why?" I snapped. "Because we're such good friends? Are we supposed to just hug and catch up like I wasn't hysterically crying and begging you not to leave me the last time we were together?"

His nostrils flared, eyes glossing. "I didn't want to leave."

"Could have fooled me."

"I thought I was doing the right thing."

I scoffed. Because him standing here now — injured, sidelined, his future suddenly uncertain — it was impossible not to notice the timing. Hockey had been taken from him, and only then had he come looking for me.

And maybe that wasn't fair of me. Maybe grief was warping everything.

But I couldn't shake the truth burning in my chest: if hockey were still an option, he wouldn't be standing here.

"You were choosing hockey over me," I corrected him. "You still would be, if you had the chance."

"That's not—"

"Fair?" I laughed, releasing a puff of white breath into the night. "Yeah, well, if I've learned anything in my life, it's that nothing is fair." I pulled my scarf up against the wind. "I should get back inside to my friends."

I turned to the sound of crutches scraping the sidewalk, and then a hand found my elbow, pulling me to a stop.

"Wait."

I didn't shrug him off, afraid I might cause him to fall. And maybe for a moment, I wanted to let myself feel him again — his warmth, his scent, the safety and comfort I once found in him.

My eyes trailed up from where he gripped my arm to where his eyes were watching me.

"I don't deserve it, Ariana, but I'm going to ask for it, anyway. Please, forgive me." His voice broke a little, and he sniffed, straightening as much as he could. "I was young. I was fucking stupid. I thought I was protecting you. I thought..." One of his crutches slipped an inch on the wet sidewalk, and he caught himself with a wince before he continued. "I know none of it matters now. I know we're in the past and you're happy and you've moved on, and I want that. I do. I want your happiness. But I also *need* your forgiveness." He swallowed. "Please. Please, Ari, forgive me."

I didn't realize I was crying until the first tear slid down my cheek. It was so cold it stuck to my jaw, never falling to the ground, but instead marring my face like a tattoo.

"I forgive you for leaving," I said, my voice stronger than I felt. "But I'll never forgive you for staying gone."

The impact was immediate.

His shoulders slumped, like I'd knocked the last bit of air from his lungs. His grip loosened, his hand falling away from my arm as if he'd forgotten it was there. For a second, he just stood there, glassy-eyed and stunned, staring at me like he'd finally understood it was too late to fix what happened between us, too late to right his wrongs.

I left him standing there in the snow, retreating back into the restaurant and pretending I was fine when I rejoined my colleagues. I drank my wine. I ate my pasta. I convinced myself I was proud of my response.

But I cried until I couldn't breathe that night, curled into a ball and clutching my pillow like it was Shane.

I knew I'd never see him again, that those would be the final words between us.

I had been strong. I had defended my heart. I had denied the man who hurt me the privilege of forgiveness.

But alone in my bed, I only wished I'd been weak. I wished he were here with me now, holding me, kissing me, telling me he'd never leave again.

I'd lost him for a second time.

And I was the guilty one now.

## CHAPTER 18

### THE MAN WHO WALKED AWAY

Shane
Present

"You would go to Mars?!" Ariana asked, jaw popped open.

"You *wouldn't*?!"

"No!" She laughed, staring at me like I was insane. "Absolutely not."

"Not under any circumstance?"

"I can't think of even one."

I sat up in the hammock we were sharing, one that was sprawled between two tree trunks on the edge of the University of Tampa campus where it hugged the Hillsborough River. Boats and kayaks passed us as we swung, Curtis Hixon Park alive with activity across the river from where we sat.

The hammock was large, but it didn't matter the size. It was still impossible to put much space between us. Even when we tried, the way the hammock hung pushed us back to the middle, our thighs touching, Ariana's hands wrapped tightly together in her lap like she was afraid to accidentally brush mine.

"Not even if you were ninety-nine years old, slowly dying, and they offered you the chance to be the first to go?"

Ariana considered it. "No, not even then."

"Why on Earth would you say no to that?!"

"Because I'd want to spend my last moments with the people I love," she answered simply. "With Georgie."

"And Nathan," I finished for her.

She flushed a deep red. We'd somehow managed not to talk about him all day. "Yes, and Nathan. I wouldn't want to be alone. Wouldn't you feel the same?"

I sat back again, bringing our bodies closer together. My eyes wandered to the water in front of us. "I'm pretty good at being alone."

That quieted us both, but I quickly cleared my throat and laughed it off.

"Besides, I've watched too many space documentaries and read too many books not to be curious enough to say *fuck it*. If I'm going to die anyway, might as well die among the stars."

"It *would* be cool to see Earth from space," Ariana conceded.

"Just a marble floating around," I mused. "Puts things into perspective, doesn't it?"

My day with Ariana was flying by as quickly as I anticipated. I knew just having one day with her wouldn't be enough, but I didn't know how easy it would be to talk to her the way I used to, to catch up and hear about who she was now. I reveled in anything she gave me — how she liked her coffee now, how she'd become a big fan of sushi, how she'd ended up at the same party as Michael Jordan once by happenstance.

Some things didn't sit right with me, like the gaps she wouldn't fill about why she never ended up pursuing her career in social work. She'd had gigs within the space, that was for certain, but it was like her path was interrupted somehow. Of course, she hadn't *stopped* working in the nonprofit sector, but it had changed, her work tied up with her husband's.

*Which makes sense, you idiot*, I chastised myself internally. *Of course their lives would intertwine.*

I couldn't put my finger on why I didn't like it.

I was sure it had something to do with the fact that I'd always imagined me in her life, and this didn't fit any picture I'd had in my head.

"I can't imagine going to college here," Ariana said, her eyes crinkling at the edges as she smiled at a group of college kids passing by us. Two of them held blankets under their arms and the third had a Frisbee. They traipsed past us, oblivious to the world before setting up camp a few yards away.

"It's kind of like Boston," I mused. "On the water, a city with its own vibe."

"It's a lot warmer," Ariana pointed out.

"And has beaches."

"But no train."

"And no North End."

She groaned at that. "What a shame. Poor kids. I actually feel sorry for them now."

I smiled, taking in her profile. This woman had aged so goddamn beautifully it hurt. Every soft line on her face, the weathered skin of her hands — all of it told a story. I could close my eyes and envision her laughter, her time in the sunshine, all the nonprofits she'd worked for, all the memories she'd made with Georgie.

She was so strong. She'd fought so hard for the life she had now.

I ached to be a part of it in a way I didn't deserve.

"I got you something," I said after a moment. "At the market."

"What? How? I was with you the whole time."

"When you went to the bathroom," I answered easily. "Close your eyes."

"Shane." She laughed.

"Oh, just do it."

She narrowed her eyes at me, but she was smiling when she finally did as I asked.

"Hold out your hands."

Even with her eyes closed, I could tell she rolled them, but then she plopped her hands out.

I dug into my pocket, fishing out the delicate gift wrapped in tissue paper. I unwrapped it and then pressed it into her palm.

"Okay, open."

She peeked one eye open and then the next, gaze drifting from me down to what she held in her hands.

A wooden page holder.

"Wait, is this...?" She smiled, holding the trinket up and tilting it this way and that.

"A page holder," I answered, taking it from her long enough to show her the hole through the middle. I took her hand in mine without hesitation, sliding her thumb through the hole to demonstrate. "So you can hold your paperback open with one hand."

She let out the most pleased laugh, soft and light, and then pulled the device closer to inspect it. She ran the fingertips of her opposite hand over the script engraving that read *just one more chapter*.

"How do you know I even read anymore?" she asked, arching a brow at me. "We haven't talked about that. Maybe I haven't read in years."

I scoffed. "Please. If you were breathing, you were reading. No way could you live without books."

I smiled wide, my cheeks flushing at the truth of it.

"I still remember the ugly look you gave me when I borrowed your copy of *Meditations* and returned it not in perfect shape," he said.

"You had bent, like, twenty page corners!"

"I was highlighting the ones I liked most!"

We both laughed, the two sounds mingling to create my favorite old song.

After a beat, Ariana shifted on the hammock, then leaned back slightly, bracing herself with her hands before letting her shoulders rest against the fabric. Her feet stayed on the ground, but her posture relaxed, gaze tipping up toward the sky above us.

I followed her lead a second later, the hammock creaking softly as I reclined beside her, the late-afternoon sun warm on my face. There were clouds in the distance now, slowly rolling in.

She lifted the small wooden page holder toward the sky, holding it up like she was sighting something far away through the hole in its center.

"I still have that, you know," she said. "Marcus Aurelius always seems to know what to say to calm me when my mind starts spinning." She turned her head to say something else — and stopped.

Because I was already looking at her.

The moment stretched, quiet and charged. Her pupils flared just slightly, her breath catching before she smoothed it out, and I felt the shift in the space between us as clearly as if she'd reached for my hand.

"Sometimes, I open up to one of the pages you tabbed and try to figure out which one spoke to you," she admitted softly.

My throat was tight with my next swallow. *She'd held onto me, too.*

We were so close, our eyes searching one another, our breaths shallow. There was an aching heaviness between us that I wanted so badly to point out, but was afraid I'd lose the day entirely if I acknowledged its existence.

"Well, now you can just ask me," I said.

The corner of her lips twitched and fell. "I guess I can, can't I?"

I could have stared at her forever. I could have let the sun set and the night take the city and stayed right there in that hammock with her.

Unfortunately, the moment was cut entirely too short by the clearing of a throat behind us.

Ariana and I scrambled to sit up in the hammock and peeked up over the side to find a young college student, barefoot and holding a notebook under his arm.

"Um... that's my hammock, dude."

I turned to Ariana, whose brows shot up into her hairline, and then we both burst out laughing.

• • •

An hour later, after having a beer each at Sail Bar, Ariana and I walked the riverwalk from the convention center toward Curtis Hixon Park, our paper bags from the market swinging on either side of us. The sun was setting on the day I'd asked for, and I felt greed swelling in my chest.

I wanted more.

I wanted another day with her. I wanted a night. I wanted a week and a month and a year after that.

It would never be enough, no amount of time I had with her. I could never know all I wanted to know. I could never hear her laugh enough to satiate me. I could never find enough excuses to touch the small of her back or slide my hand into hers.

I knew this day would be a dangerous one even when I asked for it. Still, I couldn't resist. And it made sense, why I would want to torture myself just for the chance to reconnect with her.

She'd always been it for me.

But what I had struggled to figure out, more and more as the day progressed, was... why had *she* agreed?

She was married. And yes, I'd practically begged her to come, I'd sworn it would be all innocence, and to be fair, it had been.

Still, I was her ex. Even if it was a lifetime ago, we had been in love.

Why had she agreed to spend the day with me when her husband was away?

And had she told him about it?

These questions plagued me to the point that I couldn't ignore them as we walked the river. The clear-sky day we'd had was now turning gray, clouds rolling in, wind sweeping over us. It wasn't cold, but the weather was whispering a warning, humidity filling the charged air around us.

I ignored it like the fool I was.

"So... when does Nathan get home?"

Ariana's steps faltered for just a half-second, barely noticeable unless — like me — you caught every flicker of change in her. She tucked a strand of hair behind her ear, eyes fixed ahead.

"Tomorrow," she said lightly.

I hummed, pretending like I hadn't just felt a crack splinter through the day we'd built. "You two doing okay?"

That had a puff of a laugh coming from her nose. "We've been dancing around this all day, haven't we?" she asked softly.

"Maybe." I shoved my hands in my pockets. "Maybe I wanted to see how long it would take you to bring him up."

Her lips curled and fell again. "We're... fine. Great. I mean, he's busy with the team and his new position, but I'm busy with getting the house in order, and now with Sweet Dreams, so... yeah. We're good."

"Are you answering the question or trying to convince me?"

Her gaze cut to mine, sharp and wounded. "Shane..."

I held her stare. "Are you happy?"

I watched the answer ripple across her face — the real one — before she shoved it down so quickly I almost doubted I'd seen it.

"Of course I'm happy," she said, a smile sliding into place like a mask she'd worn a thousand times. "How could I not be?"

It landed wrong in my chest, heavy as wet sand.

I told myself to move on, but I couldn't.

"How did you two..." I waved my hands in the air, unable to even say the words.

Ariana exhaled, slow and steady, like she was bracing herself before diving into cold water.

"We met at a nonprofit fundraiser," she said finally. "One of the youth outreach programs I was running. He came as a representative for the financial organization he worked for at the time. He gave a speech, shook hands, made everyone laugh. You know how he is."

Her voice tilted fondly, but there was something else underneath that seemingly affectionate sentence.

"I remember thinking he was... steady," she continued. "Everything in my life back then felt like it was one loose thread away from unraveling. Georgie was in middle school, he was struggling with some stuff from the trial, and I had him in therapy, but it was still a rough patch, and I was working two jobs and going to school full time. I barely slept."

She laughed quietly to herself.

"And then Nathan walked in," she said. "He was so... confident. So sure. He listened to me in a way no one had for years." Her eyes darted to me quickly before they were on her shoes again. "He told me I was extraordinary, that I'd done what most people couldn't do."

I could hear it in her voice, how much she'd needed that then.

And it killed me.

Because he gave her what I couldn't.

I took away her safety and her comfort, her trust.

He brought it all back in.

My ribs tightened like a fist around my lungs.

"He asked me to dinner that night," she said, smiling a little at the memory. "And we ended up in this awful little diner at midnight, eating greasy eggs and talking about books and kids and life. It was easy. Easier than anything had been in a long time. He... took care of me." She swallowed, shrugging. "And I let him."

The wind pushed her hair across her cheek, and she tucked it back again with trembling fingers.

"For the first time in years, I didn't feel like I was drowning," she said. "He came over, had my apartment cleaned, cooked dinner, helped Georgie with his science fair project. He was older, settled, established. Georgie relaxed around him, finally acting like the kid he was. I relaxed, too. He made everything feel... safe."

Safe.

That word split me open. Because that was what I'd stolen from her. The very thing she'd craved since childhood, the thing I'd sworn to give her and then robbed her of by leaving.

"You deserve all of that," I said quietly.

She looked up at me with her brows pulled tight, like she wasn't expecting kindness from me right then. Her eyes softened for a breath, then shuttered.

"He was good to me," she said. "Really good. For a long time." A pause. "Long enough for me to believe it was everything I'd ever wanted."

And there it was, the reason my stomach never quite settled around Nathan, the reason I couldn't stop picking at why Ariana was with him.

It was small, almost enough not to notice, but I caught it — a hint of truth slipping between the seams.

A hint she didn't mean to share.

"And he still is?" I asked carefully. "Good to you?"

Ariana blinked at me. I swore I saw fear in her eyes before she smoothed it away with a practiced ease that made my stomach drop.

"Yes," she said brightly. "Of course. He still is."

But she didn't look at me when she said it.

Lightning flashed in the distance, silent at first before a distant roll of thunder found us. Tourists and locals alike reacted with hurried movement, gathering their belongings, everyone ready to head inside a restaurant or shop or back to their cars.

But I was frozen, my breath stalled in my chest.

She'd married the idea of safety.

But maybe she didn't feel safe at all.

"I followed the trial."

My words had Ariana frozen now, her gaze stuck somewhere around my chest like she couldn't look me in the eye.

"I was so proud of you," I said, throat tight with the honesty. "The day of Jay's conviction, I tried texting you."

I could see it in real time, how Ariana was shutting down more and more with each word I said, but I couldn't stop.

"It bounced. The text never went through. I tried calling, and it said the number was no longer in service."

Another crack of lightning, and this time, close enough that the thunder rolled immediately. The wind picked up, blowing Ariana's hair wildly.

I swallowed hard. "Ari... I hate how everything went down. I know you say it's in the past, but I—" I paused, searching for breath that suddenly felt scarce. "I think about it. All the time. That day. Don't you?"

A cloud passed over her expression just like the ones darkening the sky. She finally lifted her eyes to mine, and they might as well have been a knife to my kidney. "The day you left? There. I finished the thought for you. And no, I don't think about it. I haven't thought about it in years."

*Lie.*

It was there in the way she tore her gaze from mine, in how she crossed her arms hard over her chest.

"I didn't have a choice," I tried.

"You always have a choice," she shot back.

"I was trying to do what was best for you."

"Yeah, well, thanks for letting me have a say in what that was."

Thunder rumbled, and the sky opened.

"Great," Ariana muttered, and then she was off.

"Ariana," I started, but she was already walking again, steps furious and quick.

Rain fell in brutal, heavy sheets, so sudden it was like someone tipped the entire goddamn bay on top of us. Ariana broke into a run, sprinting for the nearest bridge, the paper bag in her hand quickly becoming soggy. I chased her, soaked instantly, water plastering my shirt to my chest.

We ducked under the arch just as the downpour intensified, and there we were — alone, breathless, dripping.

The river churned beside us. Lightning flashed again, closer this time.

She had one hand braced on her hips, chest heaving. I was a safe arm's length away, though every nerve in my body begged me to close it.

"Ariana..." I tried again, softer now. "Talk to me. What's going on?"

She didn't look up, but her voice broke. She shook her head. "This day was so good. It was nice. And then you—" She stopped, breath sharp. "You ruined it."

"I ruined it by asking if you're happy?"

She scoffed, glaring at me before she whipped out her phone and started thumbing away at something.

"I'm serious, what did I do but ask how your marriage is? I didn't realize that was an off-limits topic."

"You didn't ask because you actually care," she said, closing her phone screen. "You say you want my happiness, but admit it — you were hoping I would say I wasn't happy. You were hoping for my misery."

"Fine!" I snapped.

I dropped the paper bag with my candles in it, not caring if they broke. I needed my hands for more important things.

I invaded her space with my breath hammering in my chest, tilting her jaw with my knuckles as she gasped. "You're right, okay? I want you happy, Ariana, I do, but not with him. And I can see right through the lies you tell me. There's something wrong between you two. There's something you're not saying."

Her eyes darted between mine, wide and almost... hopeful. Like she was relieved someone saw it.

But in the next instant, her face was blank.

"You don't know me anymore," she said, swatting my hand away and taking a step back. "You think you do, but you don't."

"I know you better than anyone."

"No." She backed up another step. "You *knew* who I was. Past tense. You don't know who I am now. You don't know my life. My marriage. You don't know anything!"

"Ari, please." The word cracked out of me. "Don't shut me out again."

She barked a laugh, but it broke in the middle. "Again? Shane, you—"

Her phone buzzed in her hand. She looked down.

*Uber arriving: 1 minute.*

My chest caved.

"I can take you home," I said quickly, stepping forward. "You don't need—"

"It's fine. I called a car," she cut in.

"It's pouring," I argued desperately. "Let me—"

"Let you what? Take me on another cute little trolley ride back to Ybor where your Jeep is parked? Don't you think we've played pretend enough today?"

The rain drummed harder, echoing off the concrete. Her phone buzzed again, and she looked down at the screen showing her approaching ride.

"Ari," I tried again, reaching out. "I don't want today to end like this. Please—"

She jerked back like my touch burned. "This day shouldn't have begun at all. The whole thing was a mistake."

That gutted me.

Before I could react, before I could grab the thread slipping between us, she turned and jogged out from under the bridge, straight into the downpour. Her silhouette blurred into the sheets of rain as a car pulled up beside the walkway.

The driver hopped out with an umbrella popping up, holding her door open so she could dive inside.

She didn't look back.

I stood there beneath the bridge, rainwater dripping from my hair, my chest heaving as I dragged a hand back through it, water slicking down my neck. My jaw locked. My fists curled at my sides, knuckles aching with the effort not to chase after her.

The rain hammered the pavement, loud enough to drown out the city — but not the truth crashing through me.

She wasn't fine.

She hadn't been for a long time.

And whatever cracks she tried to hide behind that bright smile... I saw them.

I saw her.

I didn't know what she was walking back into, or what waited for her behind the door of that house, but I knew the look in her eyes. I'd seen it once before on a girl who had learned too young that safety could be taken from you in an instant.

I'd failed her back then.

I wouldn't fail her again.

That girl was still everything to me.

And I'd be damned if I'd be the man who walked away from her twice.

## CHAPTER 19

### MORE THAN YOU'LL EVER KNOW

Ariana
2007

"Merry Christmas Eve," I sang, practically skipping into the living room of the apartment I shared with Shane. He'd made a perfect cup of coffee for me and left it on the bedside table, its scent luring me awake.

I nearly spilled that sweet cup of joe when I took in the scene of the living room.

"Christmas Eve?" Shane repeated, frowning. "Never heard of it. HAPPY BIRTHDAY!"

He spread out his arms, showcasing how he'd transformed our living space overnight. The Christmas tree was still there, yes, and a string of white lights still framed our window. There was still a poinsettia on our coffee table and a few gifts under the tree.

But an explosion of birthday decorations muted it all.

There was a giant hand-painted banner strung from one end of the room to the other, a bright yellow with neon pink letters — my two favorite colors. Balloons littered the floor and floated in bunches of five or six around the room.

Framing the poinsettia were bouquets — plural — of my favorite flowers.

White and yellow daisies and pink carnations.

On the floor, there were two pink pillow cushions serving as chairs, and Shane had turned a box into a table, covering it with a cloth and a breakfast spread right out of a magazine: French toast, bacon, fresh berries, and perfectly scrambled eggs.

In the center of that table was a small box wrapped in yellow paper with a pink bow.

"Shane..." I covered my mouth, eyes wide and fingers trembling as I looked around and tried to take it all in. "What is all this?"

My boyfriend — *boyfriend*, God that word still made me giddy — looked as cozy as ever in his gray sweatpants and *The Fray* hoodie. We'd seen them together over the summer and he'd bought us both the same one in the hopes that I wouldn't steal his.

Futile hope, that was.

His hair was a mess from sleep, but his grin was that of a boy who'd pulled off the perfect surprise. He crossed the room and took my coffee cup from my hand, setting it on the table next to my breakfast before he swooped me into his arms.

"This is your birthday celebration," he answered easily, hands smoothing my hair from my face so he could plant a proper kiss on my nose. "One you've always deserved."

I shook my head, blinking over and over and trying to make sense of it all.

"You told me last year when we left for Christmas break that no one ever really cared about your birthday," he reminded me. "I wasn't your boyfriend then, but I was still pissed. It killed me to think that a day that should be all about you was instead focused on a holiday. A *pre*-holiday! It's not even the real one!"

I laughed. "I mean, technically, it's the night Jesus was born."

"*Technically* no one actually knows what night Jesus was born, and it was probably April. *Anyway*," he said, waving his hand like we'd gotten off topic. "The point is that we were apart last year. You were with your family, and I was with mine. But this year, and every year after this, we'll be together. And I promise that I will always make your birthday special. I will always celebrate you." He swallowed, his eyes searching mine. "I love you, Ari."

Tears flooded my eyes. "I love you, too."

"Now," he said, waving his hand over his elaborate setup. "Please, m'lady, have a seat and let your boyfriend serve you. After breakfast, we're going to build a snowman — complete with a party hat — and then I'm taking you to see the new *National Treasure*."

"The sequel that's in theaters?!"

"The very one. You can drool over Nicholas Cage all day and live out your puzzle-solving fantasies."

"Can we make snow angels, too?"

"Would it be a proper birthday without snow angels?"

"And can I get Butterfinger Bites at the movie theater?"

"You can, as long as you save some sweet tooth for the cake I stayed up all night baking for you."

"You baked me a cake?!"

"Funfetti. Your favorite."

I threw my arms around his neck, kissing him deeply. "You really do love me."

Shane framed my face with his big hands, thumbs smoothing my jaw, his eyes on mine.

"More than you'll ever know."

## CHAPTER 20

### CIRCLE OF TRUST

Ariana
Present

"You made it!"

Grace wrapped me in a fierce hug before welcoming me inside, taking the batch of cookies I'd made from my hands as soon as I was in the door.

"And you brought cookies?!" Grace beamed before turning to yell down the hall. "Ariana brought cookies!"

There was a cheer of joy from where I assumed the rest of the girls were gathered, and I smiled, my cheeks flushing with heat.

I was so nervous I wanted to puke.

I hadn't had girlfriends in so long, I couldn't remember what it was like to have a girls' night. The last time I'd had anything even remotely similar was when I was thirty.

Almost a decade ago now.

But after I moved in with Nathan, I found myself going out with my friends less and less. I was obsessed with Nathan, for one, and fully in love with falling in love. I wanted him to take up all my time. I craved it.

When the honeymoon phase settled, I realized it had been a long time since I'd seen a lot of my friends outside of work or a group gathering. And when I did get brave enough to make plans with them, Nathan would lament my leaving, making a big show of wrapping me up and begging me not to go in a playful, teasing manner. It always ended with us making love before I'd go, and then I was ready to hurry back home to him.

Eventually... I just stopped leaving.

And then when I did want to, it was no longer a playful show of him not wanting me to leave — it was a threatening one. It was him suspicious of me going to a bar without him, asking me how I would feel if he did the same? He twisted innocent nights into me not wanting to spend time with him. He used the fact that he was busy against me, like I should want to spend any time he had at home together. How could I want any more alone time when he was already gone so much?

So, yeah... friends had rightfully given up on me. Who wanted to keep inviting the person who never came, who never invited you anywhere?

My topsy-turvy stomach situation wasn't helped any by the fact that I'd been a wreck the last week since I'd spent a day with Shane.

I'd felt so guilty that night when I went home, taking a long hot shower as if I could scrub the impure thoughts from my head. I'd tucked the wooden page holder away between books I knew Nathan would never touch, and I lit the candle I'd bought, burning it down to the wick before throwing it in the trash and taking the trash out to the garbage can outside just in case.

When Nathan came home the next day, I swore he'd see right through it, like I was standing there at a crime scene red-handed.

But he didn't notice a thing.

In fact, he'd been more preoccupied than ever since he returned from his trip. He hadn't even batted an eye when I'd reminded him of craft night tonight. He'd kissed my forehead before he left for work and told me he'd be out late anyway and to have fun.

I knew he was busy with his new team and staff, but it was rare for him to leave me alone so much.

Not that I was complaining.

It was a nice break. I didn't mind at all that I could spend my days working on Sweet Dreams and my evenings working on the house. I loved when Nathan texted me that he wouldn't be home for dinner, and I could order in or make a bowl of pasta and rot on the couch watching Bravo. I especially loved the nights he was so late that I was fast asleep by the time he made it home.

My gut churned again at that.

What kind of wife would wish to never see her husband?

I tried not to let myself dwell on it too much as I followed Grace inside. I didn't need to think about Nathan tonight. I didn't need to think about Shane, either — whom I'd insisted leave me to deal Sweet Dreams on my own unless I specifically needed help with players. The *last* thing I needed was time alone with him in close proximity.

One day had proven how dangerous that could be.

It was strange, how quickly my emotions had warped after that day. I'd left angry and sad, storming home with smoke fuming from my nose. But even that night, my anger had subsided, leaving only sadness in its wake. And by the next day, I found I just...

I just missed him.

I missed the Shane I spent nearly two years of my life with at a time when I felt like possibility was endless.

I thought the worst of my life was behind me and I had nothing but brighter days ahead. I'd lost myself in that boy and the promises he made so easily, because I trusted him. I never had a reason not to.

Until the day he showed me how fair-weather love can be.

I shook my head, determined to let it go. No thoughts of Nathan or Shane allowed.

No, tonight was about making friends. It was about building community in my new home. It was about me.

That was probably why I felt so uncomfortable.

It had been so long since I'd done anything for myself that I felt guilty for even considering it.

"Welcome to Craft Night Chaos!" Grace said when we made it to Maven's living room.

I was stunned enough to stop walking, my lips parting as I took in the gorgeous space. The sliding glass doors along the back of the room led out to a private beach on the Gulf, which was currently showcasing a stunning sunset. Pinks and purples darted across the sky, the sound of the waves crashing just barely audible over the soft music playing on the speaker.

Sitting at the dining table near the kitchen was Maven, along with two women I didn't recognize.

And one who had me even more shell-shocked than the beach view.

"Is that..."

I pointed at the pop star, who looked deceivingly normal at the moment with a messy bun of hair piled on her head and an oversized t-shirt. Her tan legs were folded beneath her, and she was painting ghosts onto what appeared to be an old, vintage painting of a farmhouse, her tongue out as she focused. She sat back with an appreciative smile at her work before her eyes met mine.

"Oh, yeah, I forget that she's kinda famous," Grace said, waving her hand at her friend like she was just an everyday person. "But yes, that is the one and only Mia Love."

"You say that so casually like you didn't fangirl so hard you nearly passed out the first time you met her," one of the women at the table quipped with an arched brow. She was working on a delicate necklace, it looked like, her earthy-brown hands meticulously threading beads onto a chain. She had gorgeous black hair that framed her face in a flowy blowout, her makeup flawlessly applied like she was set to hit the runway rather than hang out at a friend's house. "Hi, I'm Livia," she said to me, her smile warm.

"And I'm Chloe," the last of the unknown said, and the curvy little redhead popped right out of her seat and skipped over to me, crushing me in a hug. She had metallic pink eye masks under her eyes and brought a set for me, too. "I have heard so much about you. Welcome to girls' night."

"Thank you," I managed, smiling despite the way my neck felt like it could fry an egg.

"So, you already know Maven and my connections to the team," Grace said, placing my cookies at the center of the craft table before she invited me to sit. She immediately plucked one off the platter and took a huge bite, moaning with approval before she continued around a mouthful. "Livia here is Maven's bestie and is now engaged to Carter Fabri."

"She had his baby first, though. Scandalous," Maven teased.

Livia threw a bead at her.

"And then Chloe here somehow softened our very own Daddy P into the mush ball he is today."

"Is that how you'd describe him?" I asked, folding my hands tightly in my lap. I hadn't thought to bring anything with me to craft night.

Idiot.

"Because I'm pretty sure I've seen him smile a total of two times."

"He was even more of a grump before Chloe here, if you can imagine that," Grace said.

Chloe beamed, pressing her fingertips into the eye masks above her cheeks. "It's true. You should have seen the man at Disney World. You would have thought we'd dragged him to prison rather than the most magical place on Earth."

"And this one," Grace said, nudging *Mia Fucking Love* — I still wasn't over that. "She actually grew up with Aleks Suter. And they started dating out of nowhere and had, like, the fastest engagement of all time."

I remembered, though I wouldn't dare say a word about it here. I'd followed their whole relationship, fawning over the photos the paparazzi leaked. I especially lost my mind over the one of them kissing on the beach.

"It was so romantic," Chloe swooned. "I'll never forget that speech he gave on the yacht when he proposed."

"So... I actually have a confession," Mia said, looking around the table with her lip between her teeth. She dropped her gaze back to her painting when she said, "What if I told you we were actually kind of faking it..."

Grace laughed. "Oh sure, so fake." She rolled her eyes, but then her smile fell when Mia didn't give in. "Wait. You mean to tell me it was all a publicity stunt?"

"I mean... kinda?" Mia winced. "Until it wasn't. Obviously."

"I knew it!" Livia snapped her fingers, pointing across the table at her literal popstar friend. "I overheard your publicist talking to Suter's agent at your album release party in California, something about getting *the money shot*."

"But you two are so in love!" Chloe whined.

"We are. And we were then, too. We were just also both really stupid and thought it was fun to torture ourselves thinking the other was just pretending to like us for a few months." Mia shrugged. "Sounds crazy, but it was actually kind of fun."

"You're all crazy," Maven said, looking around the table. "And that's exactly why I love you so much."

I smiled, looking down at the empty table in front of me. I decided to put on the eye mask Chloe had given me just so I had something to do with my hands.

When I looked up again, all eyes were on me.

Shit.

"Here," Grace said, sliding a coloring page of Idris Alba over to me along with a box of colored pencils. "I don't craft, either, but I like to color attractive men sometimes. I have a Keanu Reeves coloring book if he's more your style?"

She tore a page out of that one and handed it to me as I laughed. "Thanks. I... I didn't even think about bringing anything."

"Do you do any kind of crafting?" Livia asked, working on her necklace again. "I'm a lover of fine jewelry, but Maven roped us into working on her wedding, and I absolutely hated that shit."

"She did. She protested until I hired a planner," Maven confirmed.

"And you thanked me for it, didn't you?" Livia tilted her wine glass to her lips, and then her eyes went wide. "Oh! We're so rude. Someone pour Ariana a drink."

Grace hopped up. "On it!" And then everyone was waiting for my answer.

"I'm not really a crafter," I said. "But I love to read."

"Ick, Jaxson loves to read. I don't know how you guys do it," Grace said, bringing me a glass of white wine. "Bores me to tears."

"Yes, well, you don't know how to sit still without some form of vivid entertainment for longer than two seconds," Mia pointed out. "Hence why we've only recently managed to get you to stay in Tampa for more than a month at a time."

"I'm still debating the trip to Italy next month," Grace said.

"I'll allow it only if you set a wedding date." Maven arched a brow at her friend before turning her gaze to me. "What do you like to read?"

"Oh, lots of things. Anything, really," I said, and the first easy smile bloomed on my lips.

I could talk about books all night.

"I'm a huge lover of classics. I have pretty much every book you can think of that your English teachers made you study. Hemingway, Brontë, Austen. I'm a pretty big nerd for fantasy. Tolkien changed my life when I was a kid."

"You read *The Lord of the Rings* as a *kid*?!" Chloe asked in disbelief.

"Middle school," I answered with a shrug. "It was a great escape from real life."

The room quieted, the girls sharing looks like they wanted to know more about *that* little comment, but I brushed hurriedly past it.

"Memoirs are a guilty pleasure of mine, too. And historical fiction. Oh, and cozy mystery! I *love* a cozy mystery."

"What about romance?" Maven asked with a waggle of her brows. "You read any spicy books?"

I flushed so hard the table erupted with laughs.

"That's our answer, I think," Livia teased. "Don't be shy, my love. Trust me — nothing you've read is kinkier than what I've lived in real life."

"No lies told there," Grace said, tilting her beer toward Livia.

"Romance books are my favorite to read," I said, a faint smile finding my lips. "They get such a bad rep, I think. Literary snobs turn up their noses at the entire genre. But it's the bestselling one there is — and it makes perfect sense. We're all looking for love, aren't we? Whether we desire it from a partner or a parent or a sibling or a friend. We all crave acceptance for who we are. We fantasize about not just being seen, but being chosen. We wonder what it would be like for someone to look at us, with all our quirks and flaws, and think, '*Yeah. That. I like that. I want that in my life.*'" I shrugged. "And with romance books, you get to experience that feeling of falling time and time again — the butterflies, the stomach flips, the longing, the heartbreak and pain — only to know you'll be put together in the end. It's quite lovely, actually. No happy endings are guaranteed in real life, but with romance books, you know it'll all turn out okay. And it fills you with hope, doesn't it? That maybe things will be okay for you in the end, too."

I'd picked up a colored pencil somewhere in my ramble, and I smiled as I colored in Idris Alba's shirt. When no one said anything, I paused, looking up with my neck heating again.

"Okay, Miss Poetry," Livia said with a curl of her lips. "Is this how you reveal that you write, too?"

"Oh God, me? Never," I said on a laugh.

"Well, after that little spiel, you may want to consider it," Chloe said. "As a teacher, I feel like I'm certified to speak on these things and you, my dear, have a gift."

"She probably speaks so eloquently of love because she's getting dicked down by the hot general manager," Grace said, doing a little dance in her chair. "Big Boss Daddy Energy right there, ow owww."

Everyone laughed.

I nearly puked.

Somehow, I managed a smile despite the urge to vomit. "He's quite the man," I answered carefully.

"Okay, but I have a question." Maven shared a glance with Grace before she opened her mouth, shut it again, and then tapped the table with one long nail before asking, "How do you and Coach know each other *really*?"

The table went silent, all eyes on me.

Double shit.

"We went to college together," I said.

"Well, we know that." Maven waved me off. "But were you just classmates or friends or…?"

Again, everyone leaned in, and I felt my skin prickle at the back of my neck.

I wanted to trust them. I wanted to share with someone and talk about it, to have a safe space.

But were they safe?

What if they told Nathan?

If he found out Shane and I used to date and I didn't tell him…

I shuddered, hands wrung together in my lap again as I stared at them.

"I…" I wet my lips before looking up at them. "If I tell you all, will you promise not to say a word to anyone? Not even your husbands or boyfriends or—"

"You can stop right there," Livia said, holding up a finger. "What happens at girls' night stays at girls' night. We are a fortress, this crew. Trust me."

"I mean, Maven was married to my brother when I asked her to keep my secret that I was shagging his best friend. And she did," Grace pointed out. "Without question."

"Circle of trust," Mia promised.

And maybe it was stupid, maybe it was a little careless... but I believed them.

I wanted so badly to have someone to talk to about it all that I was willing to take the risk.

"Shane and I were a couple," I said, and just admitting it out loud lifted a weight off my chest. "We... we were in love once."

Again, I was greeted by silence, and when I looked up, the girls were all slack jawed.

Then, all at once, the table broke into chaos.

"Oh, my God!"

"Did she just call him *Shane?!*"

"Okay, we need all the details right now."

"I knew he looked at you like a sad puppy dog who'd lost his human!"

"How long?! When?!"

And against all logic, I answered every question.

The girls listened. They swooned as I walked them through how we started dating. They cursed and hit the table when I explained how we'd broken up — though I did leave out the finer details on that one. And by the time I finished my story, I felt something I hadn't in years, though I couldn't quite place it.

"Thank you for sharing that with us," Maven said when I'd finished. "It's nice to know the background."

"Do you think he still loves you?" Grace yelped when Livia flicked her arm. "What?!"

"She's married, you dummy."

"And?!"

I chuckled, focusing on where I was coloring. "No. Shane and I had... well, it was just young love." The lie felt sour in my gut. "It's in the past."

"So you're friends now?" Mia asked.

I sighed. "I wouldn't say that, either."

The girls quieted, but thankfully, Chloe must have realized how we were crossing into a territory I was uncomfortable with because she smiled and cleared her throat. "I want to hear more about Georgie."

"Oh, yes! Tell us about your baby brother!" Grace said.

"I can't believe you raised him," Livia marveled, shaking her head. "I haven't even survived one year of motherhood, but it's the hardest job I've ever had. And I had a stint of doing root canals when I was in school."

The girls chuckled, and I smiled, the conversation easy from there. It was effortless to talk about my little brother, about how he felt like my son more than anything. I loved telling them about how smart he was, how caring, how funny. I promised them they'd get to meet him when he came to visit for Christmas, and then blessedly, the conversation moved away from me.

But I didn't miss the way the girls watched me at different moments that night, the way their gazes lingered, thoughtful, like they could sense the things I didn't say and the parts of myself I kept carefully tucked away.

I knew they were curious about my past, maybe even my present, but they didn't push. They gave me space. They let me choose what to share and what not to.

And suddenly, with a clarity that made my chest tighten, I understood why Nathan had never liked me having friends.

It wasn't just that people might see *him* more clearly, that they might notice the cracks in the polished version of him that he worked so hard to present.

It was that friends meant witnesses.

It meant voices outside his own.

It meant I might have someone to talk to besides him.

Without them, he was the only place my thoughts could go. He was the only version of reality I'd hear. There was nothing to challenge him, nothing to compete for my attention.

Anything that pulled me away from him had always felt like a threat.

And that was the part I hadn't fully seen before.

If I had friends who were too close, someone else might notice that he wasn't the Prince Charming everyone thought he was.

And worse—

I might notice it, too.

# CHAPTER 21

## BLOOD ON MY HANDS

Shane
Present

A week into November, the season had my full attention. Almost, anyway.

It was hard to let go of Ariana, and I realized I likely didn't have the strength to actually do it entirely. But I did have the respect for her to leave her alone when she asked me to — and she had. Point blank.

She wanted me to stay away from Sweet Dreams unless she specifically asked for something. She warned me not to bring up the Sunday we'd spent together, even when all I'd tried to do was apologize. Basically, she'd stayed away from me, muttering excuses to leave the room whenever I entered it.

It ground on me like pumice stone.

I wanted to apologize. I wanted to have the chance to explain. But then I'd ask myself... explain what? Was I actually sorry for asking about her happiness?

No.

But I *was* sorry for upsetting her.

I was sorry for how I'd left her.

I was sorry I'd stayed away.

I was a sorry piece of shit, basically, but she didn't want to hear it. And I couldn't blame her.

So, like I always did, I threw myself into hockey.

It was easy to do. The season was fully underway, my schedule packed with travel and practices and games. Currently, I was at the arena well after hours, which wasn't anything new. When everyone else had gone home — players, trainers, PR, even the janitorial staff — I stayed, eyes glued to the monitor in my office as I reviewed video from our last game.

Tonight, it was Ben Sandin who had my attention.

Daddy P's hip had been acting up again — just enough to pull him from the last couple of games, which didn't sit right with me. I knew the hip was tender, but not tender enough for this. He was doing the PT, staying on his regimen, taking what the docs gave him... and still gritting through pain he couldn't explain.

And so, Sandin had become less of a backup and more of a routine player for us.

I watched him guard the net on the screen, replaying the moment he missed a block I'd seen him stop a thousand times — in practices, in scrimmages, in the AHL, even here in The Show. It was muscle memory for him. A layup. A routine save.

But he didn't make it.

I slowed the playback, rewinding and pausing as the puck flew in. I watched his eyes track it, watched him drop into the crease and slide his leg out perfectly.

And still... he missed. He didn't slide wide enough, the puck slipping past the blade of his skate and right into the net.

The Detroit team swarmed in celebration. Sandin hung his head, grabbed his water bottle off the net, and took a long drink before resetting.

I searched for any sign of something — pain, hesitation in his push-off, a misread.

I found nothing.

I sighed, leaning back as the video kept rolling, though I wasn't watching anymore. I didn't know what the hell I expected to find.

He'd missed a block.

So what?

Daddy P had plenty of goals scored on him and I never poured over tape like this. Sometimes a puck goes in, even one that should've been stopped.

But I couldn't shake the suspicion clawing at me. And it wasn't just Sandin.

There was the rookie Nathan rostered when he put Wood on waivers — Ivan Baranov. Annoyingly, the kid was playing like a damn all-star. And that shouldn't have annoyed me; I was his coach. But it did. Because Nathan had handpicked him, and now that he was performing, Nathan looked like some all-seeing genius with prophetic hockey intuition. Everyone trusted him implicitly.

Baranov was quickly becoming someone we could rely on to score. Twice now he'd earned star of the game.

But he'd also fucked up when it mattered most.

When I finally pulled Carter Fabri after he'd been stuck on the ice for nearly four exhausting minutes against Toronto, thanks to penalty kill chaos that wouldn't let him change, I sent Baranov over the boards. Within twenty seconds, he lost the puck in our own zone, coughing it up right inside the blue line.

Toronto jumped on it instantly. And Sandin failed again.

We'd gone from up by three to tied with a team we should have walked all over, and then lost in a shootout after a scoreless overtime.

Was it a shit-luck game? Yeah. Did it happen? Of course.

But my *something-is-off* radar wouldn't shut up.

I didn't voice it. I reminded myself of everything I'd learned from my years in college and my decades of coaching — how life bleeds into performance, how even the most reliable guys have off nights. I checked in with my players, centered them, and did my job.

But inside, I was stewing. And I felt insane because everyone else seemed to be under Nathan Black's spell.

Staff loved him. They thought he was a genius for shaking things up, giving us an edge Richard Bancroft had lost years ago. He was "fresh" and "fun" in their eyes, and they ate up everything he served.

Players respected him — even the ones I hoped would see through his shit. But Nathan had brought in sponsorships and more money, which meant better equipment, upgraded recovery systems, and new therapy amenities. Hard to hate a guy who gives you cutting-edge hydrotherapy and a cryo chamber.

And the fans practically worshipped him. He'd launched the "fan of the game" program, sending PR out before puck drop to pick a lucky fan from the crowd outside — a crowd that grew bigger every game as people dressed up and camped out for their shot at rink-side seats and a spotlight during second intermission.

Then he opened one practice a week to the fans. Richard had always said it was too distracting — and he'd been right. But Nathan announced it at a press conference without telling a single damn person on staff. We just had to smile and pretend it was the plan.

Now I had weekly meet-and-greets when all I wanted was to prepare for whomever we played next.

It was good. All of it was good. The city was invested. We were in the news. We were being talked about. We had a winning record.

Which was why I wouldn't voice my concerns out loud, and why I felt like I'd slipped into insanity. Because somehow, I was the only one who saw he was a snake dressed as a saint.

I pinched the bridge of my nose, letting out a long, calming breath as I squeezed my eyes shut against the headache building.

I had no *actual* reason to feel like Nathan was a problem other than the fact that he was with Ariana and I didn't like it.

Basically, I was acting like a jealous fucking teenager, and yet no amount of common sense could snap me out of it.

A loud thump and subsequent rattling snapped my head up, and I whipped around with my heart hammering and my hand curled into a fist ready to fight.

Only to find Ariana standing with a giant box in her arms.

"Oh, sorry," she said, a bit breathless as she tried to balance the box. She teetered again, this time the rattling amplified as her eyes shot wide and she saved the box before it tumbled to the ground. "I... I didn't think anyone would be here."

I hopped up, rushing to the door to take the box from her hands. It was surprisingly heavy, and I laughed a little as I grunted and carried it to the desk I'd just been sitting at. "No one should be at this hour. What the hell is in this box? Bricks?"

"The trophies for the Skate for Change event," she said, her cheeks pink, hands hanging on her hips now as she caught her breath. "I accidentally had them shipped to our house instead of the arena. Classic ditzy move. They showed up earlier tonight and Nathan didn't want them cluttering our…"

Ariana's words faded, and she cleared her throat, smiling like she thought better of finishing her thought. My attention was stuck on the fact that she'd called herself a ditz.

She was so far from that, it was laughable. Why would she insult herself that way?

"Anyway, we needed them here, so I just thought I'd bring them up myself," she said.

"At nearly midnight?"

She shrugged, and her eyes finally met mine. "Couldn't sleep, so I figured now was as good a time as any."

Time slogged when she looked at me like that, her diamond eyes piercing straight through my battered soul. She hadn't looked at me in weeks, and I savored that gaze like it was a hard-earned championship title.

*Why couldn't you sleep?*

I wanted to ask so badly, but I had a feeling by the way she watched me that her words weren't an invitation to pry.

I let myself indulge in my greed instead, soaking in everything about her — the matching lounge set she wore, mustard yellow, the color bringing out the gold in her hair and setting off the blue in her eyes. I wondered if yellow was still her favorite color. The fabric hugged her curves and fell around her silhouette, the image one that had me flashing back to her in her dorm in college. She wasn't wearing makeup, and her hair was unkempt, like she'd literally rolled out of bed and thought, *"Well, nothing better to do, so I guess I'll just run this heavy ass box of trophies up to the arena."*

She looked so damn cozy I had to stuff my hands into my pockets to keep from reaching for her just to see if she felt as soft as she looked.

Ariana's cheeks burned a deeper shade of red the longer I looked at her, and I was ready for her to frown and snap at me and storm out of the room.

Instead, she folded her arms over her chest and cleared her throat. "What are *you* doing here so late?"

I shrugged, nodding to the screen that was still playing the Detroit game. "I'm always here late. Watching video."

"You don't do that in your office?"

"Sometimes I do," I said. "Sometimes I need a change in scenery. Or a bigger screen," I added with a grin.

"It doesn't hurt your eyes to stare at this thing?" She pointed to the monstrous screen behind me.

"Oh, everything hurts my eyes at this point in the day, but I'm a masochist, I guess. I just... I don't know. Sometimes it's hard to leave when I feel like I'm missing something, or like the team needs something from me that I haven't delivered yet."

"And what is it you're missing tonight?"

*You.*

The thought shouldn't have surprised me, but it did. I opened my mouth, shut it again, and laughed, blowing out a breath before I ran a hand through my hair. "Your guess is as good as mine."

Ariana smiled, looking down at her feet. "Well, I should leave you to it."

"You don't have to go." The words shot out of me so fast I should have been embarrassed. "I mean, you're probably tired. You probably want to go home. But if—"

"I am tired," she said on a sigh. "But I'm having a hard time sleeping."

"Why?"

I couldn't help but ask this time, and she leveled me with a gaze like I should know.

*Should I?*

Stupid hope ballooned in my chest.

I wondered if she was losing sleep because of how we left things between us.

How fucking idiotic I was to hope to be the subject of her insomnia.

"I just have a lot on my mind, I guess," she said with a sigh. "Do you mind if I just unpack these and check them over?" She pointed to the box of trophies. "I'd like to make sure none of them are damaged, and then I'll get out of your hair."

"Stay as long as you'd like," I said, waving my hand toward the box.

Ariana silently went to work, and I sat behind the desk again, eyes on the screen as I pretended I was focusing on the game and not on her. It was torture to stay quiet when I finally had her alone again, when I had the chance to rectify what had happened between us.

After about ten minutes, I couldn't resist.

"Ari, I'm sorry about that day on the riverwalk."

Her hands paused where she was unpacking the box, eyes focused on the trophy in her hands.

"I know you said not to bring it up and I promise, after tonight, I won't. But I upset you and it's eating me alive. I shouldn't have pushed about Nathan," I said, turning the chair toward her. "I shouldn't have pried into your life. It's none of my business. I just... I miss you."

*Fuck.*

The words pushed through my lips like inmates who saw an escape and refused to miss their chance.

Ariana closed her eyes, holding them shut as she let out a long breath, and maybe I should have backpedaled but I didn't.

I meant what I said.

"I've missed you for decades," I admitted softly. "And I never thought I'd see you again, not after that night I stumbled upon you in Boston. I guess I just... I look at who you are now, at the life you're living, and I want all the missing pieces of the puzzle that I don't have. I don't deserve it, but I want the whole story of your life. And I... I was rude. I was assumptive and I'm sorry."

Her eyes fluttered open, gaze still on the trophy in her hands, and she nodded. "It's okay. I'm sorry, too. For running out like that."

"You had every right to."

She nodded again, and then silence fell over us, save for the soft sounds from the game.

"It still hurts," she admitted after a while, and her eyes flitted to mine before going back to the box. "That's why I left. Thinking about that time in my life is just... hard."

My throat was lined in sandpaper with my next attempt at a swallow.

"You said you followed the case," she said. "That you tried reaching out... but I don't understand. Why?"

"Because it was over," I said in a rush, standing. She still wouldn't look at me, but I had to be closer to her when I said it. "The case, the trial, all of it. You were safe. Georgie was yours. Jay wasn't able to hurt you, and I... I didn't feel like a threat to any of that anymore. I didn't feel like a threat to your safety."

"You never were."

I bit down the words I wanted to snap back because we both knew we disagreed on this point.

Her legal team, my coach, me... we all saw what Ariana refused to back then. I *was* a threat to her security in that case against her stepfather. If we'd have stayed together, she would have been flying nonstop, pulling Georgie out of school or leaving him in childcare too often. The court was looking for stability, and I would have ruined that for her. I was the most publicized rookie in the NHL at the time. I had cameras following me everywhere — and that meant she would have, too.

"When the texts I sent bounced, I tried calling you. Then, I sent a letter to your house, asking if I could see you," I said, deciding to tell her how I'd tried to find her again instead of defending my choice to leave. "The letter was returned. I even tried reaching out to the school, Ari. I was ready to get on the next flight, but I couldn't find you." I swallowed, inching closer to her. "It was like you disappeared."

"I did," she said, her voice surprisingly calm. She checked another trophy before setting it beside the box. "That was what my legal team advised. Jay's family was harassing us all through the trial, and we knew they wouldn't stop once the verdict was reached. If anything, it would be worse." She paused, shuttering like she was reliving those horrid years. "I changed my number. Georgie and I moved.

It doesn't surprise me that you couldn't get my information from the school because they knew I had people after me. They were protecting me." She shrugged. "The whole point was to disappear, and I guess it worked."

"And you didn't have social media," I said. "Or at least, I couldn't find you if you did."

She shook her head, wrinkling her nose. "God, no. I still don't."

"I looked in the phone book," I said on a laugh. "The *phone book*, Ari, in fucking 2009. I spent hours on Google. I paid some scammy guy to try to find you. I even looked for Georgie."

"We changed our name," she said, her gaze sliding to mine. "We didn't want Jay's last name anymore. So, after the trial, we changed it to my mom's maiden name."

"Campbell," I mused. "I was looking for Ariana Ridley, but she didn't exist."

Her smile was tight before falling altogether, and then her eyes were back on her hands. "It's probably a good thing you didn't find me. Not like it would have mattered, anyway."

She dug into the box.

Her words dug into my heart.

She was saying what I'd always assumed, but hoped, I was wrong about. Even if I had found her, she wouldn't have wanted to see me. She wouldn't have wanted me back in her life.

Could I blame her?

What was I expecting?

I left her to fight alone. Even if I did think it was the right thing to do, even if I somehow had proof that I would have jeopardized her case... did it matter?

I *left*.

I'd negated every promise of love and security I'd ever given her.

Why *would* she give a fuck if I'd tried to find her when the hardest part was over?

My nose stung, chest aching with the pressure mounting against it. So long, I'd wanted to tell her how hard I'd looked for her. And now, I knew that it didn't matter.

I needed to let it go — to let *her* go. My time had passed. I'd fucked up my shot with her and I didn't deserve another.

But now, she knew the truth. It was all there between us. She had the full story.

Maybe, if luck was on my side, she would at least afford me her friendship.

"Ari?"

"Hmm?"

"Can I hug you?"

Her eyes slid to mine, wide and soft and searching.

"I really need to hold you, Ari. Just for a moment. Please."

There were so many unsaid words in her eyes flicking between mine.

"Just for a moment," she echoed on a whisper.

I nodded, an unspoken promise to behave, and then I pulled her into me like a lifeline.

My arms enveloped her, the scent of her hair invading my nose as I closed my eyes and wrapped her up tight. I couldn't pull her in enough. I couldn't get close enough. I held her with the longing of two decades and the regret of one decision that had altered both our lives forever.

She was right.

It wasn't my decision to make alone.

I'd acted like a fucking saint, sacrificing us at the altar like I'd be regarded a hero in the end.

Instead, I'd killed us — our youth, our innocence, our hope, our love.

The blood was on my hands even still.

"I'm so sorry," I whispered into her hair. "I shouldn't have left. I was wrong. You deserved better. You deserved me staying and being there with you through all of it."

Her fingers curled in my hoodie, knuckles grazing my back as she buried her head deeper into my chest.

Tears flooded my eyes, nostrils flaring, the truth gutting me like a fish.

But I held strong, sniffing my emotion back and making a new vow to myself, and to her, to be her friend now. I couldn't change the past. I couldn't rewrite what happened.

I only had now, and I would make the best of it.

"I promise to leave it alone now. I won't keep trying to revive something I know is dead." I swallowed, pulling back just enough to press my lips to her forehead. I squeezed my eyes shut as she let out a shaky breath at the contact. "Friends, Ari. That's all I want. Just let me be your friend."

Another squeeze of her hands at my back was her only reply.

## CHAPTER 22

### THE FIRST CRACK

Ariana
2017

It was an accident, the first time I saw Shane on my television after that night he found me in Boston.

I was a newlywed, happy as a clam as I sat cross-legged on the floor of my new bedroom and unpacked boxes of clothes, the two-carat diamond ring glittering on my finger. 2013 felt like a lifetime ago. Since then, I'd met Nathan, fallen madly in love, been engaged and married and was now moving into our first house together.

It would be a lie to say Shane never crossed my mind. He did. I had a feeling he always would. But that cold winter night in Boston four years ago had cleansed me of him in a way. I'd been able to look him in the eye and tell him how I felt, and it helped me move forward.

I didn't follow what happened to him after his injury. I didn't want to know. Any time I thought of him, I tried my best to *unthink*. It was a wound I didn't want to poke, a scab I knew better than to pick at.

But Georgie had become a hockey fan in the last few years, thanks mostly to Nathan and his affiliation with the league through his job. Nathan worked in finance, and his firm specialized in alternative investments — money that moved quietly, through channels most people never saw. Sports were just another asset class to him, another place where numbers could be bent, optimized, and leveraged.

And right now, my little brother was sprawled out on my king bed, hand buried in a bag of chips and a game on the TV as he kept me company while I unpacked.

Part of me wanted to tell him to shoo so I could listen to an audiobook or some music, but he was fifteen now, a sophomore in high school and quickly becoming too cool for his older sister. If he wanted to hang out with me, I was going to take it. I had a feeling those days would come to an end far before I was ready.

I was sorting through a box of Nathan's, folding his night shirts and pajama pants, when a reporter said a familiar name and made me freeze mid-fold.

"Shane McCabe, assistant coach for the Jacksonville Barracudas, joining us now."

My heart stuttered so hard I felt it in my teeth.

The camera cut to him, and I stopped breathing.

The last time I had seen him, he had been on crutches outside that restaurant in Boston. He'd been pale, too thin, and hollowed out by pain — both physical and mental. That boy had looked defeated and lost, the kind of broken that made me ache just to witness, even if I was still mad at him.

But the man on my television looked nothing like that.

"Whoa," Georgie said from the bed, suddenly sitting up. Chips spilled onto the comforter, but he didn't seem to notice. "No way. I had no idea Shane was still in the league."

"Me either," I managed on a breath, the corner of my lips curling as the reporter asked him question after question.

And it wasn't a lie. I didn't know what happened to him after his injury. He'd told me he was done playing, but I knew there was no way he'd let hockey go forever. It was in his soul. It was who he was.

So to see him now, still able to be a part of the sport he loved so much...

I couldn't help but smile.

"Man, look at him," Georgie said, grinning as he shook his head and popped another chip in his mouth. "Hard to believe I used to ride around on that guy's shoulders. What a stud."

I laughed.

It felt like shaking rust off my ribcage.

Shane's hair was slightly longer now, swept back in a way that looked effortless. A neatly trimmed beard sharpened his jaw. His suit jacket stretched over broad shoulders that spoke of strength rebuilt over time. His cheeks were flushed from the game, and his loosened tie made him look relaxed and confident in a way I'd never seen before.

He looked good.

He looked healthy.

He looked sure of himself.

It felt as though the injury, the depression, and the broken pieces I had seen in Boston had been smoothed over and reforged into someone steady.

It felt as though he had healed, and he had done it without me.

"Is he really an assistant coach now?" Georgie asked, turning to me with wide eyes. "That is insane. He's like, what... thirty-three?"

"You called me *old* when I turned thirty," I teased my younger brother. "Now thirty-three is young?"

"To be an assistant coach in the NHL? Yeah." Georgie shoved a handful of chips in his mouth. "And you threw your back out like the day after you turned thirty, so…"

I grabbed one of my t-shirts and tied it into a knot before chucking it at my little brother, who laughed and caught it with ease. The brat.

When I looked back to the TV, Shane lifted his chin toward the reporter, and the familiarity of the gesture made something deep inside me twist.

"Coach McCabe, there are rumors swirling that you may already be in consideration for head coaching roles as early as next season," the reporter said. "Anything you want to comment on?"

Shane smiled, and the sound of his quiet laugh reached directly into a part of me I had tried so hard to seal off.

"Rumors are just rumors," he replied. "My focus is here with this team. Tonight's win belonged to the players. They earned it."

"That's humble talk," the reporter teased. "But you're one of the youngest assistant coaches in the league. What would it feel like, to become one of the youngest head coaches in the future?"

"We will take the future as it comes," Shane said with a small shrug. "For now, this is where I want to be."

My fingers closed slowly around the shirt in my hands. I felt my pulse beating in my throat, sharp and unsteady. The reporter said something else to dismiss Shane, and he smiled at the camera, giving a little wave before he excused himself.

I found myself smiling, too.

"Good God, Georgie."

I jumped a little at the baritone of my husband entering the room.

*Husband.*

I wasn't sure I'd ever get used to that.

My heart bloomed even as it beat double time as Nathan swept into the room, like I'd been caught doing something I shouldn't have been doing rather than folding laundry. But I also beamed at his presence, at my handsome husband joining us. Any time he walked into a room, I lit up like a firework.

Nathan swiped the bag of chips out of Georgie's hand. "We *just* had dinner."

"That was thirty minutes ago!" my little brother defended with a grin.

It was then that I noticed the tumbler of dark liquor in Nathan's hand.

*That's odd*, I thought. *He doesn't usually drink at home.*

"You're going to eat us out of the house," Nathan said, which made us all laugh, even if the joke did sound a bit aggressive. "Might be time to get a job so you can contribute to the grocery bill. God knows your sister doesn't."

That comment killed the laughter.

Both my and Georgie's smile faltered. He glanced at me, a question in his eyes, and I flushed furiously before smiling to cover my confusion.

*What the heck was that?*

"I'm just messing with you, kid," Nathan said, grabbing a chip before he handed the bag back to Georgie and ruffled his hair. "Eat all you want. You've got it good now."

I blinked repeatedly, my stomach sloshing with anxiety soup. I thought it was from Shane being on the TV, but now...

Nathan crossed to me next, plopping down on the floor next to where I sat. He wrapped me up from behind and kissed my hair. "That was a nice smile you had when I walked in," he said, eyes flicking to the TV. Thankfully, it was on game highlights now, Shane no longer on screen. "Wish *I* got more of that smile."

I swallowed, trying to shake off the weird feeling in my gut. "What do you mean? You get all my smiles."

"Not that one. I wasn't even in the room."

I blinked again.

*What was he getting at here*?

Before I could wrap my head around the confusing comment, Nathan chuckled, leaning his chin on my shoulder and looking at the folded clothes in front of me.

"You're so cute when you try to be domestic," he said, picking up one of his night shirts I'd folded. He eyed it with amusement as he took a sip of the liquor in his glass. "Georgie, did you teach your sister how to fold, or did she learn from watching another toddler?"

Georgie's smile was strained, and again, his eyes caught mine, like he was unsure what to say or how to react.

*That makes two of us*, I thought.

"I'm teasing you!" Nathan said, elbowing me.

I laughed, but it felt stranger than anything that had ever left my lips before.

My heart was pounding in my ears, but I didn't know why.

"Here, let me show you," Nathan said, and he kissed my cheek sweetly before holding up his shirt and instructing the proper way to fold it. Once he'd finished, he watched me re-fold three shirts before he seemed satisfied. "There you go. You'll get the hang of it."

He stood then, saying he needed to do some work in his study before he was humming his way down the hall like nothing had happened.

I stared at the shirts I had refolded, every edge sharp and straight, exactly the way he wanted them.

A thin line of unease coiled beneath my ribs.

It was small enough to ignore.

It was easy enough to swallow.

But it was the first crack in the glistening picture he'd painted for us.

I felt it — even if I didn't realize what it was.

# CHAPTER 23

## FINISH THE JOB

Ariana
Present

"Okay, charcuterie and antipasto are out and ready," I murmured to myself, ticking items off on my fingers as I paced around the kitchen. "Chicken Marsala is prepped to go in the oven... which is preheated... orzo and broccolini ready to go in right after... tiramisu chilling in the fridge... wine decanted..."

I exhaled, a nervous, excited laugh slipping out.

It was a Friday night in mid-November, one of those rare Florida evenings where the air felt cool enough to pretend it was fall. The windows were cracked, letting in a breeze that carried the faint scent of orange blossoms and saltwater. And I was hosting my first real dinner since our move.

Nathan had sprung it on me last minute, giving me only a few days' notice, but I didn't mind. I loved hosting. I loved the ritual of it: crafting a menu, setting a table, choosing a playlist that felt effortless but intentional. I loved the glow of the candles, the clink of glassware, the hum of conversation that wrapped around a room like a warm blanket.

And tonight, I'd get to be a part of it too — not just the woman behind the curtain pulling strings, but someone at the table.

It was an executive dinner for twelve: Nathan and me, obviously, Nathan's assistant and associate general managers, his senior advisor, the director of amateur scouting, the director of player development, and five members of the coaching staff — our three assistant coaches, the goaltending coach, and the head coach.

Shane.

I should have slapped my own hand for the way my stomach fluttered at the thought of him being here tonight, for how my cheeks warmed and my smile spread like butter melting on a hot roll. Things between us had settled into something resembling peace ever since I crashed his video review at the arena last week. Our apologies that burned as much as they soothed had paved a new road for us, or so it seemed, and we were both committed to leaving the past in the past.

It felt like smoothing out a wrinkled page to start writing again, a new chapter ahead of us.

This time, as friends.

And *God*, was I excited to have a friend.

That was perhaps my favorite part of the move to Tampa — how Maven and Grace and the rest of the girls had wrapped around me with effortless warmth. And now, somehow, I had a fresh start with a man who knew me in a way no one else here did. It was a strange kind of comfort, that familiarity. Like finding an old sweater or hearing a song you used to play on repeat but haven't heard in decades.

So yes, my nerves were kicking around over the timing of the dinner courses, and the pressure of wanting everything to be perfect buzzed under my skin. But mostly? I was excited.

I had new people to talk to tonight. A new friendship to rebuild. A chance to do something I genuinely loved.

Perhaps what had me buzzing most was that Nathan had promised I'd get a moment to talk about Sweet Dreams.

My smile widened just thinking about how I'd have the chance to tell the executives about the Skate for Change event next week, about the Christmas gala, about everything else we had planned.

As much as I loved hosting, I loved nonprofit work more. I missed being in the social-work sector with an ache deep enough to carve a canyon out of. But Sweet Dreams had lit that part of me up again. I had purpose. I had an organization I believed in to throw myself into. I was flush with new ideas and creativity.

Tonight, I'd get to share that with important people — people who could help.

The thought had me giddy as I straightened a candlestick on the dining table, smoothing the linen runner with proud hands.

I was preening.

I took a moment to sneak around the corner and check my appearance in the hallway mirror. The deep green dress skimmed my curves without clinging, elegant but understated, the kind Nathan preferred for nights like this. My hair was swept up, loose tendrils softening the look, my makeup carefully done — enough to feel polished, not so much that it would invite commentary.

I adjusted the delicate gold bracelet on my wrist, letting it settle just right before lowering my arm. Then I made my way back into the dining room to double-check everything was in its place.

"Oh, sweetheart. You've outdone yourself."

Nathan swept into the dining room still fastening his cuff links, eyes taking in the warm, sparkling scene I'd set. A deep red table runner with stunning floral design stretched over a cream tablecloth, each place at the table framed neatly with a gold charger and delicate china plates. Wine glasses and candles were perfectly placed, soft piano jazz flowing in from our speakers above, the scent of dinner enough to make any mouth water.

"I've set the antipasto out on the bar," I said, folding my hands together as I looked at the same scene with pride. "I made sure we have that tequila you said Jared likes best. I still think wine would pair better with the meal, but..."

Nathan slid his arm around my waist and pulled me in, kissing my hair. "He will appreciate the thoughtfulness, and so do I."

His eyes dipped briefly, taking in my dress, my hair.

"You actually made an effort tonight," he added lightly. "I like this look on you."

I held my smile despite how the compliment felt sour, my hands finding his chest as I looked up at him.

For a moment, a deep sadness came over me. I longed for the days when I used to touch this man and feel desire, for when I would look into his eyes and feel nothing but comfort and safety. But I didn't let myself linger in those thoughts. "Thank you for letting me be a part of tonight."

His face screwed up a bit at that, like I was being silly. "Well, we needed a dinner, didn't we?"

Nathan laughed, and my stomach sank.

I ignored it.

Tonight was going to be great. He was just teasing.

"You know what I mean," I said, swatting at his chest playfully. "I wish you knew how excited I've been all day knowing I get to talk about Sweet Dreams this evening."

Nathan patted my hand, surveying the space once more like he was checking to make sure all was in order. "I'm sure you are, honey."

The doorbell rang, and I smiled wide, bouncing a little as I let out a giggle. "First guest is here!"

"Okay, okay, calm down," Nathan said with a laugh.

I was ready to skip to the door, my heart beaming. "Hang on one second. I just want to check the—oh!"

I giggled as I ran into one of the chairs, knocking the table and making the glassware shake, the candles flickering.

"Easy," Nathan said, smiling though his eyes were wide now, his hands up. "Let's take a breath."

"Sorry," I said, covering my smile with a hand. "Okay, I want to greet them at the door with you. I just need to quickly—*ouch!*"

It happened so fast, I barely registered it.

One second I was on my way to the kitchen to triple-check my prep list, and the next, my wrist was snagged in a vise grip and halted back over my head, the force so sharp it whipped me around.

Nathan had his fingers wrapped tight around me.

A burning ache seared from the point of contact all the way to my elbow, and when I tried to pull free, it only made the pain worse. I cried out.

"Nathan—"

"I mean it, Ariana, calm. *Down.*" He seethed the words, holding my wrist tight as he yanked me close enough to whisper his next threat.

"You're hurting me," I whispered, like I was afraid to say it out loud, like if I only said it quietly, it wouldn't be true. My brain was already arguing with me. *You're fine. It's not that bad. You're being dramatic.*

"This is an important dinner, and I need you to play your role of doting wife. Okay? I've got important deals to discuss tonight, and I don't need you tripping over yourself and causing a commotion. The table looks great. You're beautiful. The food smells lovely. Now, finish the job and *quiet down.*"

I stared at him slack-jawed, blinking rapidly like I was sure I'd misheard him. But he held fast to my wrist and lifted a brow until I nodded my understanding.

And I felt it.

My soul faded like a candle flame burning down to the bottom of a wick, the remaining wax snuffing it out silently, and with just a small wisp of smoke. My mind was retreating inside me, burying itself deep, leaving my body to bear the brunt of what was happening so it could protect itself.

"Good," he said, releasing me with a flourish. He smoothed his hands over his suit and adjusted his cuffs. "Now, I will go greet our guest. You check whatever you need to check. And when I see you again, I expect tranquility. Yes?" He shook his head. "This isn't some chaotic family dinner, it's a business meeting. Speaking of family, let's do our best not to bring up yours. The last thing I need is to have to explain a dead mother, a deadbeat stepdad, and a brother you raised like some sort of single mom before I met you."

He didn't wait for me to respond. With practiced ease, he slid a politician's smile into place and skated toward the foyer. I heard the door open a few moments later, followed by a loud, booming welcome and laughter.

I was still rooted to the spot, my wrist aching, heart pounding in my ears.

All the excitement drained out of me in an instant, my hopes and dreams for the night swirling into an endless black hole in my heart. Somehow, I managed to move, to put one foot in front of the other until I was in the kitchen. There was nothing to check. Everything was perfect. But I stayed in there as long as I could before it could be considered impolite.

Now, it was me with the practiced smile in place, gliding into the foyer to join my husband and greet our guests one by one. I stood at his side. I laughed when it was appropriate. I thanked each person who complimented my home, or the appetizer spread, or the wine.

I played my part.

Right up to when Shane walked through the door and saw through the act.

# CHAPTER 24

## SHE'S MINE

Shane
Present

I should have been enjoying the meal.

Objectively, it was one of the best home-cooked dinners I'd had in years — hell, maybe ever. The chicken was perfectly moist, the broccolini roasted to perfection, the orzo citrusy and balanced. It was the kind of food that came from someone who cared, who planned, who put thought into the details most people never even noticed.

But the longer I sat at that table, the sicker I felt.

Something was wrong.

There was a little voice inside my head reminding me that I only felt this way because I hated Nathan for reasons that would never make sense to anyone but me. The guy was perfect in the eyes of everyone at this table, and yet I knew I'd always struggle to see him as anyone more than the man who had Ariana, the man I felt didn't deserve her even if I didn't know *why*.

But there was also a louder voice tonight, one that was practically screaming from the moment I walked in the door.

Ariana wasn't okay.

No, I didn't have proof, but I still knew it as if I had a peer-reviewed study in front of me. The evidence ticked up throughout the night in ways other people at this table wouldn't see unless they knew Ariana down to her bones the way I did.

And that's why, from the moment we'd all taken our seats, my stomach had been twisting tighter and tighter.

It started when I walked through the door and saw the smile she wore, a polished one that I knew was forced. My suspicion climbed higher when I noticed her wince when her husband wrapped his arm around her hips and pulled her into his side proudly, but didn't invite her into the conversation — like she was a trophy to be admired and silent.

Things only got worse once we were seated.

Jared — our assistant general manager — complimented the chicken Marsala and asked Ariana where she learned the recipe. Ariana inhaled, shoulders straightening, lips parting with that bright, eager smile I remembered from when we were younger...

And Nathan answered for her.

"Oh, she just found it online," he said with a laugh. "Pinterest or one of those wife-life blogs she's always on. But she nailed it, didn't she?" He rubbed her arm affectionately. "She's always been so great at throwing a party. With a little guidance from me, of course." He laughed at that, and then launched into a story about the time she'd botched a Christmas dinner with his family by undercooking a prime rib.

None of the guys thought twice about it. Jared chuckled, complimented the dish again, and kept eating.

But Ariana's smile wilted, and my pulse notched up.

The progression was so subtle I knew I was the only one to notice it.

Her voice, which had been soft but steady when she'd first greeted the room, faded as the night went on until she wasn't speaking at all. She just sat there next to her husband, hands folded neatly in her lap, eyes fixed on whoever was speaking like she was attending a lecture instead of a dinner party.

She'd looked... expectant for a while.

Like she was waiting for something.

I realized what it was when dessert was served.

Our amateur scouting director, Samuel, was regaling us all with a story about a kid on his radar — someone he said could be the next big thing out of the USHL. Apparently, the kid had been homeless from the age of twelve to fourteen.

He'd lived under the Jefferson Street overpass for a stretch, then in the dugout of a public park, then in a cardboard lean-to behind a mechanic's shop. His mother had overdosed; his father was in and out of jail. The boy had slipped through every crack the system had.

"And the crazy part?" Samuel said, leaning in, wine glass dangling from his fingers. "He was still playing hockey. Not travel hockey or club, of course, but with anyone he could at the freaking *outdoor rink*. I mean, this kid had old, borrowed skates and a broken stick someone had tossed in the trash. He'd show up to the open community sessions every winter, lacing up gear two sizes too big for him. The rink manager let him skate for free because 'the kid looked like he needed it.'"

For the first time since dinner began, I watched Ariana come to life a bit, her eyes sparking at the story.

Samuel went on to tell us about how a retired surgeon entered the picture next, Dr. Albright. He volunteered at the local rink sharpening skates and helping with learn-to-skate programs.

"One night, during a storm, he spotted the kid huddled in an abandoned house across the street. The boy had slipped inside through a missing panel in the back door. Instead of calling the police, Dr. Albright offered him dinner, then a shower, then a bed. Social services got involved, but when no relatives claimed him and his father failed to show for the hearings, Dr. Albright applied for full guardianship."

"Wow," Kozak said beside me, shaking his head. "And you think this kid has real potential to be in the league?"

"Oh, I mean, from there, it was like striking oil. The kid just exploded. Grew six inches in eighteen months. Got into AA hockey, then AAA. Now he's lighting up the USHL with Madison."

"That's insane," Coach Romanov said.

And Ariana's smile bloomed, her back straightening again as she leaned forward and chimed in for the first time. "See, this is what I think so many people don't understand. Having a safe place to lay your head at night, having an actual *bed* to sleep in... it can change everything. I've actually been working closely with—"

But it didn't matter that all the eyes at the table had shifted to her with interest. In fact, that might have made things worse.

Because Nathan cut her off, patting her hand like she was a child.

"Okay, honey, that's enough," he teased, laughing as he looked around the table and shot his associate general manager a wink. Ralph. I didn't like that guy, either. I didn't like the slimy way he smiled back like he and Nathan were in on a secret. "No one wants to talk about poor kids without beds when we're sipping high-dollar wine and eating tiramisu. Oh! Speaking of which, Jared, I know you were wondering about the Marsala recipe. *This* one, the tiramisu, is actually from my great-great-grandmother. See, when she was little..."

Like nothing had happened, the attention shifted to Nathan, everyone at the table completely oblivious to how he'd shut Ariana down.

I watched her try to blink away her disappointment before she forced a smile and lowered her gaze, swallowing whatever she'd been about to say. Her shoulders curled inward.

And I saw red, my chest tightening along with my fist under the table.

I couldn't put my finger on it, but every instinct I had — every coaching radar, every old muscle memory of knowing her in a way no one else ever had — was screaming at me that something had happened before we arrived.

And for the first time since Nathan Black kicked his way into our team, I didn't let myself second-guess my gut instincts about him.

This motherfucker was trash, and I was ready to take him out.

Somehow, I kept my cool at the table, biding my time to when I could somehow get Ariana alone. My opportunity came in a way I least expected that had my stomach churning more.

Ariana was still silent next to Nathan, but she was absentmindedly rubbing her wrist, wincing a bit as she rotated it and wiggled her fingers.

I wasn't the only one who noticed.

"You good, Ariana?" Kozak asked from beside me, nodding to where she was rubbing her wrist.

Her eyes flicked to Nathan so fast I almost missed it.

He was smiling and pleasant, but I saw the flash of warning in his smile.

My stomach dropped through the floor like an anvil.

*Oh, God...*

*No.*

*No, please, no.*

Ariana straightened with a shaky breath and forced a laugh. "Oh, I just aggravated it lifting the chicken out of the oven. I think I'll grab some ibuprofen. Excuse me a moment."

She stood, barely brushing the back of Nathan's chair as she passed.

Her gaze met mine for a split second, just long enough for me to see it: the unspoken plea.

*Help.*

And then she disappeared down the hall.

"God love her," Nathan said the moment she was gone, shaking his head with a chuckle. "The woman gets so flustered trying to host these things. I keep telling her she doesn't have to impress anybody."

There was another wave of laughter around the table.

My jaw flexed so hard it hurt.

Impress anybody?

She had impressed *everyone*.

The entire evening was perfect because she'd planned it down to the minute.

But that wasn't the point.

The point was the way he spoke about her like she wasn't a full person — like she was a prop, an accessory, something to pat on the head and manage.

I took a slow sip of my wine, trying to cool the wildfire in my chest as I bided my time. We all eventually stood, Nathan guiding us to the back patio for a cigar. Ariana still hadn't returned, but I heard the soft sound of water running from the kitchen.

"I think I'm calling it a night, fellas," I said, grinning wide and hoping like hell no one could see through me as I shook hands and clapped backs in firm hugs. "Morning skate will come too early."

"And we all know you'll be there hours before the first player shows up," Coach Timberland added fondly.

"You know me well. See you all in the morning."

I made sure to thank Nathan profusely for the night, inflating his already swollen ego as much as I could before I quietly made my exit. The conversation picked up the moment I turned, Nathan showing off his selection of cigars.

I slipped inside the house, shutting the sliding glass door behind me. For a moment, I looked around at the house Ariana shared with Nathan, looking for signs of life. Other than one photo from their wedding, I didn't see much. My eyes snagged on a camera in the corner of the living room, and my heart stuttered.

I made a beeline for the kitchen.

Ariana was at the sink, her back to me, scrubbing away at the pan she'd cooked the chicken in. She yelped a little when she scrubbed too hard, letting the pan fall into the dishwater and holding her wrist.

I wanted to run to her.

I wanted to whip her around, grab her by the arms, and demand she tell me what the fuck was going on.

But I knew better. I knew the last thing she needed right now was more aggression, or another man telling her what to do.

Wordlessly, I slipped up beside her at the sink. She turned to me in surprise.

She'd been crying.

It felt like swallowing acid as I held back what I wanted to say. Instead, I reached into the soapy water and grabbed the dish. Then, my hand found hers.

I wrapped around her slowly, gently, our soapy, slick fingers gliding along one another. I took my time, savoring her warmth, heart racing in my chest as I grabbed the sponge she held fast to.

For the longest moment, she didn't let go. Her eyes trailed from where our hands touched up my arm, my shoulder, catching at my neck before they snapped to meet my gaze.

I squeezed her hand, letting her know I was there to help.

She released the sponge.

And we got to work.

For twenty minutes, not a single word passed between us. She brought in the rest of the dishes from the table while I washed the ones already piled in the sink. She wiped the counters. I dried the heavier dishes and put them away for her.

Eventually, there was nothing more to do, and I leaned a hip against the counter, wiping my hands on a dishtowel with my eyes on her.

"Thank you," she muttered quietly, her gaze on the floor between us. She tucked her hair behind her ear and folded her arms tightly across her chest like she wanted to disappear.

I couldn't let her. Not after tonight.

"I'm going to ask you this once," I said carefully, schooling my breathing as much as I could. "And I'm going to beg you not to lie to me."

I heard her swallow over the sound of the piano jazz. Her eyes stayed glued to the floor.

"Is everything okay between you and Nathan?"

Her eyes welled in an instant, two big fat tears sliding off her cheeks and down to the tile.

She wouldn't look at me.

But she shook her head.

My throat constricted. It took everything in me not to grab her right then, throw her over my fucking shoulder, and steal her away. Possession and protectiveness surged from me like smoke billowing from a building on fire.

But that wasn't what she needed.

I knew it as much as I knew my playbook.

This was a delicate situation, and I had to approach it as such.

"Can you look at me?"

She shook her head again.

Carefully, I pushed off the counter, taking three slow steps until I was right in front of her. Her gaze was on my chest now.

"Please," I asked again. "Look at me."

She blinked a few times before she did, and as soon as her eyes met mine, they watered fiercely again. She clapped a hand over her mouth. "I'm sorry."

I frowned, my heart fucking breaking at the sight of her so distraught. "Ari, what happened?"

She shook her head, again and again, like it was impossible to say, like she didn't believe her version of the truth enough to speak it out loud.

"Talk to me. What's going—"

"Coach!"

Ariana winced, jumping back, and ice slid through my veins at the familiar voice.

Nathan waltzed into the kitchen with a tumbler of brown liquor in hand. He wore a grin that spread from ear to ear, but his eyes were lazy and calculated, sweeping from me to his wife and back again.

I saw his grip around his glass tighten.

"I thought you left a half hour ago," he said with that slick smile of his in place.

"He was leaving," Ariana said, and I didn't know how I missed it, but she'd somehow cleared her tears. There was still evidence there on her cheeks, but she looked so different than she had just moments before — more put together, like nothing had happened at all.

Red flags were waving so aggressively in my head I couldn't see straight.

"But then he saw me in here with all the dishes," she said, laughing as she swept a hand over the clean kitchen. "And I couldn't lift that big cutting board since I hurt my wrist."

She gave her husband a very particular look with that last part, like she was reminding him of something I didn't know.

"So I asked if he wouldn't mind helping. And he was so kind to oblige." She smiled, nodding my way. "Thank you again, Shane. I appreciate your help. But you should get going! I know you want to get rest before morning skate." She turned to Nathan then. "Is everyone still on the patio? I can bring limoncello?"

Nathan was quiet for a long, heavy moment.

His eyes narrowed so slowly I'd have missed it if I wasn't watching him so closely. And once again, he looked long and hard at his wife.

And then at me.

Suddenly, he smiled, the gesture warping his face into the perfect picture of amiability. "Very kind of you to help, Coach." His smile slipped, his gaze hardening, and then he turned the grin on his wife. "Limoncello would be lovely, sweetheart. Why don't you pour up some glasses and I'll meet you out there?"

Ariana nodded, and she didn't so much as chance a glance at me before she was slipping out of the kitchen on her way toward their bar.

Nathan slid his free hand into his pocket, sipping his liquor. He smiled at me again. "Well, have a good night then, Coach."

The last fucking thing I wanted to do was leave, but what else could I do?

This was my general manager.

Ariana was his *wife*.

I didn't know anything other than they were maybe having a fight or an off night. That didn't warrant me doing anything other than what I had — offering Ariana someone to talk to.

And she hadn't wanted to talk.

Still, it was eating at me — the way he treated her tonight. I didn't care what they were arguing about. You didn't treat someone you loved like that, no matter what.

And her wrist...

What the *fuck* was up with that?

My instincts were blaring that he'd hurt her somehow. But as soon as I thought it, I shook it off.

Ariana wouldn't stand for it.

She'd grown up in a household watching her mother in that situation. I knew at the first *sign* of abuse, she'd be gone.

... Wouldn't she?

"Do you need me to walk you out?" Nathan asked, still grinning. "Seems like you might have lost your way to the door earlier."

I tried to smile back, but it fell flat. "Not at all. Go back to your party, sir. I'll see you next week."

Again, I didn't want to leave, but I didn't know what else to do.

So I made my way toward the door.

A hard hand slammed against my chest before I could slip past Nathan.

"And Coach?"

I angled my chin toward him, waiting, my hands curling into fists.

"Watch yourself around my wife. Understand?"

"I don't know what you mean."

He smiled, nodding with a pat against my chest where he'd had my shirt gripped before. "Test me, and you'll find out," he said.

He released me, heading back to the party.

And I drove home with murder in my veins, my foot hard on the gas pedal, knuckles white on the wheel.

I had to get Ariana alone.

I had to figure out what the fuck was going on.

I had to expose that snake of a man for exactly who he was.

And I had to start planning how to do it.

Tonight.

## CHAPTER 25

### NO PRESSURE

Ariana
Present

The arena was alive with joy.

The Skate for Change event was in full swing — skates scraping, kids screaming, whistles blowing, holiday music echoing off the metal rafters. It was loud and messy and too cold for anyone sane to call it cozy, but everything in me melted, anyway.

This was what I lived for.

All the days planning, the nights of long, hard work, the behind-the-scenes emails and phone calls and schedule management to make it all happen — it all led to this. There was nothing like seeing your vision come to life even better than you imagined, to look around at a literal arena full of smiles and know you made it happen.

"Okay, check-in tables are stocked, raffle tickets ready, donation boxes out," I murmured, ticking through my mental list as I weaved between clusters of people in the lobby. Sweet Dreams banners hung from the railings, the logo bright and hopeful. Volunteers in matching t-shirts stood at folding tables, greeting families with smiles and Sharpies in hand.

A little girl in a knit hat beamed as she slid a paper wristband up her arm. "Do I really get to skate with the players?" she asked her mom.

"Sure do," I interjected, winking at the mom when she smiled at me. "They're all out there waiting."

She squealed and tugged her mom toward the rental skates.

My wrist throbbed as I reached to straighten a banner stand. The ache pulsed under my bracelets, where the faint shadow of a bruise hid against my skin. I flexed my fingers, wincing, and told myself the same story I'd been repeating for days.

It was the chicken pan. The box of brochures. The lifting.

Not... anything else.

That dinner party felt like a lifetime ago now, the days blurred by event prep and a showering of love from my husband. Nathan had been so over-the-top helpful the last week that it made my head spin. He'd planted sweet kisses on my cheek in the morning, sent texts every afternoon: *How's planning going, sweetheart? So proud of you.*

He'd hired a housekeeper *and* a chef, telling me it would help me lean all my focus into Sweet Dreams. He'd bought the gorgeous dress I wore now, a deep, brick-red and velvet-laced number that cinched my waist and flowed like magic down to my heels. He'd come home every night all week, spending quality time with me — watching movies, making ice cream sundaes, telling me how excited he was to see what I did with the event.

This morning, there were flowers on the counter with a note: *Tonight's going to be a home run. I'm lucky to have you.*

If my life were a theme park ride, then I'd just been whipped backward and through a loop. My head was spinning and aching trying to make sense of it all.

But I didn't think of any of that tonight. All my focus was on Skate for Change.

"Look at this place," Maven said, suddenly at my side with her hands coming up to frame my arms. She looked around with pure wonder in her eyes. "This is insane."

Grace appeared on my other side like she teleported, linking her arm with mine. "I feel like I'm at some Hallmark movie event, but, like, one that doesn't suck."

I laughed, the sound coming easier than it had in days. "That's the goal. Cheesy but effective."

"Have you seen the donation numbers?" Grace asked, nodding toward the big clear box by the doors. Crumpled bills and folded checks were stacked inside, and there was a QR code for people to scan if they didn't have cash. "I cannot *wait* to see the final number on the jumbotron later. I've been clocking the people in attendance, and there's some *big money* in here. How the hell did you get Robert Jennings to attend?!"

Robert Jennings was the CEO of Jennings Financial — and there was a literal skyscraper named after his family's business just two blocks away.

"That would be Nathan, actually," I said, hating how my stomach soured a bit at the admission. It was a great thing that he'd brought in such great benefactors, but something about it ate at me. "He's been calling in a lot of favors for tonight."

"Bless that man," Grace said.

"And the players are having a blast," Maven added. "Vince is already out there trying to impress toddlers with his toe-drags. You did this, Ari."

Heat rushed to my cheeks. "We did this," I corrected. "You two, PR, the shelter, the team—"

"Yeah, yeah, yeah, you're a team player," Grace cut in, rolling her eyes fondly. "But seriously. This is all you. You look happy, and you should be. This is your baby, and these are its first steps. Soak it in, darling."

The words landed in a place that hadn't felt anything in a while.

For a heartbeat, I let myself feel it — the buzz of the crowd, the laughter, the smell of popcorn and ice and cheap hot chocolate. Kids who never got anything special were getting a night on the ice. Sweet Dreams was getting money for beds.

I *was* happy.

And still... there was a hollow space in my chest where the dinner night still sat like a stone, cold and heavy.

I must have been absentmindedly rubbing my wrist again because Grace softened, nodding toward the reflex. "You okay?"

I startled, smiling big and immediately folding my hands behind my back. "Oh, fine. Think I may have tweaked something lifting boxes of t-shirts earlier."

"Easy to do," Maven said. "Let the volunteers do the heavy lifting later, okay? Ah," she added, nodding behind me. "I think our time of kissing your feet is over, at least for now. Your leading man just arrived."

I followed her gaze.

Nathan strutted in like the arena belonged to him, and I suppose it might as well have. His suit was perfect, hair perfect, that signature GM smile turned up just enough to charm but not enough to look like he was trying. A few fans called his name as he passed, and he paused for a quick photo like it wasn't a bother at all, all polish and ease.

When his eyes found mine, they softened.

"There's my girl," he said as he reached me, arm sliding around my waist and pulling me in. He kissed my temple like he used to when we first started dating. "You are incredible. This place is buzzing."

The warmth of his praise collided with the memory of his grip, confusing everything inside me.

"Thanks," I managed. "We're nearly at our goal for the night, and we're not even to the scrimmage yet."

He beamed, like a proud husband who'd never done anything worse than leave socks on the floor. "That's my wife," he said, winking at Maven and Grace as he tucked me under one arm. "Tell me again how I got so lucky?"

"We've been asking ourselves the same since you two showed up in Tampa," Maven teased.

Grace snorted. "She's being nice. You married up, Black. Don't forget it."

Nathan laughed good-naturedly. "I know when I'm out of my league."

He gave my waist a squeeze, not a hard one, but one that was soft and affectionate.

It was just enough pressure to make me feel crazy for having been afraid of him at all.

"Channel 8 is ready when you are," our PR manager called from across the lobby, waving us over.

"Go shine," Maven whispered, bumping my hip.

"Knock 'em dead," Grace added.

Nathan steered me with him toward the camera setup, his hand warm at the small of my back. "Having fun so far?"

I let out a nervous breath as we approached the camera crew. "I am. Everything has come together perfectly."

"It really has." He paused, pulling me to a stop to check my hair and dress with an affectionate smile. "Have you seen Coach McCabe yet?"

His eyes stayed on my dress where he busied himself with smoothing the fabric that didn't need to be fixed.

I swallowed. "No, not yet, actually."

Nathan hummed, nodding. "Good. I think maybe it's best you stay away from him."

My heart lurched into my throat. "Oh?" I asked carefully. "Something going on?"

At that, Nathan smirked, the first bit of evil leaking through his perfect exterior in days. His eyes skirted to mine. "I don't know, Ariana. *Is* there something going on?"

The pulse thrumming in my ears muted everything, and I didn't know what to do but stare back at him and feign naivety.

"Mrs. Black?" a soft voice interrupted, and then the assistant with the news crew ushered me over to the camera. "You're up."

The lights were bright, the reporter poised with her mic and perfect smile. I was still trying to regain my composure after the unexpected warning from Nathan.

"We're here at the first annual Sweet Dreams Skate for Change," the reporter said once the camera was rolling, "and joining me now is the woman behind it all, Ariana Black."

I swallowed my nerves and smiled into the camera. I could do this. I knew my talking points better than I knew my own reflection. With a deep breath and winning smile, I zeroed in.

I talked about bed insecurity, about kids sleeping on couches or floors or in cars. I talked about how a good night's sleep changes everything. I talked about Sweet

Dreams and the shelter and the team's support. The reporter nodded in all the right places, eyes bright.

"And it looks like the organization has really wrapped around this effort," she said. "GM Nathan Black is here tonight as well—"

"Let's get him in!" the PR manager chimed in, already waving Nathan forward.

My husband slipped into frame beside me, arm curling around my shoulders, pulling me closer.

"Yes, please," the reporter said, delighted. "Nathan, how proud are you of your wife right now?"

"Ridiculously," he answered without hesitation, looking at me like I'd hung the moon. "She has poured her heart into this. She's always been passionate about community work, and to see her build Sweet Dreams here in Tampa, to see the impact it's already having on these kids... I mean, look at her." He turned back to the camera. "She's the brains and the heart behind tonight. I just sign the checks and try to keep up."

My heart squeezed so tightly in my chest I couldn't help my visceral reaction — tears glazed my eyes.

*Did he mean that?*

The reporter laughed. "That is so sweet. You seem like a great team."

"We are," Nathan agreed, squeezing my shoulder. "On and off the ice."

The words cradled me like a newborn, comforting and warm. If I were someone else watching this on TV, I would believe it. I'd see a devoted husband bragging about his accomplished wife. I'd think they were perfect.

For a second, I believed it, too.

Maybe that dinner party was just a bad night. Maybe I was making too much of it. Nathan was here, right by my side — saying all the right things, *doing* all the right things.

I didn't realize I'd fallen quiet until the reporter wrapped up.

"Thank you both so much," she said. "We can't wait to see how much Skate for Change raises tonight."

"Thank you," I replied, forcing my voice through the tightness in my throat.

The camera light cut off. The reporter complimented us again, talking about how good it would look on the ten o'clock segment. Nathan thanked her, shook her hand, and draped his arm around me as we stepped away.

"You were great," he said, dropping a kiss on my forehead. "Perfect, sweetheart. Just perfect."

I swallowed, nodding. "You too."

He smiled, then his eyes darted beyond me as he spotted one of the owners. He excused himself, leaving me standing in the glow of the lights, the praise still clinging to my skin like static.

*You're fine,* I told myself. *Look how wonderful he is. Look how much he supports you.*

My wrist twinged when I adjusted my bracelets.

I shook it off and headed toward the glass to check on the ice.

Kids dotted the rink, clinging to the boards, shuffling along in slow, terrified inches, or zooming past in fearless streaks. Parents and fans in jerseys filled the lower bowl, some on their feet, some taking videos. Mariah Carey belted out from the speakers, her voice bouncing around the rafters.

And in the middle of it all, I saw him.

Shane.

He was a youthful kind of handsome tonight, sporting a team jacket and a knit beanie pulled low. He wore deep-cut laugh lines at the corners of his eyes. A little boy clung to his hand, skates splayed, legs shaking like a baby deer. Shane was bent slightly at the waist, talking to him, pointing with his free hand to show him where to put his weight.

"Bend your knees," I read on his lips. "Trust your edges."

The boy wobbled. Shane steadied him with one hand at his back.

The boy tried again, found his balance, and glided just for a second without panicking.

He laughed, bright and free, looking up at Shane for approval, who met him with a wide grin and a high five.

As if he sensed me, Shane glanced up.

Our eyes locked across the ice, and my stomach somersaulted.

For a moment, the noise fell away. There was just the cold air seeping through the glass, my breath fogging the surface, and his gaze holding mine.

His expression softened, a question in his blue-gray eyes.

*You okay?*

I didn't know what to answer back.

Someone tugged on my sleeve.

"Um... excuse me?"

I blinked, tearing my gaze away from Shane to look down.

A young boy stood beside me, maybe eight or nine, cheeks pink under a too-big knit hat, Sweet Dreams wristband snug around his arm. His laces were loose, skates practically falling off his feet.

"Hi there," I said, forcing my smile back into place. "Having fun?"

He nodded so hard his hat slipped over one eye. "Yeah. I wanted to say... thank you."

"Oh," I said, thrown. "You're welcome. For what am I being thanked for?"

"For this," he said, gesturing out at the ice. "My mom said we couldn't do stuff like this anymore. But then she said this one was free." He rocked back on his blades. "I've never skated before. It's the coolest thing ever."

Warmth flooded my chest, hot enough to burn through everything else for a second.

"I'm really glad you're here," I told him. "And I hope you fall a little bit. That means you're trying something new."

He laughed. The sound took me back to when Georgie was his age, and my chest squeezed tighter. "I already fell three times."

"Perfect," I said. "You're doing it right, then."

"Mrs. Black?"

The woman I assumed was his mom approached then, balancing two Styrofoam cups of hot chocolate. She looked tired in a way I recognized, her smile soft.

"Sorry if he's bothering you," she said. "He just really wanted to say thank you."

"He's not bothering me at all," I replied quickly. "I'm happy he found me."

She hesitated, then shifted the cups to one hand so she could touch my arm. "We... um... we're on the Sweet Dreams list for beds," she said. "My son's been sleeping on the floor since we had to move in with my sister. We both have. They said... they said he'd have a bed by Christmas."

My throat was so tight I couldn't swallow.

"I know it's just a bed," she rushed on, "but—"

"It's not just a bed," I cut in gently. "It's a place to land. A place that's his. It matters. He matters."

Her eyes shone in the way of someone being understood. "Thank you," she whispered. "For this night. For... everything."

My smile wobbled. "Thank *you*," I said back. "I'm really glad you're here. And if you give me your name, I'd like to see if we can get a bed for you, too."

Her eyes widened. "Oh, no, it's okay. I really just want to make sure he—"

"Please," I said softly, hoping my smile communicated that I understood where she was at and wanted to meet her there. "I'd really love to."

With a watery smile, she nodded, providing me her name and number on the list. I jotted it down in my phone, making a mental note, too.

After, she guided her son back toward the ice, and I watched them go, my heart too full and too empty all at once.

*This is why you stay,* I reminded myself. *This is why you swallow what you swallow. Look what you get to do. Look who you get to help.*

I pressed my fingers lightly against my wrist, feeling the dull ache there.

*One does not cancel out the other*, another small, stubborn part of me whispered.

I ignored it.

My phone buzzed in my pocket, and I fished it out to find a text from Georgie.

**Little Brother:** Saw a clip of the event on social media. Wow, Sis. You really did your thing. Proud of you. Call me later!

My smile was so big it hurt my cheeks as I thumbed a reply, and then it was back to work.

By the time the scrimmage was over, the donation thermometer on the jumbotron had shot up higher than I dared to hope. The announcer made a big show of the final number: $76,208.

Our goal had been $25,000.

Kids screamed, fans cheered, confetti cannons popped. Ben and Daddy P did a victory lap with a pack of teenagers trying to keep up with them.

It was a huge win.

We did it.

The night wound down slowly, families heading out of the cold arena and into the warm Florida night. Volunteers folded tables, stacked chairs, and broke down signs. The soundtrack shifted from Christmas music to the hum of the Zamboni and the clattering of skates being boxed.

I moved through the concourse with my tablet tucked to my chest, checking boxes. Nathan had disappeared into the bowels of the arena with a man I didn't recognize and a couple of executives a while ago, and I hadn't seen him since.

My wrist throbbed when I try to lift a bin of packed-up supplies — tape, extension cords, LED lights, and the like. I should have been able to lift it no problem, but it sent a zing up to my elbow.

I breathed out slowly and sat it back down.

"You know there are interns for that, right?"

His voice slid over my shoulders like a warm coat.

Shane stood a few feet away, hands in the pockets of his team jacket, hair curling from under his beanie. He didn't look like the coach I knew everyone else saw him as — that stern, dialed-in, unshakeable man.

He looked like the boy who once taught me how to skate backward on a frozen-over pond.

"I thought you'd left," I said, fingers tightening around the edge of the table.

"One of the benefits of being an old man," he said wryly. "Nobody expects you to stick around for the big clean up — especially after nine o'clock."

I huffed out a laugh I didn't really feel. "And yet, here you are."

He shrugged. "Maybe I like defying expectations."

His gaze traveled over the half-broken-down event — empty raffle tables, sagging banners, a few stragglers in Sweet Dreams shirts laughing as they carried supplies into the tunnel. When his eyes came back to me, they softened.

*Stay away from him.*

Nathan's words echoed in my mind, but I shoved them right into the same attic I was forcing most of my thoughts into, adding to the list of warnings I chose to ignore.

"Gotta say, you blew away every expectation I had for tonight," Shane said. "This was... huge, Ari. For the kids, for the foundation. For the team, too, whether they realize it or not."

The compliment landed deep, under all the layers of numbness and performance.

"Thank you," I said quietly. "That means a lot."

He took a step closer, enough that I could see the darker gray ring around his blue irises. My heart kicked hard against my ribs.

"How's the wrist?" he asked.

The question was gentle, but it still felt like a spotlight. Instinctively, I tucked my injured hand closer to my body, my bracelets chiming together with the movement.

"It's fine," I said too quickly. "Just... sore. The pan was heavy."

His brow lifted, the faintest hint of skepticism tugging at his mouth.

"Right," he said. "The pan."

I swallowed, my throat suddenly dry. "What else would it be?"

His jaw clenched once, a tell I knew as well as my own reflection. "Nothing," he said. "Just... maybe let someone else do the heavy lifting for a bit. At least until you can open a jar of pickles without swearing."

A real laugh bubbled up, surprising both of us.

"There she is," he murmured, so soft I almost didn't hear it.

The bin on the table seemed to grow heavier just from looking at it.

"I should get this to the back before facilities locks up," I said, wrapping my good hand around the edge again, like if I kept busy enough, Shane would go away, and I wouldn't have to feel this pull between us.

Before I could get leverage, his hand came down over mine.

"I've got it," he said.

For a suspended second, neither of us moved. My skin buzzed where we touched, his fingers brushing the inside of my wrist, just above the hidden bruise. I watched his gaze flick down, lingering on the flash of discolored skin peeking out from under my bracelet before dragging back up to my face.

My lungs felt like wet paper bags.

I snatched my hand back like I'd been burned, heart racing at the thought of Nathan finding us together any second, along with the thought of Shane calling my demons to the light. "You don't have to—"

"I know," he said. "Let me anyway."

He lifted the box like it weighed nothing, the muscles in his forearms flexing where he'd shoved his jacket sleeves up. I stared at the spot where our hands had been, heat crawling up my neck.

"Ari," he said after a beat, and when I dragged my gaze up, his eyes were on me, steady and serious. "About the other night..."

My heart lurched.

"I'm not going to push you," he said quickly, clearly reading the panic that must have flashed across my face. "I just... I left your house feeling like I'd failed you. Again."

I winced.

"And I wanted you to know that if you ever need... anything. A ride. A couch to crash on. Someone to yell at a wall with you... I'm here."

I shook my head automatically, the denial ready on my tongue before I'd even thought it through.

"It was just a weird night," I said. The lie came out smooth and practiced. "Hosting stresses me out. I get... emotional. It's not a big deal. I'm fine."

He watched me for a long moment, and I had the distinct, uncomfortable feeling of being seen. *Really* seen. It made my skin itch.

"Okay," he said eventually, nodding. "If that's what you want me to believe, I'll believe it. For now."

"For now?" I echoed.

He shifted the box in his hands, breaking eye contact for a second like he was giving me a chance to breathe.

"I'm going to ask you something else," he said. "Less heavy. I promise."

I exhaled slowly, tension easing by a fraction. "Less heavy sounds nice."

"I heard Nathan is out of town next week for Thanksgiving."

The way he said it, flat and assuming, made another thread of unease weave through my ribs. He was right, of course. I wondered if that was part of the reason Nathan had been so sweet all week. Was he trying to make up for the fact that he had to go back to Vegas during the holiday?

I didn't really mind. I was looking forward to some alone time, and Georgie was going to FaceTime me.

It did sting a little that I was never *asked* about these things, though. Nathan just told me, the decision already made without any input of mine. And he hadn't asked me to join him. I'd never been to Vegas. Maybe it would have been fun. But I wasn't even a thought.

"That's not a question," I pointed out.

"What are you doing while he's gone?"

I huffed, glancing down at my heels. My feet ached after walking in them all night. I didn't even know why I'd worn them. This event didn't call for a dress and heels. I'd have been better suited in jeans and a jersey and sneakers.

*But Nathan bought me this dress...*

Probably because he wanted to control how I looked.

"I don't know," I said. "FaceTime Georgie. Maybe volunteer at a kitchen. Order takeout, watch some trashy TV, read a book."

Silence stretched between us for a beat. When I looked up, Shane was watching me with ghosts in his eyes.

I wondered if he was thinking about our first Thanksgiving as a couple, the one where I nearly burned our apartment down.

"It feels wrong," he said finally, "you sitting alone with DoorDash on Thanksgiving while half the city eats themselves into a coma."

"I won't be alone," I argued weakly. "I'll have... Netflix."

"Ari," he said, voice soft with patience and something like amusement. "You know what I mean."

*God,* I loved when he said my name like that.

"Some of the guys on the team are doing a Friendsgiving," he said. "In honor of Daddy P's last season. We have a game the night before and the day after, so it won't be anything crazy, but... they've invited me. And I'd like to invite you."

I shifted.

"You'll have other friends there, too. Maven, Grace... I don't know if you've met the rest of that crew yet."

"We had a girls' night, actually."

"See? It's perfect."

The image bloomed in my mind before I could stop it — loud laughter, crowded table, mismatched chairs, someone shouting over a football game in the background. It sounded like the kind of Thanksgiving I'd only ever glimpsed in movies, the kind I'd dreamed of as a kid, the kind where people felt safe enough to talk too loud, eat too much, stay too long.

My chest ached.

"I don't know," I said, defaulting to the only defense I had left. "Nathan—"

"Will be in Vegas," Shane said gently, not unkind. "Working. Which, for the record, is fine. That's his choice. But you get to have choices, too, Ari."

Did I?

I wasn't sure.

I wasn't sure about anything anymore.

"I don't want to cause problems," I said quietly.

He shifted the box to one arm so he could free a hand,

like he had the impulse to reach for me and was physically restraining himself at the last second.

"You coming over to eat turkey and argue about whether pumpkin pie is superior to pecan is not causing problems," he said. "It's... living. It's being with friends."

That hadn't been exactly what I'd been referencing. The problem I was thinking of was what Nathan would do when he found out I went. But I didn't correct Shane because the word he'd said landed like a stone in my stomach.

*Friends.*

That's what we were now, what we were supposed to be. That had been the neat little label I'd put on whatever existed between us, because anything else was too big, too dangerous.

Too threatening to the life I'd worked so hard to build.

Funny, because some days, I felt like that life was tearing me apart from the inside.

"I'll think about it," I said, my voice barely above a whisper.

It was the most I could give him.

His shoulders dropped a little. "That's all I'm asking," he said. "If you decide you want to come, text me. I'll send you the address and the time. You can even show up late just for dessert if you want. No pressure."

"No pressure," I repeated, like if I said it out loud enough, it might feel true.

Footsteps echoed down the concourse then, voices bouncing closer. I recognized one of them immediately, the cadence, the lazy drawl.

Nathan.

Shane heard it, too. He took a step back, widening the distance between us, body instinctively shifting into something that looked more neutral, more... professional.

"Hey," he said, his voice just for me now, low and earnest. "Regardless of... anything. You should be proud of tonight. You did something good. For a lot of people."

I met his gaze, my throat suddenly thick.

"Thank you," I managed.

He nodded once, then turned, disappearing down the hallway with the box in his arms before Nathan rounded the corner.

"There you are," Nathan said when he spotted me, his tone light, like he was complimenting a well-trained dog who'd stayed where it was supposed to. "I've been looking all over."

I resisted the urge to tilt my head at that and ask *have you?*

"Just finishing up," I said, gesturing to the half-bare table. "The volunteers took most of the stuff down already."

He slid an arm around my waist, pulling me close enough that I could smell the whiskey on his breath. His fingers skimmed the line of my ribcage, stopping just shy of my wrist.

"Good," he said. "Come on. Jennings cut a big check tonight and wants to talk to you about setting up a Sweet Dreams donation box inside the Jennings Financial Building. Smile and be charming, okay?"

I nodded, tucking whatever fragile, flickering thing Shane had just put in my chest somewhere safe.

As we walked down the concourse, Nathan talking about Vegas and meetings and sponsorships and how this event would play in the press, I let my head tilt toward his shoulder at the appropriate moment. I laughed when he tossed out a joke. I agreed when he told me what our next steps should be.

I played my part.

But somewhere beneath all that, like a quiet drumbeat under a loud song, another thought pulsed.

Friendsgiving.

I didn't have to spend the holiday alone.

I could spend it with Maven and Grace, with the rest of the girls, with the team and a couple babies and pets.

And Shane.

That was the dangerous part. Not only had Nathan warned me to stay away from him, but I knew I walked a thin line when I was alone with him. It was too easy for the time between us to wane, for the young girl I was when I was with him to try to swim to the surface of my soul.

I knew he saw what so many others missed.

What scared me most was that I *wanted* him to see.

And I was starting to think I didn't care what the consequences of that desire were.

# CHAPTER 26

## MAN UP

Ariana
2007

"**M**om, *please*," I begged, embarrassment boiling me from the inside out as Jay continued to make a complete ass of himself.

And of me.

"I don't know what you expect me to do, honey," Mom said. Her voice was just a sigh of dejection, her eyes hollowed out, skin so pale it might as well have been translucent.

It was Thanksgiving, I was hosting for the first time, and it was a complete disaster.

Shane's grandparents hadn't been able to make it, thanks to a crazy snowstorm that had flights canceled left and right. We decided to still move forward with just my family in attendance.

Only the first hour had gone smoothly.

Jay, my mom, and Georgie showed up on time, all of them smiling and hugging and ready to eat. Mom put on the Macy's Thanksgiving Day Parade for Georgie and then helped me in the kitchen. Shane was on turkey duty.

And Jay started drinking.

Things had gone straight to hell after that.

The Macy's Thanksgiving Day Parade was barely an hour in when he planted himself in front of the TV with his third beer, heckling every float that drifted onto the screen. When the giant Snoopy balloon appeared, he barked, "Who the hell cares about a depressed dog?" and when the high school performers came out, he muttered something gross under his breath about the cheerleaders that made me want to crawl into the floorboards.

Georgie had been sitting cross-legged on the rug, wide-eyed and excited, but every time he tried to point something out — "Look, Ariana! It's Pikachu!" — Jay talked right over him, yelling about how the whole thing was "a soft participation-trophy circus." Eventually, Georgie just... stopped talking.

He curled in on himself, shrinking smaller with each slurred commentary Jay shouted at the screen.

And that was only the start.

Once the parade ended, Jay decided Georgie needed to learn how to throw a football. He grabbed one of my decorative pumpkins and chucked it across the apartment to demonstrate — where it exploded against the wall, seeds sliding down the paint. He only laughed, grabbing another beer as if this was all perfectly normal.

Then came the kitchen critiques. Jay stumbled around the kitchen assessing every aspect of my perfectly planned day. He lifted pot lids, stuck his fingers into the mashed potatoes, and started gagging after tasting the cranberry sauce. It was a nice touch when he called Shane "chef boy-ar-dumb" when he asked my mom how to make turkey gravy — which he'd only done to try to include her.

Through it all, I could see how hard Shane worked to restrain himself, to be kind to my asshole of a relative when I knew he wanted to throw him right out. He let me know he was with me every time he passed — a hand on my back, a kiss to my cheek, a smile from across the kitchen.

I was still mortified.

Mom had trailed behind Jay silently for a while, fixing whatever he messed with — the thermostat he kept cranking, the fridge he left open after getting another beer, the cabinet door he let slam hard enough to rattle the shelves. But eventually, she just gave up.

By the time the casseroles went in the oven and the football games started, the beautiful holiday I'd imagined was gone. The whole day had dissolved in front of me — one humiliating, heartbreaking moment at a time.

And now, we were less than ten minutes from dinner being ready and it was pure chaos.

"Come on, Georgie. You gotta man up! Not gonna be a boy forever!" Jay was screaming so loud I was sure all our neighbors in the apartment building could hear. He shoved my little brother down to the ground, rolling his eyes when Georgie cried before Jay was screaming for him to stand again.

"Don't cry like a girl. Get mad! Fight back!"

He pushed Georgie again and my heart cracked.

He wasn't hurting him, the shoves soft enough to just land Georgie on his butt. But the kid was just barely six years old, and I could see it in his eyes — it was the same emotion I'd grown up with my whole life.

Fear.

Shane's hand swept across my lower back gently, but I still winced, my cortisol levels through the roof. I turned to him wide-eyed, and my fingers curled in his sweater as I clung to him. "I am so sorry. I'm... I'm mortified." My eyes grew wider when I spotted the water I was boiling for the stuffing spilling over onto our stovetop. "Shit!"

Jay carried on in the living room as I ran to handle the mess before I burned the whole place down. Everything seemed to be happening all at once: the stuffing needed to go in the water, the rolls needed to go in the oven, the casseroles needed to come out, I needed to whip up the gravy, Jay needed to go the fuck to sleep or something, and Mom was so useless all I wanted her to do was get out of my way.

My heart was aching beneath all the panic, the sour reality of the holiday at war with what I'd had pictured in my mind. I was naïve to think we could host a beautiful, calm holiday with my family here, that we could have a normal dinner where everyone smiled and went around the table saying what they were thankful for.

Thank *God* Shane's grandparents couldn't make it.

I shuddered at the thought of them being here to witness the disaster.

Somewhere in the background as I dashed around the kitchen, I heard my mom try to wrangle Jay. It was a feeble attempt, and he screamed at her for it before lifting his hand in warning. He seemed to remember where he was before he put it back down and sulked on the couch, draining the beer in his hand before storming to get another.

My lungs seized.

How were we supposed to do this?

How were we just supposed to sit down and have dinner with him in this state?

Panic clawed at my throat.

Suddenly, the television cut out.

"Hey!" Jay screamed. "The game is on!"

"I thought we could all play a game ourselves, instead."

Shane stood with a grin — holding two Nintendo Wii controllers in his hands.

He handed one to Georgie and then to Jay. "What do you say? Some good old-fashioned competition? Georgie, I'll be on your team. Bowling or tennis first?"

Jay grumbled, but I could see it in his glazed eyes — his interest was piqued. He was nothing if not competitive. "Bowling."

"You're on!" Shane said, and the way he was smiling, the way he bent down to Georgie and helped him pull bowling up on the screen before talking him through the controls like nothing wrong had happened all day...

It wrecked me.

Tears flooded my eyes when Shane glanced up and found my gaze across the room.

"Thank you," I mouthed.

He smirked, winking at me like it was nothing.

It was everything.

It was him seeing me for exactly who I was, for exactly where I came from, for exactly the baggage I held — and staying, anyway.

It didn't scare him.

It didn't seem to faze him at all.

We somehow survived dinner. Jay passed out not long after, and the rest of us had a peaceful evening playing board games.

And later that night, when I crawled into bed with Shane, he pulled me into his chest and let me cry. He held me through every shake of my shoulders, and then he wiped the tears away and swept my hair from my face, his hands framing my cheeks, eyes locked on mine.

"I am so in love with you," he whispered.

And then he showed me it was true until I forgot about everything else from that day.

## CHAPTER 27

### WITHOUT LOOKING BACK

Shane
Present

The first time I ever had a gut feeling about something, I was seven years old.

It was the night my parents died.

I was with my grandparents. Mom and Dad had been on a trip together celebrating their anniversary. They ended up flying home one day early to try to beat the snowstorm barreling toward the south — a region of the States ill equipped to handle what was coming.

I remember leaning over the back of Grandma's couch and staring out the window as the snow fell down. I thought it was so pretty, but it also made my stomach turn.

"I don't like the snow," I'd said to Grandma.

"That's silly. Every kid likes snow."

"It's dangerous."

She'd frowned at that, ruffling my hair. "What an odd thing to say about snow."

I think sometimes the universe tips us off. It gives us that little wriggle in our stomachs or tightening of our chest for a reason. I'd listened to that gut feeling ever since that night, no matter how ridiculous it felt, because I trusted my body. I trusted my instinct.

And now I had a gut feeling that Nathan Black was doing something to compromise the integrity of our game.

It started as nothing more than a flicker in the back of my mind, and I'd convinced myself I was being ludicrous because Ariana being back in my life had scrambled my brain. I didn't like the man because he was with her, and I was fairly certain it wasn't a good relationship.

But over the last two weeks, that flicker had grown teeth.

Nathan's sudden trips to Vegas were easy enough to write off as work-related, but now I wondered what *exactly* he was doing there. The way he strutted around the facility like he owned not just the team, but the men on it, only added to my suspicion. The way some of my players had been acting was heavy on my mind, too — jokes dying the second I walked into the locker room, eyes cutting away, tension where there'd never been any.

None of it proved anything. But it all struck the same nerve.

I had a very slimy feeling that something gambling-adjacent was happening.

I didn't tell anyone. I'd considered confiding in my assistant, Kozak, but the truth was I knew I had to be absolutely certain before I breathed a word of it to anyone.

And part of me hoped I was wrong.

Because if I was right, then it meant the mess went deeper than any of us wanted to consider — that the boys might be involved, that they may be being pressured or promised something behind closed doors.

It also meant I could lose Ariana before I'd even truly had her back.

I didn't have proof of any foul play, and I hated that I was even thinking it. But the thought wouldn't leave me alone, and I'd learned too young not to ignore that gut feeling.

So, I started writing things down. Dates of his trips and games that felt odd. Comments I heard from him or other staff members or players. Looks between people that made me suspicious. Patterns I hadn't noticed before but felt keyed into now. It felt insane, maybe even personal, but the truth was simple: once the idea took hold, I couldn't shake it.

I must have had the tension of my sleepless nights written in my expression on Thanksgiving, because Daddy P clapped his hand hard on my shoulder and shook me a little.

"Earth to Coach," he said, just loud enough for me to hear. He smirked when I blinked back to the present. "It's impossible for you to take a day off, isn't it?" he teased. "I can see video playing in your head like your eyelids are projector screens."

I chuckled, tilting my beer bottle to my lips on a shrug. We were standing in his backyard, an expansive thing with a massive pool and hot tub and pool house where Chloe stayed before they were a couple.

It was elite outdoor entertaining space — plush couches and chairs, a giant television beneath a shaded patio, Sonos speakers. Chef Patel was manning — or should I say, *womaning* — the smoker while Will's uncle watched her in awe. The house and yard were alive with holiday festivities. Maven and Livia were sprawled out in the grass with their babies crawling all over them and giggling at the bubble machine Chloe had set up. Ava — Will's daughter — was practicing her slap shot with Carter on one end of the pool while Jaxson and Vince argued about how to set the table. Aleks and Mia were cuddled up on a pool float, oblivious to the world around them, and Grace was glued to the TV like she had money on the game, her fist thrusting into the air any time the Tarpons made a first down.

It made my chest ache as much as it made me smile, seeing such a lively holiday scene. My grandparents were gone now. My parents had been since I was a kid. I typically spent Thanksgiving alone at the arena, my focus entirely on the season and whatever game we were playing next.

Sometimes I thought about what my holidays could have been like in another world, one where I hadn't walked away from Ariana because I thought it was the right thing to do.

I tried not to dwell on it.

"We both know St. Louis won't be easy on us tomorrow," I said. "At least one of us needs to be focused on how to win."

"I was honestly surprised you accepted the invitation," Will said. "And I'm glad you did. I think we all need a day off after the craziness lately."

My stomach vaulted at his words, that suspicion lying dormant inside me stirring again. "It has been an interesting season so far, hasn't it?"

Daddy P shook his head. "You're telling me. Not exactly what I pictured for my last season." He frowned, shifting his weight with a wince like his hip was bothering him. "I can't put my finger on it, why this injury has suddenly become such a... problem."

"Oh, I can answer that," Jaxson said, joining us with a grin and an elbow nudge to his goalie. "You're an old fart."

Will flattened his lips. "Maybe. What's your excuse for hitting glass more than the damn goalie?"

"His head is in the clouds planning a secret wedding," Vince chimed in, and Jaxson nut-tapped him before the guys were all laughing.

Their banter continued on, but my focus was drifting... because there it was. Another reason for my hackles to be raised.

Why *was* this injury suddenly something knocking Daddy P out of games left and right, giving Ben Sandin more time on the ice than any of us projected?

I didn't want to let my mind wander down that road. I sure as *hell* didn't want to entertain even the remote possibility that someone on our training staff was in on whatever Nathan was orchestrating.

Fortunately, all my thoughts were erased in a pinch.

Because Ariana walked through the door.

For a second, the noise around me blurred, like the world had softened its edges just for her. Sunlight spilled in behind her through the open doorway, catching in the loose fall of her hair as it brushed her shoulders, turning the dark blonde strands almost molten. She wore a soft knit sweater that hugged her in a way that made my chest tighten, paired with jeans and boots that said she hadn't overthought this, that she'd come as herself.

And her smile was just as soft.

She looked lighter than she had at the Skate for Change event, like the version of her I used to know — the one who laughed without checking the room first, who didn't carry tension in every line of her body.

Seeing it hit me harder than I expected, a quiet ache settling deep in my chest. I told myself, not for the first time, that this was all I was allowed now. Watching. Not touching. Not reaching. Just taking her in like a memory I wasn't permitted to disturb.

"Ariana! You made it!"

That squeal of a greeting came from Grace, who had her arms thrown around Ariana's neck in an instant. Ariana laughed a little as she strained not to drop or smush the pie in her hands. She'd let herself in the front door of the house and was joining us through the sliding glass door that led outside. Will and Chloe had it open so people could easily flow in and out, and the weather was perfect for it, one of those Florida days that *almost* felt like a real fall.

Her eyes slid to me, her cheeks flushing, but then her attention was pulled to the next person approaching her with a greeting. This time, it was Maven, who had a smiling, cooing Rowan on her hip.

I watched from a distance, letting everyone else welcome Ariana in. Chloe took the pie from her hands and walked it inside as everyone else handed out hugs and smiles and welcomes. Ava insisted Ariana come watch her "bring the noise" on Fabri, who barked out a laugh and said he'd like to see her try. But before they could pull her away, I slid in with my heart in my throat.

"Ari," I said.

Her blue eyes glittered as she lifted them to meet my gaze. "Shane."

"I'm glad you came."

She shrugged, tucking her hair behind her ear before she looked down at her feet. "I'm glad for the invite."

She smiled a little when she looked up at me through her lashes, and I swore my fucking heart thrummed like it was a string she'd plucked with that gaze. I opened my arms for a hug, and she slid in and wrapped her arms around me like it was nothing.

In an instant, I flashed back to when we were kids, to how I'd wait up for her the nights she volunteered late, or she'd wait up for me after games. I could still smell our old apartment, the pine-scented candles she loved to light, and the old leather of the hand-me-down couch. I buried my nose in her hair, wondering if she was remembering, too.

Ava cleared her throat. "Do you two know each other or something?"

That little girl cocked a brow at us, pointing a finger at me and then Ariana and then back to me.

I chuckled, reluctantly letting Ariana go. "We went to college together."

"Oh," Ava said, her shoulders jumping in a little shrug. "I thought maybe you were married."

"You know I'm not married," I challenged.

She shrugged again. "Yeah, but *everyone* is not married until they are." She rolled her eyes as if that was so obvious and I was a dumbass, and then bounded off without another word, running toward the hockey station she had set up — complete with a goal and everything.

Carter smirked at me and Ariana, who was covering her laugh with one hand. "I mean, she's not wrong." And with a wink, he jogged off after Ava.

"Welcome to the chaos," I said to Ariana, who was blushing furiously and still covering her mouth.

"She's adorable."

"That she is. So... I take it Nathan is gone?"

Her smile faded. "He flew out yesterday."

I nodded, searching her gaze for... what, I don't know. My mind was a mess with her here in front of me now. I thought about the dinner at her house, the way Nathan had treated her, her wrist...

But I also heard her voice from the Skate for Change event, the confidence when she'd assured me everything was fine, that it had just been a weird night and she'd been stressed.

It was a lie.

I knew it. She did, too.

I also knew better than to push.

After that night at her house, after the way Nathan talked to her in front of me and every other staff member like she was an inconvenience instead of his wife, I'd wanted to light the whole damn place on fire. But Ariana wasn't a player in my locker room I could call into my office and demand the truth from. She was a woman I cared about — still — and whatever was happening behind closed doors had her looking spooked and unsure, like she was trying to hold every piece of herself together with shaking hands.

So I played it the way I would with a guy who'd taken a hard hit and wasn't ready to admit he was hurt: with patience, presence, and no pressure. She'd talk when she was ready. The truth always comes out eventually. But until then, all I could do was give her a day where she didn't have to flinch or apologize for breathing. A day where she could just... *be*.

Thanksgiving felt like the one thing I could give her without crossing a line.

And thankfully, once she settled in, the day did exactly what I'd hoped it would.

Ariana eased into the mayhem like she'd been born in it. At first, she hovered close to me, shoulders tight, smile a little too careful and practiced. It made me think of the dinner at her house, how it had felt like a performance. But the longer she was at Will and Chloe's, the more the tension in her shoulders softened.

Grace brought her a glass of wine, claiming "doctor's orders" before pointing to Livia as the doctor. We watched football and chatted, Ariana slowly chiming in more and more as she relaxed. She told the crew about her brother, about growing up in Connecticut, about her time working in various nonprofit sectors. A little before dinner, Ava insisted Ariana help her name her imaginary team, a very serious task that involved a clipboard, stickers, and Ava's best businesswoman voice. That got Ariana laughing, a real laugh, one that made her shoulders drop and her eyes brighten.

I felt something in my chest loosen at the sight.

She moved with ease into the kitchen after, helping Chloe and Livia pull casseroles from the oven while Mia teased Aleks about sneaking a bite out of a turkey leg before Chef Patel swatted him away with a wooden spoon. Maven handed Rowan off so she could teach Ariana how to fold the cloth napkins "restaurant fancy," and Ariana showed her own method, which Maven loved so much she declared her the new napkin boss.

Through it all, I watched in real time as the ice defrosted, as her smiles turned more genuine, as her laughs came easier.

It was impossible not to see the contrast between this version of her and the Ariana from the executive dinner. A blink and I could see her that night, her shoulders tucked near her ears, eyes never moving without permission, voice held tight in her throat like she was afraid to speak out of turn.

Here, she didn't have to hold back. She didn't have to pretend.

By the time we all settled around the long outdoor table — the sun low, the pool lights glowing, babies babbling from their highchairs set up between their parents — Ariana looked like she belonged to this world more than any of us.

Will stood at the head of the table, wine glass lifted. "I know we've got a big game tomorrow," he said, sweeping his gaze around at the team, "but in the spirit of the holiday, I wanted to say... thank you. I'm not a man of many words, but I have infinite love for all of you here. You've been the best team. You've loved my kid like your own. You've welcomed my beautiful wife into our family with open arms."

"Oh, if you ever get divorced — we call dibs on her in the separation," Grace said, pointing her roll at Daddy P before popping a piece in her mouth.

"If you ever get divorced, I'll actually kill you," Livia threatened, picking up her knife. "Because we all know it'd be your fault."

Chloe flushed as Will laughed, winking at her. "She's stuck with me. Promise." He turned his attention back to all of us. "It's been an honor to be your goalie. And Coach," he added, finding my gaze.

Oh *fuck*.

I saw it, the moment his eyes watered, and I felt mine do the same.

"You are one hell of a leader. I've watched you mold this team over the years into something unrecognizable from what you first walked into. It's been my privilege to play for you, and I know you'll do amazing things in my absence, too."

I cleared my throat, holding up my glass of wine with a wordless nod.

"To the Ospreys," Chloe said, tilting her water to the sky. "And to family."

"Hear, hear!" Vince hollered, clinking his glass against Jaxson's.

Jaxson rolled his eyes. "Stop pretending you're sentimental."

"I'm very sentimental," Vince argued. "I put cinnamon in the sweet potato casserole and smothered it with marshmallows. That's love."

Grace flicked a green bean at him. "You also *ate* half the sweet potato casserole before we even put it on the table."

"I had to test it!" he fired back.

Ariana laughed so hard she nearly spilled her wine. I didn't think she realized she'd leaned into me until I felt the soft press of her shoulder against mine. And when she did notice, she straightened quickly, cheeks pink, brushing a strand of hair off her face.

*God*, I missed her.

I knew it was ridiculous, to miss someone right next to me, but I did. I missed her like I missed the leaves changing color in Boston, like I missed the way it felt to be hugged by my parents, like I missed having a hip and knee that didn't ache every day.

I missed her like she was a part of me, one I'd learned to live without somehow. But now that she was here with me, I knew I couldn't even pretend to try to live without her again.

"And speaking of family," Chloe said over the noise, her eyes skirting to Will before she stood and held her glass up higher. "Ours is expanding."

Three words and the whole table was silent — for all of a second, anyway. Then, it exploded with noise.

"You're pregnant?!" Maven asked, her eyes already welling with tears.

Chloe nodded, her eyes flooding, too, and then the girls were surrounding her while all the guys ran to congratulate Will.

"*Finally*, I can talk about it!" Ava burst, lounging in her chair like she was exhausted from holding it in. "I've been dying!"

"You're going to be the best big sister to ever live," Grace said, giving Ava a big hug.

Carter waited until the clamor of noise died down and everyone was back in their seats before nudging my ribcage with his elbow. "Hey, Coach," he murmured, low enough not to draw attention. When I hummed in acknowledgment, he grinned. "Not to be dramatic or anything, but I haven't seen you this happy since... ever."

I rolled my eyes, but he wasn't done. He tipped his chin toward Ariana, who was telling Ava she would love her help picking out stuffed animals for the Sweet Dreams toy drive.

Carter smirked. "I'm glad you came. And I'm guessing *you're* glad *she* came."

I did my best not to react, but I had a feeling it was pointless. The way Carter cocked a brow told me he'd seen right through me — which meant I'd been doing a shit job hiding my feelings for Ari.

Still, I didn't entertain him with a response. I just sipped my wine and dug into my plate while he chuckled from beside me.

Dinner went on like that — loud and fun and messy in all the best ways.

Aleks was mostly silent, but he watched Mia dumbstruck as she regaled the table with her tales from her tour; Chloe kept disappearing inside to grab "just one more thing," even though the table was already perfect, and apologizing for the cat hair that no one else seemed to notice; Livia kept swearing her daughter Lennon said her first real word ("no") when Carter tried to wipe her face; Maven and Grace ganged up on Vince about how he was, in fact, the softest girl dad in the world as he attempted to wrangle Rowan's hair into tiny pigtails; and Jaxson tried

— unsuccessfully — to convince Ava to stop calling him "Uncle Four Eyes," a nickname Vince had suggested when Jaxson had taken out his contacts and switched into his glasses.

Ariana watched it all with wide, dazzling eyes. She helped pass dishes. She teased Vince right alongside the girls, throwing in how she was soft for her brother in the same way. She let Ava braid a section of her hair with sparkly butterfly clip-ins. She somehow got Aleks to talk to us about growing up in Switzerland, which was a feat. She ended up with both babies in her lap when dessert was served, and she laughed and used her fork as a choo-choo train to shovel pie into each of their little mouths, not caring in the slightest when blobs fell onto her sweater in the process.

She was a part of them — effortlessly.

A part of *us*.

Like she'd always been meant to be here.

I watched her in the soft glow of the patio lights, the breeze lifting her hair, her laughter drifting across the table like a song I still knew by heart.

For the first time in a long time, Thanksgiving didn't feel like just another day at the office.

It felt like hope.

I did my best to squash it before it swelled too deep in my chest, but it was useless. I couldn't help but watch her and wonder if she was feeling it, too — if that joy radiating off her felt like the relief I'd been so desperate to give her.

I walked Ariana out to her car around eight. I didn't want to leave, didn't want *her* to leave, but she told the crew she needed to get home to FaceTime Georgie, and I used it as an excuse to head to the arena to prepare for tomorrow's game.

The quiet of the night surrounded us once the door was shut, a jolt of laughter following us out into the cool night. I smiled, stuffing my hands in my pockets so I wouldn't reach for Ariana.

"That was so fun," she said, digging in her purse for her keys. She unlocked her car with two beeps and a flash of the lights. "I can't remember the last time I had a Thanksgiving like that." She shook her head. "I never have, actually."

"Not even with Nathan and his family?"

She snorted. "Please. His family is so hoity toity, they wouldn't be caught dead at a table with babies. They had enough trouble the first year I brought Georgie, and he was a teenager."

Her eyes widened, like she just realized she'd said something she shouldn't have.

"Don't take it back," I said. "This is a safe place. You can say whatever you want, no judgment."

She sighed, looking down at the keys in her hand as we reached her car. "It's terrible, though, isn't it? How easy it was for me to talk shit about my husband?" She shook her head.

I wanted to say so many things, but I kept quiet, afraid she might change the subject or backtrack if I spoke too soon.

"I just..." She blew out a shaky breath, her free hand slipping into her hair. "I just don't know how I got here."

Her voice was small — not fragile, but honest in a way that made my chest tighten. She looked up at me, then down again, like the words were fighting their way out.

"One moment I'm just a young girl falling in love," she said softly, "and the next I'm... I'm this woman I don't recognize at all. I don't have any friends. I don't have any purpose outside of Sweet Dreams, which wasn't even mine to begin with. I don't feel butterflies anymore. I don't feel... *anything*."

My heart cracked open.

"And I love Nathan," she added quickly, instinctively, reflexively — the way someone says "I'm fine" after they've been limping for miles. "I do. He's... I know he's a great man, a great husband. I know I'm lucky. I just..."

Her voice thinned.

She swallowed hard, eyes shining.

"Sometimes I..." She shook her head, wiping at tears before they fell. "I'm sorry. I don't know what I'm saying."

"Don't apologize," I murmured, stepping closer. "Not to me."

She laughed — a broken, bitter little exhale — like she half expected me to tell her she was being dramatic.

But I never would. I wasn't him.

Ariana inhaled, a long trembling breath that lifted her shoulders and dropped them again.

"Tonight was... *God*, it was like seeing another life I could have had. I felt so at ease. I loved being here with this family, with Ava and Rowan and Lennon, with all these people who so quickly called me a friend. I could see Georgie here with all of them."

She paused, throat shifting before she looked at me.

"With you."

The air changed, thickening and humming and pulling tight like a wire between us.

I felt it down to the bone.

Her gaze didn't waver, even as the atmosphere sizzled between us. Years from our past flickered like highlight reels in my mind — and I knew she was experiencing the same. I saw it in the flush of her cheeks, in the way she leaned into me, the way hope flashed in her eyes.

"Do you remember the time we hosted Thanksgiving together?" she asked.

"I remember everything, Ari."

Her breath caught, and the way she looked at me emboldened me to continue, to not waste this chance. I didn't care if it was wrong. I didn't care that she bore the last name of another man, that the man she'd sworn vows to was my boss.

At the end of the day, she didn't belong to him. She never could.

Because she was mine, and I was hers, and no amount of time or distance could ever change that.

I reached up, sweeping a strand of hair gently behind her ear before my hand cupped her cheek.

She trembled under my touch, even as she tilted into it, like she was afraid to give into the desire I felt pulsing through her.

"Every day," I said quietly. "Every night. Every word and touch and kiss."

My thumb brushed her jaw, heart pounding in my throat with every syllable I uttered.

"You are embedded in me like the code that makes me operate. You were then. You still are now."

"Shane..." she whispered, shaking her head — but she didn't move away. She didn't pull back.

I framed her face with both hands, tilting her chin just enough that her eyes fluttered closed.

"If you tell me to stop, I will." My voice dropped to a raw whisper. "But selfishly... I really hope you don't. I want to kiss you, Ari. I've wanted to kiss you since the moment you crashed back into my life. Please..." I swallowed, wetting my lips. "Let me kiss you."

For a heartbeat, she hovered there — breath trembling, body leaning, soul caught between fear and longing.

And then she pressed up onto her toes, searing my mouth with the gentle brush of her lips.

It was the gunshot that set off a chain of reactions — her gasping, me inhaling a breath that burned my lungs, the night air around us pulling taut before it snapped like a rubber band.

I descended, my mouth firm against hers as my heart pounded in my chest. I wanted to go slow. I wanted to savor that kiss and each tender press of her lips against mine.

But I was like a caged beast, and she'd unlatched the door.

My fingers curled in her hair, cradling the back of her neck and holding her to me. I sucked in a breath on that kiss, and when I opened my mouth and she did the same, letting my tongue in to dance with hers, I moaned, deep and guttural.

"Fuck, I've needed this for so long, Ari," I groaned, kissing her harder, more frantic. "Needed *you*."

I backed her into her car, pinning her against the door and pressing the full weight of me into her. I wanted her to feel how my heart raced out of control, how I trembled where I held her, how every breath was shaking out of me.

"You think you're hiding it," I whispered against her mouth, brushing my nose to hers before I was stealing another long kiss.

I was greedy. I could never have enough.

"But I know you, Ari. I've always known you. I see when you're scared. I see when you're shrinking yourself to survive." Our foreheads were together, her hands knitted in my sweater as I shook my head against hers. "It kills me not to pull you out of whatever situation is making you do that."

Her breath hitched as I kissed down her throat, up over her jaw, claiming her mouth again with a kiss I hoped said more than any words could.

"You deserve to breathe, Ari," I whispered. "You deserve to speak without flinching. To exist without apologizing. I don't know what happens behind your doors, but I know what it does to you. I can see it in your eyes."

My thumb swept her cheek.

"And I swear to God, I'm trying to respect the life you chose. The vows you made. But if you ever... if you ever looked at me and said you needed a way out—" I swallowed hard. "I'd take your hand and run. Tonight. Right now. Without looking back."

I exhaled, trembling.

"I'd choose you, Ari. Over everything. Every time."

She whimpered, and then her arms were around my neck, pulling me into her. She hiked one leg up and I answered by lifting her completely. Her dress slid up, the fabric bunching at her hips, and we both groaned when I pressed against her, when the heat of me combined with the heat of her.

"Fuck," I whispered, cock hardening at the feel of her, and she thrust against me with a moan of her own.

We were ravenous, kissing hard enough to bruise, teeth sinking into skin deep enough to mark.

And then, suddenly, she pulled back.

Ariana's hands pressed firmly into my chest, her eyes wide as they flicked between mine.

And I watched the exact moment guilt flooded over her, taking out any desire in its wake.

"Stop," she panted, and she couldn't look at me as she wiggled out of my grasp. I dropped her feet to the ground gently. "We have to stop."

"Okay."

"We have to stop now. Right now."

"Okay," I repeated, calmly. Once she was safely on the ground, I pulled away, even as my body and heart and fucking soul screamed in protest. I held up my hands, letting her see I was listening, that she was in control.

Her eyes finally met mine again, and then immediately welled with tears. She sniffed them back, shaking her head. "That was wrong. That was — we can't —"

"Okay. Ariana, it's okay."

"How can you say that?" Tears spilled over, and she swatted them away. "It's not okay. Nothing is okay. I'm *married*, Shane."

Her words sliced me to the bone.

"To your general manager," she added, digging the knife deeper. "Do you realize what it would mean for me, for *you*, if he ever found out what we just did?"

She ripped her car door open, and she might as well have ripped my heart from my chest in the process.

I wanted to beg her to stop, to stay, to talk to me, to *be* with me.

I wanted to scream *I don't fucking care what it would mean!*

But I'd already crossed a line, and I knew that even though she hadn't stopped me then, the invitation was revoked now.

"And you're a liar," she said with her back turned to me. She angled her chin over her shoulder just enough for me to see the pain in her face when she added, "You wouldn't choose me every time. You didn't even choose me the first time."

She was in the car in the next breath, her door slamming shut, engine firing to life, wheels screeching as she threw it in reverse.

I stood there like an idiot — chest heaving, mouth parted, hands still lifted like I was trying to hold on to something already long gone.

Her taillights burned into the night, two red smears bleeding into the dark as she shot down the driveway and disappeared around the bend.

I didn't chase her.

God, every cell in my body wanted to.

I wanted to sprint after her, pound on her window, tell her she had it all wrong — that I'd choose her now, tomorrow, always, that I'd never make that mistake again.

But wanting wasn't the same as deserving.

She'd trusted me with something raw and trembling and secret. And then I'd kissed her like every restrained thought in me had snapped.

She wasn't running from me.

She was running from what it meant that she didn't pull away.

I looked down at my hands — the same hands that had held her face, her waist, her heart for one impossible minute — and curled them into fists.

"If you think I won't fight for you this time," I whispered to the empty drive, "you don't know me at all."

The ache in my chest sharpened. It was the kind of pain that made me feel alive, the kind that existed because what I was fighting for mattered.

*She* mattered.

I wouldn't chase her now. She needed space. She needed safety. She needed breathing room.

But I could prove her wrong.

Her taillights were long gone, swallowed by the night, but I stayed there anyway — rooted to the driveway like leaving might undo the last ten minutes.

Hell, maybe I deserved to stand there and feel every ounce of what I'd been missing for years.

Because one thing was certain as the air finally settled around me:

She could run from the moment, from the intensity, from me.

But I would never run from her again.

And I didn't care what I risked in the process.

# CHAPTER 28

## DISAPPEAR

Ariana
Present

I stared at my hands — the weathered, textured skin of them and how my knuckles were white from gripping so tightly. I had them folded in my lap, and I looked at them as if it were the first time, as if they were something to discover, as if they held all the answers.

I didn't know who I was anymore.

Those hands were once young, once smooth and pale and devoid of the fine lines that marked them now. They once held fast to a boy who loved me and made me feel safe. They once cared for my younger brother, holding him and bathing him and teaching him how to ride a bike. They once worked for me, writing grant applications and college essays. They once helped the community I cared about so much.

Now, they were cold and brittle. They trembled from fear. They ached with loss. They longed for a past so far out of reach I couldn't even see it anymore.

Nathan came home the Sunday after Thanksgiving looking like a complete stranger. His eyes were red and underlined with a deep purple, like he hadn't slept all week. He kissed me absentmindedly upon his arrival, immediately showering and then passing out until he had to work the next morning.

When he finally asked me what I did for Thanksgiving after not checking in even *once* on his trip, I told him the truth.

And it had been a mistake.

At first, I didn't think he cared. "You were gone and they invited me," I'd explained, and he'd acted like it was no big deal. But after a long, quiet dinner, he'd started in on the questions.

*"Where was it?"*

*"How long did you stay?"*

*"Who was there?"*

Every question was careful and calculated, but it was enough for me to know he was building a story in his mind. Somehow, by the end of the conversation, I was backpedaling and trying to justify why I went. I felt guilty.

*Me.*

The one who was left behind while he went to Vegas for the holiday, who would have spent that holiday *alone* had it not been for Shane's invitation.

But Nathan didn't care.

He'd have rather me been alone, if his tone was any indication.

And I *should* have felt guilty — not for spending Thanksgiving with friends, but for what I did after.

Except I didn't.

I didn't feel a single ounce of anything other than longing when it came to what happened with Shane. I wished for a world where I could have stayed right there in his arms, where I could have let him kiss me senseless, where I could have believed him and the notion that it could all be so easy.

*"I'd take your hand and run. Tonight. Right now. Without looking back."*

A chain twisted around my heart and pulled tight at the memory of those words, at how desperately I wished for them to be true.

But for the first time since the day Shane McCabe walked away from me, I understood why he did it.

It was the same reason I couldn't stay, the same reason I couldn't entertain his offer.

I loved him. Even still, maybe always, I loved him.

And I loved him enough to not let him lose everything that mattered to him just for me.

If I would have let him take me home, if we would have crossed even further over that line between us, everything would have imploded. Nathan would have lost his mind — he already was just with the knowledge that I was in the same household with Shane for Thanksgiving.

"I told you to stay away from him," he'd seethed.

"He was one of like fifteen people, Nathan," I'd explained, exasperated. "I was invited and so was he. What was I supposed to do? Walk out because he was there and just spend Thanksgiving by myself?"

"I'm not angry because you went," he'd said slowly, like he was meticulously picking each word to make sure they hit their mark. "I'm angry because you knew exactly how much it would hurt me — and you decided my feelings mattered less than your discomfort." He'd tilted his head, looking at me as if he didn't know me. "That tells me everything I need to know."

If I were the woman I was even a week ago, he would have achieved his goal. I would have died from guilt and apologized and beat myself up for days, wondering what the hell I was doing.

As it stood now, I only felt suspicious and numb.

But his reaction did solidify the truth in my mind: Nathan would have come after Shane if I were to leave. He would fire him, at the very least, and kill him, at the very worst.

And he wouldn't just let me go.

There wouldn't be an easy divorce where we just sign a few pages and go our separate ways. He would make it drag. He would make it hurt.

He'd take everything — including Georgie's tuition money.

I had nothing without him. I hated that fact, but it was true. My degree was old and unused. Every nonprofit I'd been involved with since we married had been under Nathan's thumb, which meant he held the key to all my references of the last ten years.

I didn't have a dime to my name because he managed all our money.

He promised to take care of me.

And I stupidly trusted him.

Worse than anything that might happen to *me* was what would happen to Shane.

He would have his job ripped from him, his only tie to hockey gone in a flash. And Nathan would make sure he never had another job in the league.

It would be over for him.

And I knew hockey was everything in his heart.

It didn't make any of it hurt less, and I'd felt like a ghost going through the motions since the night I drove out of Will's driveway. I wanted to talk to Shane, to explain my coldness, to make sure he knew that I didn't regret that kiss, that I wished it could be more.

But I stayed away.

Nathan was watching me like a hawk, questioning everything — and now, it was bleeding into Sweet Dreams.

He'd been different since his return from Vegas, moving through our house with a quiet, methodical purpose, like he was taking inventory of a life he suddenly suspected wasn't his anymore. He combed through the mail the moment he walked in, asked offhand questions about packages I'd already opened. He checked the bank app over breakfast, eyes flicking to me as if he expected me to flinch. He lingered in doorways when I got ready for work, watching me the way a scientist might watch something that had slipped out of its enclosure.

His suspicion was a creeping, living thing.

When he asked what kept me out of the house until nearly midnight when I was preparing for the Sweet Dreams Gala, his jaw clenched at my reply. "You were working on Sweet Dreams that long?" He'd shaken his head. "Maven didn't mention staying that late."

The day after that, he wanted paperwork — invoices, schedules, timelines.

"Something feels off," he'd murmured, scrolling through his phone when I'd given him everything he'd asked for. "It's probably nothing. I just like things to be clean."

Then came the digs, soft as tissue paper, but sharp all the same.

*"You're always tired lately. Maybe Sweet Dreams is too much responsibility for you."*

*"We should review our budget. Georgie's tuition review is next month—don't forget."*

*"You looked flustered at the rink today. You should be careful. Optics matter."*

Each comment was mild, reasonable, even helpful if I looked at them sideways. But every one carved out a little more space inside me and replaced it with him.

And now, I was sitting alone in our bedroom with my hands folded tightly in my lap, trying to recover from the blow that finally took me down.

"I talked to PR," he'd said to me tonight, loosening his tie as he sat down at the table I'd set for dinner. "Given your... emotional connection to the families, it's better if you step back from Sweet Dreams. Let Maven and Grace take point on the gala. You can help from behind the scenes."

Panic had slithered in and choked me like a snake.

"Nathan..." I wished I could say my voice was even and calm, but it was impossible for his name not to be a shocked plea.

"It's better this way. You'll have more time to devote to the house. And we have your big birthday party coming up — your focus should be there."

"Nathan," I'd begged again, shaking my head as my eyes flooded with tears. "Please don't—"

"Don't what?" He'd tilted his head, as if he were innocent, as if he didn't know he was ripping my heart from my chest. "I'm protecting you, Ari. And the organization. You've been spreading yourself too thin lately. Besides, you don't want sponsors thinking you're too close to the beneficiaries. That wouldn't be good for anyone. Especially not Georgie."

And that was it — the veiled threat not so hidden any longer. He'd locked his eyes on me with the mention of my brother's name, as if he were daring me to try him.

We'd eaten the rest of dinner in silence, and then Nathan had excused himself to meet an "important business colleague" downtown for drinks.

Which was how I ended up here, perched on the edge of our bed, staring at my hands like they belonged to someone else. Like they might listen if I silently willed them to fight, to run, to save me.

But they only trembled.

I stood, walking slowly to our closet where I dug through my clothes on hangers to a hidden shelf behind them. Wrapped in an old reusable bag and covered with spare fabric from when I'd tried my hand at sewing was Shane's old Boston College Hockey hoodie.

I slipped it over my head and let the pain sear me, my eyes welling with tears as I fell into a heap on the closet floor. I curled into the hoodie, tucking my legs under it, pulling the sleeves over my shaking hands and inhaling deep as if the scent would still be there. It had faded long ago, but my memory of what it was to be loved by Shane McCabe never would.

I thought of my mother — of all the years I'd watched her shrink inside herself, bite down on her tongue, apologize for things that weren't her fault. I used to wonder why she didn't leave. How she didn't scream. Why she didn't run.

Now, I understood in a way that made my stomach lock up like a malfunctioning machine.

It broke my heart when she died. But lately... lately I'd caught myself wondering if it wasn't mercy in the end. I wondered if she didn't long for the quiet of it, if slipping away hadn't felt like opening a door that had been locked for years.

Because sometimes, even when I was ashamed to admit it to myself, the idea of not existing at all felt easier than living in a hell no one else could see.

My fingers curled, ice cold and shaking, nails digging into my palms.

I wasn't my mother.

But for the first time, I finally understood how someone like her — someone like me — could disappear without ever leaving.

## CHAPTER 29

### VERY, VERY WRONG

Shane
Present

When the Sweet Dreams Gala rolled around, I thought I was prepared.

I was prepared to wrangle the team into dancing for charity donations. I was prepared for our away game in Boston that we'd leave for the following day. I was prepared to put up with Nathan, to grin and bear the whole event like I didn't hate the prick. I was especially prepared to keep a close eye on him, to continue watching him for clues as to what he was up to behind closed doors.

What I was not prepared for, it turned out, was seeing Ariana.

I'd been counting down to it. I hadn't seen her since Thanksgiving, since she let me kiss her and then told me I was a liar. It wasn't for my lack of trying. I'd found my way into every Sweet Dreams meeting I could, even when I knew I wasn't needed — but she was never there. And when we had games, I looked for her in the suites, only to come up empty-handed.

She'd been staying home. She'd been avoiding me. At least, that was what I'd thought.

But one look at her tonight, and I knew there was something more at play.

She stood near the edge of the ballroom, light catching on her the way it always did, like the room had tilted subtly in her direction without anyone else noticing. Her hair spilled down her back in long waves of golden blonde, framing alabaster skin that seemed almost luminous against the black of her dress. It clung to her in all the right places, hugging the generous curve of her hips and the soft swell of her waist and chest. The fabric shimmered when she moved, fine glitter woven through it like starlight, and from her shoulders flowed a sheer draped train, part cape, part veil, trailing behind her like smoke.

She was absolutely breathtaking.

She was also, undoubtedly, not okay.

I knew it with one lingering look. I'd spotted her, my heart kicking back to life in my chest as I moved toward her, and then promptly stopped again.

In an instant, I saw through the makeup and dress.

Her smile didn't quite reach her eyes — not the way it used to, not the way it did when she was proud of something she'd built. Those blue eyes were glassy, distant, as if she were looking through the room instead of at it. Her posture was perfect, shoulders back, chin lifted, but it felt rehearsed — held together by willpower alone.

She shifted her weight where she stood next to Nathan, one heel sliding back, then forward again, like she was bracing herself for a blow no one else could see coming. One hand stayed curled at her side, fingers flexing and unclenching, betraying the tension she worked so hard to hide.

It didn't make sense.

This gala was her heart on display. Sweet Dreams was her vision, her fight, her sleepless nights and relentless hope stitched into every detail — and yet she looked like she'd rather be anywhere else, like she was counting the minutes until she could disappear, like the room was closing in on her instead of celebrating her.

Something was very, very wrong.

"Coach."

I snapped out of my daze, blinking to find Maven Tanev standing next to me. She was watching Ariana, too. Her eyes slid to me, and she nodded her head toward an empty corner cocktail table.

I followed her over, unable to help myself when I looked back over my shoulder at Ariana just in time to see Nathan put his hand on the small of her back and guide her across the room. They were set to give a speech on stage any moment.

As soon as we were at the table and away from prying ears, Maven tipped her champagne glass to her lips, looking around the room with a smile like we were just having a nice chat.

"What the fuck is going on with Ari?" she asked, still smiling, the words ground through her teeth.

"You see it, too?"

"Of fucking course, I see it. She looks like a walking corpse in a knockout dress. Where has she been? I haven't seen her since Thanksgiving."

I frowned at that. "You haven't? What about Sweet Dreams?"

"She told Nathan she didn't want to do it anymore, that she was stretched too thin." Maven shook her head. "I didn't understand it. Nathan came to one of our meetings and told me and Grace the news. He apologized for dumping it all back in our laps last minute and promised he was on the hunt to find a replacement. He... he made it sound like he was disappointed, like Ariana was quitting on us and that she had a tendency to do that."

I tried. *God*, I tried to keep my emotions hidden, to keep my shit together, but I just couldn't.

My jaw tightened, fingers curling into fists as I shook my head. "That motherfucker."

Maven arched a brow at me, plucking a glass of champagne off a tray that floated past. "Here. Drink this and smile. And then tell me what the hell is going on."

"I don't know for sure," I said, and we pretended to laugh before I added, "But my gut is telling me Ariana isn't safe, and that Nathan is controlling her. Manipulating her." I swallowed. "Maybe worse."

It was Maven's turn to clench her jaw. I'd seen this side of her before — namely when she and Vince were fighting like trained MMA fighters the season she followed him around for a reporting job. Maven was laid back and cool — until you pissed her off. Then, she was hell on wheels.

"There is no way Ariana would give up Sweet Dreams freely," I said with conviction. "You've seen her. You know how much she loves this program, how much she believes in it, how much she's put into it. Why would she walk away suddenly? And what else would have her *stretched too thin* to be a part of it?"

"He wants her to be a silent, beautiful little trophy on his arm," Maven mused, her brows pinched. "But *why*? What happened? What would make him take this from her when he's the one who assigned her to it in the first place?"

"That makes the most sense, doesn't it?" I pointed out, my stomach sick even before I said it. "He didn't give her Sweet Dreams because he believed in her."

Maven's eyes flicked back to the stage as Nathan and Ariana were announced, polite applause rising around us. My heart was racing in my chest. I didn't realize how badly I needed to talk to someone about this, how much I needed someone else to know what I suspected.

And I knew I could trust Maven.

"He gave it to her because it kept her where he wanted her," I went on quietly. "Gave her something that mattered, something public, something she couldn't say no to or walk away from without looking like the bad guy."

Maven stilled.

"It's a leash," I said. "A long one. It looks generous from the outside, makes him look like the supportive husband, the man who champions his wife's passions." My jaw clenched. "But it keeps her busy, exhausted, grateful — and firmly in his orbit."

"And when she actually started excelling, when she did such an incredible job with the Skate for Change event and had put so much into making tonight happen..." Maven said slowly.

"He yanked it," I finished. "He took it all back the second she was stepping into her own."

"Because he can't stand to see her actually thriving outside of her role being his wife?"

"Or because he didn't like her having too much time away from him where he couldn't keep tabs on her."

My eyes drifted back to Ariana, to the way she stood just a fraction behind Nathan instead of beside him. A fierce ache ripped through my chest, like my heart was trying to rip itself out and fly through the air to her, like it wanted to drag me onto that stage and get her in my arms where she belonged.

I felt powerless and reckless all at once, like I couldn't do anything, and like I'd do whatever it took, no matter the cost, to get her safe.

"Jesus," Maven muttered.

"He reframed it so she looks unreliable," I said. "So he looks disappointed. So the narrative becomes that Ariana quits things, that she can't handle the pressure, that she needs him to step in and manage things for her." My hands curled tighter around the edge of the table. "It isolates her, takes her away from you and Grace and the whole team, makes her doubt herself." I swallowed. "Makes everyone else second-guess her, too."

Maven's mouth pressed into a hard line. "And now she's stuck standing on that stage next to him, smiling like he didn't just strip her of the thing that gave her purpose."

"Exactly," I said. "This isn't him losing faith in her. This is punishment. Control. A reminder that everything she has goes through him first."

Maven exhaled slowly, fury simmering just beneath the surface. "So what now, Coach?"

I watched Nathan lean in toward Ariana, murmuring something in her ear that made her smile tighten another fraction.

My heart drummed inside me, unsteady and hurried. This felt like a moment that changed everything — the point of no return.

It felt like I was ready to risk it all.

"Now," I said, voice low and steady, "we stop letting him control the story. And we make damn sure Ariana knows she's not crazy — and she's not alone."

## CHAPTER 30

### TROJAN HORSE

Ariana
Present

Nathan's voice washed over the crowd like white noise.

I knew, distantly, what he was saying — something about donor generosity, something about community impact, something about how *we couldn't do this without you.*

But it was all muted.

I stood at his side, my hand resting lightly on his arm, smiling when I was supposed to, nodding along as if I weren't hearing the same speech he'd been giving in slightly different variations for years. I chimed in at the right moments — thanking benefactors by name, laughing softly at the right jokes, letting my gaze linger on familiar faces just long enough to seem engaged.

I played my part perfectly.

Inside, I felt hollow.

The ballroom glittered around us — crystal chandeliers, polished marble floors, gowns and tuxedos and champagne flutes catching the light — but all I wanted was for it to end. I longed for the night to be over, for the weight in my chest to loosen just enough that I could breathe again.

I wanted to go home.

My stomach twisted when I realized I never could again.

Home didn't exist anymore. It was just a house that didn't feel like mine, walls that closed in instead of sheltering, silence that felt loud with things I wasn't allowed to say. There was no room in it for me unless I stayed small, pleasant, and useful.

I swallowed hard, my smile never faltering even as I felt my soul dying within me.

Nathan kept on as I took a half a step to stand behind him. I stayed close enough to look united, but inched far enough away that no one would notice how rigid I felt, how carefully I held myself together. My feet ached in my heels. The sheer train of my dress brushed against my calves when I shifted my weight, and I found myself wishing it were a real cape, that I was a superhero somehow, that I could morph into someone else in that very moment.

If I could've slipped out of my own skin, I would have.

Applause rippled through the room, and I clapped along with it, my palms meeting softly and mechanically. Nathan leaned toward me, murmuring, *"Good job, sweetheart,"* as his hand settled at my lower back in a gesture that looked affectionate and felt like a reminder.

I was aware of him constantly: where he stood, who he was watching, how close he kept me.

As soon as we were off stage, we were surrounded. People flooded to Nathan's side like they had since the day I met him. He was magnetic like that, everyone drawn to his charm the same way I'd been.

I felt like a sucker now, and I couldn't help but think they were all suckers, too.

My cheeks hurt from the smile I forced as each person who surrounded us praised Nathan, shaking his hand like he was the goddamn president. I was an afterthought, of course, but I still smiled when they acknowledged me.

"Ariana," a bright voice cut in.

I blinked out of my haze, ears clearing like I'd just emerged from being underwater.

Grace appeared at Nathan's side with Maven just behind her, both of them beaming like this was the most natural interruption in the world even as the group of highly prestigious benefactors eyed them curiously, like they weren't sure what to make of them until they figured out how much money they had.

"You did wonderful on stage," Maven said, smiling at me brightly. I thought I saw something calculated in that smile when she turned to Nathan. "As did you, Mr. Black."

"Truly. You've been amazing, Mr. Black," Grace gushed. "The donors are eating this up. We've already been asked if the gala will be an annual event. They love the holiday cheer of it all."

Maven nodded enthusiastically. "Sweet Dreams wouldn't be what it is without you. We're so lucky the team brought you in this season."

Nathan preened just a fraction, the tension in his shoulders easing as he accepted the praise. "That's very kind of you," he said smoothly. "It's been a team effort."

"Well," Grace said, looping her arm through mine before I could react, "we were hoping to steal Ariana for just a minute."

Maven leaned in conspiratorially. "There's a photo booth set up near the back, and we really want pictures of the women who put this whole thing together. You know — for memories."

Nathan hesitated.

I felt it immediately — the way his grip tightened at my back, the way his gaze slid to my face, sharp and assessing. It was a silent question, a thinly veiled warning.

My pulse kicked up, my smile threatening to crack.

Then he laughed lightly, glancing around at all the affluent people he desperately wanted to impress who were very obviously watching him. "Of course," he said, gracious as ever. "Go ahead, darling. Have fun."

His hand slipped from my back with a kiss against my temple, but his eyes didn't soften when they found mine.

"Just don't take too long," he added, voice pleasant, pleasant, pleasant even as it sent chills down my spine. "We'll need to get back on stage soon to announce the final number of the night."

My chest constricted as I managed a nod.

Grace squeezed my arm. "We'll be quick," she said breezily. "Promise."

Maven added, "You won't even miss her."

They didn't give him the chance to change his mind.

They threaded their arms through mine, steering me away with laughter and light chatter, the sound of the crowd swallowing us as we moved deeper into the room.

"You okay?" Maven asked quietly once we were out of earshot.

"What?" I replied automatically. "Yeah. I'm fine."

The words came out flat. Empty.

Grace clicked her tongue softly. "Ari. Don't do that. Not with us."

I opened my mouth to argue, to insist I was okay, really, but my lip betrayed me, trembling before I could stop it. Heat burned behind my eyes, and suddenly everything felt too tight — my dress, my chest, the night itself.

Maven stopped walking. Grace did, too. "Oh, honey," Maven said, her voice so full of concern it broke me. "Come here."

They wrapped their arms around me, quick and fierce, like they were afraid I might vanish if they didn't hold on. It took every ounce of willpower I possessed not to completely fall apart in their arms.

*They see it.*

*They see* me.

I inhaled shakily. I didn't know whether to be relieved or fucking terrified.

"Okay," Grace murmured. "Okay. You're okay. All right? We're here. You're not alone."

I didn't know what to do, what to say. I stood stock-still where they held onto my arms after pulling back from the hug.

Maven glanced over my shoulder, scanning the room. "He's not looking."

Then she nudged me gently — but firmly — toward the photo booth curtains.

"Go," she whispered. "Just for a second. We'll keep an eye out and pull you when it's time."

I frowned. "What—"

The curtain parted.

And there was Shane.

It was the first time I'd seen him since he held me, since his lips were on mine, since I ripped away from him knowing I couldn't have what he was offering, that we couldn't take what would ruin us both.

The sight of him now had my heart in my throat.

His hair was styled, perfectly placed, but one rogue strand fell over his forehead. I longed to sweep it away. He wore a tailored charcoal suit, the silver threads of it bringing out the gray in his blue eyes. Those eyes were wide and fixed on me, a thousand questions within them.

He smiled, the corner of his lips tilting up as he made room for me next to him on the small bench.

That smile knocked me back to 2006.

Why was it that my heart clung to that time in my life so fiercely, to the boy who grew into the man before me now? A whole life, I'd lived, and yet nothing made me ache inside the way those two years with him did.

Is that what it meant to have a soul mate?

Did the universe really know I belonged to him in a way I couldn't anyone else? Did it remind me every time I was near him, daring me to leap into the timeline I was meant to live in and abandon the wrong path I'd somehow stumbled so far down?

"Go," Grace whispered, and with a little nudge of encouragement from her, I slipped inside the booth.

The curtain dropped behind me, the sound of the gala dulling behind it. I didn't realize how hard I was breathing until that very moment, until my chest heaved, and my ragged breaths lingered in the quiet space between us.

Shane's eyes flicked between mine, his brows pinching together, throat constricting as he swallowed. Carefully, slowly, he lifted one hand, his fingers catching my hair and brushing it back as he framed my face. His thumb lined my jaw, his fingers curling against my scalp, and tears flooded my eyes instantly.

"Oh, baby," Shane said, his voice soft and tinged with pain.

The words broke me, and then his lips were on mine.

His other hand came up to join the first, holding me to him as he kissed me long and soft and sweet. There was no passionate urgency like there had been the last time. There was no hesitation or question of permission.

And maybe it was because he knew, just like I did, that the permission was already granted.

I was his to kiss, even if I could never be his at all. My heart beat for him the way his was bound to mine. It didn't matter if timing and circumstance were against us, if we were locked inside a reality where we couldn't exist together. We still did. We had to. There was no other choice.

I broke our kiss with a sob breaking free, my hands clutching at the lapels of his suit jacket as I pressed our foreheads together. "I don't know how I got here," I whispered. "I... I can't believe I'm... I'm in the same..."

"Don't do that," Shane said, shaking his head. He kissed my forehead before pressing his against mine once more. "This is not your fault. You hear me? This is not on you. And you don't have to face it alone."

"I'm scared."

The admission leaked out of me in a strained whisper, making fresh tears flood my eyes. Now that I'd voiced it, I'd freed it. The fear and shame burst from the cage I'd locked them in and attacked me, fierce and merciless.

"I know," he said, his fingers curling in my hair. "I know. But you don't have to be. Not anymore."

"How did you know?"

He pulled back, his eyes searching mine. "I didn't. I still don't. I won't until you let me in and tell me everything. But I... I sensed it. I felt it, Ari." He swallowed. "That's how it's always been with us, hasn't it? Since the first moment we met. I felt you. And you felt me."

I rolled my lips together, nodding, and when I closed my eyes tightly, more tears rushed down my face. "But there's nothing we can do. He... he *owns* me, Shane. He's tied up in every aspect of my life. And you," I added, touching his face with reverence like I didn't want to point out what he might not have yet realized. "If he even knew we dated two decades ago, you'd lose your job. You'd lose hockey."

"I don't care."

I stilled, my mouth hanging open. "I... of course, you—"

"I don't." He cut me off with a stern shake of his head, his hands still holding me to him. "Ari, I don't fucking care. Whatever knots he has you tied in, I'll untangle them. If he loses his shit and fires me, so be it."

For twenty years, I'd carried a truth I never questioned: that hockey had always come first for Shane. That loving me had been real, but temporary. That when forced to choose, he'd chosen the game, the grind, the future he could see — and left me behind because I hadn't fit into it.

I'd made peace with that. Or told myself I had.

But since discovering there was more to it than that, since I realized he left because he truly felt it was the best thing for *me*, it had me questioning that truth I'd held onto for so long.

And hearing this now — feeling the way his hands tightened on me, like he was afraid I might disappear if he loosened his grip — it was a balm pressed to a wound I'd learned to live with. Something inside me ached, sharp and tender all at once, like scar tissue that would always be there, but was finally fading enough for me to heal.

"Shane..." I said his name breathlessly, disbelief heavy in my exhale.

"None of it matters. Do you hear me?" He bent his forehead to mine, kissing me long and hard before repeating himself. "None of it matters more than you. It never has. I made a mistake twenty years ago. I walked away because I thought it was the right thing to do, but I was wrong. You are the only thing right in my life. You are what matters most. And now that I have you back, I will fight with everything I have left in me to keep you. Okay? I will go to war. I will burn it all down. I will die for your happiness and safety if that's what it takes."

Grace peeked inside the curtain. "I'm sorry, but we're running out of time. He's on the hunt. Maven went to distract him with Vince but..." She tapped her wrist before closing the curtain.

My heart leaped into my throat again, this time beating so hard I thought I might pass out.

Shane saw the fear in my eyes and took a deep breath, steadying me with his exhale as he framed my face again. "I know it doesn't make sense, but I need you to trust me. Okay? Everything is going to be all right. I have a plan."

"A plan?"

He nodded, and then with a cleared throat from outside the curtain, he cursed, kissing me urgently.

"We can't talk tonight. Go home. Do what you have to do to survive. I'll get a message to you tomorrow."

"How?"

"Just trust me," he said, and then with one final kiss, he was ushering me out of the booth with reluctance pulsing through his hands into mine. "And Ari?"

I turned, glancing over my shoulder before I drew the curtain open.

"If anything happens tonight, if you need me... don't hesitate. Call me. I mean it. We all mean it when we say we're in this with you. Just call, and I'll come. You don't even have to say a word. I'll know."

"I'll be fine," I assured him. "He has me under his thumb, so he's not threatened." I shrugged at that, a pathetic smile on my lips. "He's won and he knows it."

Shane's nostrils flared.

"He thinks he's won," he corrected. "But we've got a Trojan horse, Ari. We just need him to open the gates."

# CHAPTER 31

## A RISK WORTH TAKING

Ariana
Present

Two days after the gala, while Nathan was out of town on business, Shane and Maven planned my escape.

Maven arrived just after dusk, her presence intentional and visible, her car parked squarely in the driveway beneath the cameras Nathan had installed to keep the world out and me in. We ordered takeout, poured wine, and talked loudly about nothing in particular. At one point, she posted a photo to her story, the two of us leaning together and giggling as we held up forkfuls of Thai noodles. It set the stage perfectly, leaving digital footprints to prove I was in the house and nothing out of the ordinary was happening.

When we were sprawled out on the couch watching Bravo, she covertly passed me a burner phone hidden in a colorful box that should have housed macarons. It did have one macaroon in there, and I plucked it out and ate it to hold up the charade as Maven smiled mischievously at me. I turned my attention back to the TV, but read the note on the phone.

It was directions — how to set it up to forward calls and texts from my real one to it. And then there was one instruction loud and clear at the bottom.

*Leave your phone here.*

Maven left a little before ten, giving me a big hug right in the camera's line of sight. I stayed behind and followed my usual routine, careful not to rush it. When I was in the bathroom, I set up the burner phone and tucked it into the back waistband of my pajamas. I washed my face, brushed my teeth, plugged my phone into the charger on my nightstand after sending a goodnight text to Nathan, and changed into pajamas — all with my heart thudding in my throat.

I climbed into bed with a book and read for twenty of the longest minutes of my life. The house settled around me, every familiar creak and hum easing into silence. When I finally turned off the light and clicked on our white noise machine, I lay there in the dark, listening to my own breathing until even my nerves seemed to grow tired.

Only then did I move.

Tonight wasn't about my permanent escape, although everything in my being wished that were the case. It was about solidifying a plan. It was about being patient and careful, about not making any wrong moves too soon.

But I would get to see Shane.

That was enough for me.

I slipped from the bed and crossed the house barefoot, my heart pounding so hard I was sure it would give me away. The hallway was unlit. I tiptoed along the wall with the burner phone clutched in my hand like a lifeline. The door we never used that connected to the side of our house was just beyond the nearest camera's line of sight, something Shane had somehow clocked during the exec dinner, long before either of us had known how badly I would need that knowledge.

From the burner phone, I tapped into our security app, quickly disarming the system. I unlocked the door as quietly as I could, opened it carefully, stepped into the cool night air, and quickly armed the house again. I'd disabled the notifications to Nathan's phone discreetly before he left, but he still had the app on his phone. One look and he'd see whether the system was armed or not. I prayed he didn't pick that exact moment to look, that he wouldn't dig too deep into the logs.

It was all a risk — this whole thing.

But it was a risk worth taking.

Maven waited down the road with her engine idling, the car dark and unobtrusive. I didn't look back at the house as I walked toward her. I didn't let myself hesitate. The door closed behind me, and with it, something tight and painful inside my chest finally loosened.

The drive to Shane's passed in near silence, save for Maven asking if I was okay. I simply nodded, and she grabbed my hand and squeezed, a silent promise that it would all be okay somehow.

Shane was already waiting when we pulled into his driveway.

He stood there with his hands in his pockets, his posture rigid as if he were holding himself in place through sheer restraint. The moment I stepped out of the car, that restraint gave way. He crossed the distance in a few long strides and pulled me into his arms, solid and warm and unmistakably real. I sank into him, my face pressed to his chest, breathing him in as he held me.

"You're safe," he murmured, though it sounded as much like reassurance to himself as it did to me. "Okay? Trust me. I've got you. I've thought this all through."

I didn't have the heart to tell him no matter how he'd thought it through, none of us were safe from Nathan Black.

He kissed my hair before releasing me enough to thank Maven with a hug. Then he guided me inside, the door closing behind us with a soft, final click.

And I allowed myself to believe him.

# CHAPTER 32

## JUST THE WAY IT IS

Shane
Present

I watched Ariana take in every inch of my home as I walked her through it, guiding her toward the living area. She paused more than once along the way, her eyes tracking the framed team photos lining the hallway, the plaques and trophies mounted with understated restraint. She lingered longest in front of the photograph of me with the Stanley Cup lifted over my head, the Ospreys packed tight around me, all of us frozen mid-roar. Her lips quirked upward, something like pride softening her expression, before she finally moved on.

Though I'd never claim to be an interior designer, I did consider myself a man of taste. The space reflected that in a way that felt instinctive rather than curated — clean lines, dark woods, leather softened with wear. The furniture was substantial and meant to be lived on, not admired from a distance. An old-school record player sat against one wall, its walnut casing polished from years of use, stacks of vinyl neatly organized beside it. Across from that, a wide bookshelf stretched nearly from floor to ceiling, packed tight with hardcovers and dog-eared paperbacks, some hockey-related, others completely unrelated, all of them well-loved. The house had always felt grown to me; grounded and masculine without being cold.

I'd lived here since accepting the coaching job in Tampa. It was farther from the stadium than most people might expect, a newer build perched along the water in Indian Rocks Beach, but the distance had been intentional. I needed a place that created space between me and the rink, somewhere I couldn't see the stadium lights from the driveway or hear the echo of the crowd in my head the second I walked through the door. Not that it always worked. I'd lost count of the nights I'd slept at the stadium anyway, especially during playoff races, but this place had always been my attempt at balance. It was my reminder that there was a world beyond the ice.

Ariana hummed in amusement as she traced my record player, tapping her nails on the CD player perched right next to it. Her blue eyes sparkled when she cocked a brow at me. "Care to join us in the age of Bluetooth speakers?"

"Not when I have these at my disposal," I said, bending to retrieve a thick album of CDs. Ariana's jaw dropped before she stole the thing from my hands. Then, she was giggling and shaking her head as she thumbed through it.

"Wow," she said, pulling one from its protective case and holding it up to show me. "*Warm Up Mix 2005.*"

"And it's a banger, too."

"I just *know* 50 Cent is on here."

"The Game, too. But don't get it twisted," I said, holding up one finger firmly. "Fall Out Boy and Foo Fighters take up just as much space."

"What's the first song?"

"Pop it in and find out," I dared, notching my head toward the player.

She smirked, accepting the challenge, and when "Girlfight" by Brooke Valentine started playing, she held her laugh for all of two seconds before it burst from her lips.

"What?" I defended. "This shit is hype!"

She laughed harder, and then her eyes snagged on another CD in the album. She wordlessly pulled it from the case and swapped it out with the one playing.

As soon as the first song began, I knew which mix she'd picked.

"Open Your Eyes" by Snow Patrol hummed over my speakers, the familiar, rhythmic guitar strums echoing in my chest the way they always did.

"*Her*," Ariana said, reciting the word I'd scribbled in Sharpie across the top of that CD the day I'd burned it. Her eyes lingered on mine, and I shrugged.

"One guess who she is."

Ariana's throat constricted, her gaze falling to the floor between us, and then she wordlessly moved over to the couch and sat. She dropped the burner phone on the couch cushion before immediately folding her hands into her lap, wringing them together as her knuckles turned white. She was dressed in satin pink pajamas, her feet bare, face shining from what I assumed was her nightly skincare routine.

The sight of her like that sucker punched me, because I felt robbed. I could have lived my entire lifetime with that sight, with her climbing into bed next to me and kissing me before settling in to read her book while I fell asleep beside her. I could have woken to her each morning, could have held her against me and felt her warmth.

I'd been a fool to leave her under the pretense of protection. A young, stupid fool.

I quietly sat next to her as Snow Patrol serenaded us, and for a while, I let her stay silent. Then, I reached over, peeling her hands apart so I could slide my palm into hers and thread our fingers together. We both closed our eyes when I did, like we were spiraling back to the first time I'd ever grabbed her hand.

"I know it's probably the last thing you want to do," I told her, gently stroking her skin with my thumb. "But I need you to tell me everything. I need to know exactly what's been going on with you and Nathan."

She let out a shaky exhale, shaking her head. "I don't know if I can."

"Try."

She spoke slowly at first, like she was testing the ground with each word to make sure it wouldn't give way, and I stayed quiet, my hand wrapped around hers as I listened. What she told me didn't land as something that made sense all at once, but in pieces that seemed small on their own and devastating in the way they accumulated.

Nathan controlled their money. He not only reigned over their accounts but restricted her access to them. He handled every payment, laughed at her when she suggested maybe she should have a separate account of her own, and framed all of it as responsibility rather than restriction. He acted as if he was doing her a favor by taking it off her plate.

Her schedule wasn't hers either. He expected to know where she was, who she was with, and how long she'd be gone. When she stepped outside those expectations, he noticed. He always noticed.

"Did he know we were together that day when he went to Vegas the first time?" I asked.

She swallowed. "I didn't think so at first, but now... I'm sure he did. Or at least, I know he knows I was out all day. He may not have proof I was with you, but he suspects."

I nodded. "It makes sense why he was so abrasive with me at the executive dinner. If he already suspected we'd spent time together..."

"And then he saw us alone."

I nodded grimly.

"He asked me where I'd been for Thanksgiving after his trip. We share our location, so I didn't see any reason to lie." She paused. "He wasn't happy you were there. And that's when he started in on Sweet Dreams."

She went on to tell me how Nathan had questioned the time it demanded, the people involved, the way it was "draining her," all under the guise of concern. By the time his concern hardened into pressure, Ariana had already realized what his intention was.

"And then... there's Georgie."

My stomach dropped along with her shoulders when she said his name. She told me what I suspected, that everything her brother depended on had been folded neatly into Nathan's influence — his tuition, housing, stability. He'd never threatened her outright with any of it, but he didn't need to. He simply reminded her what was at stake and let the fear do the work for him.

"That part hurts the worst," she admitted softly. "Because for so long, I took care of Georgie. But then I trusted Nathan when he said he wanted to take care of both of us. I fell into the trap because I was so desperate for the release — to be free of the stress, the worry, the pressure."

That had cracked my heart like flimsy, dry clay.

Because I knew she was desperate for that because I'd left her wanting.

Affection, she went on, had become conditional. Nathan gave it to her when she complied, withheld it when she didn't, and sharpened it when she resisted. He made her feel smaller without ever raising his voice, made her doubt instincts she'd once trusted without question.

I listened as it all came together, each piece slotting into place until there was no denying the shape of it. Nathan had worked his way into every corner of her life so subtly that she hadn't realized she was losing ground until there was nowhere left to stand. He'd charmed her first, then slowly eroded everything that made her glow, leaving behind a subdued version of the woman he'd met. Every choice she made, every movement she allowed herself, had been orchestrated until he held the strings, and she was left believing it was her fault.

"He's never hit me," she admitted softly, like that somehow acquitted him, like because he wasn't the same kind of piece of shit as her stepdad, he somehow still had merit. "But... before the dinner party, he grabbed me. My wrist. Hard. He was angry, and I tried to pull away, and he—" Her breath hitched. "He wanted to hurt me. Just enough to make a point."

By the time she admitted she was terrified to leave, her voice was barely there. It trembled as she told me how she was scared of what he'd do, worried of what she'd lose, and ashamed that she'd let it happen, that it'd grown to this point.

My grip tightened around her hand. I hoped it anchored her and I needed it to anchor me, because now that I could see it clearly, I understood just how deep it went.

And there was no universe in which I was letting her face it alone.

"I don't know who I am anymore, Shane," she whispered, her eyes welling, lips rolling together as she shook her head. "I... I can't believe I've let it get here. I watched this happen to my own mother." She finally looked at me. "How did I not see it happening to myself?"

I swallowed, pulling her into me even as she shook her head like she didn't deserve the embrace. That only made me wrap her up tighter, and I sighed, kissing her hair before I rested my chin on the crown of her head and closed my eyes.

I needed a moment to steady myself. Everything inside me wanted to be desperately idiotic. I imagined myself flying to wherever the fuck he was right now and ending him. I'd do it with my bare hands. I'd watch the light leak out of his eyes and enjoy every fucking second of it.

I let that ravenous side of me exist for a moment, let myself feel that rage, and then I tucked it away. Rationality took over and I reminded myself that I had a better way to end him — one that wouldn't cost me Ariana in the process.

"You are not to blame for this. Okay?" I tilted her chin with my knuckle, eyes fixed on hers. "I know you hate hearing this word, but you are a victim. He hurt you, but that's going to stop. You're going to take back power."

"How?"

"I'm going to help." I swallowed, realizing it was now or never. What I was about to say would either make sense or it wouldn't. I either knew what I was talking about, or I was grossly misunderstanding and didn't have a single leg to stand on. "I think Nathan is involved in something illegal," I dared to utter. "Something involving gambling and manipulating the integrity of the game."

The words sat between us for a beat, heavy and dangerous. Even as I'd said them aloud, doubt crept in at the edges of my certainty, whispering that I might be reaching, that I'd let my feelings cloud my judgment.

"I don't want to scare you," I went on carefully, my thumb still tracing slow, grounding circles against her skin. "And I don't want to sound paranoid. Hell, there have been moments where I've wondered if that's exactly what I am." I let out a quiet breath. "But too many things don't add up."

Her brow furrowed, confusion flickering there, but she didn't pull away. She leaned in instead, like she was bracing herself.

"I started noticing it with the guys," I said. "Players acting off in ways that didn't track with injuries or fatigue. Daddy P hasn't been himself this season, as I know you know. He got sick unexpectedly that one game and I thought — okay, that happens. But then to have his injury flaring up so badly when it hasn't been an issue, to have Ben as his backup being incredibly inconsistent... It just raised some red flags for me.

"And then I started paying attention. Fabian Lorenz was one of our most dependable defensemen, and suddenly, he's unpredictable. He'd shut down advances one week and miss easy clears the next. James Hart, a rookie winger, shows up to a game wearing a fucking Rolex I *know* he can't afford — not even if he spent every penny of his signing bonus.

"I watched how other staff members interacted with Nathan, how many off-script meetings were happening, how the conversation would stop whenever I entered the room." I shook my head. "There were games where medical decisions felt... influenced. Guys cleared too quickly. Others held out when they shouldn't have been."

I hesitated, the words thick in my throat now. "And then there were the betting lines. They'd move in ways that didn't reflect public money or analytics. It was like someone already knew how things were going to play out."

Her breathing had changed, shallow and quick, and I could feel it where she was pressed against me.

"I heard things, too," I admitted. "When I caught the end of those conversations that stopped when I walked into a room. There was a bookie's name that came up more than once when it shouldn't have. And every time I tried to tell myself it was coincidence, something else happened. Another roster decision that felt engineered. Another game where the integrity just didn't sit right."

I scrubbed a hand over my jaw, frustration curling tight in my chest.

"I know how insane this sounds," I said, noting how Ariana was staring at me like I had more than a few screws loose. "Accusing a GM of manipulating outcomes is not something you do lightly, and I kept telling myself I needed more than instincts. That I needed proof."

"It's not crazy," she interrupted, shaking her head. "I've seen things, too."

Hope prickled at the back of my neck like the touch of a ghost, and we both sat up straighter, her hands holding fast to mine as I clung to the words tumbling from her now. "Shane, I didn't understand the signs before, but—" She swallowed. "He has a second phone, too. A burner just like how you set me up with one tonight. I found it in his bag once and he brushed it off like it was nothing. He said he liked to keep some business separate so he wasn't bothered with unimportant things when he was off the clock."

My pulse spiked.

"As I already told you, I don't have access to our money. But sometimes I'm sitting next to him when he's on his phone, and I've caught glimpses of him in his banking app." She swallowed. "Recently, I noted that it wasn't the same bank we use for everything else. I thought maybe he'd changed banks without telling me or... I don't know, that he had opened an account with someone's bank because he wanted them to donate to the team or something."

My chest went tight.

"I also saw deposits there. Big ones. Numbers that made my stomach drop. I asked him about it once, and he brushed it off like it was nothing, like I'd misunderstood what I was seeing. He told me it was bonuses, or money moving between accounts that didn't really belong to us." Her eyes lifted to mine, wide now. "I stopped asking because every time I did, he made me feel stupid for noticing. But it didn't feel right. It never felt right."

She shook her head slowly, eyes flicking back and forth like she was trying to search for more clues that she'd brushed off.

"And just like you, there have been times I've walked into a room when he's on the phone and he'll take one look at me and end the call abruptly. There are emails, too — he closes them the second he's not alone. I thought it was just normal work, but..." Her grip tightened on me. "I heard him fighting with someone once. I didn't know who it was, but he kept saying something about odds being wrong and money being lost."

Each word landed like confirmation, like the final pieces clicking into place.

I drew her closer, my arm firm around her back, my other hand sliding up to cradle her neck as I leaned my forehead against hers. "You're not imagining this," I said quietly. "And neither am I."

Her voice dropped to a whisper. "What does that mean?"

"It means we're taking him down," I said, the resolve settling fully into place now.

"Shane..." Her fingers flexed against my chest, fear threading through her voice.

"Together," I said gently but without wavering.

"How? Where do we even begin?" She swallowed, shaking her head. "Fuck, this scares me, too. It feels big."

"That's because it is," I said quietly. "If what we suspect is true, then this is federal-level, career-ending, freedom-ending shit." I exhaled, scrubbing a hand over my face. "I already filed an anonymous report with the league's integrity office. It buys us time. It puts eyes on him. And once that happens, he won't be watching you anymore — because he'll be too busy watching his own back."

Her breath hitched.

"You mean..." she started, then stopped, like she was afraid to finish the thought.

"I mean that if this goes where I think it's going, Nathan won't have power over you," I said. "Not your schedule. Not your money. Not your fear. If we can work together to gather what we need to solidify proof, he'll be under investigation. Everything he's built to control you will start collapsing in on itself."

She stared at me, something fragile and luminous breaking through her expression. I recognized it as the same emotion that had wrecked me since she'd come back into my life.

Hope, tentative and stunned yet indestructible.

"So... there's a way out," she whispered. "A real one. One where you don't lose your job. One where he can't hurt either of us."

"There is," I said, my voice steady even as my chest burned.

Then her brow furrowed again, reality crashing back in. "But that doesn't fix everything. The prenup. Georgie.

The money. I signed things, Shane. I don't have access to anything, and I don't know how long it would take to untangle all of it."

"We'll handle that, too," I said without hesitation. "Together."

She shook her head faintly. "You can't be responsible for—"

"I'm not trying to save you," I interrupted gently, forcing her to meet my eyes. "But *fuck*, Ari. I love you. I always have." The admission scraped out of me, rough and unavoidable. "I loved you when we were kids. I loved you from afar. I loved you when you rightfully walked away from me in Boston on that cold winter night, and I loved you when you walked back into my life this year. It doesn't matter that you're married. It doesn't matter that there's a risk here for both of us. I love you, and that's just the way it is."

Each word from my lips had her fingers curling more and more in my shirt, a smile spreading on her lips even as tears slipped from her eyes.

"And I'm not trying to become another man who runs your life. I know you need this to be yours." I swallowed, the words tightening in my throat. "But if you let me... I'll stand with you. I'll make sure you and Georgie are okay while you figure out your next step. And his. For as long as it takes."

Her lips trembled.

"You don't owe me anything," I went on. "This isn't a transaction. This is me choosing you."

"And Georgie?"

"And Georgie, too. I won't disappear again. Not when things get hard. Not when it's inconvenient. Not when staying costs me something. I left because I thought it was best for both of us, mostly for you, but I was wrong. I know it now."

She pressed her forehead to my chest, her hands clutching my shirt like she needed proof I was real.

"Let me stay this time," I murmured into her hair. "Let me prove to you that I'm not walking away again."

Her breath shuddered as she finally nodded, and when she looked up at me, the fear was still there — but it was no longer alone.

For the first time, it was standing beside hope.

"Kiss me," she whispered, fingers digging into my shirt and pulling me closer. "Please, Shane. Kiss me. I can't think about anything else. I just... want you. Your touch. Your warmth. Your voice. Everything about you. Let me be with you, even if just for tonight. We can live in reality tomorrow. We can fight and... *God*, I don't know, put everything on the line to try to find our way out of this. But tonight, please, just... hold me. Kiss me." She wet her lips, the next words even softer. "Touch me."

My hands were in her hair without hesitation, threading through silk and skin as I pulled her into me and covered her mouth with mine. The kiss was slow for exactly half a second before it wasn't, before weeks of restraint and years of history collapsed between us. She made a soft, wrecked sound against my lips, and it went straight to my spine.

I shifted, guiding her onto my lap, her knees bracketing my thighs as she melted into me like she'd been built to fit there. Her hands slid up my chest, her body pressing closer as I kissed her again, deeper this time, slower and more deliberate.

"It's not just tonight," I breathed against her mouth, her forehead resting against mine as our breaths tangled. "It's me and you again, Ari. It's always been us."

Her eyes shone as she nodded, her hands fisting in my shirt like she was anchoring herself to the truth of it. "It's always been us," she echoed.

The music still played softly behind us, The Fray humming through the room, but the world had narrowed to the space between our bodies and the choice we were making.

It was reckless.

It was forbidden.

It was everything I'd spent years convincing myself I could live without, only to have the brittleness of that lie break the moment I saw her again.

Years, I'd yearned to touch her. Decades, I'd longed for one more night, one more chance.

And here it was.

I kissed her again, slow and unhurried this time, like I had all the time in the world, like I wouldn't have to somehow sneak her back home tonight and stomach the fact that she had to stay put in that house with that piece of shit man — at least for now, until our plan played out.

For a moment of blissful ignorance, I pretended like everything was already okay, that we didn't have anything to lose.

And I knew, without a shred of doubt, that neither of us was turning back now.

## CHAPTER 33

### SAME. SAME. NEW.

Ariana
Present

I didn't know if it was hope or desperation, but whatever it was encompassed us like a storm.

Shane's hands on my hips were a crack of lightning. His moans against my throat were a pained roll of thunder. His mouth on mine was a frantic whip of wind. I felt his heart pounding through his chest and right into mine like the steady pelting of rain. I held fast to him like a shoreline bracing for landfall.

It was wrong. It was so, so wrong. I was married to another man. That man was Shane's boss.

But no amount of common sense or logic could stop me now.

Because in the end, it was *right* — me and him, he and I, this, *us*. We were starlight and space, water and air, ink and paper.

Strong on our own, unstoppable together.

Drawn into each other's gravity.

Unable to exist the same way apart.

We weren't whole without the other.

And some things, no matter how forbidden, are simply inevitable.

It was a symphony of sounds as Shane hauled me into his arms and carried me through his house to his bedroom. It was kisses and sighs, moans and pants, whimpers and whispered promises. The balance was somewhere between frenzied and tranquil, like we weren't sure if we should rush and seize this very moment before it slipped away, or if we had the time to savor every touch.

It was a wild love, and we held fast to the reins, determined to hold on.

"I wish I could slow this down," Shane mused against my skin, his expert hands stripping me like he'd done it a thousand times in his dreams. He had me pressed into his comforter, my thighs spread around him, his erection pressing into where I ached for him most. "I wish you could understand how much I've missed you, how badly I've longed for a redo, how much I've tried to bargain with every deity known to man to go back in time and never let you go."

I kissed him silent as he unfastened the buttons of my silk pajama top, and the groan in his throat when he pressed back on his knees to look at me made my neck burn furiously.

"*Fuck*, Ari," he said, voice husky with reverence as his eyes drank me in. I wasn't wearing a bra, all part of selling the *I went to sleep* story to Nathan, and now I was exposed for Shane for the first time in decades. "You are so beautiful."

I flushed deeper. "Not exactly the youthful girl you once touched."

His eyes snapped to mine, a firm line appearing between his brows. "Don't." He leaned back over me, one hand braced beside my head, the other settling warm and sure at my waist. "Don't talk about her like she's gone," he said quietly. "Like she was better because she was younger."

His thumb traced the soft curve of my stomach, slow and deliberate, like he wanted me to feel every inch of the path.

"This body," he went on, voice roughening, "has lived. It's carried years and choices and love and loss. It's held you through everything that tried to break you."

His gaze softened, something almost fierce in it now, and then he lifted my hand to his mouth and pressed a kiss over my scar. He held my gaze as he let his lips linger, telling me without words that he saw and knew every part of me and loved me still.

"When I'm touching you tonight, I'm not thinking about what you used to be," he said, swallowing hard. "I'm barely holding myself together at the realization that I get to touch you *now*. Because every line, every curve, every place time has kissed you feels like a privilege for me to experience after I've waited and wished for so fucking long."

He dipped his head, pressing his forehead to mine.

"I'm honored you let me see you like this, Ari," he whispered. "I'm honored you let me touch you at all."

"Shane..."

"I mean it," he said, punctuating his intention with a long, deep kiss and a roll of his hips into mine. "Now, let me see all of you."

It was incredibly tender and yet bursting with heat, the careful way he stripped me then. The silk of my top slid over my shoulders, pushed by his fingertips. My shorts went next, pulled to my ankles along with the panties I wore beneath them. When I was bare, Shane shook his head, lip pinned between his teeth as his gaze trailed every inch of me.

And then it was his mouth on that path, kissing the arch of my foot, the soft skin inside my ankle, along my calf, my thigh, sending chills through me as he took his time climbing all the way back to my mouth.

His tongue danced with mine, and every sweep had me caught up in a memory. He was right. I felt honored to touch him now, to feel how time and distance had changed his body. My hands explored the new dips and valleys as I wrangled him out of his t-shirt. He hopped off the bed long enough to rid himself of his joggers and briefs, smirking as he allowed me one long, appreciative glance at his naked body, and then he was on me again.

"I can't wait to figure out everything you like," he whispered against my lips, and then he was kissing down again, licking a long, hot path along my inner thigh as he settled between my legs. "I wonder what's the same. I wonder what's changed."

My back bowed off the bed as he spread my thighs wide, his gaze hungry as he took in the sight of me sprawled out for him. A satisfied groan rumbled through him as he reached up to play with my tits, thumbing my pebbled peaks and squeezing just tight enough to make me moan.

"Same," he mused, smirking against my thigh as I squirmed under his touch. He remembered how much I loved having my nipples played with, how those little sparks of electricity got me wet faster than anything else.

He took his time there, playing and teasing and toying until I was practically shoving his face between my thighs. I kept my hands in his hair as he turned his attention, and with the first lash of his tongue against my clit, I trembled out a moan.

"Same," he echoed, smiling wickedly up at me as he flicked his tongue back and forth, up and down, circling and sucking as I panted with disbelief.

His eyes were a shocking blue, the silver in them familiar and new all at once. His dark hair fell over his forehead just enough to drive me wild, and I fisted the bit of it I held harder in a silent plea for more.

Shane slicked his fingers through my wetness before pressing them against my opening. He slid one finger inside, curling and smiling when I rewarded him with a gasp. A second finger joined the first, and then he was pulsing them inside me, slow and rhythmic just how I liked, perfectly in sync with the swirling of his tongue and the gentle sucks of my clit.

When I was close, I reached down, guiding his fingers out of me. The middle one was still slick from my desire, and I coaxed it down an inch, heartbeat roaring in my ears as I asked for what I wanted without a word.

Shane lifted his head with his eyebrows shooting into his hairline, his grin boyish and amused. "Here?" he asked, teasing my backdoor entrance.

I nodded, biting my lip and squirming under the teasing touch.

"Mmm," he said, gaze falling to where he was touching me. "New." His grin faded into a heated gaze as he pressed against the tight hole, and then my eyes rolled back, fists twisting in his comforter as he lowered his mouth to my clit again.

It didn't take long. The forbidden shock of his finger inside my ass, the expert suck of my clit, the fact that Shane was touching me again when I never thought it possible... it was the perfect cocktail for my release.

My orgasm ripped through me like a tornado, picking up everything I was before and shredding it in the process.

I felt the old me leaving my body, willingly or not, and reveled in the feeling of being completely upended. I moaned and cried out his name, one hand in his hair and the other fisting my own as I rode out every last wave of pleasure.

I was liquid by the end of it, my limbs melting into the bed, chest heaving as I tried to catch my breath. Shane smirked against my clit before pressing one more gentle kiss to it as he withdrew his finger.

"Don't move," he instructed, and then he rolled off the bed and into his en suite bathroom. I heard the water run and assumed he was washing his hands. Moments later, he returned with a hot washcloth, and then he was cleaning me up, and the sensation of that hot, wet towel between my thighs made me moan in a whole new way.

Shane climbed into bed with me when we were both clean, maneuvering us until we were under the covers and tangled together in the sheets. I laid on my back, and he on his side, his legs weaved with mine, one arm slung over my waist as he balanced his head on the other hand.

"Please tell me we're not done," I panted.

He laughed, kissing my nose. "Just taking a little break. I want to look at you."

"You can't look at me while you fuck me?"

"Not with a clear head."

I rolled my eyes, but then my hand was on his chest, drawing circles as I took in everything I'd missed over the years. I traced the dark tattoo ink on his ribs, the dusting of hair over his abdomen, the new, grown muscles that lined his shoulders and arms.

I let my hand drift lower, following the slope of his abdomen to the hard line of his hip. His breath hitched when my fingers brushed the faint, pale scar there — a smooth crescent against his skin, almost easy to miss if you weren't looking for it.

I traced it slowly, reverently, and felt him still beneath me.

"Can I?" I asked, already shifting, already knowing the answer.

He nodded, his hand sliding to my back as I pushed the covers down and eased myself up onto an elbow. My gaze dropped to his leg, to the knee that suffered a career-ending injury. I ran my fingers over the thin line just below his kneecap — narrow, faded, a whisper of what it must've cost him.

"I'm sorry I wasn't there for you," I murmured, tracing it carefully. Then the smaller mark along the inside of his knee. "I'm sorry I pushed you away when you found me that night in Boston."

"I deserved it."

"You didn't," I argued. "But I was angry and hurt and young."

He nodded, still rubbing my back. He didn't rush me as I took in the sight of him, and when my focus shifted more to the thick rod between his thighs, the tension of the moment melted into something more heated.

I crawled my fingertips up, walking them along his thick, muscle-corded thigh and smirking at the parade of goosebumps I caused. I loved the thought of affecting him the way he did me, of bringing him pleasure from my touch.

"Ari," he warned gruffly when I got close to his shaft.

"Mmm?" I was all innocence, undeterred as I wrapped my hand around him.

His groan was guttural, his head falling back into the pillows. "Fuck."

Why was that one word exhaled on a breath so hot? Why did I feel so powerful to reduce him to nothing more than a curse word?

"I've missed you, too, you know," I said, my voice low and smooth as I stroked him, base to tip, gathering precum to slick my second stroke. "Your eyes. Your body. Your touch. Your kiss." I squeezed a little tighter, biting my lip as he rolled his cock into my fist. "This."

"You've thought about me?"

"So many times," I confessed. "I'd find my hand under my sheets, between my thighs, and you…" I shrugged, like he should know already, like it was nothing to be surprised about.

"Me, too," he said gruffly, wetting his lips before he flexed into my touch again. "I've thought about you so many times. I've longed to be inside you, to feel you wrapped around me again."

It was my turn to moan, those words shooting a spark straight between my legs.

Impatient, I crawled back up to him, straddling his lap in the process. I bent to kiss him long and deep, both of us inhaling a stiff breath when our tongues touched, when that electricity fired again.

"Let's put our imagination to rest then," I said, and then I reached between us, fisting his cock and lining it up where I was wet and aching for him.

His breath caught, but his hand slid to my wrist, stopping me only long enough to turn and reach for the nightstand. He kissed me as he fought with the wrapper, and when he was sheathed, we were heat to heat again.

"More like put it to shame," he muttered.

With a smirk, I lowered down.

We groaned together as I sank onto him, me stretching to accommodate him and him gripping my hips like a lifeline. I worked down an inch or two before pressing up onto my knees, only to sink down another inch. Over and over, slowly, I stretched and worked until I could sit all the way down, until Shane's eyes were squeezed shut and he was letting out a whole string of curses.

"Goddamn, Ari," he breathed, shaking his head as I lifted and sat again. "You feel so fucking good. Better than I—"

He couldn't finish the thought, another groan ripping through him as I planted my hands on his chest and began to work. I rode him slowly, lifting and lowering, savoring the way he stared at my breasts, at how his hands worked them perfectly. I tipped my head back and let myself slip into the euphoria of his touch.

Being connected with him again felt like a piece of my soul coming home, like I'd been wandering around this planet looking for it without even realizing. My heart beat steadier. My anxiety eased in an instant.

I was home.

*He* was home.

When I sat back, he reached even deeper, hitting that spot inside me that made me see stars. I moaned and worked my clit with one hand as I held myself steady against his chest with the other. Soon, I was bouncing, reaching, panting, aching.

Exploding.

My second orgasm was faster, a lightning bolt straight to my chest. It didn't roll like the first, it zapped, hot and fierce and all-encompassing. I cried out my release, and the way Shane gripped my hips, I knew his was close behind.

When my legs finished quaking and I dipped my head to his, Shane followed my lead, slowing a bit for me to steady out. Then, we were kissing wildly again, and he flipped me onto my back, entering me with a powerful, possessive flex.

"Yes," I breathed, arching into him, nails digging into his back.

"So fucking good," he breathed against my neck, and his pace quickened, his arms wrapping around me and crushing me to him as he pummeled in. "I want to live here, Ariana. I want to die here. You were made for me. You and this perfect fucking cunt."

I moaned, kissing him hard, and he kept that bruising kiss as he grunted out his release. I loved the way he stiffened with it, the way he groaned and gripped and fell completely apart. I was the one who drove him there. It was me he wanted so badly.

I'd never felt more desired in my life.

I didn't know how long we lay there afterward, limbs tangled, breaths syncing, the room still humming with what we'd done. Shane pressed a kiss into my hair, slow and lingering, like he was trying to memorize the weight of me against his chest.

"Come on," he murmured eventually. "You're shaking."

"I'm not cold," I protested weakly.

"I know," he said softly. "But I want to take care of you."

The bath was already running by the time he carried me in, steam curling around the room. I was still taking in every part of his home, of this place where so much of the man I didn't know yet lived, where pieces of the boy I knew like my own heart revealed themselves.

He eased us down into the water, my back to his chest, his arms circling me beneath the surface. The heat seeped into my bones, and I sighed, heart so content I could cry.

I rested my head against his shoulder and closed my eyes.

For a little while, the world didn't exist.

He washed me the way someone does when they're afraid of hurting you — careful, unhurried, reverent. When he pressed a kiss to my temple, my throat tightened.

"I could stay here forever," I whispered.

"Me too."

But time is cruel like that. It doesn't care what we want or when we want it. At the end of the day, we play by its rules, not the other way around.

Eventually the water cooled, and reality crept back in around the edges. Shane wrapped me in a towel, another around himself, and led me back to the bedroom. I saw the pain in his eyes as he helped me dress, felt the way he hated this as much as I did.

His hands lingered at my waist, my shoulders, sliding into my hair we'd been so careful not to get wet in the bath. His jaw was tight as he buttoned my pajama top, like each fastened button was a small act of violence.

"I hate it, too," I said quietly.

He nodded, taking me into him for a long hug. His words were warm against my hair. "This is temporary. You hear me?" He pulled back to look into my eyes, his desperate and urgent. "You survive for me. For us. Okay? Whatever you have to do. We're almost there. We just have to solidify the plan, and then it's over."

A plan.

Time.

Patience.

All words that felt like torture when his eyes looked at me like that.

He drove me home with the headlights off until the last turn, parking down the road like Maven had earlier. He walked me to the edge of the trees, pulled me into his arms one last time, his forehead pressed to mine.

"I want to do this the careful way, but if you need me... I'm here. You understand? Everything else can get fucked to hell in the process, but if you need me—"

"I'll call. I promise."

He nodded, and both of us held onto each other longer than we should have, our throats tight with the way each word was breaking us.

Sneaking back into my house felt more wrong than the act of cheating did. The bed smelled like Nathan, like a life I was already half-out of. My skin still hummed with Shane, my senses full of him.

I curled onto my side, staring into the dark.

*It will be over soon.*

*We have a plan.*

*I will be free.*

I repeated it until sleep finally claimed me, clinging to a promise that felt too good to be true.

# CHAPTER 34

## PATIENCE

Shane
Preset

We decided the perfect time to take Nathan down was at Ariana's birthday party.

I was already pissed the man had the audacity to use her birthday as an opportunity to schmooze the people he wanted to impress, anyway, so it felt like poetic justice. Ariana lived most of her life with her birthday on the back burner, her family never separating it from Christmas. I'd made sure when we were together to make her feel special, but it was clear Nathan hadn't done the same.

That would all be over soon.

The weeks leading up to it were a careful dance — measured, deliberate, and invisible to anyone who wasn't inside the job.

Ariana moved through her days like she always had: gracious, capable, accommodating. No one would've guessed what she was doing behind closed doors. She copied emails when Nathan stepped out of the room. Took photos of financial ledgers she wasn't meant to see. She recorded one late-night conversation when his voice sharpened just enough for her to know he was talking to someone he shouldn't have been, his threats loud and clear. She gathered documentation tied to Sweet Dreams when she realized money was moving into the organization without making its way to the final budget, which made us wonder if the nonprofit was somehow being used to hide the money he was pulling in from Vegas. She flagged upcoming "meetings" with sponsors whose names set off alarms the moment she mentioned them to me.

All the while, our conversations were scarce and too short. She'd sneak away and call me from her burner phone whenever she could, and I'd always answer scared to death that it would be her needing me rather than just a check in.

"I'm scared," she admitted more than once.

And I was, too.

But we were in it together, and we had a team.

On my end, I kept quiet and played Coach. We were well into the season now and it was easy to stay busy and off Nathan's radar. But in that act, I was able to covertly do my own digging — casual conversations with staff, a question here, a comment there. I noted every odd practice incident, every moment that didn't sit right. I screenshotted betting line shifts that made no sense unless you knew where to look. I talked to medical trainers off the record, noting which ones sweat at my questions versus which ones were confused by my implications.

In the end, I compiled it all into a timeline so clean and airtight it couldn't be dismissed as coincidence.

Will, Jaxson, Vince, Aleks, and Carter played their roles without ever needing the full picture. Same with the girls: Livia, Maven, Grace, Mia, and Chloe. Information passed between us easily, supported by our friendship over the years. I pulled Will into the mix more than the others, telling him how crucial his testimony would be in all of this. Of course, I'd had to calm him down when I told him I was fairly certain the medical staff had been pushing him toward his injury instead of away from it. He was murderous and rightly so, but I reminded him they would get theirs when the ringleader was taken down — and he could help us do it.

The crew also acted as a barrier, the girls stealing Ariana away for girls' nights whenever possible, and the guys keeping Nathan busy with our traps. Carter would be especially important. The night of Ariana's party, he would go to Nathan and pretend he'd heard about "opportunities for advancement." I knew he wouldn't have to say it outright for Nathan to pounce, eager to bring another player into his scheme, and with Carter recording the whole conversation from his phone in his pocket, it would be an irrefutable source of proof.

But it was all a waiting game. We stacked up evidence and laid low.

Ariana and I never spoke in person. Nathan had ripped her from Sweet Dreams, and there was no reason for me to see her before the party. Those late-night calls whispered into darkness were our only lifeline.

And God, the distance was killing me.

After that night with her, being apart felt like punishment, like torture, like I'd been given something holy only to have it ripped away again. Every instinct in me screamed to touch her, to pull her back into my arms, to remind her she wasn't alone.

But patience was the price we had to pay to win.

There were so many ways this could go wrong, but if it went right...

*It'll all be over soon,* I promised her. *Just hold on a little longer.*

We were setting him up perfectly. Every step was documented. Every angle was covered. If it worked — and I had to believe it would — Nathan would be gone without ever touching her again, without risking my job, without giving him a single thread to pull.

It was killing me to wait.

But some endings are worth the patience.

And this one would be final.

## CHAPTER 35

### HAPPY BIRTHDAY

Ariana
Present

I'd learned a lot about playing my part when it came to my husband, and if there was one lesson that stuck, it was that the more convincing I was, the less he questioned me.

So I leaned into the version of myself Nathan expected.

I was gracious and polished, hanging on his arm at work events and keeping the house running smoothly. I convinced him I was focused on ribbons and place settings and the logistics of hosting a December birthday. I fussed over the tree in our living room, adjusting ornaments and lights and leaning into Nathan's side as we admired it.

I pretended I wasn't listening when he took calls in the next room.

But I was always listening.

I ached for Shane. I longed for even one stolen moment with him. I imagined going to the arena under the guise of bringing Nathan lunch just to orchestrate a secret meeting with Shane, to steal away in a hidden hallway and feel his hands on me, his lips searing mine.

But it was too dangerous, and there was too much on the line to take such risks.

So, I stayed the course. I reminded myself what was at stake, what could be mine in the end if I remained focused. Shane and I snuck late-night, whispered conversations when we could, when Nathan was out of the house, or when I could get away for a girls' night.

Otherwise, we were both focused on the task at hand.

The house glowed with warm light three days before my birthday party, the Christmas lights surrounding our space and making it feel soft and safe. If I weren't masquerading in my own personal hell, I might have truly felt it. Garland wrapped along our banister. Our Christmas cards were half enveloped and stamped on the kitchen counter, waiting to be mailed.

I busied myself with those envelopes, writing each name and address in perfect script. Nathan thought the AirPods in my ears were playing an audiobook.

He had no idea they were hooked up to a recording device I'd hidden in his office.

"I told you that money was supposed to clear before the end of the quarter." A pause. "No, don't spin it back to me. If it doesn't move by Friday, we have a problem."

My pulse ticked faster, but my movements didn't change.

He was angry. And when he was angry, he was careless.

"You don't get to decide what I'm exposed to," he said, his voice low and controlled. "That organization exists because I allow it to. If I need it to absorb a transfer, it does. End of discussion."

I swallowed.

Sweet Dreams. He had to be talking about Sweet Dreams.

My fingers trembled a bit where I penned the next address.

Nathan went on, irritation sharpening each word. "If you screw this up for me, I will make sure you regret it. You know I will."

He hung up, and I tapped into the app on my phone that I'd hidden in a folder called *period cycle apps*. Quickly, I cropped and saved the recording, and then I put my phone away before Nathan's footsteps came down the hall.

This was what my weeks had looked like since the night I had with Shane. My heart was never steady, constantly pounding in my chest and vibrating in my ears as I collected as much proof as I could. I didn't know if what we had would be enough, but I knew I wouldn't stop trying. I knew I would give our plan everything I had — even if we all ended up burning in the end.

Later that night, when Nathan was in the shower, I dismantled our cameras in our shared security app and slid into his office long enough to peek at his laptop. There was a spreadsheet minimized in the corner of the screen, and I didn't hesitate.

I clicked into it immediately.

The numbers for Sweet Dreams were familiar — donations in, expenditures out — but the middle column was new. There were transfers routed through Sweet Dreams that never appeared in the final budget — and the amounts were too precise to be accidents, too consistent to be coincidence.

I snapped a few photos before slipping out of the office and turning the cameras back on before I plopped down on the couch, stomach in knots as I pretended to watch a home design show on HGTV. I was smiling because I could feel my freedom inching closer.

"What are you smiling about?" Nathan asked when he joined me.

"My birthday," I said lightly. "It's just going to be so fun, this big party full of people. Such a wonderful celebration."

Something flickered in his eyes, one brow ticking up as he watched me like he wasn't sure he could believe me. I kept my smile in place, my eyes soft.

"It will be a lovely party," he said finally, taking a seat next to me. He pulled out his phone immediately, scrolling through it. "You're going to love it."

And I knew I would.

But not for the reasons he thought.

"Looks like our cameras cut out for a bit," he mused with furrowed brows.

"I think the Internet was on the fritz," I offered with a shrug, eyes still on the TV. "We lost streaming, too."

The next few days were a blur of decorations and fake normalcy.

I confirmed the catering. I double-checked the guest list. I listened while Nathan talked about which executives would be there, who mattered, who I needed to charm. I nodded when he reminded me — again — how important it was that everything go perfectly.

"We only get one chance to make the right impression with our new team, and this is a big part of our first year," he told me the night before the party. "I need you focused. No disappearing. No silly girl hangouts like you had at the Gala."

I met his eyes. "Of course."

That night, after he was asleep, I locked myself in our bathroom and copied the ledger files from his email onto my burner phone. My reflection stared back at me in the mirror when I was through — and I was the perfect picture of calm composure, my appearance betraying the unsteady waters inside me.

*You are not trapped*, I told the woman staring back at me. *Not anymore.*

I thought about the scar on my hand, the one my stepfather had inflicted on me at such a young age I could never forget it. He'd stayed with me my entire life, not by choice, but because he'd marked me in a way I couldn't erase. And I thought about the way Nathan had grabbed me and then acted like it was nothing, like his hand bruising my wrist was deserved.

I thought about birthday candles, about Christmas lights, about how long I'd been shrinking myself to keep the peace.

And about how I was about to be the storm that disrupted everything, the hurricane Nathan would never see coming.

The evening of the party, I stood in front of that same mirror and adjusted my dress, my pulse steady for the first time in weeks.

I looked exactly like the woman Nathan believed he controlled.

But I wasn't her anymore.

This was survival. This was strategy. This was weeks of careful planning coming to fruition.

Tonight, he would be exposed. Tonight, every threat he'd ever made would come back to bite him. Tonight, the man who thought he owned me would learn what it meant to underestimate the woman standing beside him.

I smoothed my hands over my stomach and met my own eyes.

*Happy birthday, Ariana.*

It was time.

# CHAPTER 36

### SMILE

Ariana
Present

My birthday had always been a point of contention in my life.

How could it not be, when you're born on Christmas Eve? My mother always said it was the best Christmas gift she ever had — or at least, she said it when I was young, before the light in her eyes was snuffed out. The older I got, the more I realized my birthday was the worst day ever. We never truly celebrated it. I was lucky if I got a birthday cake after our Christmas Eve dinner, and usually, my birthday and Christmas gift was one and the same.

*"It was expensive,"* Mom would say. *"So it counts for both your birthday and Christmas."*

*"You're lucky to get anything at all,"* Jay would chime in once he was in the picture. *"Do you know how many kids wake up to no presents?"*

I'd learned to live with it. And honestly, I'd grown numb to wanting anything more as I got older. The first birthday I spent with Nathan, he took me out for a nice dinner and bought me a beautiful diamond tennis bracelet. He always made sure I had a gift after that, but the celebration was subpar — a dinner, usually, or sometimes a breakfast if we had a holiday party to attend with his colleagues. That happened more often than not.

I was used to spending my birthday with other people celebrating a completely different holiday.

The only one to ever make my birthday feel special was Shane.

And if everything went right tonight, he'd do it again.

It'd be the best birthday yet.

Oddly, I didn't feel nervous as I walked into the stunning event space on Nathan's arm. I expected my hands to tremble, my breaths to be shallow, but instead, I was calm and, if anything, a bit eager.

I believed in our plan. I believed in justice being served.

Still, there was something humming under the surface of my confidence as we entered the party, Nathan beaming at the guests who were already there and ready to greet us.

He'd hired multiple event planners to make his vision come to life — a winter wonderland in Tampa. The Vinoy had been an easy choice, and he'd literally bought out the bride who was set to have her wedding here tonight. The waterfront event space was one of the most luxe Tampa had to offer, and the event staff had transformed both the ballroom and the outdoor space into a magical world.

Outside, snow fell in soft, perfect drifts from hidden machines, artificial but convincing, dissolving in the warm Florida air before it could gather on the ground. A small ice-skating rink had been built along the waterfront, its surface gleaming beneath strands of white lights, guests laughing as they wobbled across it with champagne flutes in hand. Beyond it, aerial artists in crystal-studded white silks twisted and floated overhead, their movements slow and ethereal, like living ornaments suspended in midair.

Near the center of the terrace, a woman performed inside a massive glass snow globe, her breath fogging the clear walls as she danced through swirling flakes, the illusion so complete it felt like watching winter itself trapped and displayed for admiration.

Inside the ballroom, towering white florals climbed the walls, lit from below to glow like frost. Mirrored bars reflected candlelight in every direction, doubling the spectacle. The music from the band was lush and sweeping, designed to impress rather than invite.

There were nods to me, if you knew where to look — my favorite flowers tucked into the arrangements, a signature cocktail bearing my name in elegant script — but they felt like afterthoughts, like accents added once the real purpose of the night had already been decided.

This wasn't a birthday party.

It was a performance.

Nathan moved through the crowd like a king holding court, pausing just long enough at each cluster of guests to charm, flatter, and negotiate. His hand remained firm on my arm, guiding me where he wanted me, presenting me when it suited him, his smile never wavering. I couldn't help but compare how he was tonight versus how he'd been the night of Skate for Change. He'd fooled me with his admiration that night, making up for the executive dinner, playing his part of doting husband.

Tonight, his true colors shone too brightly to hide.

"Would be nice if you smiled a little more," he murmured between the teeth of his flashy smile as he toted me through the ballroom, waving to someone across the room he wanted to talk to. "It's your birthday party, not a funeral."

"Oh, it's a birthday party? For whom? Jesus?"

My sass surprised him. I saw it in how his head jerked toward me, like he was incredulous at my audacity. I never spoke to him like that.

But fuck it.

I was tired and over his bullshit, and I knew he was getting buried tonight.

"This was a very expensive party," he said, narrowing his gaze as he pulled us to a stop. "Maybe you should show a little gratitude."

"And maybe you should stop pretending tonight has anything to do with *me*."

Again, that surprise lit his face, then his nostrils flared, his skin turning red as he opened his mouth. But I didn't get to hear whatever he wanted to say, because in a sweep, my eyes were covered from behind, and I couldn't help but smile when I realized exactly who it was.

"Guess who?"

I ripped his hands away, turning to see my not-so-little brother looking far too grown in his tuxedo. He was taller than I was by a full two feet, but that didn't stop me from leaping up to throw my arms around his neck and pull him into a fierce hug.

"You made it!"

"You think I'd miss it?" He laughed into my ear, spinning me around before setting my feet on the ground again. "That whole finals bit was a lie."

"I had a sneaky suspicion, considering most finals are done by early December. Besides, you'd already promised you'd come. I knew my baby brother wouldn't bail on me."

"I thought I could surprise you. Why didn't you question me?"

"I wanted to let you think you surprised me."

Georgie grinned, taking me under his arm and threatening to dig his knuckles into my head, but he stopped short, kissing my hair, instead. "Punk."

"Brat," I shot back.

And then he gave me another squeeze, his adoration for me palpable. "Missed you."

"Missed you more."

It was the wildest thing, to look at the man Georgie had become. I still remembered the tiny baby sleeping in a crib in my bedroom. I remembered the frightened little boy who came under my guardianship. I remembered the awkward teenager trying to figure it all out.

And I saw so much in him.

I saw my mother, her bright blue eyes and wide smile. But I also saw Jay, his impressive height and shocking dark hair. I saw years of fear and terror, a child just trying to survive. And I saw the man who emerged, who went easy on me as I stepped in to care for him, who became the best man despite the horrible one who'd spawned him.

If anything was missing from tonight, it was him — and now that he was here, my heart felt whole.

"Nathan," Georgie said next, still beaming as he went in for a hug.

I didn't miss how stiff Nathan was when he returned the gesture. His eyes were hard on mine, an unspoken promise that we weren't done talking yet.

"Great to see you, kid," Nathan said when he pulled back, framing Georgie's arms and smiling with pride. "Or should I say Doctor?"

"Not yet," Georgie said, smiling, but I swore he looked uncomfortable. He shoved his hands in his pockets, his smile becoming a closed-lip one as he looked from Nathan to me and back. "What do you say, sis? Forty years old…

does that mean you can't hang and take a shot with your little brother at the bar?"

"Oh, she definitely won't be taking any shots tonight," Nathan answered for me. "There are a lot of important—"

"Please," I cut in, looping my arm through Georgie's without acknowledging Nathan. "I'll take *two* shots, and I won't grimace like a little baby the way you always do."

"It was a pickle back!" he defended.

I laughed, and then we were floating away, and Georgie waved at Nathan over his shoulder, promising to bring me back.

When we were far enough away, he covered my hand where it was holding his arm, arching a brow at me. "Trouble in paradise?"

"You and I both know damned well it's far from paradise."

That made Georgie stop. He pulled me to face him, concern etched between his brows. "I don't know, actually. I've always suspected, but you made it seem like..."

"I know," I said, unable to look at him. "I know. I pretended things were fine. I downplayed it."

"Is it bad?"

My stomach knotted. "It's not good." I finally looked up at him again, a small smile on my lips. "But it's ending. Tonight."

"Tonight?" He looked at where Nathan was locked in conversation across the room now before his gaze found me again. "I don't think he is quite on the same page as you are."

"He will be," I promised, and then I tapped his hand and pulled him toward the bar. "But enough for now. My little brother is in town and we're doing a shot."

"My choice."

"As if! It's *my* birthday."

"Fine, but only because I'm always considerate of my seniors."

I pinched his ribcage, leading him to the bar, where I didn't *actually* take a shot because I wanted to keep my wits about me. I did, however, slide the bartender a twenty and ask him to pour me a water shot so I could still show up my little brother.

And when we slammed the glasses down, Georgie wincing and shaking his head as he called me *an animal*, I laughed.

Right as my eyes collided with Shane's.

He was at the other end of the long bar, wrapped in a semi-circle with some of the other coaches.

His full attention was on me.

It was the first time my heart stuttered all night, and it had nothing to do with fear. It was the way he watched me. Like he'd been tracking me through the crowd. Like he knew every inch of me and was aching to touch it again. Like restraint was a physical thing binding him in place.

Like he loved me.

And I knew he did.

Butterflies sprung to life inside my stomach, making the smile that bloomed on my face impossible to fight. Shane was dressed to kill in a tailored beige suit with crisp lines that hugged his broad shoulders, the jacket sitting open just enough to hint at strength beneath it. His hair was styled with casual precision, stubble edged sharp along his jaw, his blue eyes dark with intent as they cut through the crowd and stayed fixed on me.

I felt the blush on my cheeks before my brother clocked it.

Georgie narrowed his gaze at me, then looked over his shoulder, and when he turned back to me, it was with his tongue in his cheek and a little pop of his brow.

"Oh. I see you and Shane McCabe have been reacquainted."

I feigned innocence, tipping my champagne to my lips and taking the tiniest sip.

"Come on, I want to go say hi."

Georgie looped my arm through his and I didn't fight him. I'd take any excuse to get close to Shane, even if just for a moment, even if I couldn't touch him the way I wanted to or feel his lips pressed against mine.

Shane pretended to look away, to be locked in his conversation until the moment Georgie and I approached. Then, he appropriately reacted with surprise, eyes widening at the sight of my little brother.

"Coach," Georgie said with that bright smile of his I loved so much. He extended his hand for Shane's. "Long time, huh?"

Shane laughed as he took Georgie's hand and shook it firmly, only to shake his head and pull my brother in for a hug. "I'll say. Last time I saw you, you were about this tall," he said, holding his hand by his hip. "And very much into *The Backyardigans*."

"Hey, that show slapped."

"I still know every word of 'Into the Thick of It.'"

"As you should." Georgie's smile turned mischievous as he threw his arm around me, ushering me closer. "Pretty crazy, the two of you back in the same place after all this time."

Shane's eyes finally slid back to mine, and the air hummed between us. "That's one word for it."

Again, I couldn't stop my smile, especially not when Shane held out his hand for mine and then pressed a slow, tender kiss to my skin.

"Happy birthday," he said. "You look stunning."

"For a forty-year-old," I supplied.

"For any age," he corrected, and I could see it, how he wanted to say more, how he longed to pull me into him as much as I wished to be held.

Georgie was too smart not to see it, too. He smirked at the two of us like a little devil as Shane and I finally broke apart.

And that was it.

That was the last little moment of serenity before my whole night imploded.

Georgie began chatting with Shane, a few of the other coaches joining in on our conversation and introducing themselves. When I felt the moment was right, I snuck in the question I couldn't hold in any longer.

"So... did the league ever confirm who's handling officiating for the next road stretch?" I asked Shane.

It was our code question, a way for me to ask him if things were on track, if the league rep who'd promised he'd be here tonight was coming through.

Shane didn't look at me right away.

It was the briefest hesitation, barely a beat, but I felt it like a shift in the air.

"Not yet," he said evenly. "Still waiting on confirmation."

My insides went cold.

He was supposed to be here by now.

Michael Reeves wasn't just some faceless league bureaucrat. He was senior counsel in the league's integrity office — the guy who handled betting irregularities, coercion, anything that threatened the credibility of the game itself. Shane had gone to him quietly, off the books at first, armed with screenshots of line shifts that made no statistical sense, the emails I'd pulled, practice anomalies documented over weeks, the whole Ben and Will timeline, and his full theory on the betting lines not adding up.

Then I'd slid in with even more — financial records from Sweet Dreams, audio from the overheard phone calls I'd recorded from the next room over, documentation of all his trips to Vegas that didn't line up with any manager meetings. It was all proof that Nathan wasn't just unethical — he was dangerous.

And he wasn't planning on stopping his schemes any time soon.

Reeves hadn't promised outcomes. He'd been very clear about that. But he had promised to show if the evidence held. He said he'd be here tonight to observe — and to intervene if necessary. He assured us he could make sure nothing could be buried once it came into the light.

*If what you're telling me is true*, he'd said, voice calm and clinical over the phone, *this won't be handled quietly*.

Tonight mattered because Nathan always overplayed his hand in public. Pressure to perform and not watching his alcohol intake made him sloppy. And we had witnesses, a whole ballroom full of them, for when we pulled our Ace.

Reeves was supposed to be here to see it.

I nodded like Shane's answer meant nothing, like my chest hadn't just gone tight enough to steal my breath. But my attention fractured instantly, scanning the room with new urgency.

When I spotted our Ace in the hole, my nerves frayed further.

Ben stood at a cocktail table near the edge of the terrace, sweat darkening the collar of his shirt despite the cool night air. A glass of brown liquor sat nearly empty in front of him, his hands flexing and curling at his sides like he didn't know what to do with them.

Shane had gotten him alone yesterday. He'd told him our whole plan, risking our necks because he trusted that Ben would help us take Nathan down. He hadn't come at him with accusations or threats, but with the kind of calm that made it hard to keep lying. He showed Ben the betting line shifts, the practice notes, the patterns that couldn't be explained away, and then he told him the truth — that this wasn't about punishing him, that it was about stopping the man who had put him in an impossible position.

Ben had tried to deny it at first, insisting he'd never thrown a game, that he'd never crossed that line. Shane hadn't argued. He'd let the silence do the work, letting the weight of the evidence settle until Ben finally cracked. When he did, it all came out at once.

Nathan had started by offering help, positioning himself as a savior when Ben's dad's medical bills began piling up, promising access and solutions Ben didn't have on his own. Then the favors came due.

Sitting a shift here.

Missing a play there.

And every hesitation on Ben's part was met with a reminder of who held the power and what would happen if Ben stopped cooperating.

Shane had listened without interruption. When Ben finally looked up, shame written all over his face, Shane told him what he hadn't realized he needed to hear — that what had been done to him was coercion, not choice, and that the league would see it that way if Ben told the truth now.

Cooperation meant protection. It meant taking down the real mastermind instead of letting him keep pulling strings from the shadows.

Tonight had been the final step in our plan: a public confrontation with witnesses everywhere, the truth spoken out loud where it couldn't be buried or spun. Ben had agreed. He'd promised he could do it.

But looking at him now, pale and unraveling at that cocktail table, it was obvious the fear had crept back in. The weight of it was too heavy, the cost suddenly too real.

When his eyes met mine across the terrace, panic flared bright and unmistakable. He shook his head once, set his glass down too hard, then shoved his hands into his pockets like he was trying to hold himself together from the inside.

And then he disappeared into the crowd.

My heart dropped into my stomach.

I turned back to Shane, and I knew he'd seen it too.

Our eyes locked, the same thought crashing through both of us at once.

This was going wrong.

Shane muttered an *excuse me*, ready to bolt after Ben, but before he could take a step, his eyes snagged on something else across the room. When I turned, dread slid through me.

His gaze sharpened, tracking past me, and when I followed it, my pulse kicked up another notch.

Carter.

He stood at a cocktail table in the far corner with Nathan, the two of them angled close together. Carter's posture was tense, shoulders hunched slightly as he spoke, his eyes darting around the room like he was afraid of being overheard. Nathan, on the other hand, looked relaxed, smiling in that smug, indulgent way he always did when he thought he had the upper hand.

This was it.

Carter was trying to get in on the betting. Trying to catch Nathan in the act.

For a split second, hope flared.

And then Nathan's smile slipped.

His eyes cut across the room and landed on me.

It was like a jaguar spotting its prey through the tall grass. His expression was cold, sharp, and knowing.

He said something low to Carter, straightened his jacket, and excused himself without another glance back. The way he moved toward me was unhurried, deliberate, like he wasn't worried about who was watching.

My next breath lodged in my throat. I couldn't look away, even as his menacing gaze tore through me like a blade.

I saw Georgie register it before Nathan even reached me — the shift in my posture, the way my smile fell away. My little brother went still, his body angling toward mine, concern flashing across his face as he took a step forward.

I shook my head subtly.

*Don't*, I warned without words.

When he reached me, Nathan's hand closed around my arm, fingers digging in hard enough to hurt. He pulled me a step away from the cluster of guests, just far enough that it looked intimate instead of aggressive. His grip tightened as he leaned in close, his breath hot and faintly alcoholic against my ear.

"If you think I don't know what you're up to," he murmured, his voice smooth and venomous all at once, "you're wrong."

My heart plummeted.

"I'm smarter than you are," he continued, his mouth curving into a cruel little smile. "You're not going to get me by sending some stupid idiot to try to trap me. And the way you've been acting tonight?" His eyes flicked briefly toward Shane, then back to me. "I'd bet you think you can just catch me in something and waltz away into the night. Run off with your college sweetheart. That right? That your big plan?"

The grin he gave me then was wicked and satisfied, especially when all the blood rushed from my face at his acknowledgment of me and Shane.

"Oh, trust me," he said softly. "I know about you and precious little Coach McCabe. I know about your past. I know you spent a day gallivanting around with him when I was out of town. I know *everything*, Ariana," he seethed. "Just like I know you thought Carter could get me to say something incriminating. Just like I know you tried to bribe Ben into playing your little game. But Ben's not betraying me. Not if he wants his dad to live."

My blood ran cold.

"And Shane's little attempt to get the league involved?" Nathan went on, squeezing my arm harder even as his voice softened a click, like we were just discussing when we should cut my birthday cake. "That's a wash, too. I've got everyone in my pocket, sweetheart. Most of all you."

He leaned back just enough to look at my face, his thumb brushing my jaw in a gesture that made my skin crawl.

"So smile," he whispered. "And give me a kiss. Or I'll make you give me much more later."

The room spun, the lights suddenly too bright, the music too loud. I could feel Shane somewhere behind me, the tension rolling off him in waves, but in that moment, Nathan was all I could see.

And for the first time all night, real fear took hold.

# CHAPTER 37

## THE COST OF VICTORY

Shane
Present

I'd been here before.

I could remember the sensation — lungs aching, throat closing in, brain shutting down. It'd happened to me once before. I was eight years old, grieving my parents, grieving the life I'd lived before, grieving what could have been. I jumped into an icy cold lake in the dead of winter just to feel something.

Shock came first. It always does. No matter how prepared you think you are, you're never ready for the way cold slices straight through you, how it steals your breath and your thoughts all at once. I was lucky it wasn't cold enough to make me inhale water, lucky I remembered to hold my breath. But I didn't last long. I surfaced, gasping, crying out, clawing my way toward shore while my body screamed at me for being so goddamn stupid.

And then — clarity.

That was the part people never talked about — the moment after panic burns itself out, when fear stops being useful and your brain snaps into something sharper. It's like survival flipping a switch.

And that's how I felt now, watching Nathan steer Ariana away, his hand around her waist, fingers digging into her hip bone.

She looked over her shoulder, and the panic in her eyes did me all the way in.

It was imploding.

Our perfectly laid plan was blowing up right in front of our faces.

"Fuck, man, I tried. I tried to get him to—" Carter zipped his lips shut before saying more than that, his fingers dragging back through his hair as he shook his head and watched Ariana go. "I'm sorry, man. I really thought I had him, and then he just looked at me and chuckled and walked away. He knew. He read right through me."

"What's going on?" Georgie asked. He followed my gaze to his sister, and when he turned back to me, his brows were bent. "Is Ariana in trouble?"

Carter and I exchanged glances. How the fuck was I supposed to answer *that*?

I took the deepest breath I could manage and decided to start with the truth.

"No," I said, squeezing Georgie's shoulder. "No, I don't think she is. But she will be. I need you to trust me, okay? I promise I'll tell you everything, but right now, I need you to just believe me when I tell you I have it under control."

Georgie didn't like that. I knew by the way his jaw tightened. He clocked his sister again and then turned back to me with a curt nod that I knew he didn't want to give me.

I felt honored that he did.

I squeezed his shoulder again, releasing it with a sigh as I tried to figure out what the fuck to do next. Carter was watching me like he wasn't sure what I'd just said to Georgie was fair anymore — not now that our plan was going up in flames.

But I had to believe.

Some people run when things fall apart.

Some freeze.

Some fight blindly and make it worse.

But there's another response — the one you earn when you've already lost everything once before, when panic has taught you its limits.

I knew this feeling.

The water was cold.

The shoreline was far.

And panic wouldn't get me there.

And so, I found stillness.

I calmed the fuck down.

And I started figuring a way out.

Nathan kept Ariana close after that, his hand never leaving her, and he paraded her around like a show pony. They posed for pictures. They grabbed the microphone from the band to thank everyone for attending. Nathan made a grand speech about his beautiful wife turning forty, and then we all watched her stand behind a lit cake as we sang *happy birthday* and she blew out the candles.

Her eyes met mine when the flames were out, a million questions burning through the rising smoke.

I checked my phone for the hundredth time, but my disappointment didn't waver.

Michael Reeves had ghosted me.

Part of me wondered if I was stupid for being surprised. Nathan had half our staff under his thumb and who knew how many players — what would make a league rep any different?

Money talked, and if Nathan was rigging bets in Vegas, my bet was he had a *lot* more money than any of us realized.

I was on high alert, looking for something, *anything*, when a familiar man walked in like a walking red flag.

I didn't recognize him the way you do a friend or colleague. I only vaguely knew that I had met him before, that I'd seen him around, that he'd been with the team at some point for something. But the moment I watched him approach Nathan, all my warning sirens sounded.

*He's not supposed to be here.*

My instincts flared.

Recognition stirred at the edges of my mind, vague and unsettling, like a name I couldn't quite place. This wasn't a donor. Not press. Not staff.

*Who was he?*

Nathan looked at the man with a forced smile, one I recognized now that I could see through his fake charm. He greeted him cheerily, but I saw the way his hand was hard on the man's shoulder as he peeled away from Ariana at last, steering his friend to the back of the ballroom and out the nearest door.

I rushed to her in an instant, and Georgie was right on my heels.

Ariana let out a long whoosh of a breath when I reached her, her blue eyes wide and afraid as she clung to me. I didn't dare take her into my arms, not yet, but I held her steady, forcing a calm breath that I hoped would bleed into her.

"Are you all right?" I asked, bending to meet her gaze.

She blinked, shaking her head. "I... I don't know. He knows everything, Shane. He saw through Carter's trap.

He has Ben back under his control. He—" She choked, shaking her head as panic started to slither in again. "He said Reeves is his friend."

That explained his absence.

I resisted the urge to curse and kick and scream and throw shit.

*Ice cold water. Distant shore.*

*Find a way out.*

"It doesn't matter. We will figure this out. Look at me." I waited until she did, and I squeezed her hand before dropping it reluctantly and forcing a big smile. The last thing we needed was to draw concern from anyone around us. "You're not going home with him tonight. This all ends here. Okay? Trust me."

She nodded, trying to mirror my smile, though hers trembled at the edges.

"This time tomorrow, you and I will be drinking the best smoothies in town and book shopping. Yeah?"

That earned me a little choke of a laugh, and she nodded again, surer this time.

I smoothed a hand over my suit, turning my attention to Georgie. "I need to check something. Can you stay with her? Don't let her out of your sight."

He didn't hesitate. "I've got her."

I squeezed Ariana's hand one more time — brief but deliberate, a reminder that she wasn't alone — and then I turned away.

I did my best not to hurry, to make it seem casual as I followed the path Nathan and his friend had carved through the crowd. When I slipped out of the ballroom, the noise from the band quieted, but the party raged on outside as I carefully moved along the perimeter, listening.

Nathan's voice reached me before I reached him.

"I will handle it."

I followed the sound, catching just a glimpse of the man who'd raised my hackles before I backed away and out of sight. I slowed my pace, angling myself behind a cluster of heaters and greenery, edging close enough to hear without being seen.

"He was supposed to sit," the man said, and though his words were accusatory, his voice was croaky with uncertainty, like he wasn't sure he could stand up to Nathan.

"I understand that was the original call, but sometimes things change."

"We had the under, Nathan," the man snapped. The edge in his voice was unmistakable now — panic sharpening into anger. "You told me you had control of him."

"I said I'd handle it, Ron," Nathan said smoothly. "Now, if you'll excuse me."

"What exactly is there to fucking handle at this point?" Ron shot back, and through the plants I was hiding behind, I saw him snatch Nathan by the arm. It earned him a death glare, and Nathan shook him off even as he continued seething. "You said he wouldn't play. He scores twice and now I've got people breathing down my neck. People who don't like being fucked with."

Ron's croaky voice was louder than he realized, louder than Nathan liked — and loud enough to draw attention. I tried to sink back farther, to be unnoticed, but there was a couple at a cocktail table who had gone silent, both of them turning to see what the commotion was.

"Things got complicated," Nathan murmured. "Now quiet the fuck *down*."

"You don't get to be sloppy," Ron hissed. "Not with my money."

Nathan lowered his voice, but now another table had angled toward them. "I'll make it right," he said, smiling and shaking Ron's hand as he grabbed his shoulder and acted like they were old pals. "Now, let's get you a drink. Hmm?"

"Are you working with another bookie? Is that what this is?"

Ron's words echoed over the party, and anyone within twenty feet turned their head.

There was no mistaking the word *bookie*.

Before Nathan had the chance to charm his way out of it, commotion stirred from inside the ballroom, the clattering of glassware and the abrupt screech of the band ceasing spilling out onto the lawn.

And then, a loud, angry voice.

"Where is he?"

The words cut through the air, raw and broken.

Heads turned. Conversations faltered.

"Where the *fuck* is he!?" Ben shouted.

I knew it was Ben even before I saw him, before he rushed through the open doors with half the team on his tail warning him to calm down.

He came through the crowd like a man unraveling at the seams, eyes wild, face slick with sweat, grief pouring off him in waves. I moved instinctively, stepping into his path.

"Ben—"

He shoved me hard enough that I stumbled back a step.

"My dad is dead!" he screamed. "My dad is fucking dead!"

Everyone froze, the party so silent we could hear the wind blow over the bay.

And my heart broke.

I knew the pain in this kid's eyes. I understood the acute ache of it, the piercing weight.

"He missed the infusion," Ben sobbed, shaking. "They said they couldn't — because he—"

"I'm sorry," I said, my hands up in surrender. "I'm so sorry, Ben. Why don't you and I go somewhere and talk about it, all right? We can—"

"*You*."

Ben wasn't listening to me at all, and when he pointed a finger over my shoulder with his entire body trembling with rage, I had no doubt who he'd spotted.

I turned just in time to see Nathan look around, as if he had no idea who Ben was pointing at.

And whatever was holding Ben together shattered completely.

He shoved past me, storming over to where Ron and Nathan were standing in the shadows. The crowd that stood between Ben and his target scattered, screams echoing as he ran right up and grabbed Nathan by the lapels of his tuxedo. "You said you'd help him!" Ben sobbed, shaking Nathan, his whole body trembling. "You said he'd be okay! I threw those games for you — I did everything you told me to do!"

Gasps rippled outward like shockwaves.

A murmur grew to a roar.

Before I knew it, Nathan was laughing and holding up his hands, trying to charm a party full of people who were now glaring at him — some of them through the lenses of the cameras on their phones.

It was the most sickening feeling I'd ever experienced in my life. My chest tightened painfully as I watched Ben unravel in front of all these people, watched his worst moment become public spectacle. I saw a player I'd coached, a kid I'd believed in, standing there with his grief exposed and his life forever altered.

This wasn't victory.

This was the cost.

I knew the look in his eyes too well — the hollow, bottomless ache that came when the world took something from you that it had no right to touch. I'd worn it myself once. I'd lived inside it. And seeing it reflected back at me now nearly brought me to my knees.

Every instinct in me wanted to shield him. To step in front of him. To take the blame, the fallout, the attention — anything to spare him from this moment. I wanted to rewind time and change the night his father got sick. The day Nathan first learned where to press. I wanted to pull Ben out of this before it ever reached this point.

But I couldn't.

Because the brutal, unavoidable truth was that Ben's pain was also the thing that finally stripped Nathan bare.

The grief that was tearing Ben apart was the same force cracking the illusion Nathan had spent years building.

Knowing that didn't make it easier to witness.

This wasn't justice delivered cleanly and neatly. It was justice born from wreckage, from a kid who should never have been put in this position, who never should've had to carry this weight.

And still... it was the moment everything changed.

Ben wasn't just breaking.

He was breaking Nathan.

And as much as it tore me apart to watch, I knew there was no stopping it now. The truth was out. The damage was visible. And there was no putting it back in the shadows where Nathan hoped it would always stay.

This was the end.

Not because we'd planned it perfectly.

But because someone had finally bled in the light.

Nathan reached for Ben, a soft laugh spilling from him like this was all some unfortunate misunderstanding as he grabbed his shoulders. "Ben, you're emotional. You've had too much to drink. Let's get you home and talk when you've calmed down."

I swore I was about to watch an NHL player kill a man with one punch, but before Ben could swing, a calm voice cut cleanly through the chaos.

"Nathan."

The man stepped forward from the edge of the crowd, his presence immediate and unmistakable. He was impeccably dressed, composed, his expression unreadable.

"Michael Reeves," he said evenly. "League Integrity."

Just as he introduced himself, I spotted Ariana standing next to Georgie near the door of the ballroom. Our eyes met, recognition widening her eyes as it buzzed through my veins.

I turned back to Nathan to find his face drained of color.

Then, reflexively, he smiled.

"Michael," he said, spreading his hands. "My old pal. Hell of a party, right? Looks like you showed up just in time to—"

Reeves shook his head once. The motion was small and controlled — an entire conversation in one tiny gesture.

"I'm afraid I'm no pal tonight," he said. "I need you to come with me now, okay?"

The panic in Nathan's eyes should have satisfied me. I should have been beaming at his demise. But I only felt sorry for the bastard.

What a miserable existence. What a fucking terrible life to live in, where you had everything you could possibly want and it still wasn't enough.

"We need to speak privately, Nathan," Reeves said when Nathan didn't move. "*Now*. You can either come willingly or we can assist you."

Security was already moving in.

Nathan looked around, searching for an ally, a lifeline. His gaze snagged on Ariana across the lawn, her face bloodless, Georgie's arm firm around her shoulders.

For the first time, he looked a little like a man regretting his choices.

"This isn't necessary," Nathan said tightly.

Reeves met his eyes. "I'm afraid it is. I'll admit, I admire your creativity. You went to impressive lengths to delay me tonight — flagging my arrival with airport security, having me intercepted the moment I landed, questioned, separated from my phone."

The explanation for why Reeves hadn't answered my texts had my heart pounding quicker. My eyes caught Ariana's across the crowd.

*He was always on our side.*

"It didn't help that you'd preceded tonight's actions with calls to the league," Reeves continued. "Claims that the situation was already being handled internally. Suggestions that my presence here would be unnecessary and disruptive."

Reeves's gaze drifted to Ben standing shattered in the open, to the guests frozen in place, to the phones raised and recording.

"It was clever," Reeves said. "And it bought you time."

Then his eyes locked back onto Nathan's.

"But all it did was delay me long enough to see the truth loud and clear. You're not the only one with influence, Mr. Black. And this stopped being something you could control a long time ago."

Security stepped in beside him.

"Now," Reeves finished, "you're coming with us one way or another. My suggestion is that you don't make more of a scene than you already have."

And just like that, Nathan Black was escorted out of his own party, the crowd buzzing with shock, whispers, and the unmistakable sense that something irreversible had just occurred.

For a beat, I couldn't move.

The adrenaline that had carried me through the last hour drained all at once, leaving my limbs heavy, my chest tight. The noise of the party faded into something distant and unreal, like I was underwater again — except this time, I wasn't panicking.

I was finding the sweetest release.

Carter moved to Ben, approaching him carefully before our goalie let Carter take him into an embrace. Carter nodded to me that he had it under control, and with that taken off my plate, my heart could follow the magnet pulling it so forcefully.

My gaze found Ariana.

She stood frozen near the edge of the ballroom doors, Georgie still beside her, one hand hovering at her back like he wasn't sure whether to pull her close or let her go. Her face was pale, eyes glassy, her breath coming too fast. She looked like she was bracing for impact that had already passed.

I didn't think.

I crossed the distance between us in long, urgent strides, my heart thundering in my ears with every step. *Go easy*, my common sense told me. *You're still in public. She's still a married woman. You've got to take this slow.*

But I just fucking couldn't.

I swept through that crowd with everyone watching me and pulled her into my arms.

She made a small, broken sound as she crashed into me, her hands fisting in my jacket like she was afraid I'd disappear if she let go. I wrapped myself around her, one arm tight across her back, the other cradling her head against my chest, breathing her in like that first sip of oxygen upon ascension.

"I can't believe what just happened," she whispered, her voice muffled against my collarbone. She was shaking so hard. "I was so scared, Shane. I thought it was over. I thought I'd have to leave with him. I didn't know what he'd do, I didn't—"

"I know," I said hoarsely, pressing my mouth to her hair. "I've got you. It's over. He can't touch you anymore."

I pulled back just enough to see her face, my hands sliding to cup her cheeks. Her eyes searched mine, raw and unguarded, and in that moment, I didn't care who was watching. I didn't care about optics or timing or consequences.

I kissed her.

It was urgent and inescapable, my mouth firm on hers, hers soft against mine, our bodies melding together as we clung to each other like the rope that led to the safety of the shoreline. I kissed her like relief and grief and love had tangled together and there was no separating them, like I'd been holding my breath under that icy water since the day I left her and finally got to exhale.

She kissed me back without hesitation, her hands sliding up my chest, anchoring herself to me.

Somewhere beside us, Georgie cleared his throat.

"Well," he said mildly, a crooked smile tugging at his mouth as Ariana and I broke apart. We still held fast to one another even as Ariana's cheeks burned from the realization of how many people were watching. "I see you two have done a bit more than reacquaint yourselves."

A few startled laughs rippled through the small cluster of people nearby, the tension breaking just enough to let the night breathe again. Ariana let out a shaky laugh of her own, her forehead resting against my chest as she exhaled. When she looked up at me, her eyes were wet but resolute.

And then, as if out of nowhere, like Mother Nature was putting on a show just for us...

It began to rain.

It was soft at first, a few warning droplets that had anyone still loitering outside moving quickly for the doors — Georgie included. But Ariana and I just looked up at the sky as it began to open, the rain falling harder and faster and soaking us to the bone.

"I don't mind the rain, you know," Ariana said, her watery smile making my knees buckle as her eyes locked on mine.

"It washes everything away," I finished for her.

With a nod, she wrapped her arms around my neck again, pulling me into her for a longing kiss as the rain poured around us. And it was there in that moment with us — our fresh start. Our new beginning. No matter how messy it was, it was ours.

"Can we go home?" Ari asked me over the thrum of the rain. Then her expression faltered, uncertainty creeping in as reality tried to assert itself again. "Or— I mean— your home. I don't... I don't know what to call it yet."

I brushed her wet hair back from her face, my thumb tracing her cheekbone, my gaze steady on hers.

"Home is what we make it," I said quietly. "My house. Your house. A new house altogether — it doesn't matter." I leaned in, resting my forehead against hers. "Wherever you are, that's where home is for me."

# CHAPTER 38

## IT HAPPENED TO YOU

Ariana
Present

"I wish I could crawl inside your mind right now."

I blinked, turning toward the deep voice that grounded me. Shane was rolled on his side, his eyes searching mine, fingers sliding up under his t-shirt that I wore and hooking around my hip. His touch was so different than the one I'd had there earlier in the night. Where Nathan's had been possessive and cruel, Shane's was tender and assuring.

He was rooting me in a time I could so easily be knocked over.

"It's not a pretty place," I muttered, the corner of my lips rising and falling again.

"Tonight was a lot."

I nodded, rolling toward him and linking our legs together. We'd left the party with all the chaos still happening. Maven and Grace had stopped me long enough to give me a big hug and promise they'd take care of everything in my absence. They assured me they'd send a full update, but insisted I go and get away from the noise.

I was so thankful for their friendship, even if I was still amazed I had it at all.

We'd taken Georgie to a hotel before coming to Shane's. We would spend Christmas together tomorrow, and then he was flying out on the first flight the following day to get back to school. Of course, he tried to change it after everything happened, insisting he needed to be here, but I assured him the best thing he could do for me was to get back to his life and not worry about me. I was his older sister, the closest thing he had to a parental figure, and the thought of him missing out on school for me was unthinkable. I promised him I'd be okay, and that I'd come visit him soon.

"I'm proud of you," he'd whispered in my hair during our last hug, one I held tight and didn't want to break.

It had made tears flood my eyes in an instant.

"I'm sorry I let it get here."

He'd shaken his head. "You have nothing to apologize for."

I wished I believed him. I wished I didn't feel just as much guilt and shame as I did relief lying in Shane's arms right now.

We'd come back to his place after dropping Georgie off, Shane running me a hot bath and playing my favorite music as he helped me undress and lower into the steaming water. He'd offered me food, but I couldn't eat. I did drink the water he gave me, though, and accepted his t-shirt. When I slipped it over my head, I sighed, content.

It smelled like him — elemental, all ice and metal and pine.

"Do you want to talk about any of it?" Shane asked, his fingers toying with mine.

I sighed. "I know I should. I just..." I bit my lip. "Shane, I feel so ashamed I ever let it get to this point, that I ever found myself in this position. When he grabbed me tonight, when he threatened me..." I held back tears, shaking my head. "I just couldn't believe I didn't see it, that I didn't realize how bad it was getting."

Shane nodded in understanding, his eyes falling to where our fingers danced together. "Can I walk you through something?"

I nodded, swallowing past the lump in my throat.

"People like Nathan don't pick their partners randomly," he said. "They're observant. They clock patterns. They notice who's learned to survive by being agreeable, who's used to carrying responsibility, who mistakes consistency for safety because they've never had anything steady."

My chest tightened.

"He didn't hurt you right away," Shane went on. "He made you feel seen. He chose you when I had walked away. He provided steady when you had been living in an earthquake. That wasn't an accident. That was him mirroring what you needed most — because it bought him trust."

I swallowed. "So I was... groomed?"

His jaw flexed, not in anger at me — but at the word itself. "I think you were studied," he said carefully. "And then slowly boxed in. That's not the same thing as being stupid or blind. It means he used empathy as a weapon."

Tears slid down my temples, soaking into his pillow.

"I keep thinking I should've known," I whispered. "I'm educated. I've read the studies. I've worked cases like this. More than that, I watched my mom." That had my chest squeezing so tightly I curled in on myself. "How embarrassing, to walk right into the situation I judged my mother for being in."

"Knowledge doesn't protect you when someone's working on your nervous system," he said gently. "Especially when they're offering the thing you've been taught to crave — peace."

I let out a shaky breath.

"And when it started to feel wrong," he continued, "your brain did what it always does. It tried to make it make sense. That's survival, Ari. Not failure."

I turned my face into his chest, my fingers fisting in his shirt.

"You didn't let this happen," he murmured into my hair. "It happened to you."

The words cracked me wide open, and finally, I found permission to break.

I sobbed into Shane's chest, his arms wrapping me up and holding me as I fell apart. I cried for my mother, for all she had to endure, for how her life ended. I cried for Georgie and what he had to go through. I cried for Ben tonight, for a young boy who was caught up in a broken system.

And I cried for myself.

I cried for that young, innocent girl I once was, for the child who had to grow up too fast. I cried for the one Shane left behind even though I understood why he did it. I cried for the woman who raised a child when she was still one herself, for the woman who clung to a monster because it was the devil she knew.

Shane didn't falter. He held me and kissed my hair and rubbed my back, letting me feel it all.

After a while, when my sobs had subsided, he added quietly, "And I think you already know this part — but I'll say it anyway. Talking to someone... a therapist who understands trauma and coercive dynamics... it will help. Someone rewired the rules inside you without your consent," he said. "And you deserve help untangling that. At your pace. On your terms."

I nodded slowly. "I know," I whispered. "I don't want to carry this into the rest of my life."

"You won't," he said, brushing his lips to my forehead. "And you won't do it alone."

I sniffed, pressing up until I was on my elbows and looking down at him. "I'm so happy you're here."

"Oh, baby," he said, sweeping my hair back and leaning up to kiss me. "I'm so happy you're letting me be in your life again."

He pressed his lips against mine, his hands in my hair, the kiss firm and comforting.

"What happens next?" I asked, wiping the last of the wetness from my cheeks. "With Nathan, I mean?"

Shane exhaled slowly, like he was choosing his words with care.

"Okay," he said. "I'm going to tell you what I know — not to overwhelm you, but so this doesn't feel like some dark, endless thing hanging over your head."

I nodded, bracing myself.

"By tomorrow morning, the league will already have started the formal process," he went on. "They don't mess around with allegations like this — especially when there are witnesses, threats, physical intimidation, and potential abuse of power."

My stomach twisted.

"They'll assign an independent investigator," he said. "Not someone tied to the team. Usually a former prosecutor or someone who specializes in workplace misconduct. Their job is to gather statements, review evidence, and figure out whether league policy was violated."

"What kind of evidence?" I asked quietly.

"Everything we've already supplied and more," he said. "Texts. Emails. Phone records. Security footage. Witness accounts. Anything from tonight. Anything from before tonight."

I swallowed. "And you?" I asked. "What happens to you?"

"I'll be questioned," he said, his jaw tightening. "Probably early. And yes — there's a good chance I'll be placed on temporary suspension while they investigate."

My heart lurched. "What? Shane—"

"Hey." He lifted his hand, brushing his thumb gently along my jaw. "Listen to me. That part isn't punishment. It's standard."

I shook my head. "But you didn't do anything."

"I know," he said softly. "And they know that too. But when someone in leadership is directly involved — when I intervened, when I confronted him — it becomes about optics and due process. They freeze everyone in the immediate orbit until the facts are clear."

Tears pricked my eyes again. "I hate that this affects you."

"I don't," he said immediately. "If the cost of taking him down and getting you in the process is a few weeks on the sidelines, I'll pay it every time. Without hesitation."

"How long does all of this take?" I asked.

"Usually a few weeks. Sometimes longer if it's complex. But you won't be left in the dark. They'll keep you informed. You'll have support — legal, therapeutic, advocacy. You won't be doing this alone."

"And Nathan?" My voice barely held steady. "What happens to him if they... if they believe us?"

"If the investigation substantiates what we've reported and what has been accused tonight, he's done."

My breath caught. I almost felt bad for how giddy it made me, to know that this could be the end of his reign of terror. I wondered how many other people were caught up in it all, who would be impacted.

"Best-case for him?" Shane continued. "Permanent suspension. Termination for cause. His contract voided. He'll never work in this league again."

"And worst-case?"

"If criminal charges are pursued — and they very well could be — then that's out of the league's hands. That becomes law enforcement. Court cases. Consequences that follow him for the rest of his life."

I stared at him, my chest rising and falling fast. "This is kind of wild."

"I know. I mean, there's no spinning it where he gets out of the situation without paying a price," Shane said. "This isn't something money or charm fixes. He crossed lines that can't be uncrossed."

I curled into him again, my forehead resting against his collarbone. "I'm scared," I admitted. "And I'm so fucking tired of being scared."

"I know," he said, holding me tighter. "This part — the waiting — is often the hardest. But you have me. Through every step. Okay?"

He kissed the top of my head.

"And here's what I want you to remember. Right now, your only job is to take care of yourself. Sleep. Eat when you can. Breathe. Let the professionals handle the process. Let me handle what I can."

I pulled back just enough to look at him. "You're really okay with all of this? The suspension and the fallout and..." I waved my hand. "All of it?"

His mouth curved into a small, steady smile.

"I've lived with worse consequences for doing nothing," he said. "This? This is me doing the right thing."

I leaned into his palm when he touched my face.

"None of this erases your life, either, Ari. This was a dark chapter, but you get to decide what happens next. The pen is back in your hands."

I nodded slowly, letting his words settle.

"Okay," I whispered.

He brushed his thumb beneath my eye. "Okay."

"I keep wondering how all of this works with me filing for divorce."

Shane's expression softened. "That's a really fair thing to be thinking about," he said. "Especially right now."

"Does everything happening slow it down? Or... complicate it?"

"In some ways, yes," he said honestly. "In others, it actually gives you more protection."

I looked up at him.

"I mean, obviously I don't know what will happen. But from my experience... I have an idea," he said. "The league investigation and the criminal side — if it goes that direction — are separate from family court. Different systems, different timelines. But they talk to each other in indirect ways."

"Meaning?"

"Meaning the court isn't going to ignore the fact that there are active allegations of abuse, intimidation, and coercive control," he said. "Especially if there's documentation, witnesses, or findings from an independent investigator."

My shoulders sagged a little in relief.

"So what happens first?" I asked.

"You file," he said. "As soon as you're ready."

"So, tonight?"

He smirked, thumbing my jaw. "Your attorney will likely request emergency or temporary orders right out of the gate — things like financial support, exclusive use of the marital home, no-contact provisions. Judges take those requests very seriously when safety is involved."

"Would they... expedite it?" I asked.

"Not the entire divorce," he said carefully. "Divorce is still divorce. But the protective pieces? Yes. Those can move fast. Days, sometimes."

I swallowed. "And the prenup?"

His jaw tightened slightly, like it pissed him off that Nathan ever made me sign one. "Prenups aren't untouchable," he said. "If there's evidence you signed under duress, emotional coercion, misinformation, or while being actively manipulated — especially if abuse can be established — then parts of it can be challenged."

"Parts," I repeated.

"Sometimes all of it," he said. "Sometimes just the sections that leave one party vulnerable. It depends on how it was drafted and what can be proven. But courts don't love agreements that were designed to trap someone."

I felt something loosen in my chest.

"And financially?" I asked quietly. "I don't want his money — but I also don't want to be... stuck."

"You won't be," Shane said without hesitation. "Temporary spousal support exists for exactly this reason. So someone can leave safely and get back on their feet without being punished for surviving."

I closed my eyes for a second, the words settling in.

*Leave safely.*

*Get back on my feet.*

For the first time, my thoughts slipped past the fear and exhaustion and landed somewhere unexpected. I pictured choices, a schedule that belonged to me, going back to school if I wanted, taking a job without asking permission.

I imagined a life that didn't require constant calculation or apology.

Freedom that wasn't borrowed.

Freedom that was *mine*.

The realization was almost dizzying, a small, bright thread woven through the dark chaos of the night.

"And if he's suspended?" I asked. "Or charged?"

"That actually strengthens your position," he said. "It limits his leverage. It shifts power away from him. And if he tries to retaliate, stall, or intimidate you through the divorce, that becomes evidence."

I let out a slow breath. "So I don't have to wait for everything else to finish."

"No," he said gently. "You don't have to put your life on hold until the world catches up. You can move forward while the investigations run in parallel."

I stared at the ceiling, absorbing it all.

"I hate that this is my life," I admitted.

"I know," he said softly. "But here's the part I want you to hold onto — this isn't you fighting him alone in a vacuum. There are systems in place now. There are eyes on him, and he's going to have to take accountability one way or another."

He brushed his thumb along my arm.

"And you're not asking for special treatment," he added. "You're asking for safety. Courts understand that distinction."

My throat tightened. "I don't want this to turn into another long war."

"It doesn't have to," he said. "Especially if the truth keeps coming out, and I have a feeling there are more people involved who will want to save their own asses, so they'll be truthful about Nathan and what he's been up to. And most people like him don't want their lives examined under fluorescent lighting. My bet is he'll do what he can to settle quickly."

That earned a weak, breathless laugh from me.

"I'll help you find the right attorney," he added quickly. "Someone trauma-informed. Someone who knows how to protect you without dragging you through hell."

I met his eyes. "You don't have to do all of this."

"I know," he said. "But I want to."

I rested my forehead against his chest. "I'm so tired."

"I know," he whispered. "And you don't have to solve the rest of your life tonight." He kissed me gently. "One step at a time, Ari. Tonight, you're safe. Tomorrow, we start building the exit."

My head was swimming, but I felt the muscles along my spine relax marginally now that I had at least a vague idea of what would happen next. I cuddled into Shane more, hooking my leg up over his hip so his thigh was between mine, his arms wrapping me up, my head against his chest.

We lay like that for a long while, my eyelids growing heavy as his fingers drew lines and circles on my skin.

And as the heaviness of the night drained away, heat slipped in to take its place.

My heart picked up its pace in my chest as my body catalogued every place we touched. A spark of electricity zipped through me, making me squirm against Shane, my hips rolling. His warm thigh gave just the briefest shot of friction to my clit, and my breath caught.

"Ari..." Shane warned, his hands tightening on my hips. But he didn't stop me. He rolled with me, helping me find that sweet build of electricity. "I thought you said you were tired."

"Not too tired to touch you," I said breathlessly. "Not when I've waited decades to feel you like this again." And then my arms were hooking around his neck and pulling his mouth down to meet mine.

## CHAPTER 39

### EVERYWHERE

Shane
Present

I couldn't get enough.

I couldn't kiss her enough, couldn't touch her enough, couldn't feel her body close enough to mine. Ariana climbed on top of me, and I slid my hands under my t-shirt that she wore, feeling the soft curves of her hips beneath it. She rocked against my erection, and I groaned, nipping at her lip and deepening the kiss.

"I need you," she panted, tugging at my shirt until I leaned up enough to pull it over my head. Her mouth was on mine the second the fabric was gone. "Need you so fucking much."

"I'm here. I'm yours," I promised, and then it was her turn to strip. I slid the fabric up over my wrists until her arms lifted, and then I peeled the t-shirt the rest of the way off, flinging it somewhere off the bed. "And I *want* you, Ari. With every fucking cell in my body."

She whimpered when I sealed that intention with a bruising kiss, when I flipped her into the sheets. She had on a pair of my boxer briefs under that shirt, and I took my time sliding them over her hips, down her thighs, and finally off each ankle.

The night had been a whirlwind, as messy as getting stuck in a storm out at sea. We were wind-whipped and drenched from fighting, our bodies aching from holding on, and yet we were both too hungry to sleep just yet.

I made quick work of my joggers and briefs before I was on top of her, sliding between her legs, my cock resting at the apex of her thighs as I kissed her greedily. I devoured her mouth, running those kisses down her neck and over her collarbone before I was sucking her earlobe between my teeth.

"I feel you everywhere," she rasped, digging her nails into my back as her ankles locked behind my hips. "Against my body. In my heart. In my *soul*." She claimed my mouth with her own, continually pulling at me like she couldn't get me near enough. "I won't ever lose you again. I *can't*."

"You never lost me to begin with," I promised, and I paused the heat between us long enough to pull back and stare into her eyes. I needed her to see I meant what I said next. "I have always been yours, Ariana. My heart has never belonged to another. And I will be right here with you, by your side, until I take my last fucking breath. You hear me? Until these bones turn to ash, I am yours."

She nodded, wincing as she pulled my mouth back to hers. We were frantic then, kissing and biting and sucking as our words dissolved into breathless pants and moans. I hiked her leg up, hooking the back of her thigh over my forearm and sliding inside her with one deep thrust. We both needed it so badly there was no waiting, no foreplay, no time to play around and tease and toy. We had to be connected. I had to bury myself inside her and she had to feel me deep.

"Christ." The word shuttered out of me as I bottomed out, withdrew, and sank back inside. "That's it, baby. This is what I want forever — to feel you stretching for me, to hear those little moans you make, to taste these pretty lips." I kissed her before leaning to one side so I could reach for her clit. "To taste this, too."

Her whimper was my reward, and she squirmed under my touch, writhing and rocking and seeking more.

I wanted to take my time, but I also craved exactly what she was begging for with her desperate scratches against my skin. I knew we'd have so many nights ahead to worship one another, but tonight we needed to claim.

"I was made for you," I groaned, thrusting hard. "If you're not mine, I don't know who I am." Another thrust. "Lost. That's what I've been without you. Hopelessly fucking lost and now I'm found." Thrust. Thrust. Moan. Sigh.

I pushed back onto my knees for better leverage, holding fast to Ariana's hips as she spread her legs wide and allowed me the perfect access to drive in. Her beautiful, full tits bounced with every pulse, her hands flying into her hair, lips swollen from my kiss.

The sight was enough to undo me.

I tried to wait, but I just couldn't fucking handle it.

"Fuck, Ari. I can't—"

She moaned and urged me on, reaching between her legs to play with her clit and come with me. And the second she tightened around me and trembled out her first cry of pleasure, I gave myself permission to follow.

I came with her name on my lips and in my soul, just like she'd said before. If there really was such a thing as soul mates, she was it for me.

Neither of us were satiated. We'd no sooner come down from the first high than we were reaching for the next. This time, Ariana flipped over, offering me a beautiful sight of her backside before she was begging me to take her from behind.

I was still wet from my release, and when I pushed inside her, my cum leaked out and coated us more.

"Fuck," I breathed, the sensation too much, the reality so fucking perfect I felt I didn't deserve it.

I lowered until I could hold her breasts while I fucked her, until I could bite her throat as each moan rumbled through it.

"You feel so fucking good like this," I breathed against her neck.

She moaned her agreement, throwing her head back against my shoulder as she met my thrust with one of her own. She thrust her ass back against me, our skin slapping together, sweat prickling the backs of our necks.

"You need more, don't you," I mused, smirking against her slick skin as I trailed a hand down her back and over the swell of her ass. "So needy. So filthy. So fucking *mine*."

I pressed a finger inside her, my cock buried in her pussy as I finger-fucked her asshole, and it earned me the sweetest demolition of her control. She trembled so hard she nearly fell into the sheets, her moans loud and unbridled, her body convulsing with desire.

"That's it, Ari," I crooned, slowing my pulses so I could push her to her edge. I curled my finger in time with my cock stretching her until she was meeting my thrusts again, begging for more. "You're so full of me, aren't you, baby? Taking my cock so well. Taking this finger in your ass."

That was all it took for her to find her second release, and the way she whimpered through it told me it hit lightning hot and fast.

For hours, we destroyed my bed. I fucked her until my thighs were weak and she was pushing me onto my back, taking over and riding me into another climax. I tasted her until she came on my tongue. She repaid the favor after only a couple hours of sleep.

We wrapped ourselves up in one another, locking out the outside world. There was so much to face when the morning light came, but the night belonged to us.

And the future did, too.

# CHAPTER 40

## ON TOP OF THE WORLD

Shane
Six Months Later

"This was a hard-fought battle, and I think our team needed the win more this season than ever before. I mean, I don't have to say it for all of you in this room to know we've had a tough go of it. A lot of changes. A lot of distractions along the way."

The room full of press murmured their acknowledgment to my statement, some of them sharing knowing looks across the room.

"I'm always proud of this team, win or lose, because I know how hard we work. I know the personal and professional sacrifices we've all made along the way. But I'm extra proud tonight. I'm..." I shook my head, running a hand over my jaw. "These guys played their hearts out in this last series, and I know they didn't just win it for themselves. They won to make a statement. The Tampa Bay Ospreys are here to stay, and we're a threat — not just this season, but every one."

Hands flew up around the room, everyone vying for my attention to be the next one to ask a question, and I couldn't help the goofy grin I wore despite how exhaustion was seeping into my bones the later the night turned. I was damp and cold from having a cooler full of ice water thrown on me. My voice was hoarse from screaming. Every bone in my body ached like I'd run a marathon, but none of it mattered.

Because we'd won the Stanley Cup.

It felt even more surreal than the first time it happened for me. I always imagined the day I'd make it there as a player, the day I'd hoist that trophy over my head and kiss it as I skated around an arena full of screaming fans. But as a coach? It hit even deeper. I felt pride like I couldn't explain, knowing what every single player had to overcome and push through in order to make the win happen.

I nodded to a local journalist in the back of the room. "What do you think this means for Perry?"

I chuckled. "Well, I guess it means he gets to retire the way all athletes dream, doesn't it? Going out on top."

The room laughed and nodded, cameras flashing.

"No, I know this means so much to him. You'll have your time with him and you can hear it from his own mouth, but no one works harder than Pickles. He's been the heartbeat of this team for years, and we're going to miss him like a limb, but Sandin is ready to step in. He's proven that this season against all odds." I balked at the choice of words. "No pun intended."

The laughter was a little uncomfortable then. It was hard to make light of such a serious situation, but at the same time, we couldn't run from it. What Nathan had done, the way so many players and staff had participated — it was as much a part of our story this season as the championship win was.

The last six months had taken the organization by storm, an investigation leading us straight into chaos. The fallout had been brutal and immediate. Ownership had moved fast with public statements, internal audits, and emergency leadership brought in to stabilize the team while the investigation tore through us. We finished the season without a general manager, the front office run by an interim committee while the league monitored every decision we made.

I was relieved to find I hadn't been the only one on our team who was suspicious. Several members of the staff and team had suspected something was off before I ever spoke up, questioning betting lines and injuries that never quite healed the way they should. But no one had imagined the scope of it. Not until it was too big to deny.

We'd found proof that there was a trainer working against Will — one who'd poisoned him the night he vomited on the ice, and then purposefully fucked with his recovery plan to make his injuries flare up rather than get better. It'd taken weeks to get him back up to top playing shape, and in that time, Ben had been suspended as he underwent investigation.

We'd survived on a third-string goalie, one pulled up from our AHL affiliate, a kid who still looked like he needed permission to grow a beard. He'd stood between the pipes like he had nothing to lose and everything to prove, and somehow, that had been enough to keep us afloat while the rest of the house burned.

Ben's name had been dragged through the mud early on. What the public never saw at first was the leverage Nathan had used to trap him. Ben's father had been dying from aggressive pancreatic cancer, and Nathan had promised access to elite care and a clinical trial that had promise. And for a while, it worked.

But the moment Ben hesitated, the moment Nathan suspected he might turn, that access vanished. Appointments were delayed. Paperwork was stalled. The next round of treatment never came.

That was what led to his father's death in the end.

The league ruled what had happened for what it was: coercion. Ben was cleared. But cleared didn't mean untouched. He lost months of his career, his privacy, his father. The punishment for him was never about the law — it was the cost of surviving someone who never should've had that kind of power.

When he came back, he played like hell itself was chasing him. I'd never seen someone channel pain so cleanly, so relentlessly. The locker room followed his lead.

Not everyone made it back.

The investigation tore through the organization with surgical precision, and there were more players in Nathan's sick game than we realized or hoped for. Trainers. Support staff. A couple of players who'd known more than they admitted at first. Some were fired. Some were suspended indefinitely. A few were quietly cut loose and would never work in professional hockey again. It hurt to look at the empty stalls, the missing faces, but it hurt worse to think about what would've happened if none of it had come to light.

As for Nathan: there was no redemption arc waiting for him.

By March, the league had terminated him for cause. His name was stripped from everything, his contracts voided, his reputation scorched. The league barred him permanently. And the criminal case that followed ensured he would never again hold a position where power could be mistaken for entitlement.

By April, law enforcement stepped in. By May, the words *criminal investigation* were no longer whispered but printed in bold type, his face splashed across screens with language that left no room for spin.

The man who'd once commanded rooms with charm and money now couldn't buy his way out of the consequences.

He tried to reach out to Ariana once, using his lawyer as the messenger. His request was a bold one: he wanted to see her, to get "closure."

Ari never replied.

She didn't owe him another word.

Later, we'd learn how close we'd come to losing everything. One of the staff members we trusted had tipped Nathan off with details that never should've left our circle. Nathan didn't know everything, but he knew enough to start watching. Enough to tighten his grip. Enough to pay attention and play dirty. That was why he'd read right through Carter's attempt to lure him at the party.

Amidst all the insanity, the Tampa Bay Ospreys rebuilt.

Piece by piece. Line by line. Trust by trust.

We played angry hockey. Honest hockey. Hockey that didn't fuck around or give anyone room to doubt us. We showed up every game with something to prove — and we did it.

So tonight, somehow, impossibly, we stood on top of the world.

The press conference wrapped up in a blur — handshakes, flashes, congratulations shouted over the din. When I finally stepped back into the hallway, the celebration roaring from the locker room down the way, I let out a long, relieved sight.

And then I saw her.

Ariana stood just beyond my office, her hands clasped in front of her, shoulder leaning against the wall. She wasn't wearing team colors — an oversized blue and white sweater paired with jeans, hair loose around her shoulders, her smile soft and real in a way I hadn't seen in years.

My heart galloped at the sight of her.

Six months ago, she'd been counting her life in court dates and survival breaths. Now she lived in a small place of her own, sunlight pouring through windows onto the library she'd built herself, and a bed she could sprawl out in without fear of the person crawling into it with her.

The divorce was finalized.

It had been mostly clean and quiet, especially in comparison to the investigations into Nathan's activity with Vegas. Georgie was still in med school, his future intact, paid for without strings attached thanks to a judge who understood all too well what Ariana had been put through.

And Ariana was back where she belonged — working in social services again.

She'd started working with the local hospital, Sweet Dreams too tainted with Nathan for her to pick up where she'd left off with it. Instead, she passed it to the very capable hands of our organization and turned to community work, specializing in helping women and kids find their way out of the very hell she'd survived.

She was turning pain into purpose without letting it swallow her whole.

Therapy was a part of that journey for her, and I was so proud of how vulnerable she was being not just with her therapist, but with me, too.

We were taking it slow. She lived at her place, and I lived at mine, but there were many nights we stayed over. Mostly, we were having fun dating again — drinking smoothies as we walked the beach, buying books from the used bookstore downtown, going to concerts as we found new artists to fall in love with.

Learning each other again.

We were uncovering the people we'd been together all those years ago, clinging to the connection that had made our foundation so strong. We were exploring who we were now, who we'd grown into in our time apart. And more than anything, we were building the people we'd become — the people we wanted to be together.

Her eyes met mine, and her smile widened, pride bursting through those bright blue eyes.

"Not bad, Coach," she said as I approached. "Second period was kind of sloppy, but hey, we can't all be perfect."

I smirked, taking her under my arm and kissing her hair. "Keep up that bratty behavior and I'll have to bend you over my knee."

"In that case... your speech on the ice kind of sucked, too."

I grinned, tickling her sides as she squirmed beneath my touch, giggling and swatting me away. When I finally took her in my arms, it was with a long breath of a kiss, my hands clasping behind her hips.

"I love you."

She smiled, trailing her arms up around my neck. "And I love you. More than anything."

"More than Coldplay on a rainy day?"

"More than that."

"More than the perfect smoothie?"

"More than that."

"More than your first edition of *Pride and Prejudice*?"

"Don't get greedy now."

A cheer erupted from the locker room as I bent to kiss her with a laugh, and then I was getting ripped backward.

"Come on, Coach! Plenty of time to kiss that beautiful woman of yours later. But right now, we've got a victory boat parade to plan, and Jaxson has a *brilliant* idea."

It was Carter Fabri, his hair soaked and grin wide as he waved at Ariana and threw his arm around my neck to drag me into the locker room.

"By brilliant, he means absolutely idiotic," Daddy P grumped.

"You're just mad you didn't think of it," Vince chided.

"Picture this—" Jaxson held up his hands wide. "A zip line strung between two yachts, and we pass ride back and forth *hanging from the trophy* before doing a keg stand on the other side and tapping the next player in."

Aleks blinked at his teammate, shaking his head. *„Der spinnt doch."*

"Exactly!" Jaxson exclaimed, pointing to Aleks. "What he said."

"Pretty sure he insulted you," Daddy P pointed out.

"But he didn't say he wouldn't do the zip line," Vince added with a finger aimed at Aleks's chest.

The bickering continued on, and I chuckled, crossing my arms and taking in the glory of a rowdy team who'd earned this night.

My eyes flicked back to the hallway just in time to see Maven loop an arm through Ariana's, Grace and Mia falling in on either side of her, laughter spilling from them as easily as it always had.

She wasn't watching from the sidelines anymore.

She had her own team now.

This was the love I'd always dreamed of.

It was support and comfort, safety and encouragement, room to be ourselves while also carving out an existence together.

The Cup was right there in the center of the noise, and the night was loud and electric and unreal — but somehow, the best part of winning wasn't the trophy at all.

It was knowing we'd both made it here together.

Time and circumstance had ripped us apart, but we'd found our way back — as if there was no other option, as if our souls were tied to one another.

And here we were. Still standing. Still choosing each other, even when it was impossible to do. Still building something honest out of the wreckage that tried to claim us.

It all started with a hand flying into the air, with a girl who captured my heart the second I laid eyes on her.

And from where I was standing, there was no ending in sight.

# EPILOGUE

## NEVER LOVE AGAIN

Ariana
One Year Later

"I feel like this should be shocking, but alas... I feel nothing close to surprise," Vince said, smirking as he took in the ridiculous chapel we were sitting in. He had one arm around Maven, who was holding fast to the hand of Rowan, who was no doubt planning her escape so she could run around freely.

"I mean, nothing screams Grace quite like bedazzled pews and an Elvis officiant," Livia agreed.

We were in Las Vegas, the whole crew, to *finally* celebrate Jaxson and Grace getting married. Grace had been reluctant to set a date at first. As much as she couldn't wait to marry Jaxson, the very act of "settling down" went against every fiber that made up who she was as a person.

She was meant to roam, to travel, to spread her wings and fly.

When she finally did decide on a plan, Chloe had been too pregnant to fly during the offseason. And so, Grace had handed us all a very conspicuous *save the date* with the Las Vegas sign on it.

Here we were, one year later, each of us dressed in our sparkliest outfits — at Grace's insistence — ready to celebrate the newlyweds.

Jaxson stood at the front of the chapel, hands clasped behind his back, wearing a white suit jacket that glittered under the lights like a disco ball. Rhinestones traced the lapels. His loafers shimmered. I was fairly certain there was actual fringe involved.

"This is the happiest I've ever been," he announced to no one in particular. "If I die today, tell my story. Carve it on my gravestone. Write it in the obituary."

"You're not allowed to die until after the honeymoon," Grace shouted from somewhere behind the curtain behind us. "I've already packed your outfits."

Livia chuckled beside me, her gaze flicking up to Carter like they were sharing an inside joke.

Then, a dramatic crescendo of piano played over the speakers before Grace stepped through the curtain behind us. The song was a classical remix of "100,000 People" by Kings of Leon.

Grace stepped out wearing something that could only be described as art. There were layers of tulle, sequins in at least three clashing shades, and a dramatic high-low hem that revealed sparkly boots. Her hair was piled high, unapologetically wild, with a short veil pinned in at a crooked angle.

She looked stunning.

She looked ridiculous.

She looked exactly like we all imagined she would on her wedding day.

Jaxson turned, took her in, and promptly started laughing even as tears flooded his eyes. None of the guys in the pews around me dared to tease him for getting mushy — Shane already told me before the ceremony started that none of them had any room to shit talk when they were all so weak for their women.

"You are the most beautiful thing I've ever seen," Jaxson said reverently as Grace literally skipped down the aisle to him. "I knew you wouldn't disappoint."

"And I've never seen anyone look so dashing in sequins," Grace replied, and against all the rules, she threw her arms around his neck and kissed him, Jaxson dipping her dramatically as we all whisked and clapped like the ceremony was over.

Elvis cleared his throat into the microphone. "Ahem. Thank you, thank you very much."

A chorus of laughter followed, then we all fell quiet, listening as Elvis gave a surprisingly heartwarming speech about love and commitment before he launched into vows. In the back of the chapel, Chloe bounced baby Everett on her hip. He was nearly one now, all chubby cheeks and bright eyes, and had learned to walk far sooner than either of his parents were prepared for. Will, retired from playing for just over a year now, looked happier than I'd ever seen him where he stood beside his wife, ready to take over should she need a break. He'd recently accepted a coaching position with the Ospreys in the fall, a fact Shane had told me with so much excitement I thought he'd won the lottery.

In his eyes, he had.

Beside me, Maven knelt to whisper something in Rowan's ear that made her giggle. Vince and Maven's daughter was two-and-a-half and already plotting chaos. But it was Lennon — Carter and Livia's daughter — who was the true wild one of the pair. They were already inseparable, two tiny forces of nature who would undoubtedly terrorize us all for years to come.

Mia looked the most at home in her bedazzled pink dress, one I was fairly certain she'd worn on tour before. She and Aleks sat across the aisle from us, Aleks's hand possessively holding Mia's thigh as she leaned into him and did her best not to cry at Jaxson's vows. Her latest album had just dropped, and she was heading out on tour in August. She and Aleks were glowing in that dual-income, no-kids way — both sun-kissed from their getaway before tour, relaxed in the way Aleks could only be during the off-season, and both of them wildly in love.

Life had kept moving for all of us after the craziness of last season.

As Elvis continued the ceremony, I felt Shane's hand slide into mine.

The past year had been everything I expected it to be. It had hard times and soft ones, too. It was scary and exhilarating, happy and sad in tandem. And maybe that was the biggest lesson I'd learned through all of this — that duality existed in all of us, and it was okay to hold all the emotions at once.

I'd rebuilt my life piece by piece. I lived on my own in a space that felt safe and entirely mine. I helped support Georgie through school and he helped by applying for scholarships. I was growing in my job working at the hospital in social services, advocating for families navigating domestic violence, especially children. After just one year, I'd moved into an executive position. Some days were heavy. But I knew I was exactly where I was supposed to be.

Shane and I had taken our time. We were still dating, falling in love, relearning each other.

He'd shown me the world, flown me to places I'd only ever seen on postcards, took me out on the water in the bay, introduced me to the Tampa he loved. With Georgie cheering him on, he'd dragged me out for multiple beach days. And while I still didn't have the kind of skin that would ever catch a tan, I enjoyed our time in the sun.

But my favorite moments were the quiet ones, the way we would lose entire afternoons or evenings at each other's homes. I loved how things started to be forgotten — toothbrushes left behind, pajamas found in the wrong dryer. Our lives were blending whether we named it yet or not.

We'd started talking about moving in together, about what home could look like, and I'd never felt so excited for the future as I did thinking of that.

Nathan had been charged with multiple counts of fraud, conspiracy, and coercion tied to the betting scandal and financial crimes uncovered in the investigation. He was sentenced to twelve years in prison, though we were fairly certain he'd serve half of that when it all came down to it. It wasn't nearly enough to erase the damage he'd done — but it was enough that the world finally saw him for who he was.

I hadn't seen him again after that night at my birthday party.

I didn't want or need to.

As Elvis pronounced Jaxson and Grace married and the chapel erupted into cheers, confetti cannons went off, startling the kids and sending Rowan shrieking with laughter. Grace kissed Jaxson like the world was ending. They were running off for a two-week honeymoon immediately after this — no plans, no itinerary, just them and a little game of airport gate roulette.

I squeezed Shane's hand, emotion swelling in my chest as he turned to me with tears in his eyes. He pulled me under his arm and kissed me, helping the butterflies in my stomach take flight even after all this time.

There was so much we still had in front of us. We'd talked about what it might look like if we started a family — not in the conventional way, but in the way that felt right for us. We had Georgie's graduation to look forward to, a home we would build together, and who knew what else.

I'd gone from a life where I woke up every day wishing to disappear to one where every hour filled me with hope and possibility.

A lifetime ago, in that psych class where Shane and I had first met, we'd talked about resilience. About grit. About whether it was something you were born with or something you built.

I'd thought strength meant standing alone. I thought it meant enduring and surviving when all the odds were stacked against you.

Now I knew better.

Resilience wasn't just internal. It was shared. It was found family and steady hands and people who refused to let you fall through the cracks.

I had grit.

But I also had them — this chapel full of friends who had become the best family I could have ever imagined.

And standing there, surrounded by love and laughter and a man who chose me every day, I knew something deep and unshakable.

I wasn't just surviving anymore.

I was living.

And the best was yet to come.

• • •

## One Year Later

The auditorium was packed, heat and anticipation pressing in from every side. Folding chairs filled every aisle, programs fluttering, names whispered and repeated like talismans. I sat on the edge of my seat, hands clasped tight in my lap, my heart already racing even though Georgie's name hadn't been called yet.

Shane, on the other hand, looked like he was preparing for battle.

"I need you to promise me something," I whispered, glancing sideways at him.

He didn't look away from the stage. "Depends."

"Please don't get us escorted out."

He grinned before sucking a breath through his teeth. "Afraid I can't promise that, my love."

I arched a brow and poked his side in warning, but truthfully, I was smiling inside.

I'd learned long ago that Shane loved Georgie almost as fiercely as I did. And it wasn't out of obligation, but because Georgie had always been part of his world, woven into the fabric of his love for me from the very beginning. We'd always been a family, even those years we were apart, and Georgie had always mattered to him.

I could still remember that first Thanksgiving we shared together, how Shane showed Georgie how to play bowling on the Wii and somehow calmed a situation that could have turned into disaster.

And now here we were, watching my little brother graduate medical school.

When they announced his residency match earlier this spring, I cried so hard I had to sit down on the kitchen floor. Children's Hospital Los Angeles. His top choice.

He was going to pursue pediatric oncology, just like he'd always said he would.

Georgie had always gravitated toward the hardest medical situations, the rooms where patients were broken, where hope was fragile and desperately needed. He knew what it meant to be a scared kid. He knew what it meant to watch someone you loved fight a battle you couldn't win for them.

When his name finally echoed through the speakers — *George Campbell* — Shane was already on his feet.

"THAT'S MY BOY!" he shouted, a smuggled-in air horn blasting loud and proud as Georgie stepped onto the stage, startled and laughing, scanning the crowd until his eyes found us.

He grinned so wide, it was like he couldn't ask for a single thing in that moment.

My chest ached with the sight.

I clapped and cried and laughed all at once, my hands shaking as Shane cupped them between his, squeezing like he knew exactly what this meant to me. And he did — more than anyone.

That was the thing about us now.

We didn't have to explain the big feelings. We just held them together.

After the ceremony, we found Georgie in the crush of families and flowers, Shane pulling him into a hug so tight Georgie groaned.

"You're going to save so many lives," Shane said roughly, voice thick with pride. "I know it."

Georgie's smile softened. "I hope so."

Two days later, we were home in Tampa, Georgie heading off to enjoy a brief trip with his friends to celebrate making it through med school before they'd all go their separate ways for residency. Shane and I were already making plans to fly to Los Angeles and get Georgie set up in his new apartment when he returned.

But for now, we were at *our* home — the one we shared together.

The house greeted us the way it always did, with sunlight spilling through wide windows, the slow sway of palms visible just beyond the glass. We'd bought it together on the intercoastal, a place that felt both expansive and deeply ours. We had open spaces softened by overstuffed furniture, books everywhere, and a record player in the corner with stacks of vinyl we argued over lovingly. It was the kind of house that invited bare feet and long conversations and quiet mornings.

I dropped my bag by the door and sighed.

"I know we had breakfast before the flight, but are you too full for a smoothie?" Shane asked, already moving toward the kitchen.

I laughed. "Never."

While he worked in the kitchen, I put on a Billie Holiday record and kicked off my shoes, sighing with content at being home. I couldn't help but wander the halls down to the room we were remodeling, the one we hoped would house a child or two for however long they needed.

We were going to enter the foster care system.

It was something I'd brought up to Shane thinking it might lead to our first argument, that he'd think I was insane for even entertaining the thought. Instead, I'd been met with excitement and joy, with him pulling me in for a hug before launching into all the logistics before I could even finish my initial thought.

We both wanted a family, and we were going to do it our way.

For many reasons, including biological ones, having kids of our own was out of the question. But what mattered to us was that we could make a difference for children when they needed it most. We could have an impact on a life — on *multiple* lives — that would have a ripple effect.

There was nothing more powerful than that.

"Okay," Shane said when I ambled back into the kitchen. He turned to me with two deeply purple smoothies in hand. "I think there's magic in this one."

"Oh yeah?" I teased.

One sip, and my eyes widened.

And then I was promptly sent back in time.

The taste dancing on my tongue was a snapshot of 2006, of me and Shane in an old Pontiac, of baby faces and wide-open hearts.

"No," I breathed. "No, no, no. Shane." I shook my head, taking another sip that had that same nostalgia laced in it. "*How*?!"

He leaned against the counter, arms crossed, trying and failing to look casual because he was gloating like a sonofabitch.

"It tastes exactly like it," I whispered. "The Berry Blast from the Smoothie Guy. *Exactly* like it."

Shane continued to gloat. "I tracked him down. Turns out he's running a food truck in Santa Barbara now. It took some bribery, but I convinced him to share the recipe."

My heart stuttered.

"You really went out of your way," I said, and it was like my body knew before my brain did that something big was happening. I started to shake. My breaths were shallow.

Shane cleared his throat and reached for the straw wrapper he'd discarded before handing me my glass. He didn't toss it in the trash.

He folded it, very carefully, into a perfect little ring.

My breath caught as he knelt.

"Ari, there are a million words I could say to you to convey my undying, unyielding love. I could write an entire book on how much I care for you." He swallowed. "But truthfully, we've already had enough time stolen from us, and I want to use every second we have left just being together the way we always should have been."

I covered my lips, eyes blurring the vision of him knelt before me.

"I've loved you through time and distance and mistakes," he said, voice steady even as emotion lined every word. "We were torn apart by circumstance, by fear, by choices we thought were necessary. But we found our way back. We fought for our second chance. And we earned it."

He held up the straw wrapper ring with a grin.

"It's always been you, Ari. And it will always be you. I want you to pick your own ring. I want us to do it together. I want you to know that now, and forevermore, your life and all the big decisions that come with it are yours to mold."

My heart burst with what those words implied, with how this man knew me better than anyone.

"I can't wait for what comes next for us. I dream about what a great mother you will be, about how you'll continue to do good to everyone you come in contact with. But before we expand our family, I want to make ours official."

Tears streamed down my face as I nodded, laughing through the ache in my chest.

"Yes," I whispered. "Yes, Shane."

"I didn't ask you yet."

"Well, hurry up!"

He chuckled, pulling my scarred hand to his lips for a kiss before he reached for my left hand and held fast to it. "Ariana, will you marry me?"

"Yes. In this lifetime and every one after it, yes!"

As he slipped the ring onto my finger, I felt it — peace. True, unfiltered, unwavering peace, the kind that only comes after surviving something that tried to break you, and choosing to rebuild despite all the hurdles you faced in the process.

We'd lost so many years, so much time, so much love. But when it really came down to it, none of that mattered.

We weren't defined by what we'd lost.

We were defined by what we chose to give.

Standing there in our kitchen, sunlight warming my skin, the future stretching open in front of us, I knew we'd give this life all we had.

And that was more than enough for me.

\*\*\*

## A NOTE FROM THE AUTHOR

Thank you for reading the *Kings of the Ice* series! I hope you've loved living in this world as much as I enjoyed creating it.

**Fall in love with the other**
***Kings of the Ice* couples!**

**MEET YOUR MATCH**: Vince & Maven
*Book 1*
**TROPES:**
Pro Hockey Romance
Forced Proximity
Opposite Sides of the Track
Interracial/Multicultural Couple
Workplace Romance
Enemies-to-Lovers Vibes

**WATCH YOUR MOUTH**: Jaxson & Grace
*Book 2*
**TROPES:**
Pro Hockey Romance
Teammate's Little Sister/Brother's Best Friend
Road Trip
Forced Proximity
One Bed
Age Gap
Opposites Attract
Forbidden

**LEARN YOUR LESSON**: Will & Chloe
*Book 3*
**TROPES:**
Pro Hockey Romance
Single Dad/Nanny
Forced Proximity
Spicy Lessons
Grumpy Sunshine
Age Gap
Opposites Attract
Found Family

**SAVE YOUR BREATH**: Aleks & Mia
*Book 4*
**TROPES:**
Pro Hockey Romance
Fake Engagement
Athlete & Pop Star
Childhood Friends to Lovers
Forced Proximity
Unrequited Love (or so they think)
Opposites Attract
Slow Burn

**STAND YOUR GROUND:** Carter & Livia
*Book 5*
**TROPES:**
Pro Hockey Romance
Spicy Lessons
Virgin Hero
Opposites Attract
Reverse Age Gap
He Falls First
Workplace Romance
BDSM

# ACKNOWLEDGEMENTS

I have to begin with Rhiannon Gwynne and her husband, Josh Brittain. This series simply would not exist without you. Thank you for opening your world to me and giving me an authentic, behind-the-scenes look at life in the professional hockey circuit — on and off the ice. Your generosity, insight, and constant willingness to answer my endless questions have shaped this series in more ways than I can count.

To my husband and daughter — thank you for giving me a life so beautiful it still takes my breath away. Your love, patience, and unwavering support are the foundation beneath everything I create. I am endlessly grateful for you.

To my mom, Lavon, and my best friend, Sasha — I swear I will never write a book without leaning on you both. Thank you for being my safe place, my sounding board, and my constants. I love you more than words.

Huge thank you to the Weird Babes, who give me the best inspiration to write girl gangs like the one in this series. I am so lucky to have the best friends in the world.

To Tina Stokes — my executive assistant, my friend, and my rock — thank you for carrying so much of the weight while I disappeared into the writing cave. You keep everything running smoothly while also bringing creativity and vision to this series in ways that directly shape its success. I love you big, and I'm so grateful for you.

To my writing sisters who were right there in the cave with me — Laura Pavlov, Lena Hendrix, Catherine Cowles, and Staci Hart — thank you for your friendship, your encouragement, and your honesty. This industry is brighter, kinder, and far more fun because of women like you. I'm lucky to walk this path alongside you.

To my alpha and beta readers — thank you for your sharp eyes, your thoughtful notes, your patience when I inevitably paused at the worst possible moment, and your unwavering enthusiasm for these characters. Your feedback made this story stronger at every turn. Endless thanks to Rhiannon Gwynne, Allison Cheshire, Frances O'Brien, Carly Wilson, Nicole Westmoreland, Nicole McCurdy, Janett Corona, Jayce Cruz, and Gabriela Vivas. I couldn't do this without you.

This book also required immense care, and I am deeply grateful to my sensitivity readers for domestic violence — Stacey Kelley, Christina Otero, Julie Kitzmiller, Jackie Nolan, and Misty Unser. Thank you for trusting me with your insight and helping me approach these themes with honesty, respect, and responsibility. Your guidance mattered more than you know.

To the dream team who turns my vision into something tangible — Elaine York at Allusion Graphics, Nicole McCurdy at Emerald Edits, Nina Grinstead, Kim Cermak, the entire Valentine PR squad, Ren Saliba, and Staci Hart at Quirky Bird Cover Design — thank you for every detail, every late-night brainstorm, and every ounce of care you pour into this series. You make the impossible possible.

To my agent, Ariele Fredman — thank you for believing in me, championing my work, and pushing these stories farther than I ever dreamed they could go. You are magic.

To Saida, Alice, and the entire team at Curtis Brown/Dialogue/Renegade Publishing — thank you for bringing the Kings of the Ice series to the United Kingdom and its territories. Seeing these books find readers across the world is a dream come true, and I'm so grateful for your passion and care.

To Sophie, Ethan, and Elsa at UTA — thank you for the doors you open and the belief you bring to my work.

To Janelle and Bonnie — the Lyla June cards and character stickers you've created are pure joy. Thank you for bringing these characters to life in such whimsical, heartfelt ways. And an extra thanks to Staci Hart for stepping in to make character art when Bonnie was on mat leave.

And finally, to you — the reader. Thank you for reading, for sharing, for reviewing, for recommending these books to your friends, and for showing up again and again. You are the reason these characters breathe, the reason this dream is real. I never take that for granted. Thank you for choosing my stories out of the millions available to you. I will forever cherish you.

# ABOUT THE AUTHOR

**KANDI STEINER** is a *USA Today* and #1 Amazon Bestselling Author living in Tennessee. Best known for writing "emotional rollercoaster" stories, she loves bringing flawed characters to life and writing about real, raw romance — in all its forms. No two Kandi Steiner books are the same, and if you're a lover of angsty, emotional, and inspirational reads, she's your gal.

An alumna of the University of Central Florida, Kandi graduated with a double major in Creative Writing and Advertising/PR with a minor in Women's Studies. Her love for writing started at the ripe age of 10, and in 6th grade, she wrote and edited her own newspaper and distributed to her classmates. Eventually, the principal caught on and the newspaper was quickly halted, though Kandi tried fighting for her "freedom of press."

She took particular interest in writing romance after college, as she has always been a hopeless romantic and found herself bursting at the seams with love stories she was eager to tell.

When Kandi isn't writing, you can find her reading books of all kinds, planning her next adventure, or pole dancing (yes, you read that right). She enjoys live music, traveling, hiking, yoga, spending quality time with her family (fur babies included) and soaking up the sweetness of life.

## CONNECT WITH KANDI:

NEWSLETTER: kandisteiner.com/newsletter
FACEBOOK: @kandisteiner
FACEBOOK READER GROUP (Kandiland):
facebook.com/groups/kandilandks
INSTAGRAM: @kandisteiner
TIKTOK: @authorkandisteiner
WEBSITE: kandisteiner.com

Bringing a book from manuscript to what you are reading is a team effort.

Renegade Books would like to thank everyone who helped to publish *Right Your Wrongs* in the UK.

**Editorial**
Saida Azizova

**Contracts**
Stephanie Evans
Sasha Duszynska Lewis
Isabel Camara

**Sales**
Megan Schaffer
Kyla Dean
Dominic Smith
Sinead White
Georgina Cutler-Ross
Ellie Walker
Jess Harvey
Natasha Weninger-Kong

**Rights**
Ben Fowler
Emma Thawley
Catherine de Mello
Alexis Alderton

**Design**
Fran Hambling
Andrew Smith
Sara Mahon

**Production**
Tara Hodgson

**Operations**
Jairiza Rivera

**Inventory**
Victoria Stephenson
Dan Jones

**Finance**
Chris Vale
Jonathan Gant

**Audio**
Carrie Hutchison

## RAISING READERS
**Books Build Bright Futures**

Dear Reader,

We'd love your attention for one more page to tell you about the crisis in children's reading, and what we can all do.

Studies have shown that reading for fun is the **single biggest predictor of a child's future life chances** – more than family circumstance, parents' educational background or income. It improves academic results, mental health, wealth, communication skills, ambition and happiness.[1]

The number of children reading for fun is in rapid decline. Young people have a lot of competition for their time. In 2024, 1 in 10 children and young people in the UK aged 5 to 18 did not own a single book at home.[2]

Hachette works extensively with schools, libraries and literacy charities, but here are some ways we can all raise more readers:

- Reading to children for just 10 minutes a day makes a difference
- Don't give up if children aren't regular readers – there will be books for them!
- Visit bookshops and libraries to get recommendations
- Encourage them to listen to audiobooks
- Support school libraries
- Give books as gifts

There's a lot more information about how to encourage children to read on our website: **www.RaisingReaders.co.uk**

Thank you for reading.

hachette UK

---

[1] OECD, '21st-Century Readers: Developing Literacy Skills in a Digital World', 2021, https://www.oecd.org/en/publications/21st-century-readers_a83d84cb-en.html

[2] National Literacy Trust, 'Book Ownership in 2024', November 2024, https://literacytrust.org.uk/research-services/research-reports/book-ownership-in-2024